ASHES

LAURALANA DUNNE

THE PHOENIX RISING SERIES

BOOKS

Published in Canada by Engen Books, St. John's, NL.

Library and Archives Canada Cataloguing in Publication

Title: Ashes / Lauralana Dunne.
Names: Dunne, Lauralana, 1985- author.
Description: Series statement: The phoenix rising series ; 1
Identifiers: Canadiana (print) 20200277693 | Canadiana (ebook) 20200277707 |
ISBN 9781989473573
  (softcover) | ISBN 9781989473580 (PDF)
Classification: LCC PS8607.U55365 A92 2020 | DDC C813/.6—dc23

Distributed by:
Engen Books
www.engenbooks.com
submissions@engenbooks.com

First mass market paperback printing: June 2020

Cover Image: Kelsey Power

To my parents, the Bookmasters

For helping me to grow my wings
and encouraging me to soar.

PROLOGUE

"There's nothing more dangerous than a storm-teased fire," Marla recited under her breath.

The sky had become a smear of black. The countless stars, tiny pinpricks of light in the endless darkness, had winked out of sight when the heavy clouds rolled across the horizon.

Marla hefted her bag to her shoulder and struggled to keep ahead of those clouds as she hurried towards the Cobber's stead. She picked her way along the flooded path, her boots squelching in the rivers of mud as she sped up the slick hill. The wind twisted ominously along the horizon, lashing above the distant forest as it churned against itself, but still only the lightest breeze ruffled the loose strands of Marla's hair. Impossibly dry flakes swayed in the air like falling snow, clinging to the sheen of sweat on her skin as she barrelled up the steep incline. She had to hurry. The storm's eye would blow past them soon enough. She didn't know what they'd do then.

A gasp slipped past her lips as she crested the hill. Devastation was everywhere. Large plumes of smoke billowed dry ash into the darkening sky. Splinters of wood fanned across the ground in front of the main structure, as if pieces of the framework had shattered. Ahead of her, the burning remains of the Cobber's house stood on skeletal legs. Blackened and foreboding as death, it was a promise to the smouldering barn next door as the remnants of the wind-whipped flames grew along the edge of the roof.

Marla cast her eyes around the area until they landed on the Speaker. "Thomas!" she called.

"Ho, Marla," Thomas returned her greeting without enthusiasm. He was a stocky man with bulging arms from years spent working in the fields. She could see that one of them was now in a make-shift sling, hanging uselessly in the dirty fabric. He leaned back against a covered wagon and surveyed the scene, nodding to Marla as she splashed towards him. He eyed the medicine bag slung over her shoulder. "I hope th' rain comes soon." His voice was mournful, low enough that it reached only her ears.

Marla touched his good arm in sympathy and looked around.

One section of the house's roof had collapsed entirely. The main supports had been burnt out from underneath, snapping in half from the weight of the structure. Large slivers of charred wood thrust out of the mud where they had gouged the ground between the scattered shingles.

Two groups of men moved in a flurry of activity - the first attempted to pry open the barn's locked doors, while the second tried to douse the flames and scrambled to move the large sections of the roof as quickly as possible. It was too early to tell if it was a rescue or a recovery operation, and Marla felt her stomach turn at the thought of the latter.

"All tha's left is th' barn," Thomas nodded at the structure. Then, as an afterthought, he added: "It's been awful quiet."

Marla's mouth went dry. She could only nod and gesture to his injured arm. Silently, he held it out for her to tend to.

The wind picked up. The scattered drops of rain became

thick sheets of water that hissed as they smothered the dying flames of the house. It was too late for the barn. The fire ate its way into the loft and caught the hay that was stored there. It acted like kindling to the flames as they spread unchecked under the roof where the rain was unable to reach it.

Marla worked quickly, assessing his arm and adjusting the sling to the correct angle. "Tha'll need t' be set once we get some light."

He nodded absently, his attention on the barn.

The men had not stopped their struggle against the locked doors. Loud curses filled the air around the chopping. After what seemed like an eternity, one of them roared and lifted his axe above his head, signaling that he had made it through one of the thick wooden doors. Those closest to him joined him, their renewed efforts increased the size of the opening until a man-sized hole was formed.

"There's somethin' blockin' th' way!"

The eye of the storm passed. The winds increased in intensity, gusting against the barn ferociously, but the squalls did little to drown out the clamor of frightened animals inside.

"It's a rafter," a man named Dylan shouted back to Thomas, frustration coloring his voice. "It's barrin' th' way! We can't get in..." His usually sunny face was haggard and covered with mud. Marla could see that all of the men were in the same condition after long hours of fighting against the weather. They were exhausted.

Thomas opened his mouth, but he was interrupted before he could respond. Another group of men, the ones who had remained shifting through the rubble, gave a yell as they lifted a collapsed wall out of the house and dumped it in the mud.

A sobering silence followed as they stared at their discovery. The closest men removed their hats and held them to their chests, bowing their heads. One of them dropped to the ground and retched into the mud.

Marla jumped up and started forward. Thomas grabbed her arm with his good hand, keeping her from getting any closer. She tried to pull away but he held fast.

"They're gone," Thomas said to her gently.

He was right. She could see the broken bodies, immobile, in the mud. She turned away from the tangle of twisted limbs, bile rising in her throat.

The grisly discovery took the fight out of everyone.

"Alrigh' then," Thomas called back to Dylan, rolling his one good shoulder. "We ain't doin' much good here. There's no sense in continuin' on fer a bunch o' low-brow animals." He said the next part quietly to Marla: "They've been haulin' well-water since th' squall came on; fightin' th' blasted wind when it was blowin' th' wrong way. One o' them will be th' next casualty if we don-"

A high-pitched cry cut him off and everyone paused. Another thin wail split the air, slicing through the noise of the storm, causing the hair on Marla's arms to stand on end. Her head snapped up as everyone looked towards the barn.

"Thomas!" she cried. "Someone's in there!"

Thick smoke poured out through the door's man-high split. Air rushed in through the hole, feeding the flames and causing them to swell against the inside walls. Whoever was in there didn't have much time left.

Ignoring his injury, Thomas ran forward and grabbed an axe with his good arm, shoving through the crowd of men. "Aim fer th' bottom o' th' door," he yelled, fighting to be heard above the wind and rain. "If we can't get 'er open we'll go under!"

The men roared with renewed energy and vigorous pounding filled Marla's ears. They needed to hurry, she thought, willing them to somehow go faster. The wailing had stopped, and Marla didn't know how much more smoke they could breathe in before they stopped breathing permanently.

Thunk.

Something banged against the double doors, rattling the heavy chains that Farmer Cobber had used to lock them together. Marla ran forward, but the men stepped backward as the force of the knocking spat wood chips on the ground by their feet. Dylan was close enough that she could see his knuckles turn white around his axe as he slid away from the barn. She came to a halt. What was happening?

The hole became larger. Chunks of wood the size of small logs crumbled away from the opening. Wood splinters trickled down the path carried by the running water, floating with the current to pool around Marla's boots.

The men crossed themselves with the sign against evil, and Marla caught herself wanting to do the same. Even Thomas's ruddy face was pale.

Another bang and her entire body went cold. No one was moving. No one was anywhere near the door.

It was coming from inside.

Someone - *something* - inside the barn was trying to get out, and whatever it was it was big, and it was angry.

It roared.

Marla felt her blood thicken and turn to ice in her veins. It pounded dully in her ears. She was rooted to the spot, unable to move her feet, unable to even think about trying to get away. Her thoughts were sluggish, and it was a struggle to remain upright where she stood.

A bestial scream of fury came from the burning structure. Desperation added to the strength of the creature, and its blows became stronger and faster. At last, the door broke with an eruptive crack. The creature gave a savage snarl and leapt out of the choking heat and into the rain.

It was massive. Its eyes glowed like an animal's in the dark, catching the flickering flames and reflecting their light back into the night. It raked an impassive gaze through everyone assembled, pausing when it landed on Marla.

Cold reptilian eyes stared into hers without blinking. Oval-slitted pupils commanded her attention, and Marla found that it was impossible for her to look away.

Her breath hitched in her throat. The idea of screaming entered her head, a brief moment of clarity before it tumbled from her mind, and she dismissed the idea when she realized how hard it would be. She couldn't even recall how to do it.

No one moved.

It - he, Marla realized - stood taller than any man here. His clothing, thick hides and stitched leather, was singed black in places from the flames. He was covered in large smudges of blood that showed up as dark lines on his green-grey skin. He bared his fangs at the men closest to him, those who still had their axes clutched in their fists, and they immediately fainted. The Fear stupefied Marla, but one word still remained after all other thoughts had left her head.

Gargoyle.

Everything went silent. The entire world stood still. Marla was unsure if the fire had been put out, or if it was still burning the barn before her to the ground. She was unable to focus on anything. She was mutely aware of her heart beating, she could feel its sluggish pounding throughout her entire body, but all of her concentration was centered on the creature before her.

The gargoyle looked over his shoulder to the burning barn. The wind battered the rain in through the large opening, causing the water to pool on the wooden floor. The smoke still hung heavy in the air, but the flames were slowly dissipating into darkness.

The gargoyle hesitated with a growl. His expression was torn. Almost reluctantly, Marla thought, he lowered himself to all fours and sprinted towards the trees. With a snap, two large bat-like wings unfurled from his back as he launched himself into the air. He grabbed an overhanging branch and, with superhuman strength, threw himself into the raging winds. Riding on the chaotic gusts, the gargoyle lifted into the sky until he disappeared into the clouds. Marla could feel a *pop*, as if air rushed to fill in a space that had been suddenly and unexpectedly emptied.

The spell was broken. The terror experienced melted away in mere moments. Warmth ran through Marla's veins and it was as though the Fear had never existed. She took a shaky breath, trying to calm her burning lungs. She blinked repeatedly to clear her vision, wondering when it was that she had stopped breathing.

Chickens, as if released from an invisible barrier, scattered from the barn; distracting everyone and putting the men to work chasing them. A few withered sheep followed, bawling their displeasure, and Dylan, being the closest, tried to grab one before it ran back into the barn from confusion.

Countless cattle and pigs stampeded into the mud. Marla knew that the Cobbers dealt with animals instead of crops, but the sheer volume of them surprised her as they crowded around everyone. Even Thomas's expression was shocked at the sight.

At the very end, after Marla was convinced that nothing else could possibly be left, a sturdy little mule came through the opening. It was more like a donkey, she decided, and it seemed too stunned to understand what was going on. It kept its head down, plodding forward with a single-minded intensity that would have led it past everyone assembled and into the woods beyond.

Marla took a step forward and grabbed its tether to halt it in its tracks. Unexpected cold bit into her fingers and Marla jerked her hand back. Surprised, she looked down to see ice remnants melting in her hands.

"Frost?" she asked incredulously, barely believing what she saw. Marla looked over the donkey and lurched forward with surprise. On his other side, almost hidden from view, stood a small red-headed child of about five years. The girl clutched the mane of the stocky donkey and walked with him calmly. Her face was dirty and tear-stained, but she seemed relatively unharmed.

"Thomas!" Marla's voice rose in pitch as she snatched her forgotten medicine bag from the muddy ground.

"Toads!" he swore, abandoning his chase of a running chicken to grab a dry blanket from inside the covered wagon. "Is she alrigh'?"

"She's in shock," Marla said, peering into the girl's blank hazel eyes. Carefully, she pried the small fist from its grip on the donkey's mane.

A thin chain was wound around the girl's open hand. Marla detangled it from her fingers and held it up for a better look. Ornate strands of darkened silver hugged a cloudy white gem that was nestled in its centre. The thin metal delicately hugged the edges of the teardrop-shaped jewel, securing the treasure in place with an elegance that had Marla hurrying to put the necklace back where it belonged. Firelight shone off the facets of the tapered white gem as Marla carefully pried open the clasp.

"Come here little lass; little darlin'," Marla said, soothingly. She slipped the pendant around the girl's neck, tucking it out of sight under her tunic. "We ain't gonna hurt you none."

The child came willingly, offering no resistance to the blanket that was wrapped around her or the worried arms that insisted on holding her. Her eyes were wide as she watched everything, but soon exhaustion began to tug at them and her blinking became slow and heavy.

"What I dun get," Marla said over the girl's smoke-darkened head, "is how th' child is th' only survivor o' a lizard attack. Why would he leave one an' not th' other two?" Her eyes strayed to where the Cobber's broken bodies had been pulled from the wreckage, the pair of outlines pronounced under the damp sheets that covered them. "And for tha' matter," she continued, almost at a whisper, "wha's a lone gargoyle doin' out here?"

Thomas grunted, allowing himself to slump against a crate now that the immediate danger was over. "Wha' I'm not gettin' is where th' lass came from. Th' Cobbers had no children. An' even if they did, she don't look like neither of 'em."

Marla knew what he meant. The Cobbers, like most in the area, shared the same pale skin and dark hair. The child dozing in Marla's lap had bright red hair, teased into thick curls from the wind and the rain, and warm brown skin that looked like it had been sun-kissed from the heat of summer. An impossible feat, considering the harvest was almost done and over with.

Thomas scratched the back of his neck where the sling was tied. "So how she survived surely issa mystery, but no less than how she got 'ere in th' first place."

Marla shared a worried look with him. The child shifted in her arms and, despite her reservations, she tightened her hold around the small body.

"We'll figure it out," Marla said to Thomas, resting her chin on the girl's curly head. "She'll be safe 'ere 'till we do."

Thomas didn't look at her, but he nodded his agreement. It

Ashes

was a statement, not a request, and no one argued with Marla once she set her mind.

The wind howled, shifting the rain and the charred wood around them. In Marla's arms, in the security of the covered wagon, the child slept peacefully, unaware of the chaos around her.

PART I
CHAPTER 1

The barn enveloped her with warmth. Soft bleating slid its way into Phoenix's consciousness, waking her from her troubled sleep. She lay unmoving, hidden in the hay pile, her eyes still closed as the rest of her senses focused. She could feel coarse straw poking through her clothing, the itch of dried sweat on her skin from the day's work.

She had been dreaming. A dull sense of fear reverberated in her chest as the sleep-terror's aftereffects settled in the old scars on her body. She rubbed her thumb against the ones between her fingers, tracing the hardened skin as if she could somehow disperse the lingering sensations of the bad dream. When that didn't work she flexed her back, trying to stretch the ache from the tightened membrane between her shoulder blades. She concentrated on the soothing smells of the stables. She deserved to rest after all her hard work.

"Wake up!" Another prod to her side made Phoenix realize what had woken her. She clawed at the straw that covered her, struggling momentarily to remove the stalks that had tangled themselves in her curls. She dashed the sleep from her eyes and glared up at Millie.

Millie towered over Phoenix like a furious queen, brandishing a stick with an air of authority that she wasn't entitled to.

"Yer presence has been requested," Millie announced, her expression sour. The stick dropped with a clatter and she eyed Phoenix with disdain. There was a moment of tense silence, then she huffed dismissively and marched towards the Lodging.

Phoenix bit back a sigh. She had been hiding in the barn since evening's meal. Becca had kicked her out with a shriek when the cooking fire burned too hot - ruining the food that was being served. Phoenix had been on the other side of the kitchens when it happened, but the blame had still fallen on her. It always did.

Maybe it was time to look for a new hiding spot.

Standing was awkward at first, her long legs protested her body's weight, and Phoenix spent a moment rubbing the feeling back into her feet before she took her first steps. Harvest had come and gone and she ached all over. She was strong for her fifteen years - as strong as any boy on the farm - and she had kept up with the lot of them to prove her worth. As the only girl working the fields, she didn't mind exerting herself... but she had planned on a rest period, no matter how brief.

She smoothed out her clothing as she moved and tucked her necklace back under her tunic. Marla had always made her keep it hidden, but that had never stopped it from coming uncovered while she slept. More than once she had found it snarled in her curls when she awoke.

"Hey, Muler," she greeted the leggy donkey, hobbling to his pen and giving his nose an affectionate rub. Muler flicked a sleepy ear at her.

He was dear to her. The crotchety creature did not like many people, so it was no surprise to anyone that Phoenix had kept him when Marla had passed. He was all she had in this world, and he meant everything to her.

"Be back soon." Phoenix leaned in and kissed him on his

bristly forehead. Giving him a pat, she adjusted his blanket and left the barn.

The wind blew stinging kisses against Phoenix's cheeks when she stepped outside. It was not long after sunsdown, but the cold season already showed signs of creeping in without the sun's light to deter it. Dried leaves danced ahead of her on the path, the slow ones crunched underfoot as she trudged to the Lodging.

She could hear sounds of celebration coming from the hall. Notes of merriment met her at the door, then trailed behind her as she bypassed the main room and entered the kitchens. Meetings always happened in the kitchens.

She was unprepared for the amount of people already assembled when she arrived. A few broke off their conversations when they caught sight of her. Several jumped when, unbidden, a door behind her slammed shut from the wind. They made the sign against evil as the flames flared in the hearth; fighting for life against the unexpected attack.

Phoenix glared. They constantly did that - blamed her for strange happenings. Marla had always told her not to mind them, and that they didn't know any better. Marla's teachings were often at odds with the practices of farm life. Why she settled here Phoenix would never know, but, once again, Phoenix swallowed her irritation and silently forgave them.

"Phoenix!" Speaker Thomas's booming voice sliced through the room. "Come here."

She heard a snicker behind her. She turned to see Millie standing next to a lanky youth named Jobe. The two were leaning against the stone wall, their postures relaxed and familiar in the crowded room. Jobe flicked his attention to Phoenix with a smirk, and Millie gave him a look of hopeless adoration.

Phoenix fought to keep the air in her lungs. It was until only recently that the three of them had been best friends. Two seasons ago they had been inseparable. So much had changed so quickly.

"Speaker Thomas?" Phoenix stopped several foot lengths in front of his seat, as custom dictated.

He looked tired. They all did.

The Speaker was well-known for his large harvests; an ambition that kept both the farmstead unified and him elected as the voice in charge. He was the one who represented them to the Proper, and he was the one who spoke to the Manor when necessary. His voice was law.

"Phoenix, sit down."

The Speaker was at the head of the table. She sat several seats down and angled her body so that she faced him, ignoring the others in the room. She made sure that she was unable to see Millie's gloating expression.

The Speaker appraised her silently for a moment, and Phoenix resisted the urge to squirm under his gaze. Phoenix became acutely aware of how dirty she was, and how unprepared she was for this meeting. She noted that everyone else in the room had cleaned themselves up and were dressed appropriately for the evening's festivities, making her stick out like a lame foal.

Speaker Thomas looked around the room slowly. A bustling sound began as those assembled started up their conversations, or became instantly absorbed in the menial tasks that they had been performing at the kitchens preparation tables.

Phoenix could still feel attention on her, but there was a look of satisfaction on the Speaker's ruddy face as he turned back to her.

"I wanted t' thank you fer all yer help wit' th' harvest. Dylan said you were quite th' worker."

Phoenix felt her cheeks redden with relief. "T-thank you."

It had been difficult convincing Dylan to let a girl work the harvest, so she had tried her hardest not to give him a reason to fault her.

Slowly, he ran his hand through his hair and looked away. He was obviously displeased about something, and Phoenix felt a tightening in her stomach.

"Th' issue now, however, is where you'll stay."

Phoenix knew what he meant. With the Healer's passing during the thaw and the seizure of her things, it had been easy enough to find places to sleep during the warmer weather. But now that the cold season was coming, the outdoors and the barn were no longer an option.

Phoenix felt a wave of apprehension wash over her. She already had her answer prepared, but she had counted on coming to him. "I have no trouble workin' fer m' room an' board, Speaker. Muler's, too." There was a long pause and Phoenix cleared her throat. "I've worked in th' kitchens every cold season. I already know most of the recipes by heart, an' Becca always says wha' a help I am..."

She looked around at those assembled to find Becca, hoping for some form of affirmation to her claim. When she located her, the woman was busily inspecting the hem of her bulging apron and seemed to be unaware of the girl's pleading look. Phoenix got a sinking feeling in her stomach.

Speaker Thomas shook his head. "Yer a hard worker, Phoenix. Any man 'ere who says otherwise is a liar." He said the last part slowly, as if it pained him to admit it. "But be tha' as it may, we can't 'ave a girl runnin' around wild. It ain't proper an' you knows it. Now, we've 'ad-"

"So if I was a boy it'd be proper then?" Phoenix's outrage guttered into embarrassment when she realized she had interrupted him. Marla had always warned her about her temper.

She would have to keep a better eye on it now that she was living on the farm.

The Speaker paused, surprised at being cut off, then his expression hardened. He opened his mouth, but was forced to pause as a clamor came from the hall.

Phoenix shifted positions in her chair, aware of the bite of the hard wood beneath her and the damp chill that clung to the stone floor. The flames flickered in the hearth as if mirroring her mood.

"We've 'ad," he continued, when the noise level died down, "an excellent offer. Herder Samuel's lookin' fer someone t' help out tendin' his home; eventually even t' run everythin' fer him..."

She stared at him in disbelief. Millie's nasty snicker was the only thing to break through her shock.

She knew of Samuel. Samuel was a goat-herder who lived between the Farm and the Proper. His wife had died during the thaw, same as Marla, and he had been left alone to rear two boys - the oldest of which was only half her age. They all kept mainly to themselves, so Phoenix had hardly ever had the chance to meet with him.

"... But he's so old."

Thomas's lips pressed into a thin line. "He's agreed t' wait until you settle in before makin' anythin' official. He's even offered space t' house yer beastie. You have t' accept such a generous offer. Don't disgrace us wit' yer bad manners."

Phoenix hated to admit it, but he was right. The offer was more than reasonable with room for Muler. She was Bloodless - she had no worth, no stature: no family to arrange marriages; no security for suitors who may be interested. She knew it was common for a Speaker to arrange a contract in this case when enlisted, but she had never entered an agreement with him to negotiate anything on her behalf.

"I don't accept," she said softly.

The following silence was profound. The wood crackling in the hearth was the only noise in the room. Thomas's word was rarely rejected, and never once by a child or girl. His reaction was instantaneous. His face flushed as he jumped to his feet, knocking back his heavy wooden chair with a large thud.

"What?" he demanded. Menace laced the single word.

Phoenix sat very still in her chair. She had never seen him so furious.

"I don't accept," she repeated, shakily. "But thank you," she added as an afterthought, remembering what he said about having good manners.

No one moved. Most were trying very hard not to draw attention to themselves while simultaneously trying to hear everything that was said.

"Cast her out," said a quiet voice with bell-like clarity. If anyone else had heard Millie they gave no sign. Thomas fixed Millie with a hard stare and Phoenix heard the girl shrink back. After a moment his attention returned to her.

"It ain't a request," he said shortly, recovering his temper.

Phoenix began to tremble. She tried hard to keep her body from shaking, but it wouldn't work. Tears filled her eyes. "I'm a hard worker. You said so yerself! Me an' Muler, we'll-"

"It ain't no request!" he repeated. Losing his composure, Thomas kicked the fallen chair. It slid across the stone floor and into the woodpile, causing a small log to roll into the fire. A spray of sparks hissed across the floor. "You got no place here! We dun want you! Yer more trouble than yer worth. You have been ever since we pulled you outta tha' barn. You an' yer cross-breed - you jus' take up space. An' only by m' allowance did tha' happen. Well, I ain't allowin' it no more!"

Phoenix held back a sob in the silence that followed. Speaker Thomas calmed himself before pointing a thick finger at her face. "Take yer mule, an' get t' th' herder's, or pay us back fer board an' feed. Either way, I want you outta here by th' end o' th' week."

More clamoring came from the hall. Several people called for the Speaker; their voices carrying a foreign cheerfulness to the room.

Speaker Thomas adjusted his tunic and turned on his heel, his boots clicking on the floor as he left the room. He'd said all that he had needed to say. There was no need for him to waste any more of his time on her.

Quietly, those assembled filed out after him. Millie sneered at Phoenix as she left, and Jobe paused long enough to spare her a pitying glance before he left the room. Becca sniffed and blotted her eye with her apron as she shuffled past, but none of the others even acknowledged her. They laughed with excitement and hurried towards the hall. Phoenix wasn't surprised. She knew that they had only been there for the gossiping rights.

She watched them go without a sound, feeling too numb to move. The idea that she owed the Lodging had never occurred to her. She had done nothing but work from sunsup to sunsdown, and, somehow, she still owed for the time that she had stayed here.

Alone, Phoenix hung her head as helplessness washed over her. Her breathing became ragged and she began to cry in earnest. Avondale Farm was the only home she had left. These were the only people she had ever known. How could they do this to her?

None of this would have happened if Marla were still alive. She would still have somewhere to belong and someone to care about her. Someone to vouch for her.

An angry pop from the hearth distracted her. The fire had found the new log and consumed it greedily, shedding a renewed light throughout the empty room.

Limply, she dragged herself towards it and sat in the growing glare of the fire. She outstretched her hands and felt her fingers absorb the new heat, helping to soothe her agitated state. The idea that she owed the Speaker for anything, especially after all of her hard work, was ridiculous. She had worked for her keep and then some. She wasn't about to let him trade her for any additional profit.

She had a week to work with. The Speaker's anger would be terrible, his loss of control was evidence of that, but if she could outrun it...

Her resolve strengthened with each passing moment. Phoenix waited for the drums to start up, signaling the beginning of the dancing. Standing, she slipped from the kitchens and into the back of the hall.

The long tables had been pushed aside. The center of the room had been cleared and couples had taken up with each other to twirl around on the dance floor, switching with one another as the song progressed.

Millie and Jobe were in the center of the room. The Speaker was off to the side, his back to her, clapping self-importantly to the beat. No one noticed her slink along the back wall.

Phoenix's stomach protested. Whether she was hungry or anxious she couldn't tell, but she hurried along to the back banquet table. Spying a discarded linen, Phoenix quickly filled it with the closest foodstuffs. When she finished, she wrapped the ends over each other and tied them together.

While everyone was distracted, while they celebrated the fruit of her labours, she slipped out of the Lodging and back towards the barn.

CHAPTER 2

It was raining. It had been raining non-stop for hours, the kind of rain that clung to everything and permeated through the thickest clothing layers. Even the clouds seemed tired of crying for half the day. Phoenix knew she was tired of it.

Despite the rain, and the constant flow of water, the ground remained hard with the cold, refusing to allow the smallest drop between its cracks. In retaliation, the rain pooled in the ruts and dips of the road, the puddles resembling clusters of ponds that stretched endlessly before her. They reflected the clouds, bleak and grey in the waning light.

Phoenix surveyed the road ahead with a frown. It would be sunsdown soon, and there was still no sign of the next town. She was unprepared. She was unfamiliar with this area, and as such she had no good idea of where to camp... or how. What was worse, her carrysack was already emptied of the small amount of food she had brought.

Muler shifted uncomfortably at the foot of the bridge where they stood, giving what Phoenix thought was an exaggerated snort of disgust.

They had come a long way since their flight the previous evening. She had traveled farther than she ever had before. Unfortunately for them, Phoenix hadn't realized the vastness of the land beyond the fields. She had always travelled in the other direction.

"Alrigh' then. C'mon," she said softly to the donkey. Phoenix flicked the reins and directed Muler to cross the water that marked the edge of Avondale's lands.

She had played a gamble coming this way. She was counting on Speaker Thomas to look for her in the other direction - if he looked for her at all - towards Avondale Proper. She doubted he cared what became of her, but his pride would make him angry enough to want to punish her. She hoped he'd assume she had gone somewhere familiar. She also hoped that he'd assume that she would have wasted a night of travel by sleeping.

The road leading from the bridge was well-trodden. It was easy to see where they were going in the dimming light, but Phoenix could feel a sense of unease as the little donkey's pace put the bend of the river behind them.

The darkening trees on either side of them cast a foreboding gloom over the roadway.

Phoenix found herself starting in her saddle as small movements from the bracken caught her eye.

This was where the Darkened Wood spilled from the mountain ridge into the little valley. She frowned at the thick trees that crossed her path. They used to be a smudge in the distance but now they intersected with the road, their new growth spreading to choke out the original forest.

Phoenix knew that Angoria was controlled by whoever sat on the throne. As a child, Marla had taught her that King Benedict took care of the Land for them, this was why they sent tithes every year as thanks for the harvest and the ability to provide for their families. Phoenix was confused as to how sitting on a chair in some castle had helped Avondale to grow anything. Still, every year they praised the King and sent a portion of their work in thanks for another harvest.

The harvest this year was big, but many of the crops had failed. And now… She was surprised that no one had sounded an alarm about the Wood. Stories were constantly told about the evil that lurked in the trees; of travelers that went missing along this stretch of road even when the treeline still hugged the horizon. There was never any clear indication as to what the danger was. The monster usually changed from telling to telling, the familiar stories escalating with each retelling. Still, even seasoned hunters steered clear of the Darkened Wood whenever possible.

"It's pro'lly jus' bears, anyhow," Phoenix muttered to herself as they approached the treeline. Muler flicked his ears back and gave a grumble, but continued forward at his steady pace.

The weather began to worsen. The intensity of the rain increased and the wind rose in response. The falling water whipped at her and Phoenix pinched her hood closed across her face, shifting the fabric so that just enough of a gap was left to see through.

A low howl carried on the wind. Phoenix felt a whisper of fear skitter down her spine. She looked around carefully but couldn't see anything moving around her. She ignored it, telling herself that it was just the moaning of the wind pushing through the trees. Regardless, she knew that they were running out of options. Soon they would have no choice but to try and find shelter within the forest.

"Or maybe jus' really big hares," she added without humor, her smile dying before it reached her lips. She made the sign against evil in front of her chest.

Darkness began to descend, and with it came a drop in temperature. The wind whipped at the pair, slicing through the cold of Phoenix's wet skin and breathing a chill into her bones.

She pulled her cloak around her torso tightly, but the sodden material did little to help. "Oh, Muler," she pressed her forehead against the back of the donkey's neck. A wave of panic washed over her. "Wha' 'ave I gotten us into?"

More than anything she longed to be warm in a bed, or standing by the big hearth in one of the kitchens eating a bowl of soup. "I shoulda jus' went wit' th' stupid goats..."

A gust of wind threw the words back into her mouth. More howling began off in the distance, far into the forest on her right. Gripping the reins, she peered in the direction of the sound. The trees were nothing but a dark blur beside her.

Squinting against the rain, she was just able to see a large shadow stretch across their path. She studied it intently. A wall? She clicked her tongue at Muler. "Almos' there, boy." Even if no one would give them shelter for the evening, they could sneak into a barn and leave before the town awoke. Then she could look for work in the morning. That way, if Speaker Thomas came to look for her, he wouldn't be able to force her to return.

Renewed hope flowed through her. "We can do it!" she said, patting the back of Muler's neck. "Jus' a little further..."

The wall began to take shape. It stretched the width of the path and beyond, disappearing into the forest on either side of it. At this pace it wouldn't take too long to get there...

The howling started up again, closer this time. Louder. A thunderous rumbling accompanying each one that reached her. Phoenix was still unable to see anything out of place, but she could feel the hairs along her neck stand on end. "Wha' was-"

Muler brayed with alarm and slipped in the mud. Grabbing the saddle knob, Phoenix managed to remain in her seat as the donkey slid to a halt.

"Woah! Okay, boy. It's okay. Almos' there, now." She stroked his neck as they stood a moment in the path to rest.

"Jus' a little further."

The rumbling came closer, and Phoenix was unable to dismiss it as thunder any longer. The trees around them shook, and a lone bird of prey screamed a challenge to the unseen offender. Whatever it was, it was moving fast.

"C'mon," she called above the wind. She turned Muler's lead and nudged her heel into his side. "Let's go!"

She could hear it now, the sound of multiple footfalls quickly coming towards them. It put her in mind of the dogs the Lodge men used when hunting game for the farm.

Muler picked up his pace without hesitation. The donkey's ears flicked back and forth towards the strange noises around them. Whatever was causing them was following the pair intently.

The wall loomed ahead of them. Slowly the shape solidified out of the shadows, and Phoenix welcomed the thought of being safe and dry inside of it.

The darkness was near complete. She found it hard to make out the edge of the road from the trees, how close the two sat next to one another. She wanted to get to the town before they completely intersected, but she was unable to tell where they merged.

A chilling howl prickled the hair along her arms. It was much closer, and Phoenix finally had to admit that it wasn't the wind. Another howl, then another, joined with the first. Wolves. A whole pack of them by the sound of it. They were hunting, and they had picked up a scent.

They were hunting her.

Muler kick-jumped and shot ahead a few paces. He slipped again in the mud but still did not falter. He ran as fast as he could along the path.

"Woah! Careful!" The last thing she wanted was for them to

slip and fall out here in the dark. Muler, however, was spooked and there was no way to reason with him.

She could hear the pack easily above the weather, moving with the wind. The heavy footfalls sounded like thunder as they broke twigs and knocked against branches in their haste to reach their prey. Short yips of excitement skittered out from in between the trees. Phoenix gritted her teeth and clutched the reins tightly. The wall was getting closer.

"Help!" she called towards the town, hoping that someone on guard would hear her above the storm and open the gate. "Someone! Please, help! Oh, let us in," she wailed.

Phoenix used her arm to dash the water from her eyes. The storm was in full force. She could no longer tell the trees from the sky anymore, whether or not branches or empty air cushioned the space above her head. Despair welled up in her throat and she berated herself as she choked down a sob, angry that she let her foolish pride get them into this situation.

Muler squealed and stopped running, all but sitting down in an attempt to slow himself in time. Phoenix screamed with fright and was thrown against him. They slid for a moment, Phoenix clinging to his neck, almost turning in a complete circle before coming to a stop.

Her body frozen with fear, Phoenix took several deep breaths before she peered around Muler's neck to see what had panicked him.

In their path was a fallen tree, the width of its massive trunk stretched so high above them that, when Phoenix craned her head backwards, she was unable to see where it ended. It was easily ten times the size of any of the surrounding trees. It's bark was a sickly green, and it showed no sign of the brittle paleness which was evident in dead trees. Looking at the trunk caused Phoenix's stomach to clench. It was out of place. It was wrong. And it exuded such a sense of *wrongness* that Phoenix didn't stop Muler as he began to back down the path.

The enormity of the situation overcame her, and the last strands of Phoenix's resolve broke.

"No," she moaned. Defeated, she surrendered to her sobbing and buried her head in her hands. There never was a wall. There was no town. They had run blindly instead of looking for safety and now they were trapped.

The sound of snarling made her jerk her head to her right. Phoenix could see shapes forming among the trees: shapes that wove easily through the forest, moving like shadows with the wind. The countless, impossibly large silhouettes ran towards them on four legs, their eyes glowing red in the darkness. Phoenix felt a cold stab of fear in her belly as those eyes grew larger the closer they came.

Muler lurched to the left. Veering off the path, he crashed through the underbrush and into the trees.

Phoenix kept a hand in front of her face to shield it from branches. Normally, she would have been afraid of going into the Darkened Wood, but she felt only a grim determination the deeper they went. They had no choice. In here death was a possibility, but out in the open it was a certainty.

Phoenix could hear the pack yip and howl with excitement behind them. Slumping forward, she wrapped her arms around Muler's stout neck and buried her face in his bristly mane. "I'm so sorry, boy. I shoulda took' Samuel's offer..."

Muler's pace did not falter so she gave him his head. Phoenix clung to him while trying to hide her face from the back-snapping boughs.

It was calmer in the forest. The rain fell less frequently among the branches, and the strength of the wind was buffered by the trees. The snapping of twigs behind them became louder as the predators grew closer. Muler continued on at the same speed, moving with purpose ahead of the pack. The trees gave the little animal no trouble in the darkness.

To Phoenix's astonishment, the forest melted away into a grassy clearing. Rain fell evenly around them but the area remained untouched by the wind.

She straightened with surprise in her saddle.

At the edge of the meadow a large rocky hill rose out of the ground, its top camouflaged by the moss and weeds that had reclaimed the surfaces closest to the sun. Her mind raced, jumping in panic between thoughts so quickly that she nearly missed it: there was a pull in her stomach that reverberated in her bones when she looked at the rocky outcropping. She didn't know why, but she needed to go there.

Muler nickered and made his way unerringly towards it.

Growling reverberated all around them. Phoenix gasped as the great, glowing red eyes watched their every move. She could barely make out the outline of the bodies that they belonged to, but she could tell from their height that they were almost as tall as her.

Savage snarls, more than she could count, joined them as the rest of the pack flanked their sides. And yet, for some reason, they did not step onto the grass. The wolves chose to remain in the trees, running back and forth along the edge in excitement. They howled their displeasure with a chilling note.

Muler flicked his ears back but his canter did not falter as he approached the rocky hill. Just as Phoenix thought he was about to collide with it, Muler squeezed them through a split in the rock's face and the vicious sounds of the animals behind them died away.

Darkness enveloped them. Phoenix's head brushed the roof of the tunnel, but there was not enough room for her to dismount. The rock walls seemed to press against them as they continued but, despite the unpleasantness of the feeling, it was still preferable to what prowled around outside waiting for them.

The pathway was small but manageable and the noise from Muler's hooves made empty echoes against the walls.

"Well," she murmured, feeling at a loss. "Now wha'?"

The darkness lifted the further down they went. Shadows took shape in the cramped tunnel and, eventually, Phoenix could make out the widening outline of the rock ceiling above her. She straightened her back with a groan, grateful that she no longer had to fear hitting her head against the stone.

The tunnel curved out of sight up ahead. Whatever was lighting it was brightest beyond the bend. The soft glow reached towards them, making her painfully aware of how cold the dark felt around her. They crept along the tunnel and around the corner.

They entered a large underground cave. Carefully, she dismounted and stood there for a moment. Enjoying the feeling of being able to stand on her own feet, she rubbed the stiffness from her legs as she stared at the scene before them.

Muler flicked his ears forward and gave an eager snort. He rolled an eye to look at her, as if to ask what they were waiting for, and pawed at the ground.

With a sigh, Phoenix led him into the hollow, her eyes barely believing what she was seeing.

A small fire crackled in the center of the alcove. A thin metal pot hung from a spit over the flames next to several blankets that were arranged on the ground, creating what she assumed to be a make-shift sleeping space.

The ragged desperation that had gnawed at her disappeared. The instinct that had pulled her into the cave switched to a feeling of safety in the cheery light.

A pale mare stood by the wall of the cave, watching them as she chewed her feed.

Phoenix had never seen such a fine horse in her life. The mare was small, but well-fed and obviously well cared for. The mud had been brushed from her long legs and her coat shone. She remained calm in the presence of the unknown pair that had entered without warning, watching them lazily without pausing her eating.

The hairs prickled on the back of Phoenix's neck. Slowly, she turned to see a man with a bushy beard staring at her in astonishment.

He looked to have about forty years to his age. He was dressed for travel, and he had the weary look about him of someone who had just spent several days in a saddle. His face was dirty and his hair was unkempt, but the curious eyes that studied her were crystal clear in the flickering light.

He stood at the entrance to the cave, blocking them from the only way out.

"Hello," he said, simply.

CHAPTER 3

He was a tall presence in the cave. His dark hair was long and unkempt, secured away from his face by a strip of dark leather that did little to tidy his appearance. His bushy beard obscured most of his face, but there was no mistaking the glint of intelligence in his gaze as he appraised her. His posture held a dignity that was not reflected in his baggy attire. His nondescript clothing hid his form much like his hair hid his face, and Phoenix couldn't help but think that he looked as though he were trying to hide in plain sight.

The strange man wasn't threatening - just dirty and wet, much as she was. Phoenix became keenly aware, however, that she had no way to defend herself.

"Hello," he repeated. He seemed just as surprised as she was. His dark sapphire eyes peered at her brightly.

"S-sorry," Phoenix took a step back. "I didn' know you... tha' anyone was 'ere." Phoenix moved so that Muler was between herself and the man. She clutched his reins tightly, prepared to drag him back outside somehow if they needed to make a break for it.

"That's all right. Anywhere is fair game when you're traveling on the road." He smiled with a shrug and gestured to the fire. "Would you like to dry yourself? It's awfully wet out there."

He moved to the opposite end of the fire in slow movements, putting it and Muler between himself and Phoenix.

He seemed completely at ease with her being there, showing only curiosity instead of apprehension. She realized with a
start that his careful movements were for her benefit and not
his.

"I'm Malcourt," he offered.

The name clanged through her. Its familiarity *pulled* at her
but, try as she might, Phoenix was unable to put her finger on
why. His accent proved that he wasn't from around here. Still,
in the strange circumstances of her surroundings, the security
of the cave and the openness of his expression made her relax.

She realized he was waiting for her to respond. "Marie,"
Phoenix replied, deciding at the last moment to give a false
name.

Malcourt smiled, and Phoenix thought it seemed sincere
enough. "A pleasure. Would you like some soup? I was about to
sup, and I've discovered that I have too much for just one person… And, between you and me," his tone turned conspiring,
"I don't think Powder here is going to be much of a help." He
used his thumb to direct Phoenix's attention to the pale mare
resting by the back wall. Powder, for her part, completely ignored everything around her except for her food.

Phoenix nodded despite herself. Haltingly, so as not to
show how badly she was shaking, she sat on the packed earth
across from the man. She stretched her rain-swollen fingers towards the heat of the fire, feeling grateful for the warmth that
began to energize her body.

"So, my dear," Malcourt said, ladling some soup into a tin
cup. He set it and a chunk of bread on the ground next to her
before withdrawing to the opposite side of the fire. "What are

you doing out so late on an evening such as this? Especially in these parts? Oh! Careful. The soup is hot." He added the last part as Phoenix, overcome by the rumbling in her belly, used the heel of the bread to scoop up as much of the food as was possible into her open mouth.

"Me an' Muler," Phoenix paused to work her tongue around a hot piece of taproot, "were headin' t' town. We was tryin' t' get there a'fore it got dark." He raised an eyebrow, and she could tell that he didn't believe her. "Musta lost track o' th' time," she muttered before attempting to shovel another large portion of soup into her mouth.

He nodded slowly. "Yes, you must have, to be traveling at this hour." He sat down and watched her curiously as he chewed his bread.

Phoenix made herself slow down her eating. Marla would've scolded her endlessly for such bad manners.

She cleared her throat of the unexpected lump at the thought of the Healer. "So... you travel th' woods often? I didn' think anyone did tha'..."

Malcourt chuckled dryly. "Not many do anymore. Too many hungry beasts for most people's tastes these days. I do travel them now and then, but I never expect to see anyone else while I'm out. I guess we have the weather to thank for our meeting." He smiled at her, and she was surprised to see that he meant it.

Phoenix nodded. "Tha's true. We were aimin' t' get t' th' next town a'fore we stopped, but we got caught in th' storm. Probably woulda kept goin' if it weren't fer th' wolves."

Malcourt paused. "Wolves?" he asked, his eyes bright. "There are wolves out there? Did they follow you into the clearing?"

Phoenix shook her head. Using her bread, she sopped up the

last of her broth. "They stayed in th' trees. We heard 'em how-lin' in th' woods earlier, but once they gave chase we looked fer somewhere t' hide. Muler found here, wit' you." She felt a small wave of embarrassment for intruding on his campsite.

"Did he, now?"

The both looked towards the donkey, who had left the main area and was sniffing Powder in a friendly fashion. The mare ignored him except to give her tail a flick of annoyance.

"Well, I'm glad he found us when he did. It's dangerous out there." Malcourt added more sticks to the fire. "You're welcome to share this cave with us, my dear. Both you and Muler. Powder and I would love the company, and we can all head to town together in the morning - if you'd like."

Phoenix, now that her belly was full and her body warm, felt the stress of the day evaporate. "Well..." The idea of return-ing to the cold outdoors to be trapped in a clearing surrounded by hungry wolves was not exactly appealing.

Malcourt chuckled. "The two of you can think about it and let us know in the morning." He stood and rummaged through his things, a pile of supplies stacked neatly behind him. "In the meantime, there's more than enough food for your friend."

Sure enough, as if on cue, Muler sidled up to Power and sampled some of the mare's feed.

Now that the adrenaline had finally worn off, Phoenix could acutely feel her body aching all over. The idea of stand-ing, of heading back out into the freezing cold, seemed almost impossible. The heat felt too good on her face. Even her tremors had finally stopped.

She cleared her throat. "Thank you," she told Malcourt soft-ly. He disappeared from sight for a moment, only to reappear behind her to drape a heavy blanket around her shoulders. She was conscious of how soft it was and made a noise of surprise.

None of the blankets at Avondale were anywhere close to being as nice.

"Get some rest, my dear," Malcourt said. "You must be exhausted after such a terrifying evening. It's not every day someone has to outrun a pack of wolves."

He went back to his side of the fire and settled in his blankets, looking strangely vulnerable lying on the ground. He curled up in his sleeping roll next to the dying flames and smiled at her, his eyes twinkling.

"Sleep well." Malcourt pulled his blankets up over his shoulders and rolled over, presenting his back to her. Once again, Phoenix was struck with the notion that he was doing it more for her comfort than for his.

Phoenix watched as his breathing became deep and even. She was unable to tell if he had actually fallen asleep or if he was just pretending for her benefit.

Her eyes felt heavy and Phoenix bit her cheek to keep herself alert. She pulled the blanket tight around her, savouring the feeling of the heavy material around her, the scratchy wool against her cheek.

She straightened her spine and fixed her gaze on Malcourt's slowly expanding torso.

His breathing was a soft whisper in the cave, one of the only sounds save for Powder and Muler's quiet munching.

Phoenix rested her chin in her hands, determined to stay awake until she found herself and Muler a safe place in the next town.

***

"There's one left," a rich voice said in a hushed tone.

Phoenix's senses rushed back into focus. She could hear someone talking behind her, the deep voice soft and gentle, and she was intensely aware of both the hard rock under her back and the pounding in her head. At some point during the night she had fallen asleep, that much was evident from the way she was slumped back onto the blanket, but she couldn't say how long she had been like that. Phoenix cracked open her eyes and looked around.

The tiny fire was no longer lighting the cave. The morning's light dimly lit the sheltered space, casting long shadows towards the rocky back walls.

Malcourt stood across from her, next to Muler, stroking the donkey and talking to him softly.

"Sorry about the slim pickings," he apologized to the donkey, his tone serious. "We only have treefruit left. There will be extra for lunch, though. I already notified the chef."

Muler sniffed his hand eagerly and took the offering with a wet crunch. Malcourt chuckled before turning to find Phoenix staring at him. "Ah! You're awake! Wonderful. Did you sleep well? I hope you don't mind, but I took the liberty of giving Muler a treat with his breakfast."

Wiping his hands on his trous, Malcourt bustled over to the fire to stir a pot that rested on the embers. He moved fluidly, confidently, as he crouched down next to the fire pit, but Phoenix could see that he was watching her out of the corner of his eye. Hastily, she tucked her pendant back under her tunic before he noticed the jewellery that had become visible during her sleep.

"Uh, yes. Thanks." Feeling self-conscious, Phoenix removed the blanket that she was wrapped up in and began folding it.

"Oh, don't mind that. It'll be washed soon enough." He poured water from the pot into a cup and held it out to her. "Tea?"

"Thank you." Grateful for his kindness, she accepted the tea even though the cave was stuffy and she was still warm from sleep.

"You're very welcome. I hope I steeped it long enough... I'm not very good at making it, despite my many adventures on the road."

"Thank you. It's wonderful. Really." Phoenix blinked back sudden tears, surprised at her reaction to his concern, and looked around the cave slowly to avoid his gaze. "Issit late?"

"A few hours to mid-day." Malcourt shrugged. "But I do have to be on the move shortly," he sounded apologetic. "Did you want to accompany me to the town? I could use the company. Powder isn't much for conversation..." Malcourt looked at her hopefully.

He seemed so forlorn at the idea of being left alone with his horse that Phoenix found herself nodding quickly. "I'd be delighted."

"Splendid!" His eyes twinkled as he began to pack up his things.

When his back was turned, Phoenix poured her tea into the campfire, dousing the glowing embers with the hot liquid. She was unable to enjoy it in the heat of the cave as it did little to slake her thirst.

Phoenix kicked dirt over the embers, smothering the red-hot glow into oblivion, thankful for her good fortune at meeting Malcourt. Even if Thomas was searching for her, he would never think to look for her with someone else.

Feeling her hope renewed, Phoenix went to check on Muler.

Malcourt tied his bag to Powder's saddle and hoisted his satchel so that the strap rested across his chest. The bag had strange pictures embroidered across its top flap, and Phoenix was surprised to see that everything, including their blankets, had fit easily within the two bags.

He secured Powder's reins. "Ready?"

Phoenix secured her small carrysack and nodded. "Ready."

Malcourt took the front and led them from the cave.

The sun was blinding at first. Drops of dew adorned the plants around them, slipping down to land on their heads as they exited the tunnel. Phoenix found the fresh breeze a refreshing change to the cave. Even the light, which hurt her eyes, was a welcome feeling on her face.

The terror of the previous night almost seemed impossible. Everything looked fresh and new after the storm; even the animals seemed to appreciate being back out in the open. Happy noises from the forest bombarded them from every direction.

Phoenix became aware of how badly she had to relieve herself. She cast her eyes around the clearing for an opportune spot, finally spotting a gap in the thicket behind the rocky hill.

"I'll just be at the edge of the clearing," Malcourt informed her, leading Powder towards the road.

Saved from the embarrassment of explaining her detour, Phoenix scrambled into the sheltered spot, making sure she was hidden in the leaves.

On her way back to Muler, Phoenix paused to inspect something that caught her eye. Withered strands of grass and thistle had turned grey where they clung to the rock. Their roots were bared to the elements as if the soil itself had recoiled from the grass, their remaining stalks ashen in between the rot.

Phoenix frowned, tracing the path of decay with her gaze, noting how some places were so grey it appeared as if the plants had turned to ash.

"Everything all right?" Malcourt called. He sounded cheerful, yet urgent.

Phoenix hurried back to Muler and led the donkey to where

the pair were waiting.

Malcourt was toeing the ground lazily in a shallow arch, but stopped when he saw Phoenix approach.

He whistled softly to Powder, clicking his tongue at the pale mare as he led her through the trees, her flanks pearlescent in the dim, dappled light of the forest. Phoenix assessed him as they walked, now that she was able to see him fully in the light. He wasn't as dirty as she'd first imagined; unshaven and travel-worn, but his clothes seemed surprisingly new, and his horse was of a fine standard. Phoenix felt a prickle of apprehension coil in her gut. Who was this man?

Abruptly, Malcourt stopped. "What did you say was chasing you?"

"Wolves." Wary of his tone, she searched the surrounding area. "A big ol' pack o' 'em. I could hear 'em howlin'." Her apprehension turned to fear and she struggled to keep her voice steady. "Why? Are they still here?"

Malcourt ignored her question and continued to stare at the ground in front of him. "And how was it that you knew where to find me?" His words were chosen with care, and when he turned to look at her she found herself rooted to the spot.

His eyes were dark sapphires. He watched her suspiciously, eyes narrowed as if he were trying to see through her somehow, see into her, as though he were searching for her thoughts.

"I didn'," she reminded him, slowly. "Muler did. P'rolly smelled Powder in th' cave an' thought it was a barn... Why?" She didn't like the expression on his face.

Malcourt looked at her, then nodded and relaxed. "Sorry." He gestured in front of him. "The tracks just surprised me, is all."

Phoenix took a few steps forward to see what he meant. She blinked a few times, not understanding what she saw. "Wha' are they?"

Several hand-lengths away, a multitude of paw prints were stamped into the now-dry mud. They curved down into the earth, as if large claws had retracted to gouge into the ground, and even with the shrinking of the mud each one was as large as her own footprints.

"Stormhounds," Malcourt murmured. He looked troubled as he scanned the area.

Phoenix felt the hairs along her neck stand up. "Wha's a Stormhound?"

"You don't know?" Seeing her look of confusion, Malcourt sighed and rubbed his face. He looked very tired all of a sudden. "No," he muttered, more to himself than to her. "Of course you wouldn't." Clicking to Powder, he led the mare through the trees and onto the road.

"Stormhounds," he said finally, when Phoenix had caught up, "are hunters. They are given the task of finding a certain thing, or person, and they are unstoppable until they reach it."

Securing Powder's reins, he hoisted himself up into the saddle. "They travel with the storm. It's impossible to detect them until they are on top of you. And if they consider you prey... You were very lucky, my dear."

She swung into her saddle. Even in the heat of the day, Phoenix could feel a shiver run down her spine. Something that large and dangerous seemed surreal, and she found herself making the sign against evil despite herself. "Where are they now?"

Malcourt gave her a smile, eyeing her hand gestures with amusement. "They can't conjure storms in light. They can only travel at night until they return to their maker. Don't worry. We're safe." Clicking to Powder he set a brisk pace for the two animals.

"And you Heard them..." he said softly. His words carried

back to her unintentionally.

Phoenix didn't respond and they rode on with silence between them.

***

It wasn't long before Phoenix found that she had to rearrange her carrysack in order to remove her cloak. Malcourt, for his part, seemed quite content bundled up in his traveling clothes. She watched him as he scanned the area frequently. If he was uncomfortable in the heat he gave no outward sign of it.

"What's your business in town?" Malcourt asked, as if he could read the curiosity in her mind.

Phoenix was caught off guard by the question. Quickly, she tried to come up with an answer. "Oh! Uh, I'm meetin' m' Aunt - at th' inn. She's expectin' me." The lie rested on her tongue like a foreign object, and Phoenix swallowed with a wince. "Hopefully she's not worried… wit' my bein' late an' all."

"Your aunt lives in town, then?"

"No! No, we're jus'… meetin' there." Phoenix felt uneasy as the lie grew. "I dun think she knows anyone there."

"I see." Malcourt nodded absently, his thoughts elsewhere. He offered her a friendly smile as an afterthought.

They rode on in a pleasant silence. The pace was not grueling and the little donkey had no problem keeping up with the larger mare.

After a time, however, her curiosity got the better of her. "Are y' meetin' someone?"

"Yes," Malcourt replied easily. "A friend at the very same inn, I believe… We have urgent business elsewhere, however."

Phoenix took this as a subtle hint that they would be parting ways there. She gave an absent minded nod that mimicked his own. "I see." From the corner of her eye, she saw Malcourt's lips twitch into a small smile.

"It's just over that next rise." He pointed ahead of them. "The inn is toward the center of town; just off the main road. That's where your Aunt should be waiting."

Phoenix peered ahead of them with interest. Too late she realized that they had not come across the giant tree that blocked her path last night. She pushed aside her discomfort when she realized he was looking at her expectantly. "Yeah," Phoenix said hurriedly. "She was s'posed t' get there yesterday." She felt her face flush, but Malcourt looked ahead without noticing.

The forest began to thin before them. Phoenix watched as the town's wall came into view. It started as a smudge on the horizon, a lip of grey among the dwindling trees, then the shadow stretched and grew until it was all that could be seen. It wasn't as tall as she expected - she could still see the peaks of the building-tops over - but the walls were thick enough that the guards patrolling their tops were deterrent enough for anyone thinking about climbing them.

Two guards were posted at the entrance. They stood in light armour, their postures relaxed as they chatted between themselves. The one furthest from her held a long spear, but was hanging off of it so thoroughly that Phoenix wondered if he was able to stand on his own. Apprehension swirled in Phoenix's stomach as they rode closer.

"Halt!" One of the guards stepped into the path. "State your business in Pine's Haven." They both wore thickly woven outfits, the pieces a mismatch of colors and style except for the boiled leather chest pieces that prominently displayed large tree emblems on the front.

The guard that started towards them inspected the pair intently.

"Harv? Guard Harv, is that you? I'd recognize you anywhere! How are you, my dear boy?" Malcourt's voice seemed strangely high-pitched as he dismounted and offered his hand in greeting. His dark blue eyes were squinted as he came forward, their stamp of recognition hidden by his unkempt hair and suddenly-terrible posture.

Guard Harv looked confused, but returned the greeting with his own hand. His eyes roamed Malcourt for any hint of recognition. "Ye passed through 'ere... a few weeks ago?"

"Yes! Saunders. We spoke then. Such a delight. Yes." Malcourt continued to talk in the peevish voice that Phoenix found so strange. She could see something shiny pass from his hand to the guard's.

"So, y'know 'im, then?" the other guard asked while leaning lazily against his spear.

Phoenix had to wonder if he knew how to use the weapon or if it was just for show.

"Aye. 'E passed through las' moon. Headin' t'wards th' Narrow Pass 'e was."

"Narrow Pass, eh? By th' Crystal Forest? Tha's a bit uv'a trot, innit?" The other guard didn't seem as friendly as his counterpart. He straightened his shoulders and eyed them suspiciously. "Wha' wuz yer business tha' far away, Mr. Saunders... if I can ask." It was a statement more than a question. By his haughty demeanor, he knew he had every right to investigate the pair.

Unaware of the scrutiny, Malcourt gave a dopey smile and sighed. "Love." He continued to beam like a simpleton and Phoenix had to avert her eyes, finding it hard to keep a straight face as she watched him.

The guard snorted and rolled his eyes. "'Enpeck'd," he muttered in disgust.

Guard Harv gave Malcourt a sheepish grin before focusing

on Phoenix. "An' 'oo be ye?" he asked. "I ain't seen ye a'fore."

Phoenix opened her mouth, but Malcourt interrupted her before she could speak. "My niece, Malinda. She's come to stand at the joining."

Malcourt beamed at the guards. He inclined his head ever so slightly to her as an introduction, giving her a private wink when his profile allowed it. Phoenix smiled at the guards and nodded with excitement so as not to spoil Malcourt's story. "She doesn't say much," Malcourt continued, giving the guards a humorous smile, "but she doesn't complain much, either."

"A'righ', a'righ'. Git a move on," the second guard growled, waving them on. "Dun 'ave time t' be talkin' t' ye all day." He looked past them to an approaching traveler. A large ornate carriage approached the entrance to the town from a different direction than they had arrived from.

Malcourt gave a little bow, then he turned and hauled himself back into his saddle. He clicked to Powder and continued past the gates.

"Good luck, Saunders!" Harv called after them as they made their way into town.

Phoenix held her tongue until they could no longer see the guards at their backs. "Malinda?" she asked finally, incredulously.

Malcourt rubbed the back of his neck sheepishly, his posture back to normal. "I'm sorry about that, my dear. I was hoping I wouldn't have to involve you." Looking around at the houses they passed he lowered his voice. "Sometimes it's important for me to travel unnoticed. I need to be able to move around without leaving a trail. And I didn't want anyone to track me back to you. Do you understand?"

Phoenix, strangely stung by that statement, regarded him disdainfully. "Are you a thief?"

Malcourt threw his head back and laughed so loudly that a rock dove fluttered off its perch.

Phoenix felt her cheeks grow hot from her rudeness. "I'm sorry. I shouldn't've-"

He waved his hand, chuckling. "It's quite all right. And, no, it's nothing like that I assure you." Malcourt looked thoughtful for a moment. His free hand snaked under his cloak, brushing his fingers against a pouch that was secured to his belt, as if checking to see that it was still there. He rearranged his cloak so that his belt was hidden from sight. "Sometimes I have to be secretive in order to protect the others involved. Does that make sense?"

Phoenix frowned as if in thought. "Are they thieves?" she asked dryly. She grinned to herself when Malcourt's answer was to start laughing again.

Phoenix glanced around as they plodded down the road, trying not to stare. The houses were small but mostly in good repair. They huddled together in haphazard clusters, the winding roads that divided the different areas the only marker between the different properties. The streets were not made of stone, as Phoenix remembered the outskirts of Avondale Proper boasting, but the dirt had been tamped down from years of wagon wheels and hoofprints to the point of being smooth. Much easier to navigate than different shaped stones set permanently for a road.

She made note of the different businesses they passed, creating a plan so that she could double back later to ask for work.

"Leave 'er alone!" A shrill cry cut through the air, snagging Phoenix's attention and interrupting her train of thought. "She didn't do nothin'!"

A young boy was howling at a group of older boys while running around them. The older boys, formed in a loose circle with their backs to him, turned to jeer and shove him away.

Phoenix was surprised by the behavior of the juniors. "Is tha' normal?" she asked, nodding to the group of boys.

"Unfortunately," Malcourt sighed, making a face. "There's not a lot to do here this time of day, so everyone fills their time however they can."

Phoenix frowned. She may have over-anticipated the amount of people looking for a willing set of hands.

One of the older boys pushed the screaming child down in the dirt. "Get outta 'ere, Sammy!"

"I'm tellin' Modder!" Sammy shrieked as he jumped back up, dashing tears from his eyes with the back of a hand.

One of the other boys stepped forward and grabbed his shirt collar. "Like toads y' are!"

"'Ey! Leave off!" The first boy balled his hands into fists. "Dun touch m' brodder!"

Phoenix was appalled. No one would dare act anything like this back on the farm.

"The inn is just over there," Malcourt informed her, motioning to a large building just back from the main road.

She nodded and directed Muler towards the inn. Her attention remained on the group, eyes following the scuffling boys to make sure that they remained a safe distance away. The donkey had been known to kick people for coming too close.

Something caught her eye, causing her to rein in Muler more sharply than he was used to. He huffed, then turned around to give her a baleful look.

"Sorry," she murmured, stroking his neck apologetically.

The crowd of boys - half a dozen at least - were gathered in a loose circle around a stout post, the type used for hitching horses outside of shops. Tied to the pole, secured by what looked to be a battered hunter's snare, was a small animal.

Phoenix assumed it was a dog. Its thin legs were long enough that at first glance it looked like a miniature foal, but it had a thick muzzle which put her in mind of a bear. Its ears were pressed against the side of its skull in a warning to anyone who came too close. Large splashes of white, tan, and black were patterned across its body, marbling against each other oddly as if the colors had dripped from an errant painter's brush.

The pup was trying its best to hide by backing into the wooden post that secured it. Sticks and rocks littered the ground at its feet, stacked so high in some places that the creature tripped over them in its haste to try and get free, and Phoenix realized that the boys had been throwing them at the animal.

The pup yelped as a stout stick flew through the air and intersected with the tip of its nose.

"Hey!" Phoenix's outrage snarled out of her as she shouted at the group. "Wha' do you think yer doin'?"

Startled by the new voice, the group turned towards her. Even the pup looked at her, head still lowered in defense.

There was a brief moment as their eyes met, as though everything had gone quiet around them, and Phoenix felt a strange *pull* in her gut from the little creature. Sympathy flooded her senses from the sight of it.

"Wassit t' ya?" a boy sneered. Two haughty eyes looked her up and down. "This dun concern you, girl. Best move on a'fore it do."

Enraged, Phoenix nudged Muler towards the group.

"What's going on here?" Malcourt's voice was hard with authority, surprising her with its closeness. He had followed her when he noticed she had lagged behind.

The boys scrutinized Malcourt's scruffy appearance, looking less sure of themselves now that they had his attention. Some of the older ones eyed Powder appreciatively. The one that spoke to her, a boy that looked like he matched her age, kept his attention fixed on Malcourt, assessing his interest in the situation.

"They've got a pup tied up," Phoenix said, her voice dark. "They're hurtin' it an' it can't get away."

"No we ain't," the first boy said sullenly. Phoenix glared at him until he looked at his feet. "S'just a wild stray, anyways," he muttered under his breath. "Ain't no proper dog."

Phoenix touched her heels to Muler's flanks. With a surprised lurch, the donkey charged through the boys blocking their way. They scattered with startled yelps, diving out of the way of the donkey's incoming hooves.

Phoenix came to a halt at the center of the circle. She glared at the group before she swung down from her saddle and turned her attention to the pup.

The pup backed away from her and bared her tiny teeth in warning. She was dirty as well as underfed. When she moved, Phoenix could see that she held her back paw off of the ground to protect it, refusing to put any weight on it as she stood there, hackles raised to make herself seem bigger than she was.

Phoenix felt revulsion in the pit of her stomach. "Hey now," she murmured. "S'okay. S'gonna be alrigh'." Phoenix took a step forward.

The wind picked up behind her, buffeting her hair and blowing Phoenix's scent towards the pup. She paused, two long round ears snapped forward like large bat wings as she assessed her. Slowly, Phoenix moved to the pole and began to pull at the thin snare. "Good dog," she murmured.

"Hey!" one of the boys protested, weakly. "What d' y' think yer - Ow!" he cried, when the youth next to him kicked him in the shin.

"All right. That's enough. Playtime's over." Malcourt dismounted and slowly walked through the boys. He gave them time to move out of his way; his stride never faltered, but his expression dared them to challenge him. Wisely, no one did. "All of you get home to your mothers."

The boys began to mutter. They looked even less sure of themselves than they did before. "Ha!" the sneering boy spoke up. "Who're ye t' tell-"

"Go!" Malcourt cut him off. His tone was hard and his stare on the offending boy was steady. There was no hint of the kindness on his face that Phoenix had become accustomed to.

The boy tried to hold Malcourt's eye, but he quickly dropped his gaze and muttered something to the boy next to him. With shrugs and angry glares, the boys sneered and disappeared along the streets of the town.

The young child, Sammy, had stopped crying and was watching everything with wide eyes. As the older boys disappeared, he ran over to where Phoenix was struggling with the knots. "Here." He offered her his belt knife. "Is she gonna be okay?" he asked as Phoenix used the dull blade to saw through the snarled hunter's snare.

Malcourt crouched down and let the little dog sniff his hands. "She'll be fine," he assured the child. "Thanks to you. It was brave the way that you stood up to those boys." He spoke to Sammy, but his gaze included Phoenix as well. "You'll be able to take her home soon enough."

Sammy shook his head emphatically. "If I take 'er 'ome, Patrick'll jus' give 'er back t' dem bullies. Plus modder seys I can't never 'ave no dogs." He looked upset as he contemplated the pup. "The guards'll just put 'er down if they sees 'er."

Finally cutting through the restraint, Phoenix handed the blunt knife back to Sammy.

"It's okay," she said reassuringly. Her head pounded as she

took in the condition of the pup standing with one paw raised. Phoenix rolled her shoulders. "I'll take 'er."

Malcourt pursed his lips. "Your Aunt won't object?" he probed.

"It's fine," she said, shrugging. Slowly, she extended her hand to the pup. The pup looked ready to bolt, but she gave the hand a sniff and wagged her tail slightly.

"Great!" Sammy jumped up and clapped his hands together. "'Ear tha', girl? Yer gonna be a'right!" He beamed at Phoenix and she couldn't help but smile back, feeling a flicker of warmth from his exuberance. "Well, see ya!" He spread his fingers in farewell, then turned and ran around the corner.

Malcourt watched him go with a chuckle. "Ah. The energy of youth." He turned to Phoenix and motioned to the inn. "Shall we?"

She nodded and took Muler's reins. Holding the snare in her other hand, she led the two in the direction of the inn.

"That was a very brave thing that you did back there, standing up to those boys like that," Malcourt said. He walked next to her as he led Powder. "And kind, too," he added. "If you want I can explain everything to your Aunt. I wouldn't want her to be upset."

"She won' be mindin' much," Phoenix assured him. She was feeling uncomfortable with the amount of interest Malcourt continued to show in her non-existent Aunt. "She has lotsa animals. One more ain't gonna upset 'er."

"Ah," he replied. As they approached the inn, Malcourt led them around the corner to a courtyard at the back. "The stable's back here. If you know what room your aunt is staying in, they'll room Muler accordingly." He nodded to the stableboy, who opened the door for them with a bow. "I'm only staying for a short while, myself. Just long enough to rest Powder before we continue on our way."

The boy followed them in and, with another bow, took the reins and led Powder down the row of stalls. The mare's hooves echoed dully, and Phoenix began to feel light-headed in the enclosed space.

"You're sure you'll be fine here by yourself?" Malcourt asked, his voice kind. "I can wait with you, if you'd like. I'd hate to leave you alone in a strange town..."

"I'll be fine," she said, looking around. Her gaze settled on a dappled brown and white horse. "M' Aunt's here already. Her horse's feedin' righ' there."

Following her gaze, Malcourt raised an eyebrow when he saw the horse. He inclined his head with a slight smile. "Then this is where we part ways, I'm afraid."

With a shy smile, Phoenix spread her fingers in farewell. "Thanks fer everythin', Malcourt."

"Be well, my dear. Take care of yourself." He splayed his fingers in response. Then, after giving her a quick bow, he turned and strode towards the inn.

With a sigh, Phoenix dropped Muler's reins and rested an elbow on the saddle. "Tha's th' nicest we was treated since Marla was alive, eh, Muler?"

Muler flicked his ears towards her, then swiveled them as the sound of Powder's feed bucket could be heard.

Phoenix tied the pup's rope to Muler's saddle and wondered what to do next. She assessed the stables. Well-kept, no draft, enough food for all the animals... She eyed the stalls, hoping to find them full so that the inn would be more interested in her offer to work. Instead, only a handful of horses occupied the space, their soft nickering the only sound in the otherwise dismal quiet.

She decided to ask the stableboy if the inn was looking for

any help. Hopefully she could clean or cook for an evening or two in exchange for a place for Muler in the stables.

A rustling caught her attention. Phoenix looked up to see two round yellow eyes peering down at her intently. The large owl tilted its head to the side and settled in the rafters, watching her.

Phoenix sighed and rubbed her face. Muler was hungry. She needed to find him something to eat and somewhere proper to rest where she could brush him out. The stables smelled homey, dredging up recent memories, but they were far too warm; much warmer than it was outside. The heat was giving her a headache and Phoenix was starting to feel uncomfortable. It reminded her of the stuffiness of the cave this morning. Sluggishly, she fanned a hand in front of her face.

The room had grown visibly darker. Her eyes were wide open, but somehow she was unable to see anything except outlines and shapes. Even the colours seemed drained.

Was it the Stormhounds? Did the Speaker send them after her? Did they find her? Panic gripped her as her mind raced. She reached for Muler and took a step to leave, but she found that she was unable to tell one direction from the other. The light had completely vanished, and she didn't know which way to go.

Something hard and cold crashed into her cheek, sending reverberations along her jaw and shooting into her skull. Wincing, she squinted her eyes to see what had hit her.

It was the floor. She lay there, feeling where her knees had buckled beneath her, her entire body dead weight as she struggled to move.

Wildly, she tried to force herself to get up. She found that it was of no use. Her senses had completely faded. She could no longer see or hear anything; no longer feel the pain in her cheek or head. Her eyelids were closing, and she had no energy to keep them open.

The room spun around her. She was falling, as if the floor had opened up and swallowed her whole. Phoenix tried to scream but no sound came out. She couldn't catch her breath.

She felt the hard floor under her limp body, and then, slipping into unconsciousness, she felt nothing at all.

CHAPTER 4

You found it then?

The gravelly voice scratched at the inside of Phoenix's skull. She winced as the question pounded against her temple.

Yes. I have it. We're on our way.

Only now, Malcourt? What was the delay?

These things take time. Malcourt's tone was mollifying. *Worry not. It is under control.*

I hope so. Your quest is an important one. I need not remind you of what's at stake.

No. You need not.

Is the Healer with you?

I'm here. The woman's voice was soft, yet just as strong.

You know what needs to be done?

I do.

And you're up to the task?

I am.

Very well. Good luck to you both. Keep me apprised.

Farewell, Malcourt and the woman chorused. Phoenix felt some of the pressure in her head recede.

You didn't mention the girl.

I felt no need. She is not slowing us down. It's none of his concern.

You didn't even know she was sick!

I was preoccupied. I take full responsibility for that… I didn't know if she was a threat or not.

Phoenix felt confused. She wasn't near the speakers, but try as she might she couldn't block out the sound of their voices.

A child? A threat? To you?

She Heard the Stormhounds.

You think she sent them?

I was undecided.

And now?

She seems too… genuine.

Coercion? The woman's tone hardened. Did you see her scars?

Perhaps… She was able to enter the guard ring around my camp.

You mean it didn't stop her?

It didn't even detect her.

Impossible!

It would appear not.

Well… I can see why she interests you. It seems you have a puzzle on your hands, Tolen.

I always do.

***

A slight bump caused Phoenix to open her eyes. The air was cool and crisp, its heaviness clung to her like a second skin. Above her, long inky clouds clawed their way across the sky, as if trying to catch the sun before it escaped below the horizon.

She swallowed painfully. Her tongue felt thick in her mouth, swollen and dry from lack of use. Her skull ached, throbbing in time with her left cheekbone as she pressed a probing finger against the area. Nothing broken, just tender.

Despite these discomforts, Phoenix found that she was able to move with relative ease. Her limbs no longer felt weighed down.

"We should stop soon," a woman's voice said from somewhere up ahead. Phoenix recognized it but was unable to place it. "It's almost dark, and I don't enjoy the thought of travelling if I can't see where I'm going."

"I agree," a second muffled voice replied. "We'll make camp soon. Another day or so and we should be there. Hopefully we're not too late."

"We would know if we were," the woman reminded him. "You know that. The Land would have reacted if we were too late."

"Yes, I know." The muffled voice grunted, as if moving something heavy. "I just worry. I feel like we're approaching the point of no return."

"You doubt my skills." The woman's tone was ambiguous, and Phoenix couldn't tell if she was asking a question or making a statement.

The response was a warm chuckle. "Never."

Phoenix turned her head carefully. She was lying on a pile of hay that spread across a wooden surface. There was a constant vibration in her bones that was punctuated intermittently by bumps and dips that mirrored those of a road. She could only assume that she was in the back of a moving wagon.

Phoenix tried to prop herself up to get her bearings, but she found that she was too dizzy to do so. She could feel the wagon begin to slow as it changed direction. The sharp jolts were replaced by gentle bumps as they left the road and veered into the grass.

They came to a halt. There were a few moments of silence, then a creaking noise as someone dismounted from the front of the wagon. Panicked, she sat up as quickly as possible.

The slight movement sent pains shooting through her head.

She waited for them to subside, then used the palms of her hands to push herself along the wooden planks to freedom.

She had to find Muler. She had to get out of here.

Sliding to the lip, she stretched her legs until her toes touched solid ground. Giving herself a final shove, she landed on the balls of her feet and spun quickly to look behind her.

The movement caused her to lose her footing in the slick mud. She narrowly avoided hitting her head, but managed to crack her elbow on the wagon's edge.

"Toads!" Phoenix hissed, the oath slipping past her lips. She wrapped a hand around the throbbing area to lessen the pain.

"Are you all right?" The familiar soft voice was sprinkled with both amusement and concern. Phoenix looked up to see a pale, willowy woman peering down at her. Her hair, which glowed silver in the dimming light, was bound in a long braid that reached her waist. Warm brown eyes surveyed Phoenix. It was hard to tell in the dusky light, but Phoenix guessed the woman had about forty years to her age.

Phoenix resisted the urge to back away from the strange woman. "I know you. " When the woman raised her eyebrows Phoenix lifted her chin, hoping that the motion hid the tremble in her voice. "You're the one who was talkin' in m' head."

Surprise flashed across her features, easing the foolishness that Phoenix felt from her accusation.

"So you Heard that, did you?"

Phoenix felt the familiar *pull* in her gut as Malcourt came into view, his hands clasped behind his back as he assessed her. "Interesting."

Relief rushed through Phoenix's body. She didn't know why, but the sight of Malcourt standing there eased the apprehension she felt at the idea of travelling with two complete strangers.

"Behave, Tolen," the woman murmured.

Phoenix fixed the man with a glare. Emboldened by her outrage she drew herself up to her full height. "Who are you?"

He looked impressed at her bravado - a reaction that annoyed her - and bowed with a flourish. "Tolen Malcourt, at your service, and this is Sylvia Vanrose," he gestured to the woman, "Masterhealer of Angoria, and the unfortunate holder of my moral compass."

Sylvia made a noise in her throat that Phoenix assumed was in protest, but she didn't have time to assess it as she quickly looked around. "Where's th' other man?"

She looked confused, but Malcourt looked curiously delighted. "Gone," he answered smoothly.

She shot Malcourt a look before changing the subject. "You collapsed," she told Phoenix seriously. "The stableboy sent for Tolen when he found you. I was able to get your fever under control, but your body was exhausted. You needed to sleep yourself out. We couldn't leave you there alone, so we took you with us since we were unable to find your Aunt."

"Yes," Malcourt agreed, "your mysterious Aunt. Strangely no one in Pine's Haven had heard of your Aunt before..."

Phoenix blushed despite herself. The lie had caught up with her, causing embarrassment to settle in her stomach like a stone. She had put herself in a dangerous situation without realizing it.

"You're distressing her, Tolen," Sylvia chided him. "Wait for her to feel better before you start poking around inside her head."

Rummaging next to the opening, Sylvia grabbed a waterskin hidden in the hay. She held it out to Phoenix. "You were feverish for a long time. I imagine you're quite thirsty. You're welcome to join us. We have more than enough food, but if you want to leave we understand. We did drag you along without any warning."

Malcourt's raised eyebrows disappeared underneath his hair. Sylvia gave him a look, one that he wisely chose not to dispute, and nodded. "It's up to you," he called over his shoulder, heading towards the front of the wagon.

Phoenix took the offered waterskin with a grateful word of thanks and, nearly spilling it down herself in her haste to open it, had swallowed several mouthfuls before she thought about it.

The water was the most amazing thing she had ever tasted. It was marvellous on her dry tongue, and it tasted as fresh as if she were drinking directly from a stream. Phoenix couldn't swallow it fast enough.

"Join us when you're ready," Sylvia chuckled, walking towards the front of the wagon. "And don't forget to breathe..."

There was a soft yip, and a furry shape immediately tackled Phoenix with a torrent of wet kisses.

"Pup!" Phoenix laughed and batted the pup away until she calmed down. With a whine of protest, the pup sat down in front of Phoenix and pawed at her for attention. "Yer 'ere!" Phoenix reached out with a smile and ruffled the pup's ears. The puppy wagged her tail and rolled over to show Phoenix her belly. "Glad t' see you're alrigh'." Phoenix talked softly as she scratched her. The pup's tail thumped in response to Phoenix's voice, but her eyes remained blissfully closed as Phoenix scratched her.

The horses nickered as they were unhitched from the wagon yolk.

Phoenix frowned, contemplating. She didn't relish the idea of traveling alone in the dark, and she had already shared a fire with Malcourt before... Surely he or Sylvia would know what the next town ahead of them was. Pine's Haven didn't seem particularly welcoming. She didn't even know if she could get back into the town without Malcourt's bribe.

Phoenix took several steps before deciding that she was in no danger of falling over. She squared her shoulders, then walked around to the front of the wagon.

Sylvia had unhitched the horses and tethered them to graze. Malcourt was off in the distance, using a stick to draw in the ground as he walked around the campsite. Phoenix watched him in confusion for a moment before her attention slid to the donkey tied to the side of the wagon.

"Hi, boy," Phoenix greeted him softly. She blinked back the tears of relief that had gathered in her eyes. Muler nuzzled her in greeting and Phoenix rubbed his nose affectionately in return. She pressed her forehead against his neck and stood there silently for a moment, breathing in his familiar smell.

"Dizzy?" Sylvia asked, coming to stand next to her.

Phoenix shook her head with a smile. "Wha's he doin'?" Phoenix asked, getting herself under control. She nodded to Malcourt who was still several wagon-lengths away.

"It's a protection circle," Sylvia replied, grabbing a bag out of the wagon seat. "It keeps harm away from travelers, making them hard to find. It allows them to sleep easier at night."

Sylvia pulled several treefruit out of the bag, offering them to Muler and the two horses. Phoenix groaned inwardly when she recognized the new horse as the dappled mare she'd pointed out to Malcourt at the inn.

"How do a circle in th' dirt protect people?" she asked, trying to hide the embarrassment of her discovery.

"Tolen has many talents," Sylvia replied vaguely. The woman pulled the bag for a few feet before dropping it on the ground. Phoenix could see an old fire pit next to it, a singed circle of rock left from previous travelers.

Phoenix trailed behind the woman, feeling lost. She rubbed her thumb against the bumps of the scars on her fingers, contemplating, then blurted: "Can we camp wit' you? Jus' until morning?" Phoenix might not have asked just for herself, but Muler had been traveling non-stop for several days now, and she felt a pang of guilt when she thought about him. He deserved a rest if nothing else.

Sylvia gave her a smile. "Of course. We'd appreciate your company… All of your company."

Feeling overwhelmed, Phoenix could only nod.

Warm brown eyes met hers. Sylvia assessed her for a moment before inclining her head. "Are you well enough to gather wood for a fire?"

Phoenix quickly nodded again.

"Take your time," Sylvia called as Phoenix walked to Muler. "No need to rush on the firewood."

Removing Muler's saddle, Phoenix gave him a brisk rubdown with his back cloth. She gave his hooves and mouth a quick inspection, then tethered him with Powder and the other horse.

"You get a good night's rest," she told him, carefully combing his mane with her fingertips, "an' I'll find you a nice barn tomorrow."

Muler lipped her sleeve in acknowledgement before lowering his head to graze.

Phoenix, relieved to be doing something useful, walked around and began picking up sticks that were scattered along the ground. Several times she came across the marks that Malcourt had made around camp, her toes nearly brushing against the wide circle, causing her to change directions so that she would not smudge the strange symbols.

The pup followed at her heels, finding delight in grabbing a stick and running away with it in her mouth - until she found a better one and dropped her current one to run around with her new one. Phoenix couldn't help but smile while watching her.

"You still need a name," Phoenix murmured to the pup as she trotted to the firesite, one side of the stick she carried dragging along the ground next to her.

"Pip was staying behind to keep an eye on her," Malcourt's low voice reached Phoenix's ears. "I was on my way to speak to my contact when she collapsed. He would have kept her safe until I returned. I was coming back."

Feeling guilty for eavesdropping, Phoenix made a show of noisily dropping some of the sticks. The conversation paused.

"Ho," Malcourt greeted her. "Feeling better?"

"Yes. Thanks. Jus' a bit lightheaded," she said as Malcourt took the wood from her.

"No sense in overdoing it, then," Sylvia declared, directing Phoenix to sit on a fallen log. "We don't need you getting sick on us again. After all," she took the sticks one by one from Phoenix and propped them up in a circle, "someone didn't even have the good sense to realize that you were exhausted and sick. Just because he wasn't out in the rain, it never occurred to him that others might catch their death of cold..." She shot Malcourt a look and he sighed dramatically.

"Please... It ain't his fault." Phoenix was surprised at her need to defend Malcourt.

"Now, now, Sylvia. You're distressing her," Malcourt interjected smoothly, echoing the woman's words from earlier. "Don't you realize she's had a rough day?" He winked at Phoenix as Sylvia began to sputter. "Now, then. Why don't you heat up this delicious stew that you've made? I'm sure we're all hungry. Sylvia makes the best stew. You simply must try it."

Sylvia opened her mouth in outrage, then gave a helpless laugh and waved her arms. "All right! All right. You shoo and set up the camp; leave me in peace to cook."

Malcourt gave a surprisingly boyish salute and went to the wagon to continue unpacking.

"Not you," Sylvia laid a hand on her leg as she started to rise, and Phoenix jumped at the light contact. "You stay here and rest. Tolen's big and ugly enough to manage by himself."

Phoenix stared at Sylvia incredulously, but the woman took no notice. Phoenix felt the need to protest about sitting and doing nothing while there was work to be done, but she also felt so strangely tired that she remained sitting next to the woman. The pup dropped her stick and put her head in Phoenix's lap. Phoenix scratched her ears idly. "Her limp is gone," Phoenix remarked, running a hand over the pup's front paw.

"Just some minor tissue damage." Syliva expertly arranged the wood in the fire pit. "It was an easy fix, much like your fever."

Phoenix blinked in surprise at the Healer's abilities.

It wasn't long before a small fire bloomed and crackled along the offered sticks. "What are you going to call her?" Sylvia asked after a while, sitting back on the log with Phoenix.

Phoenix gave a one-sided shrug. "I'm not sure I've known 'er long enough t' choose..." her voice trailed off as she traced the circular patterns of tan and black in the dog's fur. The pup wagged her tail happily. Unbidden, a name formed in her mind. "But I'm thinkin' 'bout callin' her 'Kit'."

"That's a beautiful name." Sylvia smiled and pulled a small pot from her bag. The pup barked her agreement and Sylvia laughed softly. "I think she likes it."

Phoenix watched the woman quietly. She had grown up with a Healer, learning how to make different poultices, how to set different bones and administer stitches. She had never had an interest in it before - usually assisting Marla under protestation - but perhaps that could be something she could do. She could find out where the woman trained and they might have a space for her.

The silence stretched as Sylvia bustled with her bag, pulling out a large metal hook and standing it over the fire. Phoenix was impressed by their forethought when it came to traveling, and also with their ability to pack. She would have sworn that the rack was far too large for the carrier.

"Is there someone you need to send a message to," Sylvia asked softly, eyes on the fire as she stoked it.

Phoenix debated telling another lie, somehow explaining the absence of her Aunt, or coming up with another story about herself. Who she was meeting; where she was travelling. Instead, she shook her head. "It can wait," she said simply.

There was a thunk, and the two looked up to see Malcourt wrestling with the blankets and supplies in the wagon. With a chuckle, Sylvia set the pot on the fire and filled it from a waterskin. Herbed broth poured into the heated pot with a sizzle of protest. Taking out some taproots, she began to peel the vegetables with her belt knife. "You're lucky you found Malcourt when you did. Stormhounds are near impossible to escape."

Phoenix nodded, remembering that Malcourt said the same thing earlier. After experiencing the terror when she and Muler were fighting to outrun them, she believed it. "What is a Stormhound, exactly?"

"The product of a powerful spell; used only for the darkest purposes." Sylvia dropped the vegetable pieces into the pot. "Blood bargaining. They're dogs, yet savage and efficient as a pack of wolves. They can track over long distances. They travel with the storm and use it to catch their prey, even adjusting their surroundings with it when necessary. Nothing can stop them. They can only be controlled by their Maker." She opened a pouch at her belt and sprinkled some spices into the soup.

Phoenix blinked in surprise to hear such superstitions coming from the woman, but she had to admit - they definitely hadn't been normal wolves, and the fallen tree that had blocked her path had mysteriously disappeared the next morning. "So... they're like huntin' dogs, then? 'Cept they hunt across th' whole of Angoria?" When Sylvia nodded, Phoenix shuddered. Fear twisted in her belly, and the growing darkness around them seemed to press tighter against her. "What's t' stop them from comin' back?"

"They won't." Malcourt had returned with the blankets. "They've already passed through this area. They'll travel the whole Land over again before they come back this way – following the night until they return to their maker. Don't worry. We're safe tonight." He sat down with a soft groan. "Now, then. Is that stew ready, Sylvia? It's been a long day for all of us. I'm sure we could all use something hot to eat." From his carrier he pulled several tin cups and handed them around.

The stew was warm and flavorful. Phoenix was surprised to find that she was starving, and she repeatedly burned her mouth trying to eat before her food had cooled enough. She sat contentedly while the adults made idle talk between them.

It became quiet for a time. The three sat without talking, enjoying the meal and the serenity of the eve around them. One by one, the stars began to appear in the sky. Kit sat by Phoenix and rested her chin on her leg. She watched Phoenix eat and gave a soft whine. Phoenix shovelled a few more spoonfuls into her mouth, then set the remaining stew down for the pup.

"So," Malcourt began, watching her, "Sylvia and I must be off at first light. We're in a bit of a hurry, I'm afraid. I trust you have everything you need to get to wherever you're going?"

Sylvia stared at him.

Phoenix felt a small twinge of panic at the thought of being alone, but she nodded in affirmation.

"Good," Malcourt said. He used his spoon to scrape the last remaining broth from the sides of his cup, then set that down for the pup as well. "Sylvia, we must make time to stop into the next village - Birchwood, I believe? - and inquire about any new spice shipments. Tessa is looking for a new source for the cold season."

Sylvia blinked at him, her face unreadable. "Oh?"

Malcourt nodded seriously, oblivious to her confusion. "We also need to look for new ink for the scribes. Masterrunner Tal is looking for new hides for the messenger drums... and Sean is looking to do some trades during foaling season," Malcourt was ticking off the points on his fingers as he spoke, "he's looking to introduce a few more bloodlines to the stock, but he just wants us to get the word out for him. No need for any contracts this early."

Sylvia nodded seriously, setting her bowl down next to Malcourt's. "Of course. I know there's a lot of room in the stables, but that's only proper. With so many workers it's hard to keep track. Sean might find one preferable over the other."

Malcourt hummed in agreement, nodding.

Phoenix couldn't help but stare at the two. She knew it was after harvest, but foreign spices were a luxury any time of year - even if they had just made their profits. And a place that boasted multiple breeding stocks as well as constant hiring... Her head swam. Where were they from?

Her gaze dropped to the pup, her snout caked with the thick broth as she happily ate her meal, before sliding to Muler, her heart swelling when she saw that the donkey had settled down for the night. Phoenix opened her mouth, the words making it just past her lips before they guttered into silence. Malcourt and Sylvia paused and turned towards her.

"Did you say something, my dear?" Malcourt's attention fixed on her, and Phoenix felt herself blush under the intensity of it.

She cleared her throat and tried again. "Take me with you."

The words came out harsher than she had meant them to, forced awkwardly into the air between them before she could reconsider.

The two adults looked at her for a moment. They remained silent. Sylvia cut her gaze to Malcourt, then leaned back as if to remove herself from the conversation. Malcourt, almost simultaneously, had leaned forward. He rested his elbows on his knees, steepling his fingers underneath his chin as he watched her. His sapphire eyes glittered in the firelight, dark and assessing as he stared at her - stared through her - without moving, but she refused to back away from his gaze. She would beg if she had to. For the sake of Muler, and now Kit, she would beg him for work.

"It seems," he drawled after a time, "that you haven't been entirely honest with me, *Marie*." He said the name with a lilt, and Phoenix realized that he hadn't used it since she first introduced herself.

Phoenix exhaled through her nose. "I didn' want t' lie – I jus' felt I had no choice." He watched her, waiting for her to continue. She took a breath. "I ran away. Me an' Muler did, I mean. My name is Phoenix... of Avondale." She added her Proper in place of a last name, as was customary. She waited for their demeanour to change, for the realization of her Bloodless status to illicit sneers, but she was only met with expressions of polite curiosity.

"Is that where your parents are, Phoenix?" Malcourt's gaze was steady as he watched her.

Phoenix briefly debated telling another lie - that they had told her to leave home, or that they had supported her leaving - but she stalled when trying to think of a good one. She didn't see the point. "Don't got none. My family - the people taking care of me - died inna fire when I was a babe."

Malcourt looked surprised, and Sylvia's gaze dropped to Phoenix's hands. "Ah," she said, as if Phoenix had answered an unasked question.

Phoenix resisted the urge to draw her hands up in to her sleeves. "Tha's wha' I was told, anyway." She stretched out a hand to see the scars creeping up the sides of her fingers. "I've had 'em as long as I can remember."

Sylvia frowned. "But where did you go after the fire? Surely you must have family somewhere?"

Phoenix shook her head. "No. No one 'cept for Muler, anyway. A woman, Marla, took me in... She was a Healer – like you, but she got th' breathin' sickness. She couldn' heal herself." A lump came to Phoenix's throat at the thought, the memory of Marla's last shallow breaths that had somehow seemed deafening at the time. "The Speaker was arrangin' t' get rid o' me an' Muler, so we left by ourselves. That's when we ran int' Malcourt - after outrunnin' th' Stormhounds."

Malcourt watched her thoughtfully. "And so you were making your way to town - why? To live?" He tapped his chin. "It is much easier to go unnoticed in larger places. Were you planning on making your living by thieving from one town to the next?"

"Tolen!" Sylvia sounded shocked.

"O' course not." Phoenix felt stung by the accusation. "I never stole nothin' in m' life. I worked hard fer m' keep - as good as any boy. I just don't got no one t' vouch fer me anymore, and

Speaker Thomas don't want no bloodless girl hangin' around t' shame him." She choked slightly on the last part, the unfairness of the situation. She had been avoiding thinking about it. Now it threatened to flood her head and pull her down all over again. "I needed t' leave. I needed t' go somewhere new. I had to."

Her breath rattled in her chest. Phoenix had always grown up knowing what she was, but now, without Marla, she truly understood how alone that made her. Pushing aside the feeling of helplessness, Phoenix straightened her spine. She didn't have the luxury of drowning in self-pity.

"Take me wit' you," she implored again, her voice stronger this time. "I ain't lookin' for charity. I'll work for my keep - and for Muler and Kit, too."

Kit, for her part, gave a soft woof and rested her muzzle on Phoenix's knee. Phoenix laid a gentle hand on the pup's head.

"Please," she added to Malcourt, who still watched her intently.

"That's enough, Tolen." Sylvia gave Phoenix a sympathetic look. "Tolen takes his tests a little too far at times, Phoenix, but I assure you he has a good heart."

"Sylvia's right," Malcourt agreed. "I do tend to push too far at times, and for that I apologize, Phoenix. You see, what we're doing - Sylvia and I - is very important. There are people out there following us; trying to stop us. I had to be sure that they weren't working through you."

Phoenix blinked. "Through me?"

He shared a look with Sylvia who gave the slightest nod in return. "We're from the court of King Benedict, Phoenix, and we're on a very important mission. An errand that some - enemies of the King - do not want to see us finish. However," he held up a hand, "I can assure you that the danger is minimal now. So, having said that: if it's work you're asking for, it's work I can provide… So long as you are honest with me, of course."

He gave her a small smile, as if to soften his words.

"Your time with me will not be easy. The tasks I assign may seem strange at times, but I will require you to finish them to the best of your ability - despite how long they take or frustrated you become. And it will not always be safe. But I will train you how to protect yourself. And, of course," he quirked a half smile, "I will be hovering incessantly."

Phoenix felt her surprise turn to shock. Her jaw dropped and she could only gape at him. It all made sense now: the fine horse; his traveling clothes; his interrogation upon meeting her. He was in disguise.

Phoenix blinked. Her thoughts fought to detangle themselves so they could catch up. Was he really saying she could live in the castle?

Phoenix slid her gaze to Sylvia. The woman seemed genuine enough. Maybe she really was his moral compass, as he claimed. And there was no denying the pull she felt around him. Meeting him had made her feel at ease. That had to count for something.

Matching his gaze, Phoenix extended her hand, palm up. She had never done it before, struck a bargain, but she had seen the men do it at the farm all the time, and Marla had done it whenever she had been agreeing to payment for her services.

She was proud of her steady hand as she held it out, even when he raised his own hand to line his palm above hers. She was worried that she would look foolish, but Malcourt looked strangely delighted for some reason.

"To having the courage to look for somewhere new," he murmured, sealing the deal.

And Phoenix was positive she felt a jolt from his palm to hers, even though there was a buffer of air between their hands.

CHAPTER 5

A soft growling next to Phoenix's ear woke her, causing her eyes to snap open. The field was tar-black. She was unable to see anything, including the hand she waved in front of her face, and it took a moment for her to realize what had woken her.

"Kit?" she prodded the pup in the ribs to wake her. "Quit it."

Kit was already awake, and she was agitated. Her round ears were pressed flat against her head and her fur bristled as she growled.

"Wha' issit, girl?" Phoenix asked.

Kit stopped and tilted her head, ears pricking forward for a moment before they flattened again and another soft growl rose from her throat.

As if in answer to her warning, an owl shrieked, unseen from the darkness. Phoenix laid a hand on the dog's back to comfort her. She jerked when a twig snapped from the other side of the wagon - the direction in which Kit was growling. Her eyes slowly adjusted to the dim star light, and she strained until she could make out several shapes moving towards them in the tall grass.

"Shh!" she heard a harsh voice growl. "You'll wake him!"

"You *shh*!" a second voice hissed, sounding sullen. "We

don't even know if he's here or not."

"He's around here somewhere. I can tell," the harsh voice responded with authority.

"How do you know?" a third voice joined the two.

The harsh voice, the leader, scoffed with a sneer. "I can smell his horse. Can't you?"

"Yeah. But I can't see it anywhere."

"Of course not, idiot," the sullen voice chimed in. "You can't see him, either. He's in his circle. You just have to find it."

"Hey!" The third one was loud now. "You're the idiot!"

"Quiet!" snapped the leader.

There was a moment of complete silence before the sullen voice whispered: "How are we supposed to get into this circle if we do happen to find it, Oliver?"

"Don't worry about it," the leader, Oliver, replied. "Our employer gave me something to take care of that."

They were now close enough that Phoenix could make out their features. Three large men, wearing thick leather and weapon sheaths, were slinking into view. They moved in a crouch, the long grasses barely covering them as they crept forward from the road.

"And then?" He looked at the largest man, whom she guessed to be Oliver. He didn't respond, but he let his hand come to rest on the hilt of his sword.

Slowly, trying to stay silent, Phoenix pulled her blanket back and turned over into a crouch. Keeping the wagon between her and the men, she crawled to the dying campfire where she had left Sylvia and Malcourt earlier that evening.

Kit, slinking beside her, kept her attention on the strange men, teeth barred in a warning that they couldn't see.

Reaching the campfire, Phoenix was relieved to find Malcourt already fully awake and sitting up. Seeing her, he put a finger to his lips to indicate silence. His eyes remained narrowed as he continued to watch the three men intently.

Being careful not to wake Sylvia, Phoenix crawled to him and pivoted so that she was sitting in the dirt. "Don't worry, Phoenix," he murmured softly, barely moving his lips. "The circle is intact. They can't see us."

"Who are they?" she murmured back, one hand coming to rest on Kit's bristling back.

Another soft growl came from Kit's throat.

"Hush," she whispered to the pup.

Sylvia, hearing the growl, stirred from sleep. "What..."

The owl shrieked again from the trees, causing the men to freeze and covering the noise that Sylvia made upon waking. A tense silence settled over the clearing.

Sylvia did not speak but, instead, much like Phoenix did, she slowly pulled back her blanket and sat up. She caught Malcourt's eye, and in response he held up three fingers. She nodded silently and reached down to check a pouch attached to her belt. It was the same one Malcourt had been wearing earlier.

"They should move on soon enough," Malcourt murmured to them. Sylvia and Phoenix nodded in acknowledgment. They remained motionless as they kept watch.

The men moved forward cautiously. They walked unerringly towards the wagon and the horses, and Phoenix found herself holding her breath. Her entire body was tense from worry, but at the same time she was incredulous. How could they not see the wagon mere foot-lengths from where they stood?

The men continued moving for what seemed like an eternity. Malcourt watched them intently, his fingers tapping purposefully on his crossed knee. Finally, when it seemed like they were going to run right into the wooden cart, the three turned sharply without warning and continued on in a straight line.

Phoenix's mouth opened in surprise. A quick glance at the other two showed that they were expecting this to happen. This was what Sylvia meant when she said that Malcourt's circle protected travelers from harm. She knew the men couldn't see them, but to have their direction change without realizing it...

The men disappeared behind a slope in the ground, and Malcourt rolled his shoulders and chuckled softly. "We should be all right."

"That was close, Tolen." Sylvia shook her head. "That was much faster than I expected. How did they know where to find us?"

"Someone from town must have tipped them off. They probably just followed the road between there and Castle Angor." He gave a shrug. "No matter. They're gone. Still, I think we should be ready to leave at first light."

Sylvia nodded in agreement. "How are you feeling, Phoenix? Any better, aside from all the excitement?"

Phoenix gave a weak smile and nodded. "I'm fine. Jus' a bit spooked, I guess. I never seen anyone like tha' a'fore."

"Did you get a good look at them, Phoenix?" Malcourt asked her.

She shook her head. "Not really. Kit woke me up," she ruffled the dog's ears, "an' I could only make them out a little, but I moved away a'fore they got too close. The leader is 'Oliver', but I dunno about th' others."

"Oliver?" Sylvia asked Malcourt.

"Could be anyone," he shrugged. "Hired thugs, maybe." He smiled at Phoenix. "That's more helpful than you might think. Thank you, Phoenix."

She gave a shy smile which was followed by a big yawn. Sylvia and Malcourt chuckled, and Phoenix felt her cheeks become warm.

"We still have several hours before we have to get on the move. Why don't you get some rest?" he asked. "You've had an exciting few days."

"Bring your blanket over here, Phoenix," Sylvia offered, sensing her hesitation at leaving the campfire. "I think it would be better if we stayed close tonight - I know I'd feel better, anyway."

Nodding gratefully, Phoenix stood and first went to check on Muler and the horses. Muler greeted her happily enough with a sleepy nudge, but he remained lying on the ground so she left him to continue sleeping.

Yawning again, she made her way around the wagon and gathered the sleeping gear. Holding the bundle of blankets out in front of her, she looked down and walked carefully over the wagon tracks to ensure that she wouldn't stumble in the darkness.

Lifting her foot to skirt a particularly deep rut, Phoenix's gaze followed the tracks away from the wagon towards the line that Malcourt had drawn in the ground several hours beforehand. He had filled in the tracks to draw the circle along even ground. She paused, her eyes lingering with a sense of dread.

Slowly, as if willing herself not to believe it, her eyes followed the broken tracks in the direction of the little hill that the men had disappeared behind. There, crouched down to the ground, the men were creeping back towards the camp along the ruts. The closest, Oliver, paused and looked up.

For a moment, the world went entirely still as their gazes locked. His eyes passed through her, searching along the edge of the circle as if he could see it. Phoenix froze in terror as she caught sight of the sword in his hand.

Malcourt and Sylvia were still by the fire pit. Kit had remained with them, so Phoenix knew she was all alone. She tried to think of some way to warn them; some way to let them know the danger that they were in, but she was frozen in place and unable to move.

She could think of nothing to say, so Phoenix did the only thing that she could think of.

She screamed.

"They're here!" Oliver reached into his pocket and threw a handful of red powder ahead of him. The powder hit the circle and separated, traveling along the markings in the ground until it met at the other side with a crash. The red light blinded Phoenix and she held up her hands to protect her face. "Now!" he yelled.

Phoenix felt her foot fall into the rut and she stumbled sharply. A thick hand grabbed the back of her tunic and yanked her into a standing position. "Got one!" the sullen voice called out.

There were sounds of a struggle coming from the direction of the fire. Desperately, Phoenix tried to pull free.

"None of that, girl," the man growled, shaking her roughly.

A savage snarl erupted next to Phoenix. A body of fur and fury crashed into them and Phoenix fell from the impact. Dashing her hand across her eyes, she looked to find Kit on top of the man that had held her.

She was a fearsome sight standing on his chest, pinning him to the ground, fur bristled and fangs bared savagely at his throat. She looked like a creature that had been born from a nightmare.

"Good girl!" Phoenix cried. She kicked the man's dropped sword out of reach and ran towards Malcourt and Sylvia.

Both were struggling with their own assailant. Oliver, the largest of the men, lifted his sword and lunged at Malcourt. Malcourt held his hand out flat in front of him and, both to Phoenix's surprise and horror, a yellow light crackled and expanded from his palm to form a shield. The sword slid harmlessly along its surface and slammed into the ground. Malcourt's free hand punched his attacker solidly in the face. Oliver grunted and fell back a few paces, his face twisted into a snarl.

The other man, the smallest one, screamed hysterically. Phoenix jerked her attention to Sylvia, who was in a defensive position and carefully watching as the thug scraped and clawed at his face helplessly. A strange yellow powder covered his eyes and nose, spreading rapidly to cover his mouth. Phoenix could see the remnants of the powder in Sylvia's hand. Despite the man's best efforts, the film continued to grow until his entire face was covered. His screams were muffled by the thin yellow material that covered his face. He ran around in a short circle and then, falling silent, dropped to the ground and became still.

Sylvia pivoted. "Tolen!" she cried.

Malcourt was using his free hand to pull a string of the yellow energy from his shield and throw it up into the air. Distracted by this task, he was unable to react in time to Oliver diving towards him in another attack.

Phoenix moved before she had time to think about it. Desperately, she grabbed one of the fist-sized rocks that surrounded the fire pit. With a grunt of effort, she used all her strength to throw the rock in Oliver's direction just as his sword thrust towards Malcourt's stomach.

It all happened at once. The string of light left Malcourt's hand before Oliver reached him, shooting into the sky at an astonishing speed. It moved through the air, illuminating the clouds around it with a muted glow as it rose. Phoenix gaped as the light continued to an impossible height. Just when she thought she would lose sight of it, the front of the beam hung motionless as if waiting for the rest of it to catch up.

It didn't have to wait long.

The tail-end collided into the front with a loud crash. The light expanded into a sphere, swelling until it looked like a small moon hanging in the sky. Yellow light exploded with a thunderous roar. The force of the blast lashed the trees around them, frightening the horses and causing them to rear against their tethers with shrill whinnies. Phoenix clapped her hands over her head as her ears were assaulted by the deafening noise.

The sky lit up. The entire clearing was illuminated with the eerie half-light, and Phoenix was momentarily blinded again for the second time that night. When her vision cleared, Phoenix found that both Oliver and Malcourt were laying on the ground several foot-lengths away from her.

Phoenix searched the ground in desperation, trying to locate the rock and figure out what had happened.

Sylvia screamed.

Oliver jumped up. Grabbing his fallen sword, he turned and advanced on Sylvia. Hastily, she picked up a stick and swung it at him. He caught it and wrestled it from her control, using it to pull her close when she tried to wrench it out of his hands. She turned to run, but he grabbed her arm and held her in place, twisting it until she cried out and fell to her knees.

"I know you have it," he snarled. "Give it to me."

"I don't know what you're talking about!" Sylvia cried.

"Don't play dumb with me!" He twisted her limb roughly, causing her to scream. "Do you want me to break your arm?" He grabbed her hair with his sword-hand for emphasis, gripping her scalp tightly. Sylvia screamed again and fell into him.

"Ah ha!" Triumphantly, he spied the pouch at her belt and sliced the cord that kept it attached. Phoenix recognized it as the one that Malcourt had been carrying earlier.

"No!" Sylvia yelled. Feebly, she reached out for it, only to be thrown to the ground once he had secured the pouch. Desperately, she grabbed at his feet but he only snarled and kicked her away.

Angrily, Phoenix picked up another rock. It wasn't as heavy as the first, and it closed the distance between them much more quickly. It hit the back of his head hard enough to cause him to stumble.

He turned slowly and fixed Phoenix with a dark glare. "You," he snarled. Gripping his sword he strode towards her.

A bright spear of light shot from behind her and hit him square in the chest, knocking him backwards. She turned to see Malcourt standing behind her, his hand raised to create another weapon.

Oliver rolled to his feet. He took off in a sprint to try and outrun the second spear, but it overtook him easily. This time it slammed into his back and he fell to the ground with a shriek.

"Stop!" he cried. He rolled over and threw the pouch on the ground. He held his sword over it. "Stop, or I'll destroy it!"

A large shape swooped down from the sky. With a scream, the owl descended upon Oliver's upheld hand and dug its claws into his arm. Oliver cried out and shook his arm to try and dislodge the bird. The owl let go and dove in front of the man, snatching the pouch from the ground and out of harm's way. With a flap of its great feathered wings, it rose easily out of reach.

"You were saying?" Malcourt asked. With a vindictive smile, he created another spear. The yellow light crackled powerfully along his hands, snaking between his fingers as it pooled in his palms. Malcourt waited a brief moment, then threw the energy across the clearing towards the man.

Oliver crossed his arms over his torso and braced himself for the impact. The light shot across the space and hit him square in the chest, the lightning spreading over his entire body. With a scream, he lost consciousness and fell to the ground.

Sylvia groaned.

Malcourt reached her first with his long legs and helped her to stand. "You are hurt," he said simply, looking worried.

"I'm fine," she said, brushing out her skirts. "Nothing permanent." She placed her hand on the bruise forming on her cheek from Oliver's boot. She winced and wiped the small trickle of blood that had formed where the skin had split. "What of you? I was so worried when you were just lying there..."

"I had the wind knocked out of me from Phoenix's rock. Nothing more."

He gave a half-smile, and Phoenix realized that she'd missed her target entirely.

"Sorry," Phoenix blushed. "I wasn' aimin' for you..."

"Nonsense," he brushed aside her apology. "If it wasn't for your quick thinking, I'd have had a sword in my belly instead of a stone. And, as luck would have it, he stabbed the stone and dropped his sword as well." He clasped his hands together - hands that only moments earlier were sending a furious arsenal towards their enemies - and gave her a slight bow. "I am in your debt."

There was a screech from the skies. An owl flapped over to Malcourt and perched on his outstretched forearm, the weight of the animal causing his arm to dip. "Hello darling. Thank you, Pip. Good girl." He removed Sylvia's pouch from the sharp beak and stroked the creature's head with appreciation. He looked up to see the expression on Phoenix's face. "Phoenix? What's wrong?"

Phoenix was aware that she was staring but she couldn't

help herself. A man who could shoot lightning and control animals? A woman who both fought and healed? And both of them had just been the subject of a deadly attack. What kind of people was she traveling with?

"She's in shock," Sylvia said of the girl, who was now gaping at the tame owl.

Pip looked at her with her large golden eyes before chirping at Malcourt and ignoring Phoenix completely.

Phoenix looked at the owl thoughtfully, positive that she had seen that pair of eyes watching her before.

"What about them?" Sylvia asked, nodding to the bodies of the two attackers. They remained still, their only movements were the rise and fall of their chests as they remained unconscious. "I've set up the alarm," Malcourt replied, stroking Pip's wingtips idly. "Rolf and the others will leave the guardstation to meet us here."

Phoenix sat down quickly, feeling overwhelmed. She looked down when she felt a pressure on her leg and saw that Kit was resting her chin on her. She frowned, looking around for the man the pup had been standing on earlier. Quickly, Phoenix ran her hands down the dog to check for any injuries. "Th' other man..."

"He took off," Malcourt replied, "while we were busy with these ones." He sighed, "which is unfortunate, as I would have liked to have had a chat with him..." His words were light enough, but the steely blue of his eyes showed an anger that his voice did not.

"No matter," Sylvia said, briskly, using a stick to coax the still-glowing embers back to life. "We've got two of them, and the Guardscaptain will be here soon, now that our position has been announced. He'll get answers from them soon enough."

Sitting down on the overturned log, ignoring the chaos that

had just erupted, Sylvia smiled at the two. "Now, then. Who wants tea?"

***

It was hours before the Guardscaptain arrived. The morning's early light had started to creep along the skyline when Phoenix first heard the horses. She looked up as Kit pricked her ears forward. "Someone's comin'," she told the other two.

The multiple sets of hoofbeats became thunderous as five riders came into view. Four armed soldiers rode in formation while one, the captain, led the charge in the front. All of the horses were lathered from the exertion of carrying fully armed men at top speed. After Malcourty had announced their location, stealth had obviously not been a priority.

Coming to a halt, the first man swung down from his saddle and gave a bow. "Master Malcourt," he greeted the man stroking the owl with practiced courtesy. He turned to Sylvia. "Healer. We came as quickly as we could..."

"You are a credit to your rank, Guardscaptain Rolf," Malcourt replied smoothly with a nod in return. "Our guests are currently recovering from the excitement in the back of the wagon. I didn't wish to disturb them until you had arrived. Fortunately, the three of us are barely worse for wear."

"Three?" Distrusting light brown eyes fell upon Phoenix. "A girl?" His tone was disapproving as he drawled the last word. Kit, as if picking up on his disdain, growled softly at Phoenix's side.

"A friend," Malcourt said simply: a soft rebuke. "She is *my*," he emphasized the word pointedly, "concern, and no one for you to worry about." Malcourt held the Guardscaptain's eye until he looked away with an abrupt nod.

"That's all well and good, but if you had given me my way," the Guardscaptain said heatedly, already ignoring Phoenix's presence, "you would have had an armed escort the entire way."

"And risk being discovered from the beginning?" Malcourt shook his head. "No. It had to be done this way. That is why you had to wait for us to meet you. They would have been watching to see if you altered your routine."

"A lot of good that did," the Captain growled. "Everything is all right, then?" His eyes switched haltingly between Sylvia and Malcourt.

"Everything is fine," Sylvia assured him in a voice that held more weight than her simple words.

"Very well then. Master Malcourt, Healer Sylvia, as Guardscaption of Angoria I insist that my men and I escort you back to Castle Angor." His words had a formal ring to them, as if he were telling them instead of asking.

"Captain Rolf," Malcourt replied, with a smooth bow. "It would be our pleasure."

With a nod, the Captain signaled to one of his men. "You. Keep an eye on our new friends in the back. Make sure they remain comfortable during the trip."

The guard dismounted with a grim nod and walked to the back of the wagon, his hand resting on his sword.

"And mind the supplies in the back. They are of utmost importance to the Healer, and to the King." Captain Rolf turned back to Malcourt. "Were you able to get anything out of him?"

Malcourt shook his head. "He's subject to a binding spell - it's how he found us. Whoever cast it was very careful. He doesn't remember anything. He couldn't answer my questions if he tried."

Captain Rolf's expression turned dark. "Even binding spells can be broken."

Phoenix felt a thrill of fear at the Guardscaptain's threat.

Malcourt inclined his head and said nothing.

The Guardscaptain turned to his soldiers. "Take your positions. And keep a sharp lookout - there could be others lurking around." The men moved about, securing themselves in a defensive position around the wagon. Phoenix, at a loss, began to pack up the camp's belongings.

"Phoenix," Malcourt beckoned to her. "I'd like you to ride in the seat with Sylvia. We're going to be traveling at a fast pace, so I'd like you to remain close."

She nodded, feeling relieved that she'd at least have some company during the ride. Rolf's eyes burning uncomfortably into her back as he watched her.

"Muler won't have no problem keepin' up tied t' th' side," she told him.

He squeezed her shoulder, as if she'd answered his unasked question. "Splendid."

With so many hands the work was completed in no time. Phoenix was so nervous by the time she climbed up into the seat next to Sylvia that she nearly fell back down while hoisting herself up.

Sylvia gave her a sympathetic look and helped her to settle with her things. "Don't mind the Captain," she told Phoenix, under her breath. "He takes his job very seriously. Just stay out of his way and he'll leave you alone." Phoenix nodded, and Sylvia smiled.

"All right." Rolf swung into his saddle and took the position up front. "Move out!"

With soldiers on either side, Malcourt bringing up the rear on the extra horse, and Pip flying overhead, it was hard for Phoenix not to feel safe traveling as she was.

CHAPTER 6

Large trees framed the road in an orderly fashion. The spaces between the shadowed trunks were illuminated by tall lanterns standing brightly against the dark, their dusky glow tickling the underside of the season's thinning leaves. The procession was hushed - whether silent or sullen was unclear to Phoenix - as the horses pulled the wagon and carried the surrounding soldiers at a fast shuffle. The sound of every kicked stone and creak of armour bounced back at them from the berth of trees. Everyone seemed tired after a day of nonstop travel.

They had met up with additional guards mere hours after Captain Rolf had led them from their camp early that morning. There had been different groups of them stationed in different Propers, some without their uniforms, waiting inconspicuously for Malcourt to arrive so that he could collect the added security on his way to Castle Angor. Secrecy had been paramount in the beginning, Sylvia explained to Phoenix during the long day that they spent being jostled by the wagon's movements. It made sense. Malcourt didn't want attention drawn to him by a security detail. He moved faster on his own.

A few of the soldiers gave Phoenix cursory glances now and then. Either they assumed she was with Sylvia, or they had been warned beforehand about saying anything. She couldn't tell. Regardless, Phoenix did her best to draw as little attention to herself as possible – even going so far as to find Kit's rope and securing the pup to the seat next to her.

Eventually the trees ended, but the dirt road continued on, disappearing into the darkness. No lanterns were placed along the road, and Phoenix found that her eyes were slow to adjust to the dark.

The soldiers continued on at the same pace, oblivious to the blindness around them while possessing knowledge of the path which they didn't share with Phoenix.

Kit was stretched out on the seat next to her. Her head was a heavy warmth in Phoenix's lap, untouched by the chill wind that reached them once they were past the protection of the trees. Gently, Phoenix stroked the dog's head.

"We're in the Grasslands," Sylvia said to Phoenix, leaning close to speak next to her ear. "They're what surround Castle Angor's protective walls. The Guardscaptain makes sure that the area stays well-cleared against any attacks."

Phoenix peered around but could not make out anything past the road. Her stomach began to churn uncomfortably. "Are we close, then?"

"Fairly close, yes." Sylvia wrapped her arm around her in a quick half hug. "Don't worry, Phoenix," she said, sensing the girl's nervousness. "They'll take good care of you here."

The procession began to slow. Several men moved to the head of the wagon and took hold of the horses' bridles, one on either side guiding the animals. Powder snorted a protest, but Sylvia's horse slowed immediately to match the pace of the surrounding soldiers.

"Position yourselves men!" Captain Rolf bellowed, his voice a giant's roar in the darkness.

Kit startled and clambered to her feet, howling at the excitement. The soldiers swelled around the wagon and flanked it on all sides. Hands on their hilts, the men kept pace with Sylvia and Phoenix in the cart.

"Halt!" Rolf shouted, his voice projecting over the moving men.

The soldiers slowed to a stop and Sylvia tightened the reins. The wheels creaked and one dipped into a large rut, causing the wagon to tip to one side. Phoenix grabbed Kit to keep her from falling out and getting trampled by the surrounding hooves.

"Have you seen the Castle during the eve before, Phoenix?" Sylvia asked.

Phoenix shook her head. "I've ne'r been this far from Avondale a'fore."

Far off in the distance, the Grasslands sloped upwards into a giant plateau, atop which Castle Angor sat like a stone ruler upon a throne. Thick spires stretched up into the clouds, their windows illuminated like distant suns against the night sky. Phoenix gasped at the sight.

The castle was huge. The outlines of the walls were obstructed by the darkness, making it impossible to see how long they extended. Light spilled out of Angor's deep windows, splashing against the surrounding stone, allowing Phoenix to see the activity within the castle grounds.

"Signal the pyres," Captain Rolf ordered, nudging his horse to the front of the party. "Last thing we need is to break our necks outside the gates.

A guard held a thin bugle to his lips and blew. The brash notes tumbled over themselves into the night air, climbing steadily in pitch and tempo to announce the arrival of the procession. The darkness hung in silence when he finished. The sound of a single horse prancing out of formation was all that could be heard.

"Can they really hear tha'?" Phoenix asked Sylvia.

"It was certainly loud," she answered. "But..."

"Wait for it," Malcourt told them, his horse coming to a halt at the front of the wagon. Phoenix could detect a smile in his voice when he said it.

A muffled shout rolled across to them from Castle Angor. The clanging of a metal gate carried easily across the distance, heralding the spots of fire that multiplied and danced into life across the tops of the battlements. They arranged themselves in a row and stood suspended in a flickering line.

Powder snorted and pawed at the ground restlessly.

"Hold," Captain Rolf commanded, unmoving in his saddle. Phoenix didn't know if he was speaking to the horse or to the soldiers around him.

Another muffled shout accompanied by muted whistling. The line of fire shot into the air, arching gracefully in different directions away from the castle, disappearing into tiny points of lights that were swallowed by the shadows. Phoenix stood in her seat to see if she could follow them in the dark.

"Arrows fired!" rang out a voice.

Several hollow thunks rang out as the arrowheads found their targets. There was a whoosh of air, and several pyres burst into life across the fields. One by one they ignited, tar and tinder spreading pools of light out into the darkened path.

Captain Rolf lifted his fist. "Steady men!"

Distant pyres burst into flame on a delay, spreading outward in a web of light so that the entire meadow was bathed with a muted glow.

"You may want to sit down, Phoenix," Malcourt cautioned her, making a show of peering over the rocky lip at the edge of the road. "I don't want to lose you down there."

Phoenix sat back down and gathered Kit up in her arms.

She felt embarrassed thinking that everyone was waiting for her, then foolish when she realized that Rolf wasn't paying her the slightest bit of attention. His gaze was captured by a dark spot in the distance.

The group remained motionless in silence until one last pyre sputtered into life. Rolf snorted with disgust.

"Go see what the holdup was," he ordered to no one in particular.

The soldier next to him clapped his fist to his chest and spurred his horse forward, two others following in his wake. The bugle wailed shrilly, and the rest of them began their descent at a much slower place.

Phoenix's nervousness made the ride pass too quickly, while also making it seem exceptionally slow. The Captain was not rushing them, but the pace he set seemed faster than it should have been for horses that were traveling all day. Especially for ones that had been pulling a wagon.

All too quickly, they reached the gates.

The heavy wooden doors - each one as wide as Phoenix was tall - stretched open in welcome. The thick metal lattice in front of them had already been retracted up out of the way, secured in position by a heavy chain. Phoenix eyed the metal points suspiciously as they rode under them, as if expecting the heavy spikes to break free and crush the wagon beneath them.

The grounds were expansive. She'd heard that whole farmlands were enclosed behind the stone walls, but if they were there they rested out of sight beyond the castle. Phoenix couldn't see the extent of the land in the darkness, but she could see by the lit space alone that all of Avondale Farm could easily settle inside.

They came to a second set of gates. Another set of walls – this set higher and thicker than the previous ones – acted as a barrier between the travelers and the castle.

Kit's ears twitched from all of the noises rushing out to greet them. She gave an inquisitive bark and gathered her legs to launch herself out of Phoenix's arms. Phoenix quickly tightened her grip on the young dog.

"Try to keep her out from underfoot," Sylvia cautioned. "You don't want her getting lost in all of the commotion."

"Sylvia's fans get rather excited when she arrives," Malcourt added in an even tone. Sylvia opened her mouth to respond, but a trumpeting of brass from one of the soldiers next to them interrupted her before she could say anything.

Shadows stretched across the courtyard. They flickered and danced, becoming smaller as more torches were lit around them. It was hard to see much of what was going on. Phoenix was conscious of all of the men around her, and the warmth of Kit straining in her lap. Another fanfare echoed the first, this time subdued and coming from the top of the wall ahead of them.

"The greeting bugle," Sylvia told her. "They've recognized the Captain and now they will open the secondary gates."

"That should get everyone excited," Malcourt added dryly. Noticing Phoenix's confusion, he gave her a smile. "Usually once the gates are closed for the night they tend to stay that way."

There was a great screeching as the metal doors moved under protest. A welcoming beacon of light spilled out onto the field.

Captain Rolf took the front and led them through the main gates into the inner cloister of the castle.

Phoenix was surprised to find yet another courtyard between them and the building. The entire Proper could hold here if needed.

The castle towered above them. Flaming pyres were spread across the grounds, illuminating the courtyard and the walls around them. Two towers stood imposing on either side of the courtyard, and Phoenix could only guess that there were others from the glints of roofs that could be seen in the distance.

What captured her attention was the life-sized statues that lined the walls and spouts of the castle.

Various creatures in an assortment of poses stared back at her. They all had reptilian faces. Arched wings and lashing tails splayed from their bodies, making the carvings seem larger than life against the plain backdrop of the stone walls. No two were alike. Their expressions and poses changed from one statue to the next. Even their outfits were unique. They were so lifelike that, at any moment, she expected the stone to shift and slither away with the day's lengthening shadows. Phoenix stared at them apprehensively. She had grown up hearing that the gargoyles would get her if she misbehaved. How strange it was that the castle embraced them as decorations for their walls.

Onlookers peered out of doors and windows to watch the late arrivals. Several came forward to assist with the horses and belongings.

Kit wiggled out of Phoenix's arms, slipping out of her leash, and hopped down next to the wagon. She ran circles around it excitedly.

"Kit," Phoenix hissed, embarrassed by her barking. "Hush! You'll upset th' castle!"

Malcourt chuckled as Sylvia reined in the horses. "She's young and excited. We'll give her a pass. Besides, I doubt that anyone's concentrating on what they're doing with all that foolish trumpeting going on. Ah, Camden, there you are."

A lanky youth with a shock of dark hair had joined them silently. "Camden, this is Phoenix. She'll be joining us for a time.

Will you take her donkey and settle him and Powder for the evening? It's too late now to sort things out properly." He said the last part almost as an explanation, but the boy nodded and, with a bow, unhitched Powder from the yoke and led the pair away.

Phoenix watched Muler go with a twinge of apprehension.

"Master Malcourt!" An out-of-breath runner stopped before him. "They're waiting for you in the royal bedchambers, sir."

"Yes, of course they are. Thank you. Alan, this is Phoenix. Take her to the girls' dorm and get her acquainted, will you? Ruby will know what to do with her." Malcourt gestured to Sylvia, and she hopped down from the wagon as he dismounted from his horse, clutching the pouch that was attached to her belt. Without another word, the two hurried towards a winding side staircase and disappeared from view.

Phoenix smiled nervously at the runner, who was eyeing her clothes with a look of disdain. "C'mon, then," he said, jerking his head curtly, giving her the impression that he had better things to be doing than escorting her around. "Leave the dog," he added, seeing her struggling to untie her lead. "Ruby'll rage if she sees it. One of the stableboys'll take care of it." He started across the courtyard without another word.

A young boy of about twelve years gave Phoenix a smile. "I'll see to her."

Phoenix returned the smile and watched him pat Kit on the head, then she grabbed her carrysack and hurried to catch up with Alan.

They trudged silently through a main corridor. People paused to look at them; most offered her a smile in greeting before turning back to their tasks.

Phoenix felt strangely heartened by the friendly atmosphere. It was a welcome change after the hostility on the farm.

"Why's the Mastercaller care how you get on, anyways?" Alan asked, almost accusingly, as he led her up a set of wide stone steps.

"Who?" Phoenix asked, pulling her attention towards him. She was only half-paying attention as she was trying to remember the turns they had taken. She wanted to be able to find her way back to the courtyard on her own.

"Mastercaller Malcourt," he repeated carefully, as if he thought she was slow. "You came with him, remember?"

Stung, Phoenix opened her mouth to reply in kind, but as they came to the top of the stairs her retort died on her lips.

A set of double doors opened in front of them, offering a view of a large furnished chamber. They entered the room without pausing, and Phoenix hastily glanced down at her boots to make sure that they were clean enough for her to enter.

The room was immaculate. Multiple couches and cushioned chairs were set up, their focal point being a carved stone hearth that was heaped high with wood. A large rug tied the room together with a warm splash of color, accenting the large woven pictures that hung on the walls. Phoenix gaped as she looked around the room in awe.

"Hey! What are you doing here?" A girl of about fifteen years had entered from another door and was regarding the pair with her hands on her hips. Her dark blond hair was tied back out of the way, but several defiant curls had escaped to frame the sides of her face. "You're not supposed to be here." She spoke loudly, and with an authority that surprised Phoenix.

Phoenix stopped walking, feeling unsure, but the girl's eyes were focused on Alan. "This is the girls' dorm. Get out."

"The Mastercaller told me to find Ruby," he replied with just as much authority, as well as a hint of consternation. "And you ain't the boss of anyone, Raena. So help or get outta the way."

"Yeah? Well, Ruby ain't here. I am."

"Well, you shouldn't be!"

"Ha!" Raena laughed. "You're one to talk."

Phoenix was shocked by their squabbling. Feeling at a loss, she was about to interject when the sound of a steady drumbeat cut through the air.

Arrested by the triumphant look on Raena's face, Alan glared at her. "Toads," he muttered and, turning sharply on his heel, ran back down the way that they had just come. Phoenix stared after him in surprise.

"Don't mind Alan," Raena told her. "He just started looking to Masterrunner Tal and now he thinks he owns the place. The drums let him know there's a message that needs delivering. I think it's perfect because it's a great way to get rid of him. Anyway! I'm Rae. What did you say your name was?"

"Didn't. It's Phoenix." Despite the girl's earlier posing, Rae seemed downright friendly as she looked at Phoenix. "I was sent t' look for Ruby?"

"*Mistress* Ruby. The Dormmaster. She runs the girls' dorm, so I wouldn't leave off her title in her hearing. She's nice enough, but proper when it comes to rules." Rae glanced out the window, taking note of the level of darkness outside. "She's probably escorting the other girls from their lessons to evening's meal. It's far too dark out for them to walk the halls by themselves. Their parents pay for a leader, so she watches them like a hawk." Her expression was both smug and dismissive at the same time, and Phoenix was unsure of what to make of it. "So, why's Master Malcourt taking care of you?"

Rae's look was intensely curious and Phoenix felt slightly embarrassed. Why *was* he taking care of her? "He said I could come 'ere t' th' castle with him when we met out on th' road."

Rae's eyes widened. "You only just met him out traveling? Seriously? What did you do - walk up and introduce yourself and talk to him and everything? That's so brave."

Phoenix couldn't tell if she was joking or not. "I found his camp out in th' storm by accident. I was already travelin', but I ran into a pack o' hounds-"

"Stormhounds?" Rae squeaked. Phoenix thought the girl's eyes were going to pop out of her head "You fought Storm-hounds and survived?"

"Not fought. Jus'... outran. Me an' Muler. He's m' don-key."

"Outran? On a donkey?" She looked impressed. "No won-der Malcourt brought you here. Hey," she looked at Phoenix thoughtfully, "you don't have the Calling, do you?"

Phoenix was confused by her question. "Am I callin' wha'?"

"No, silly. The Calling. You know..." She wiggled her fin-gers, and then waved her arms dramatically for a moment be-fore finishing off with the sign for warding off evil. Her half-smile gave the impression that she did these things in jest.

Phoenix stared at her.

"Or not," Rae said. "Never mind."

They looked at each other for a moment, the silence awk-ward between them, then Rae burst out laughing. Even Phoenix felt her mouth curve upwards.

"C'mon," Rae told her. "I'll show you around."

***

The dining hall held more people than Phoenix had ever seen before. The room stretched open before her, the hum of various conversations a welcoming buzz.

Tapestries much grander than those in the girls' dorm brightened the walls, their dyed threads a bridge between the large colored-glass windows. The weavings depicted noble-blood, in various scenes - hunting or posing in suits of armor. Most of them boasted crowns and finery that were heavily-laden with jewels.

The scalloped ceilings arched into darkness above her. Back at Avondale, some of the men had to duck when they entered the Lodging. Here, even the glow from the hearths couldn't touch the inky shadows that pooled between the rafters.

Phoenix dropped her gaze, following where Rae led. Multiple long tables and benches were set up in the room, the diners striding purposefully towards them as though they had pre-assigned seats. A quick assessment had her guessing that they sat according to rank.

"All o' Avondale Farm could fit in here," Phoenix breathed.

"This is only the small one." Rae plunked herself down on the bench next to Phoenix. "The big one is used for celebrations."

"Yeah, but we haven't had any since old Benedict got sick," a boy across the table interjected.

Rae hissed at him to be quiet. "That's King Benedict, Toby. Do you wanna get in trouble?"

"Yeah, right," he sneered, but his eyes darted around the room with the warning. "My Da says he won't be King for long if he don't hurry up and sit back on the throne. The Land's going to forget all about him."

"Well you and your Da better keep those thoughts to yourselves. Are you looking for trouble?"

"Wha's wrong wit' th' King?"

Everyone around her turned to stare in disbelief, causing heat to bloom in Phoenix's cheeks.

A gong sounded, and a line of scullers began to carry laden platters from the kitchens to the Head Table.

The small boy next to Toby leaned forward. "Hey, Rae. How come you're not serving tonight?"

"I cooked all day so Tessa gave me service off," Rae answered. Her tone turned conspiring and she lowered her voice. "Hester made broth." Everyone within earshot gave a knowing nod and pushed their bowls to the side.

"Hester?" Phoenix asked, as baskets of bread circulated among the lower tables.

"One of the older cooks. She's kind of... past her time, but Tessa still lets her help out with the food - and I help out in letting people know when she helps out." Rae gestured to those sitting around them.

Now that the food was being passed around, conversations became smaller as everyone concentrated on eating. She turned to Phoenix. "So, you really don't know about the King?"

Phoenix shook her head, breaking open a bread roll. "No one ever tells a... farmgirl anythin'."

Rae nodded, taking that as a logical explanation. "Last year King Benedict became ill. It wasn't bad at first - you could barely tell if you passed him in the halls - but last season he stopped coming to meals. Now he never leaves his room."

"It's from a Caller's curse, if you ask me," Toby said intently, nodding meaningfully towards the Masters' Table. Phoenix followed his gaze, expecting to see Malcourt, but several of the chairs on the dais remained empty.

Rae shushed him again.

Phoenix ignored him, but it was harder to ignore the snickers from the youths around them.

There was a sound of growling as two dogs fought over a morsel of fallen food. One of the scullers ran towards them and clapped his hands, shooing them from the hall.

"They should be locked up with the hunting dogs," Toby

muttered disdainfully, stuffing half of his bread into his mouth. "I dunno why they're even allowed at evening's meal."

"Probably because no one asked you," Rae answered sweetly.

"Aw, lay off, Rae," the small boy next to him drawled. "He's just jealous that the dogs are more popular than him."

"Shuddup, Dustin," Toby sputtered, showering the space in front of him with crumbs. Everyone around him laughed.

"You came with a dog, right, Phoenix?" Rae asked, seeing her scan the floor. Phoenix nodded quickly, feeling her guilt turn to surprise. Rae laughed. "News here travels fast. The Huntswoman always takes care of all the new arrivals. Her Apprentice took her when you arrived? Don't worry. Your dog's probably settled in the kennels already."

Relieved, Phoenix took a bite of her roll. The bread was fresh, crusty on the outside and warm and soft on the inside. She would have filled her empty stomach on it alone had Rae not deposited a large slice of meat pie on her plate as well.

"Tessa let me help with the meat, so I know it's expertly spiced." With a wink, Rae snagged her own piece before passing the platter down the line.

Gratitude for the girl threatened to overwhelm her. To distract herself, Phoenix forked a bite of the pie into her mouth and nearly groaned from the taste. Expertly spiced indeed. It was all she could do not to cram the entire wedge into her mouth with her fingers.

She didn't have to worry about navigating the rest of her meal. The scullers continued to leave the laden platters with Rae, who served both herself and Phoenix before passing them along.

After she had stuffed herself, Phoenix sipped her tea and took in her surroundings.

"The Head Table," Rae told her, noticing her scrutiny and nodding to the largest table next to the hearth. "That's where the royal-bloods and their guests eat.

"The High Table," she continued, motioning to a second large table, "is for nobles and their guests. Masters' Table; Servants' Table; Youth, and Juniors'." She motioned to each in turn and Phoenix could see that even the children seemed to be assembled by rank. The end of the table where she sat was the farthest down, so Phoenix had to guess that she was sitting with the common-blood - the appropriate place. Farther up the table she could see Runner Alan from earlier. He whispered intently with a well-dressed girl who batted her lashes at him. No wonder he had wanted nothing to do with Phoenix if their ranks were that far apart.

Another gong sounded, signaling end-of-meal, and workers came from the kitchens and began to clear the tables. Phoenix drained her mug and grabbed her carrysack.

"Ugh. I have so much dorm work to do," a boy next to Phoenix complained loudly as they all stood. "Stupid Westy wants all that written work for tomorrow."

"Master Weston assigned that a week ago, Randy," Toby said, rolling his eyes. "How can you not be done yet?"

"Dunno. I just ain't."

"Well, hurry up, then. Best run to your dorm so the gargoyles don't get you."

"Shut up!"

"No need to be scared. I'm jus' saying you'll have more time to work if you run-"

"And I said to shut up!"

"Phoenix," Rae said, letting the shoving boys go on ahead of them. "I have to see to Tessa before late call. Can you get back to the dorm by yourself?"

Phoenix looked around. The deepening shadows made everything look the same. It took her a moment to locate the way they came from, but she gave a nod. "I think so."

"Great! If you get lost just ask for directions - there's always somebody walking about. See you soon!" Rae splayed her fingers in parting before running towards the kitchens.

Phoenix shifted her carrysack over her shoulder. Backtracking the way they had come earlier, Phoenix walked slowly along the corridors. She wondered about going to the stables to check on Muler, or the kennels to visit Kit, but when she saw that the doors to the outside were bolted shut she decided against it and returned to the girls' dorm instead.

The common room was surprisingly full. What had been empty and quiet before was now filled with girls who fluttered about noisily. When Phoenix entered the room, they all stopped what they were doing to look at her with surprise.

An older woman glanced up from where she was stitching in a chair by the fire. "Yes? May I help you?" she asked Phoenix primly. Her salt-and-pepper hair was tied back in a thick bun, adding a severity to her appearance that made Phoenix nervous.

Phoenix was acutely aware of the stares and swallowed uneasily. All of the girls in the room were dressed so much better than she was, and they were looking at her as if her very presence offended them. "Please, Ma'am. I was told by Master Malcourt t' report t' Ruby t' get settled."

There was a pause. One of the girls tittered, but Ruby's stern eye was unable to catch the culprit. "I take it you are Miss Phoenix, then?"

"Yes, Ma'am."

She nodded and rose. "I am Mistress Ruby."

Phoenix winced visibly, berating herself for already forgetting to use the woman's title.

"I understand that you'll be staying with us for a while?" Mistress Ruby asked. She waited for Phoenix's affirming nod. "Very well, then. I will show you where to put your things." Flicking a speck of dust from her skirts, she turned to one of the older girls.

"Miss Brianna," she addressed the dark-haired girl, "please watch the room while I see to Miss Phoenix."

The girl was beautiful. She was meticulously dressed; her dark hair was done in perfect plaits, and Phoenix recognized her as the one who was talking to Alan earlier in the dining hall. "Yes, Mistress Ruby," Brianna replied respectfully, straightening her shoulders. She seemed pleased with the task of being in charge, and she smiled, but as Phoenix was led from the room she noticed the girl measuring her with a smirk.

"There are more than a dozen girls under my charge," Mistress Ruby told her as they walked down the corridor, "all with different blood and ranking. However, for the most part, all are equal when they are in my charge. I don't abide any disrespect in my dorm." She said the last part firmly, as if daring Phoenix to contradict her. Wisely, Phoenix said nothing.

At the end of the corridor was a short flight of stairs. "My room is here." She nodded to a doorway along the corridor at the base of the stairs. "Those students who are fortunate enough to be able to pay," Mistress Ruby continued as they went up the stairs, "have their own rooms down this way." She nodded to the right. "Am I to believe that it was Master Malcourt who sponsored you to the castle?"

Phoenix felt unsure. "He asked me t' come, if tha's wha' you mean... ?"

"Yes. Exactly so." They walked along the corridor to the left. "Those whose families cannot afford to pay for their own rooms, or those who work to earn their keep, stay here."

Phoenix could see that there were several rooms off the hallway; all with varying numbers of sleeping spaces.

Mistress Ruby rapped smartly on the door farthest down the hallway, opening it when there was no answer. "You will bunk here," she announced, entering the farthest room along the little hallway.

There were four beds in the chamber, each with their own small vanity and woven rug to protect bare feet from the cold stone floor. Each bed was recessed into an alcove with heavy curtains hanging next to it that could be drawn across for comfort and privacy. A spacious hearth stretched along the empty wall closest to the door. "You will take the unoccupied one on the right. There is a shared closet by the door for hanging your finery. The staircase at the end of the hall will lead you down to the cleaning rooms. The bottom floor is for bathing."

Phoenix nodded attentively. It wasn't a lot to remember, but she was already feeling overwhelmed in general.

"We have a curfew, here in the girls' hall," Mistress Ruby continued briskly. "No one is to turn in later than last call. No visitors are to be here later than late call, and absolutely no boys are allowed past the common room - and even then I will be in attendance. Last checks will be done by me, personally."

The woman looked at her so sternly for a moment, that Phoenix began to think that she had done something wrong. Then, without warning, her expression softened. "Have you eaten?"

Relieved, Phoenix nodded. "Yes, Ma'am. Rae showed me t' th' hall earlier."

Mistress Ruby gave a nod. "Rae's one of the good ones. She has a smart head on her shoulders. You'd be wise to make a friend in her." Before she could explain the cryptic remark, another bell sounded and the Mistress nodded. "That's the late call. All youths should be getting ready for turn in. I have to see to the other girls, but you may as well stay here if you've no further business within the castle?"

There was a pause, and Phoenix realized that the last part was a question. "No, Ma'am. I ain't got any business in th' castle." Belatedly, she thought of Kit and Muler and instantly regretted her hasty statement.

"Very well then, Miss Phoenix. Morning's meal begins promptly at second call, which is five hours before median light." The Mistress paused and offered Phoenix a small smile. "Pleasant dreaming, Miss Phoenix. You know where to find me if you need me." Phoenix nodded, and the woman swept from the room and back to the common area to reclaim her duties.

Phoenix padded to her alcove and set her carrysack down. Left to herself for the first time in nearly two days, Phoenix savoured the silence and sank down into the comfort of her new bed.

Her head was swimming. She had already met more people than she had ever known, and they all had such different roles at Castle Angor. It was a lot to take in. And then there was Malcourt... She had expected to see him again before evening's end, but he had been absent from the dining hall. What could the Mastercaller possibly want from her that he couldn't get from anyone else in the castle?

Two girls around her age shuffled into the room, their conversation trailing off as they looked at her in surprise.

"I'm Phoenix," she offered into the silence, raising a hand in greeting. She fervently hoped that they were the last new faces of the day.

"Elise," the first girl responded softly, raising her hand as well. Twin black braids zigzagged across her scalp before coiling together down one shoulder. She smiled shyly, the action causing her rich brown skin to crinkle at the corners of her dark eyes. It was the first time Phoenix had met someone darker than herself.

"Sophie," said the shorter, tan-skinned girl. Her pale brown eyes were wary as she eyed Phoenix, not returning the greeting gesture. Her curtain of dark hair was swept to one side, held in place by a comb that matched her bright, embroidered skirts.

The three looked at each other awkwardly. Phoenix was unsure how to proceed, as she had never met any youths other than those who had grown up with her on the farm.

"You're staying in here, with us?" Elise asked, looking at Phoenix's little bag of belongings next to her on her bed. "Did you arrive today?"

"Where is it that you're from?" Sophie asked before Phoenix could answer Elise. "I didn't see you in the meal hall."

"I was sittin' with Rae. An', yeah, I came today."

Elise's eyes widened. "Were you the one who arrived with the Mastercaller?"

Sophie stiffened and took an involuntary step backwards. Confused, Phoenix drew back from the look that the two were giving her.

The sound of slapping feet in the corridor interrupted them, and Rae slid into the silent room. "Ha!" She exclaimed, raising her palms in triumph. The girls stared at her, then the other two couldn't help but grin as the bell for last call rang. The tension in the room disappeared immediately.

"You've got to be more careful, Rae," Sophie scolded. "You're going to get in trouble one of these days."

"Yeah, probably," Rae agreed, keeping her arms outstretched and falling backwards onto her bed. "Hey, Phoenix," she propped herself up on her elbow. "Are you staying in our room?" When she nodded, Rae's face lit up. "Great! We could use another friendly face around here." She gave the other two a knowing look, and Phoenix could see their expressions shift from distrust to curiosity as they watched her.

"Friendly face?" Phoenix asked nervously.

"Yeah," Rae said, jumping up to shed her clothing for sleep. "Some of the other girls are too concerned with rank to make friends."

"Brianna," Elise muttered, folding back her covers before getting ready for bed.

Phoenix followed suit and set her carrysack on the unused vanity next to her. "The girl who was talking with Alan all meal?" Phoenix sat on the edge of her bed, pulling off her boots and wiggling her toes with satisfaction.

"Oh ho!" Rae laughed. "Was she now?" The other girls looked at each other and Rae erupted into such a loud fit of giggling that she had to clap her hand over her mouth to muffle the sound.

Sophie sniffed, her pert nose flaring with the action. "It's not funny, Rae. Poor Alan."

"Poor Alan indeed," Rae snorted, rolling her eyes. "Couldn't happen to a nicer guy."

"Don't be unkind," Elise chided, but Phoenix wasn't sure how much the girl meant it. "She probably has him wrapped around her little finger just for fun. You know how she is."

Rae shrugged. "You know how they all are." She gestured widely, and Phoenix was unsure if she meant the dorm or the surrounding castle. "They both know what they're doing."

Seeing Phoenix's confusion, Rae dropped her hands. "I dunno how it was done back where you came from, Phoenix, but the noble-bloods like to play with each other here at Angor. They're into the sport of Ranking."

"Not only nobles like the sport," Elise murmured, changing into her sleeping shift.

"It's not very sporting if you ask me," muttered Sophie, climbing into her bed. She pulled the curtain across her alcove, signaling her departure from the conversation.

"Ranking?" Phoenix asked softly, mindful of the girl's privacy.

Rae nodded. "Kingdom rank. Rank in the castle. Everyone loves trying to get to the top." She rolled her eyes expressively.

"For wha' purpose?"

"The higher up you rank, the more people rank below you," Elise shrugged. "That means more people have to listen to what you have to say."

"Not that what you have to say gets any better," Rae muttered. "Basically, it means that more people have to do stuff for you if you tell them to... I'm guessing that's not how it worked where you came from?"

Phoenix shrugged a shoulder. "I stayed with a woman, Marla. We lived by ourselves, but we had a Speaker who represented us t' th' Manor, otherwise we jus' did stuff fer ourselves."

Elise's soft laughter tumbled out of her, and Rae flashed Phoenix a grin. "I think you're going to fit in just fine," Rae told her, her eyes dancing.

CHAPTER 7

Phoenix was shaken awake. She gave a soft groan of protest, then felt a moment of panic when she realized she was in unfamiliar surroundings.

"Phoenix?" It was Rae who was shaking her in the pre-morning light.

"Mrr?" It had been a long time since Phoenix had slept in a bed, and she was finding her body was protesting the need to be awake.

"I gotta take you to the kitchens," Rae's voice was quiet as she shook her again. "C'mon."

With another soft groan, Phoenix rolled out of bed and began to dress.

"Don't you have any clean clothes? Oh, never mind. C'mon. Tessa's waiting."

They padded quietly from the room, easing out into the hallway while being careful not to wake the other girls. Once they passed through the doorway, Rae quickened her stride and bolted down the corridor, ignoring Phoenix's hiss to slow down. She had no choice but to run to keep up.

They flew down the first set of stairs, all but sliding down the bannister in their haste.

"Miss Rae. Miss Phoenix. Am I to understand that both of

you will be working in the kitchens this morning?" Mistress Ruby had appeared at her doorway, her unbound hair crinkled from sleep, coiling around the edging of her nightgown. Her eyes were narrowed against the lantern lights, and Phoenix felt a pang of guilt for waking her so early.

The girls skidded to a stop. "Yes, Mistress," Rae looked as guilty as Phoenix felt. "Kitchenmaster Tessa asked me to collect Phoenix to help with morning's meal."

"Did she now?" Mistress Ruby looked disapprovingly between the two, as if waiting for one of them to confess a more mysterious motive. Finally, she gave a clipped sigh. "Very well. But please make sure that in the future, Tessa discusses the schedule changes of my charges with me." Mistress Ruby held Rae's gaze until she blushed.

"Yes, Mistress," Rae said, helplessly.

Satisfied, Ruby nodded and gestured for them to continue on their way.

"Ladies do not run!" She instructed after their rapidly-disappearing backs.

The two were out of breath by the time they reached the lower kitchens.

A tall woman stood at a large prep table with a serene expression on her face. Even though she barely moved, her actions seemed to dominate the entire room. Others bustled around her and tended to their tasks, yet she was able to keep perfect track of them while expertly kneading and shaping the floured dough in front of her. "Stef," she called, barely looking up from her work, "flip those eggs, please. They'll burn if you don't. Marsha, wipe up that spill by your foot. We don't need anyone cracking their skull before morning's meal. I'm sure the Healers wouldn't mind the luxury of sleeping until a proper hour for once."

There was a chuckle from someone nearby as the woman identified as Marsha bent to clean the floor.

Rae led Phoenix towards the woman. "Ah, Rae. There you are. You're almost late." She placed the dough by the hearth to rise, then turned to look at them, wiping her hands in her apron. "Did Ruby give you a hard time about the schedule change?"

Flour dusted her cheeks and her spiked short black hair. Her face was rosy from the warmth of the kitchens, but her eyes were exceptionally bright and her gaze perceptive, contradicting her look of disarray.

"So you're Miss Phoenix? Tall for a girl, aren't you? Well, come closer, child. Let me get a look at you. I don't bite." Phoenix flushed, aware that those immediately around them were staring. She stepped forward to be inspected, feeling self-conscious. "You're who all the talk is about? Hmm."

"Mistress?" Phoenix asked shyly.

Tessa smiled. "No rank here in the kitchens, Phoenix. 'Tessa' will do just fine. And pay no mind to all the curiosity you'll be getting. Everyone loves a bit of gossip around here - especially about one who arrives in such an... unusual fashion." She dismissed her own remark with a wave of her hand.

"Rae, will you go help Stef, please? I'm going to show Phoenix around."

Rae winked at Phoenix, then grabbed a metal spatula and went to go stand by an older woman cooking eggs.

"Now then, Rae tells me that you grew up on a farm?" Tessa led Phoenix away from the curious onlookers, stopping at a small closet to pull out an apron and a hide tie. "You're familiar with the workings of a kitchen, I assume, being a rural girl?"

"I worked there for th' cold seasons, when there weren't nothin' t' grow or t' harvest," she acknowledged. Phoenix used the hide tie to secure her curls away from her face before don-ning the apron.

Tessa stared at her a moment. Surprise tinged her features. "Your mother let you work in the fields?"

"I worked in th' fields. Me an' Muler." She purposefully skirted the question of her blood.

Tessa blinked, then nodded her head slightly. "Well then," she continued, "tell me what experience you have in cooking."

Phoenix did so as Tessa led her on a tour around the kitchens. She pointed out a few of the pieces of equipment that she was familiar with, and for the most part Tessa listened, interrupting with a question or two at various points of Phoenix's explanations. Several times, she positioned her at a station and had her continue the work of the cook who was there.

"You're already ahead of some of the workers here," Tessa told her when she had finished shaping the dough that the woman had left to rise. "Rae was right to bring you."

Phoenix felt relief flood through her body. "Y'mean... I can stay on?"

Tessa patted her arm. "I'm not one to turn away a good worker. I'll help Master Malcourt keep you occupied, and if it's a good fit you'll have a place here regardless of who you're looking to."

Relief washed over her. Work was not a problem for her. Somewhere that would accept her and allow her to earn her keep was better than she had hoped for.

"Now, you go eat and get ready for the rest of your day. You're supposed to be in the hall with the other girls, but I expect you here with Rae bright and early tomorrow morning, understand?"

Phoenix nodded again. A woman by the spit called out for help, and Tessa gave a suffering sigh before giving Phoenix a smile. "Hurry, now, or you'll be late." She shooed her in dismissal and joined the woman by the hearth. Rae gave Phoenix a thumb up, and then Phoenix was speeding off to their table in the dining hall.

"You left early this morning. I didn't hear you get up." Elise sat down next to her, offering her a smile. Sophie sat next to Elise, balancing an open book on each knee as she compared the writing on their pages. "I'm guessing Rae dragged you to the kitchens? How did it go?"

"Tessa wants me t' report t' her tomorrow."

"Does this mean that you look to her?" Sophie's expression was one of disbelief.

"Look t' her?" Phoenix asked, noting how Tessa herself had used the exact phrase only a few moments ago. "Does tha' mean somethin'?"

"Of course," Sophie sniffed critically, but not condescendingly. "Those who work here look to someone - an established worker or Master who is in charge of them until they are able to work unsupervised. Then they're given permanent residence."

"Rae looks to Tessa, too," Elise told her. "Sophie looks to Minna, the Masterclothier, and I look to Master Weston - he's the Masterscripter."

"Masterscripter?" Phoenix blinked. She began to wonder how many titles floated around Castle Angor.

"He teaches language as is 'proper for a person of stature!'" Elise's voice took on a grand tone, and Phoenix could only assume that she was mimicking Master Weston. "You'll meet him after meal," she continued merrily. "He's great. Sophie especially thinks so."

"I do not!" Sophie protested loudly. "If he would teach the lesson properly the first time..." she trailed off, blushing, as her outburst grabbed the attention of those around her. She shot Elise a furious look. "Not funny!" she hissed, but Elise was grinning good-naturedly from her teasing.

"Hush now," Elise told Sophie. She inclined her head meaningfully towards the Masters' Table to indicate that he was already seated.

Sophie huffed and said nothing.

A gong sounded and the meal began.

Phoenix helped herself to some bread and eggs, pouring herself and the other girls a glass of fresh juice as she did so.

"Would you look at that!" The boy next to her exclaimed to his tablemates. Phoenix followed his gaze towards the Head Table.

There was a muted hush of surprise at the front of the room. A man with about thirty years wove between the chairs before seating himself at one that afforded him a view of the entire hall.

He was striking, with dark hair and bright vibrant eyes, and he moved with a grace that made her stop and stare. Which, admittedly, most of the room was already doing.

It took Phoenix a moment to realize she was still standing from pouring the juice. She sat back down with an unceremonious plop. "Who's tha'?" she breathed.

"Prince Hallan," Elise replied slowly, as if unsure of what she was seeing.

Phoenix felt relieved when she realized that the girl was paying as much attention to the Prince as she was.

"But he hasn't been to the hall since the King fell ill." Sophie, who was shorter than those around her, craned her head to try and get a better glimpse of him.

Prince Hallan's manner was relaxed. He smiled easily as he conversed with his table mates, the ones nearest to him tipping their head back in laughter when he spoke.

"Does tha' mean th' King is better?" Phoenix watched the

Prince with fascination. "Surely his own son wouldn't be so happy if he were still sick?"

Elise and Sophie stared at her with wide eyes. "You mean, you don't know?" Sophie gaped.

"Know wha'?" Phoenix asked, the question coming out more testily than she meant it to. Phoenix was starting to get tired of all the things that people already assumed she knew.

The girls exchanged a look.

"No one tells a farm girl anythin'," Phoenix added. She used the same excuse that she had used before on Rae, and both girls relented with looks of pity.

"Right. Of course. Sorry, Phoenix. It must have been awful, being so isolated like that." Elise extended her hand.

Phoenix shrugged and tried not to think about her previous life. "Forget it," she said, accepting the apology.

"Well, anyway," Sophie began, "Prince Hallan isn't King Benedict's son. He was brother to Queen Helena - the King's wife. They're not from Angoria. They're royalty from the next kingdom over..."

"Kaltor," Elise supplied.

Phoenix didn't know where that was, but she nodded and Sophie continued. "He was very distraught once the King took sick. He said that with the deaths of the Queen and the Princess, the King was the closest thing he had to family. He never left his side. But that means that King Benedict must be doing better if the Prince is here eating in the hall."

"He must be very kind," Phoenix murmured. She found that she couldn't stop her eyes from darting back towards the Head Table while she ate. She surprised herself by wishing that she were closer in order to hear what he was saying to his laughing table companions.

"He's a gentleman." Elise's smile was sly as she finished her morning's meal. "No one's been able to turn his head - despite all their best efforts." Both girls looked pointedly at Brianna and the gaggle of girls that surrounded her at the other end of their table.

Another round of tea began to circulate, and Elise stretched quickly and stood. "I have to set up the Scripting Room for to-day's lessons. See you soon?"

Phoenix remained silent as Elise looked pointedly at Sophie, but Sophie nodded an affirmative for the both of them, hanging the girl one of the books on her lap. "We'll be there." Elise raised her hand in parting and strode quickly from the hall.

"Scripting Room?" Phoenix asked Sophie over the empty chair between them.

"Yeah. all the Angor girls have lessons with him first thing in the day." Her voice took on a stern tone that mimicked that of Mistress Ruby. "It is important for every Lady, no matter of standing or stature, to be able to express themselves with pro-priety and distinction." She then shrugged to dispel the imper-sonation.

"All th' girls get taught th' same time?"

"It's done by age, usually. If you're smart you get bumped up a level." Sophie scanned the hall, her face unreadable. "C'mon. Let's get there before the others. I hate getting stuck sitting by the drafty window."

Phoenix drained her mug and followed Sophie from the hall.

It was a long walk to the Scripting Room. It was the deepest that Phoenix had travelled into Castle Angor, and her head was spinning as she tried to remember her way. She wished that they would slow down so she could get her bearings, but So-phie had set the pace and she seemed reluctant to slow down.

Rae and Elise were already in the room when they reached

it. "Apparently he's even asking for food!" Rae was saying as they entered. "He hasn't wanted to eat in ages! It always made him sick."

Phoenix helped Sophie arrange the chairs next to them. "Who?" Sophie asked.

"King Benedict!"

"I was wondering. Prince Hallan was in the hall for breakfast today."

"No!" Rae clapped her hand over her mouth.

Phoenix listened to the girls chat while she looked around the room. No tapestries adorned the walls here. Instead, large parchments of different colors were nailed to the stone, each with different flowing symbols brushed onto them. The squiggles reminded Phoenix of spiders, and she felt that it was a strange choice of decoration in comparison to the rest of the castle.

There was a bustling in the hall, and Rae and Sophie fell silent as the rest of the girls arrived. Phoenix sat in the empty seat next to the now-subdued Rae, staying as quiet as she was, but she couldn't help but stare as the rest of the girls entered.

They were dressed in a kind of finery that she had never seen before. Their clothing was elegant; flimsy and brightly colored. The dresses were modest and revealed nothing, high-necked with skirts down to their ankles, but they were tailored to flatter the shapes of the girls who wore them. Many of them wore headscarves to protect the intricate designs that they had woven into their hair.

Phoenix became acutely aware of her dirty clothing and simple-bound hair. Unconsciously she smoothed a crease in the lap of her pant leg.

Brianna, her dark hair shining with the window's sunlight, led the group across the room to the remaining chairs. Spying Phoenix, she stopped halfway across the floor to evaluate her with a calculating glance.

The girl was beautiful. Her dark hair hung in perfect ringlets, framing her face under her scarf, the wispy material holding it in place expertly. Her pale skin contrasted her full pink lips that were pursed in thought as she assessed Phoenix.

Phoenix offered a smile and spread her fingers in greeting. Brianna's leaf-green eyes flashed and, with a sniff, she led the rest of the girls to their seats.

The silence was uncomfortable. Elise and Sophie fidgeted nervously while Rae just looked straight ahead of her, lips pressed together tightly.

To Phoenix's relief, an older man bustled in as the rest of the girls took their seats. He struggled with an overflowing armful of ledgers, and would have dropped them on the way to his desk had Elise not jumped up to assist him.

Once they stood in a precarious stack, he turned to assess the room with a scowl. He was a bit more dishevelled than Phoenix had expected. His Master's robes were clean, but rumpled around his torso from the ledgerwork he had carried. His skin was pale, his back held a slight hunch, presumably from years of sitting at a desk, and his white hair stuck out in unruly tufts over his ears. His appearance would have been comical if not for the permanent frown that was etched on his face.

"Good morning, ladies," he greeted the room, and Phoenix was astonished to hear a rolling sound come from his mouth when he pronounced the 'r'.

"Good morning, Master Weston," the girls chorused in reply.

"Miss Jenny. Would you be so kind as to take attendance while I set up the lesson?"

"Yes, Master Weston." A slight blonde girl dressed in pink, rose and dipped into a curtsy to the Master. She plucked a led-

ger from the pile, standing poised at the front of the room, and
began calling names amongst muffled titters from the other
girls.

Jenny checked off each name as it was acknowledged. Then,
when she had finished, gave a smirk and returned to her seat
next to Brianna.

Only then did Phoenix realize why they were laughing.
Jenny had not said her name.

"Splendid!" Master Weston's words were precisely enun-
ciated, but the tone didn't match the expression on his face.
"Now, then, please turn your workbooks to page twenty-eight,
and have your dorm work out and ready for inspection."

It was then, while everyone turned the pages of the books
on their lap, that Phoenix realized that she didn't have a workbook.

Clasping his hands behind his back, Master Weston walked
around the room, glancing at some while reading others more
thoroughly. He stopped when he came to Phoenix.

"And where is yours, young miss?" he asked, peering down
at her from under his bushy white eyebrows.

Phoenix blinked as he scrutinized her. Surely he must realize he'd never seen her before...

"I don't got any," she replied, starting to feel flustered.

He clutched at his chest. "What! You don't got any?" He
jerked backwards, as if repulsed.

"Yes, sir," she said meekly. "I'm Phoenix. I'm new."

He stared at her, as if trying to decide whether she was lying or not. "I see," he said finally, somewhat stiffly. "And where
is it that you grew up in order to learn such an atrocious way
of speaking?"

Giggles came from behind her, and Phoenix felt her face
become hot, but Master Weston seemed oblivious to the dis-

comfort that he was causing.

"Avondale Farm... sir."

"Harrumph!" He walked back to his desk and picked up the ledger. "Your full name, please?" His face was polite, but his tone had a hardness in it she couldn't identify.

Phoenix straightened in her chair. "Phoenix... of Avondale."

There were audible gasps from the girls behind her, and Phoenix felt what little confidence she had left gutter into nothingness.

"Spell that for me please."

Phoenix blinked. "Sir?"

He sighed. "Is it with a P or an F... ? Nevermind. You can adjust it later. Recite your numbers please," he instructed in a bored tone, writing her name in the ledger.

Haltingly, aware that everyone in the room was watching her - with the exception of her friends, who were doing their best to look anywhere else - Phoenix began counting.

"And your letters," he interrupted when she started to repeat the higher patterns.

Embarrassment twisted in her gut. Phoenix kept her back straight as she sat in the chair, staying respectful as she answered his questions. Taking a shaky breath, as if that would somehow calm the fluttering her in stomach, she recited the letters from the song she'd learned as a child.

"How many years are you, Miss Phoenix?"

"Fifteen, sir."

He gave a disgusted sigh and wrote several lines on a separate piece of parchment. "Very well, Miss Phoenix. Your farm provided you with the most basic of lingual beginnings – which is no small miracle, let me assure you - so I feel that we can continue. See me after class for your assignments. You'll have to work hard to catch up on your dorm work. Now then, please read the fourth paragraph down on page thirty, but replace the subject with your own name."

Phoenix stared at him, entranced by his eloquent way of speech despite herself. She wondered if she had to learn to roll her 'r's as well.

She realized that he was looking at her expectantly as if waiting for something. "Sir?" she asked.

"Open your workbook to page thirty," he repeated, carefully, "and find the fourth chunk of - yes, thank you Miss Rae. Your generosity is boundless. Miss Phoenix, can you read Miss Rae's workbook and tell me what the subject is, please?" He looked at her expectantly, but she only stared at him blankly.

"Never mind," he said in a disgusted tone. Master Weston pinched the bridge of his nose with a long-suffering sigh. "I see we have more to catch up on than I previously thought. Just read the paragraph."

Phoenix looked down at the workbook in front of her. Small squiggles, much like those on the walls around them, swooped across the page. She looked at them desperately, trying to decipher them, but try as she might she couldn't understand what he was asking of her.

Master Weston cleared his throat and she looked up at him. He was staring at her in disbelief. "Am I correct in assuming that you are unable to read?"

The scorn in his voice brought tears to her eyes. Immediately, Brianna and the others fell to whispering among themselves. She was aware of Rae giving her hand a squeeze.

"I can do nothing for you. You obviously need a more... remedial setting." Poorly-stifled giggles erupted from the back of the room. Phoenix felt a hot tear run down her cheek and she watched it land on Rae's workbook before her.

Master Weston glared at the girls until they fell silent. "Please excuse yourself," he said to Phoenix, his voice scathing. "You've wasted enough of our time for one day."

Rae squeezed her hand again, but she barely felt it. Locking her spine, she rose without looking at anyone and quickly slipped from the room.

"Now then, ladies. Please direct your attention to page thirty..."

Master Weston's voice drifted away as Phoenix all but ran down the hall. She looked straight ahead as she walked, willing herself invisible so that no one would stop her to demand where she was going.

She walked blindly, taking no note of where she was going until she reached a dead end and threw herself down on one of the many stone benches that lined the hall. She sniffed softly.

She felt like Speaker Thomas had just finished yelling at her. If everyone at Castle Angor knew how to read and write - and if she was truly as hopeless as Master Weston had indicated - then how much longer would it be until they, too, kicked her out? Where would she go this time? And where was Malcourt? He had wanted her to come, yet he was quick enough to pawn her off as soon as they arrived.

Angry, she blinked away her tears, wiping her face with the heel of her hand. No sense in crying, she told herself firmly, there was no help for it now.

Unless... Unless she could speak with Tessa. Surely she could work in the kitchens until she got sorted out. Maybe she could move out of the dorms and away from Brianna and her cronies. Before she had to spend too much time around them. Before she became too attached to the rest of the girls there. Before she made more friends...

With a sigh, Phoenix straightened her shoulders and looked around. She had no idea where she was. She must have gone in the opposite direction she had come from. She must be on the other side of the hall, otherwise her surroundings would seem at least a little familiar.

Phoenix stood and tried to get her bearings from a nearby window.

Looking outside, she was struck by the enormity of Castle Angor's lands. She watched the wind play in the yellowing fields, causing the grass to dance and bow in waves.

The castle was making Phoenix feel claustrophobic. She was used to the open air and the sunshine, not stuffy halls and thick-walled rooms. Perhaps she could work for Tessa until she had enough to pay for traveling supplies...

Phoenix turned determinedly from the window and began to look for an exit. She noticed a cramped stairway in the wall to her left and quickly slipped into it. The winding stairs led down to a corridor that seemed familiar, but with so many of the halls looking similar she realized that she was still unsure how to get back to the dorms.

Something nudged at her leg, and Phoenix looked down to see a wagging tail and bright eyes looking up at her.

"Kit!" Phoenix exclaimed. Excitedly, she knelt down to rub the pup all over as Kit wagged her tail harder and licked Phoenix's face.

"Where'd you come from, girl?"

Kit gave a yip and scampered away a few paces before stopping to look back at her. Phoenix followed her curiously.

Kit led her through a doorway and down a side corridor. A moment later, the pup squeezed through a thick wooden door that was left ajar. Phoenix paused, then pushed on the heavy wood and was rewarded with the morning's sun on her face. Quickly she slipped outdoors.

The air was cool against her skin. She took a deep breath, savouring the chill as it filled her lungs.

Kit trotted ahead of her, across the open courtyard and towards the stables. Smiling, Phoenix lengthened her stride to catch up.

The barn was cozy with the smell of hay and animals. Feeling comfortable for the first time since she arrived, Phoenix trailed her hands along the stall doors as she walked down the aisles. The horses barely registered her presence, their temperaments mild enough that they flicked an ear or tail as she walked by, still chewing their feed uninterrupted.

They were far grander than she was accustomed to seeing; even grander than Malcourt's mare, Powder. Phoenix realized that he must have thought his disguise had been a good one, and she chuckled softly to herself as she continued down the line.

A pen was next. She could see several donkeys, as well as hinny and mule foals munching contentedly on their oats. Muler stood off to side on his own, a warm blanket fastened over his back. Breathing a sigh of relief, she unlatched the door to his stall. Muler nickered a greeting and nudged his nose into her hands when she approached.

"Hey there," she greeted him quietly. She picked up the currying comb in his stall and brushed out his mane. He had already been tended to, but she felt guilty for not being the one to clean him after their travels so she gave him a thorough grooming anyway.

"I'm sorry I've been gone so long," she told him softly. "Angor's a confusin' place.. . I dunno if I like it much. Everyone's so prim an' proper. I dunno... Rae's nice. And Tessa. But everythin' seems so busy all th' time. I jus' wanna be left alone. I wanna spend m' day wit' you an' Kit - not be stuck inna stuffy ol' castle."

Phoenix sighed. Kit perked her round ears towards her

and came to sit by her feet. She gave a whine and lifted a paw. "Don't you start," Phoenix berated half-heartedly. She ran a finger up the black stripe that ran between Kit's eyes. "I'm glad you found me," she told the pup.

Kit's tongue lolled out in a wolfish smile. Phoenix felt a soft breeze move her hair, and she looked up as Kit's ears swiveled forward.

A large owl had entered the barn. It swooped past them on silent wings and perched on a rafter above their heads.

"Pip?" Phoenix asked. Pip looked at her silently with large yellow eyes. Looking away, the owl flipped her wings to her back and began to preen.

"Why issit I have more friends inna barn than I do inna buildin'?" Phoenix asked Kit. The pup wagged her tail and yawned in reply, stretching out on the floor of Muler's stall.

The sound of a bell could be heard from the castle. It was time for mid-meal, but Phoenix was feeling more sick and tired than anything, so she made no move to join the others in the hall. Instead, with a sigh, she sat down next to Kit. "Glad t' see you're alrigh' sleepin' inna barn," she told her. "Me an' Muler have a bad habit o' stayin' in them."

Phoenix reached out to scratch Kit's ears. She felt herself calming down the longer she sat there stroking the velvet fur. "We'll be all right," she told the two resolutely. "We don't need anyone else."

Phoenix made herself comfortable in the hay next to Kit. She decided that she would speak to Tessa after meal's end, after the commotion had died down. There was no sense in putting it off any longer than that. If she was lucky, they'd be able to leave before the snows came.

Phoenix pointedly turned her head so that she was unable to see the golden eyes watching her from the rafters.

CHAPTER 8

"I'm tellin' ya: she's not in 'ere!" Phoenix heard a gruff voice exclaim as two sets of footsteps drew closer.

"And I'm telling you that she is," replied a familiar patient voice. A moment later, Sylvia stuck her head over the side of the pen. "Ah, Phoenix. There you are."

A man with a ruddy complexion stuck his face in as well. "What're you doin' 'ere?" the stocky man demanded.

"Maybe if you'd stayed at your post, Sean..."

"Horses dun jus' clean themselves!" The short man glared at Sylvia, then Phoenix, before turning on his heel and stomping back the way he came. Phoenix could hear him muttering to himself.

Pip chirped a question and peered down at the two women. "Yes, thank you, Pip," Sylvia said. "And you," she continued, turning to Phoenix. "What are you doing here? Mistress Ruby has been looking everywhere for you. Why didn't you return to the dorms after your morning's lesson?"

Sylvia leaned against the pen door as she regarded the girl with a level gaze. She had cleaned up since their travels, her fresh outfit reminded Phoenix of her dirty appearance, but she looked exhausted, and Phoenix felt a pang of guilt that the woman had come looking for her.

Phoenix fought against the embarrassment that coiled in her stomach. "Tha' was no lesson." She resisted the urge to clench her hands into fists. "Master Weston dismissed me early. He said it was no place fer me; that I was wastin' everyone's day." She blinked furiously against the tears, tilting her head forward so that her hair hid her brimming eyes. She didn't know what she'd do if she started crying in front of Sylvia. She couldn't handle any more embarrassment.

Sylvia's face darkened. Her expression tightened around her eyes, and Phoenix had a momentary image of the woman yelling at her. Instead, when she did speak, her voice was soft and even. "It's okay, Phoenix. It's not your fault." Sylvia smiled at her, but it didn't quite reach her eyes. "There's no help for it, now. But we'll get it sorted. Don't you worry." She extended her hands to help Phoenix stand. "It's almost time for evening's meal. We might as well get cleaned up for that, at least."

Phoenix nodded and accepted the help, brushing the stray straw from her trous.

"Did you bring any clothing with you besides that?" Sylvia asked, only just realizing that Phoenix wore the same outfit that she had been wearing while traveling. When Phoenix shook her head, the woman gave a small frown. "Come with me, then. There's bound to be some discards in the share room..."

Sylvia turned to Kit. "You stay here," she told the pup, pointing at the ground. "Minna would have a fit if you showed up as well."

Kit gave a growl that pitched upwards into a whine, but ultimately settled on the floor next to Muler. Satisfied, Sylvia patted Kit's head and led Phoenix from the stables.

Gargoyle statues peered down at the two as shadows stretched across the courtyard, lanterns and lights having already winked into life in the castle. Phoenix became aware that she had been with Muler for much longer than she had realized.

Castle Angor busted with activity. Scullers were furiously cleaning walls and watering plants; old Masters were seated at tables debating each other with words that Phoenix could neither recognize nor understand. A lone Runner she didn't recognize zipped past them and bounded up the stairs, a crumpled parchment clutched in her fist.

"Just down here," Sylvia informed her, steering them towards an out-of-the-way room at the end of a long corridor. She rapped smartly on the door before opening it, then wordlessly ushered Phoenix inside.

The musty room didn't seem large enough to hold everything that was in it. Abandoned pieces of clothing and furnishings occupied any spare place that they could fit. Unorganized items were stacked in haphazard piles around the room, making Phoenix nervous that they would topple with the slightest nudge. She made a point of holding her breath as she slid between two looming stacks of leather.

"We're closed," a muffled voice called out from behind a pillar of broken chairs.

"Minna?" Sylvia asked, looking around.

"Healer Sylvia?" the voice asked, incredulously. A large woman with flushed cheeks came into view. How she maneuvered between everything was a mystery to Phoenix. "It is you! I'd heard you were here, but I hadn't seen you around. Is it true that you're treating... Ah." She stopped when she noticed Phoenix standing there. "Who's this?"

"I'm Phoenix," Phoenix supplied, trying not to wince as a damaged saddle slid to the floor by her feet.

"Yes. This is Phoenix. Phoenix, this is Masterclothier Minna." Phoenix was saved from attempting a curtsy as Sylvia laid a hand on her shoulder. "Phoenix came with Tolen."

The Masterclothier straightened in surprise and looked at Phoenix thoughtfully.

"Unfortunately, she didn't have time to bring a change of clothes with her..." Sylvia continued, almost as an after-thought.

The woman's bright eyes sharpened speculatively. "I see. Well, I'm sure we can find something for one who arrives with the Mastercaller."

Minna came closer to appraise Phoenix's frame. "Tall bit of a thing, aren't you? Boys clothes might be more appropriate. And you've already got trous on. Far more practical than skirts if you ask me..." She trailed off, and Phoenix certainly wasn't about to point out that the Masterclothier was currently wearing skirts herself. "Are you working while you're here, Phoenix?"

Phoenix nodded. "I'm helpin' in th' kitchens," she replied, deciding not to mention Malcourt's plans for her until she knew what they were.

If Minna heard her she gave no acknowledgement. She reached out to take measurements with her hands, measuring finger lengths between shoulders and waist, but she stopped short of actually touching Phoenix. "I have a few things that might do. At least in the short term."

Taking one last look at Phoenix's worn outfit, Minna pursed her lips and disappeared behind the stacks in the room. Phoenix barely had time to scrutinize her harvest work clothes before Minna reappeared with an armful of clothing.

Depositing them onto a lopsided chair, she motioned for the two to inspect the items. She grabbed a mirror and positioned it while Sylvia began handing Phoenix the different items of clothing.

"Some of them are still dirty," the Masterclothier said, by

way of apology, "but they should be fine once they're freshened up a bit."

"It's far better than wha' I got," Phoenix assured her gratefully.

Sylvia smiled and held up a flared brown tunic. "This one should fit, and there's only one button missing."

"There's a pair of trous that'll go with that one, too," Minna told her. Phoenix stood still as the women chose different clothing items and held them up to her.

"There," Sylvia said after a while, appraising the pile of garments set aside for Phoenix. "They might not turn heads, but they're practical and warm, at least."

"I had that set aside as well," Minna told them, pointing to a skirt draped over a broken chair back, "but I believe it's too big."

The skirt was pale green in color with a darker ivy pattern creeping up the sides. "Tha's far too grand fer me," Phoenix protested. In truth, she was relieved that the skirt was too large. Girls at Avondale married in plainer clothing.

Sylvia folded it back up and set it aside dismissively. "You could fit two of her in there," she said. Minna looked thoughtful and nodded. "Well, we must be off if Phoenix is to get to the hall in time for evening's meal."

"Thank you for takin' th' time t' help me, Masterclothier Minna. I'm sure you must be very busy." Phoenix attempted a curtsy, then quickly wished she hadn't. She wondered if Rae could give her a few pointers.

Minna stared in surprise. She looked at Sylvia before giving Phoenix a genuine smile. "My pleasure, Miss Phoenix. Do come back at any time. That goes for you as well, Healer." Minna fixed Sylvia with a long look. "You still owe me a tale or two from last visit."

Much to Phoenix's surprise, Sylvia laughed. It was a joyful, bell-like sound, and it transformed her whole face - momentarily erasing the exhaustion that had started to etch itself into her expression.

She handed Phoenix the clothes.

"I'll come back before I leave. I promise," Sylvia called over her shoulder, chuckling as she steered Phoenix back towards the dorms.

***

"She has a good heart," Sylvia told Phoenix as the two climbed a small staircase, "but she doesn't get out much. Don't mind her if she seems small-minded at times. She means well enough."

Phoenix was confused by the last statement but was too preoccupied by the pile of clothes in her arms to say so.

It was only a short walk to the entrance of the dorms. To her surprise, Sylvia didn't leave Phoenix at the entrance but walked with her into the girls' common room.

"Miss Phoenix!" a prim voice called out. The chatter of those present was silenced and the assembled girls looked up expectantly. Mistress Ruby regarded Phoenix with a scowl of displeasure. "When you are dismissed from class, I expect you to report back to me! I don't know how you did it back in Avondale, but here we obey the rules!"

Phoenix could see Brianna watching her intently. She felt her cheeks get hot when she saw the smug look on the older girl's face. Did Brianna know that the rules had never been explained to her?

Mistress Ruby stopped short when she saw Sylvia standing there as well. Phoenix watched her school her expression as she halted whatever it was that she was about to say next.

"Ah, yes. My apologies, Mistress," Sylvia said, curtsying fluidly. "I detained Phoenix by request of the Mastercaller. There were a few things that she needed to attend to."

"I see," Mistress Ruby said, flustered by the curtsy. At a loss, she mollified her tone. "That is understandable, of course, but I do expect to be advised of the whereabouts of all of my charges - even the new ones."

"Of course. I'll be sure to let Master Malcourt know. It's my understanding that he will be setting Phoenix's schedule as soon as he has the moments to finalize it. I'm sure you will be the first one he informs."

The women exchanged a silent look. Sylvia's gaze was steady, her smile so perfectly bland that it was impossible to find any slight with it.

Mistress Ruby looked away first with a small huff. "The call for the evening's meal will ring shortly," she informed Phoenix, eyeing the clothing in her arms. "Now would be the best moment to get cleaned up, if one were so inclined to do so."

"Yes, Mistress," Phoenix said, bowing her head. She could feel everyone's eyes on her as she stood in the middle of the room. No one dared to whisper.

Sylvia curtsied again. Without another word, she clasped Phoenix's elbow and steered her towards the rooms.

"I knew something like that would happen," Sylvia said upon entering Phoenix's room. She looked around slowly, her expression unreadable as she eyed the empty beds. Phoenix set her new clothing on her vanity.

"How are your dormmates?" Sylvia asked her. "Pleasant?"

Phoenix nodded quickly, surprised by the question. "They've been very kind. Rae's been showin' me around, an' Elise an' Sophie sit with us at meals..." Phoenix felt touched that she cared enough to ask.

Sylvia nodded and sat on Phoenix's bed. Her shoulders

slumped, her body showing a fatigue that she had been hiding earlier. "You'd tell me if it was otherwise, right?" When Phoenix nodded under her scrutiny, Sylvia smiled warmly. "Good," she said simply. "Now go and get washed up."

Phoenix nodded and dashed down the hall. She grabbed a drying sheet from the shelf and took it to the bathing pools. She shed her clothing quickly, leaving only her pendant on, and hurried into the water. She was pleasantly surprised to find that the water was heated and didn't carry the outside chill that she was expecting. With a soft sigh, Phoenix slipped the rest of the way in and pushed herself around the shallow pool. Dunking her head under the water, she used her fingers to pull the dirt and the tangles from her hair.

She was dismayed to realize exactly how many snarls her curls had produced over the past few days working the harvest and running from Stormhounds… No wonder people were looking at her strangely.

Surfacing, she took a liberal amount of powdered scrubroot and vigorously rubbed her scalp and skin until she felt clean. Rinsing the lather from her body, she reluctantly climbed out of the pool and dried herself off with the sheet.

Loathe to redress in dirty clothes, she took the chance that no one was around and ran up the stairs and back to her room in only the towel.

"And then he just told her to leave!" Rae vented angrily to Sylvia. She looked up as Phoenix entered the room. Her face colored and she stopped, embarrassed.

"All right you two. Think no more on it," Sylvia said briskly, standing and flicking her skirts with more force than was necessary.

Rae bit her lip and avoided Phoenix's gaze. "It wasn't Phoenix's fault," Rae cried desperately.

"Leave it," Sylvia said firmly. "I mean it. It'll be taken care of." She fixed Rae with a stern glance, then, giving Phoenix's shoulder a pat, she left the room.

Phoenix watched her leave, feeling mystified. "Wha' did she mean 'it'll be taken care of'?"

Rae shrugged and ground her foot into the floor, watching it intently as she did so.

Phoenix returned her attention to getting ready and walked over to her bed. She felt giddy as she looked through her new clothing and picked out an outfit. She'd never had her choice between so many clothes before! Somehow the problems from earlier seemed farther away compared to her current excitement.

"Oh, Phoenix, I'm sorry!" Rae breathed. "She was asking questions about the lesson. I didn't know what to do…"

Phoenix dropped her towel and changed quickly, slipping a worn belt around her waist to secure her tunic over her trous.

"S'okay," she told the girl with a shrug. "She would've heard about it anyways. I'm jus' glad it's from someone on my side."

"So, you're not mad?" Rae asked hopefully.

"Nope."

"Promise?"

"Promise."

Rae threw her arms open and hugged her, and Phoenix couldn't help but realize that the idea of personal space was a lot different in Castle Angor.

"I'm so glad!" Rae exclaimed excitedly. "If you're ready, we can head down to the hall. The rest of the girls have already left, and Sophie and Elise have seats saved for us. You must be starving."

Phoenix ran her fingers through her clean hair and sighed

happily. "Let's go!" she agreed, her stomach grumbling at the mention of food.

Grinning, Rae swung open the door and led the way to the hall.

***

Rae and Phoenix joined Sophie and Elise, who were already gossiping in their seats. They were giggling and shooting coveted glances towards the Head Table. Phoenix looked around the room and noticed that many of the girls from different tables were doing the same thing.

"He's here!" Sophie hissed as the two sat. She gave a giddy giggle and looked back to the front of the room. Phoenix followed her gaze to see Prince Hallan talking amicably to the noblewoman next to him. She seemed to be just as enamored with him as the rest of the girls. She kept smiling at him, and laughingly touched his arm whenever he paused talking in order to take a sip of wine.

"Are you okay, Phoenix?" Elise asked with concern, her full attention on Phoenix. "We couldn't find you after you left Master Weston's this morning."

"I'm surprised she'd show her face at all," a voice said haughtily.

Phoenix turned to find Brianna standing behind her; Jenny at her side. She eyed Phoenix's wet curls with disdain. "I hear that the babes of Castle Angor start their lessons soon - maybe you can join them." Brianna smirked, and Jenny snickered beside her. "I'm sure they'd be able to help you with yours."

Stung, Phoenix clenched her hands under the table. "Wha's your problem anyways, Brianna?" Phoenix demanded. "I ain't done nothin' t' offend you!"

Brianna stalked forward, leaning in so that her seaglass eyes were a hand length from Phoenix's face. "Your very presence offends me," she hissed.

Hastily, Phoenix drew back from the girl's venomous expression.

"You show up, unannounced, without even a decent pair of clothes to your Bloodless name, blunder your way into the castle, and then we civilized ladies get stuck with you while others who are more deserving are forced to wait. It makes me sick." Brianna's cheeks were flushed with an anger which her low voice could not fully express.

Rae looked outraged. "Master Malcourt brought her, Brianna! You know the rules. If a Master—"

"Ha!" Jenny cut her off. "'Master'? More like 'Freak'!"

Brianna shot Rae a smoldering glare. "You stay out of this, sculler, or I'll set to you, too."

Rae's face turned bright red, but she drew herself up and returned Brianna's glare.

A gong sounded, signifying that the meal was about to begin. Straightening with a wicked smile, Brianna and Jenny gave the group a mocking wave and went to sit with their rank.

With a huff, Phoenix turned her attention back to the table and the platters of food that was being passed around. Reminded of Millie and the condescending way in which the girl treated her back at Avondale, resentment washed over her, souring her mood.

Picking up a cutting utensil, she speared the offered food with more force than was necessary and caused the meat platter to tip and fall onto the table. Rae, coming to her rescue, righted it nimbly and passed it on while Elise used her napkin to mop up some of the spilled juices.

"Pay no mind, Phoenix," Rae said lightly, putting on a bright face. "Once we get you settled in the kitchens you'll be so busy you won't have time to worry about what Brianna thinks."

She looked to Elise and Sophie for encouragement, and the two nodded their heads in agreement. "Besides," Rae continued, her eyes twinkling. "You heard what the Healer said. Leave everything to her."

Phoenix sighed loudly, then gave a sheepish smile. "Okay," she conceded, trying her best to shove the encounter from her mind. "Who asked Brianna, anyways, right?"

The three nodded their agreement. Despite her skipped meal earlier, Phoenix found that her enthusiasm for her food had vanished. She picked at the food in front of her until she found an opportune moment to slip her sliced meat to one of the dogs under the table.

Sullenly, she scanned the noisy hall. Malcourt was still unaccounted for, and Sylvia was nowhere to be seen. The woman barely mentioned him earlier, or what he had been doing since they arrived.

Phoenix squashed the feelings of frustration that were threatening to take over. He was very encouraging that she come here considering he had been absent since she arrived.

Even with her new friends' encouragement, she was unable to rid herself of the sick sensation in her stomach.

At the end of the meal, servers walked between the tables with platters full of delicate cakes. Sophie took two and handed the larger one to Phoenix. "Sorry about earlier," she said softly, her dark eyes downcast. It was the first time the girl had spoken to her since morning's meal. "I didn't realize... I didn't think Master Weston would single you out like that."

Phoenix forced a smile. "It's alrigh'. It wasn't your fault."

Sophie smiled at her bravado. "Everyone has it rough the first week or so, but you'll find your place soon. It'll take a little while, but once you get settled nothing else will really bother you."

Phoenix was taken aback by the girl's serious tone, but she found that it made her feel better. "Thanks Sophie."

Sophie grinned and took a bite of her cake.

Phoenix did the same. The cake was delicious, but the dryness in her mouth made the crumbs stick to the back of her throat. Hastily she washed it down with a mouthful of tea.

She watched her new friends talking around her, but every now and then she glanced over to Brianna's end of the table. Watching. Assessing. Something needed to change if she was to live with the girl all next season, and Phoenix was determined to figure out what that could be.

CHAPTER 9

The kitchens were busy despite the early hour, and Phoenix wondered how the rest of the castle was not awakened from the noises of the morning's activities.

She hadn't slept well the previous evening, so she helped herself to an extra splash of tea as she and Rae changed into their kitchen clothes.

"All right! Here are your assignments, people!" Tessa's voice cut through the din and silenced all but the most necessary of noises. "Rae, you're helping Hester this morning." Phoenix heard Rae's soft groan. "You two are to concentrate on desserts, so make sure that the pie crust is actually edible, please. Abby, you're to head up meats. Jesse, you're veg. Stef: breads. The rest of you, report to your section leaders. Section three are the runners for this morning's shift. Let's feed a hungry castle, people!" She clapped her hands and the kitchens became busy again.

"You're with me, Phoenix," Tessa beckoned to her. Phoenix nodded and followed her. "We're going to cook morning's meal." Tessa led the way to the giant cooking stoves. "Eggs," Tessa told her, pointing to a large bowl that held what Phoenix thought was a week's supply of eggs, "and meats. We cook the main orders here, then pass it down the line to be completed. Understand?"

Phoenix nodded. She was used to cooking morning's meal, but she was unprepared for the quantity that she had to make. She was thankful that Tessa was there to keep her from falling behind. At first the individual orders didn't seem too overwhelming, but once more of the castle was awake, Phoenix was hardly keeping up when Tessa announced that they had to begin preparing the hall meal.

Phoenix wiped a stray hair out of her face with the back of her hand and cleaned the large iron pan in front of her. She was unaware of the man standing by her elbow until he spoke.

"Excuse me," a deep voice asked. "Am I too late for a meal?"

Tessa jerked to attention upon hearing the voice. Setting down her spatula, she wiped her hands on the front of her apron.

"No, Your Highness. Of course not."

Phoenix looked up to see Prince Hallan standing beside her, waiting patiently with his hands clasped behind his back.

He smiled at her, a dashing smile that lit up his face, and Phoenix felt her legs lose some of their strength. He was much more attractive than she'd first thought. Up close, his vibrant eyes were a striking emerald green. They were bright as they watched her, assessing her - making her feel like she was the only person in the room - and Phoenix understood why his dining companions were always so enraptured when he spoke.

She was dimly aware of Tessa asking her to put some fresh loaves on a tray. Once she realized that the two adults were looking at her, she moved swiftly to the baking section only to find that Rae had already assembled a tray with drinks and glasses for her. Phoenix shot her a grateful look, and Rae grinned and fanned herself with her hand.

Phoenix returned to Tessa in time for her to slide several

large plates of food onto the tray. "Thank you, Phoenix," Tessa said upon her prompt return.

"Phoenix?" Prince Hallan asked, looking at her with interest. "The same Phoenix who arrived with Tolen Malcourt?"

Phoenix could feel everyone around her staring. "Y-yes Highness," she answered. She managed the clumsiest of bobs without upsetting the tray that she held.

"I was wondering when I'd get the honor of meeting you." He smiled easily, and his emerald eyes studied her intently.

Phoenix felt her tongue stick to the roof of her mouth. "Your H-highness?"

"Well, I'm curious," he laughed, sounding embarrassed. It was an endearing sound. "Anyone who can escape Stormhounds must be fascinating." He smiled another dazzling smile, and Phoenix was convinced that she heard a woman sigh somewhere behind her.

Phoenix felt her face redden. Tessa turned to shoot a glare at the rest of the room, and immediately miscellaneous noises started up again. No one dared to look back in their direction. "Your morning meals are getting cold, Your Highness," Tessa said, taking the tray from Phoenix and looking around. "I'll get one of the scullers to help you with these."

"Nonsense, Cook. I'm sure that Phoenix is more than capable of the task..." He looked at Tessa hopefully. The words were pleasant, but they were still enough to give Tessa pause.

"Of course, Prince Hallan," Tessa acknowledged, handing the tray back to Phoenix. "Phoenix is free to assist you in any way she can."

Prince Hallan nodded and gestured for her to follow, heading towards the main foyer with long strides. Phoenix shot Rae a helpless look and hurried after him out of the kitchens.

He went down the hallway to the main set of stairs, bypassing the side ones that Phoenix was accustomed to. She found herself struggling to keep up.

"You are not from here, are you, Phoenix?" The Prince asked her, ignoring those who stopped in their work to bow as he passed. He continued up the main staircase at the same speed - oblivious to the fact that she struggled with the tray on the stairs.

"Avondale, Your Highness." She was careful not to trip when she came to the large landing.

"The Manor?" He asked quickly.

"The Farm," she replied, using her long legs to gain ground and take the stairs two at a time.

"Ah," he said, once she had reached the top. "Your parents must be very proud to have their daughter move to the Castle so early in life."

"I don't... have any." Phoenix remembered Master Weston's previous outrage just in time to correct her speech. "It's jus' me."

"Oh." He sounded appropriately contrite, but his expression changed so abruptly that Phoenix wondered if she had imagined it. "No family at all..." he mused.

He remained silent until they reached a set of large double doors. Guards were posted on either side and, saluting to the Prince, they opened the doors to a wing of the castle that Phoenix had never seen before.

The rooms were majestic. They were laid out much like the girls' dorm - with one main room connecting all the others - but their decorations were much more lavish.

Prince Hallan entered the common room and beckoned for Phoenix to follow. "My rooms are connected by the corridor here, but we'll leave the extra food here for the others."

Phoenix entered slowly, being exceptionally careful not to

spill anything on the expensive rugs beneath her feet.

The Prince smiled and stepped towards her with out-stretched hands. His fingers brushed against hers and paused, the warmth of his skin made Phoenix acutely aware of where their hands touched.

"Now then," Prince Hallan murmured. "Let me help you with that tray…"

"Phoenix?" a woman's voice behind her asked.

Phoenix jerked, and the Prince dropped his hands hastily. Sylvia stood against the door frame of one of the rooms, still dressed in the same attire she was wearing the night before. She gave a tired smile and opened an arm to Phoenix. "In here, child," she opened the door wider for her. "Some food would do us all a bit of good."

Prince Hallan cleared his throat. "Ah, Healer. Please don't keep Phoenix long. Tessa said that her time is mine this morning." The Prince flashed Sylvia a smile and, when she gave him a startled look, winked comically at Phoenix as he took a plate of food from the tray.

Phoenix looked between the two of them helplessly.

"Be that as it may, Your Highness," Sylvia said, recovering, "Phoenix is not in Tessa's care, but the Mastercaller's. And I believe he has other plans for her today." Sylvia beckoned for her, this time with authority, and it was enough to distract Phoenix from her fascination with the Prince. Blushing, she hurried and followed Sylvia into the room.

She turned in time to see Prince Hallan's face darken, watching her thoughtfully, before Sylvia closed the heavy door behind them.

Silently, Sylvia took the tray from Phoenix and led her across another large room, into a set of darkened bedchambers. She set the tray on a small round table a few feet from a large curtained bed.

Removing the mugs from the tray, Sylvia arranged them on the table and began to pour fresh tea into them, offering a cup to Phoenix before taking her own. Slowly, Sylvia settled into a chair and sipped the hot liquid, looking drawn out in the dim room.

Instead of joining her, Phoenix compiled a small plate of food for the woman and set it in front of her. Sylvia raised her hand in protest, but Phoenix shook her head. "You need t' eat," she dared to tell the Healer.

"She's right," a voice announced.

Phoenix felt a familiar *pull*, and she didn't need to turn to identify Malcourt rising from a cot in a darkened corner of the room. As he came into view, Phoenix found herself averting her eyes so that she was looking at anything but him.

He was topless. The lighting was not strong with the heavy drawn curtains, but she was able to see the outline of muscles that shifted with his movements. She had often seen men working topless back in Avondale, but none sported the deep scars that crossed themselves along his torso, or the fresh hollow burns that dotted his forearms.

Casually, he grabbed a tunic and tied it around himself.

"You'll wake him," Sylvia said in a soft rebuke to the Mastercaller. She poured a cup of tea and handed it to him.

"He'll sleep for another while yet," Malcourt responded, but Phoenix noticed that he lowered his tone all the same, "as you should do once you've finished eating. I'll wake you," he held a hand up to forestall her arguments, "if there is any change."

The two looked at one another a moment, then Sylvia nodded and rose. She took the plate that Phoenix had prepared for her to the corner and sat on the cot to eat.

Malcourt slid into the seat that she previously occupied.

While sipping his tea, he reached for a loaf of bread. He ripped off a large chunk, slathered it in preserves, and topped it with an egg. Then, much to Phoenix's surprise, he folded it neatly and put the whole thing in his mouth.

While he was chewing, he unhooked his belt knife to cut a thick piece of cheese, speared a segment of peeled rindfruit, and slid both pieces of food from the blade into his mouth. He then washed it all down with the remainder of his tea.

Phoenix was amazed by the skillfulness in which he was able to eat. He was stuffing himself, to be sure, yet he was doing it with such ease that he was obviously used to eating in such a fashion.

When he'd finished the rest of the small loaf, Malcourt finally sat back with a sigh and poured himself another cup of tea. He then gestured for Phoenix to take the chair opposite him, not lowering his hand until she sat.

"I trust you've been settled in the dorms," he asked, once she accepted his invitation. His blue eyes were piercing, and for a quick moment Phoenix wondered if he cared more about her answer, or the way in which she answered.

"Yes, Master Malcourt," she replied, noting his surprised blink when she used his title. "Rae's been helpin' me t' get settled - in th' dorm an' th' kitchens."

"Ah." He noted her cook's outfit. "It was you who brought up such a lavish feast for us this morning? My stomach thanks you." He placed a hand on his stomach and, without standing, bowed to her from his chair.

She found herself smiling at the display.

"So you've made some friends, then? That's good. Rae's got a good head on her shoulders, unlike some of the other young ladies here." He made a knowing face, but he did not elaborate any further. "And your lessons?" He asked her. "How are they coming?"

Phoenix dropped her eyes to her untouched drink.

"I see," he said, softly. She looked up to see him tracing the rim of his mug with a finger. "I forgot that not everyone starts off in life on the same footing. It was my mistake to assume that you had been forced to revel in the same benefits that most here have enjoyed, which makes it my fault that you suffered such embarrassment. And for that, Phoenix, I am truly sorry."

Phoenix couldn't think of a time when anyone had ever apologized to her in such a fashion. She shifted in her chair, realizing that he was waiting for her to speak. "Master Weston said I don' belong here," she blurted, unsure of what else to say. "He said I'm jus' a waste o' time." As she repeated the words, the bitterness she felt made it hard for her to swallow.

"I dun wanna leave - at least, I don' think I do - but I'll go if I gotta. Jus' let me work fer m' keep durin' th' snows... Please?" Her voice trembled on the last word, and she lowered her eyes, afraid that she might cry from the look on his face.

The room was silent. Phoenix nearly startled out of her chair when Malcourt reached across the table and took her hand. "You do belong here, Phoenix, despite what Master Weston may think." He paused, letting his dismissive tone set in. "No, Phoenix. I," and he tapped on his chest, "brought you here. It is for me to decide; no one else. His opinion is none of your concern. You," and he jabbed his finger towards her for emphasis, "are my concern, now. Do you understand? You belong here because I say that you do. Don't listen to anyone who tries to tell you otherwise." He smiled at her kindly. "You truly have a place here for as long as you want it. I want you to stay."

She looked at him, wide-eyed. All the shame and resentment that she had kept down over the last few days rose to the surface. Hot tears filled her eyes and overflowed down her cheeks before she had a chance to hide them. She sniffed self-consciously.

"You've upset her, Tolen," a sleepy voice said from the curtained bed.

"I seem to do that a lot... I'm sorry, Phoenix," Malcourt said, giving her hand a squeeze, "that was not my intent."

"S'alrigh'," she insisted, with a soft hiccup. "I'm happy!" She sniffed before repeating the words softly, as if she couldn't believe it herself.

Malcourt chuckled. "You have a funny way of showing it, my dear."

"Well, what did you expect, Tolen?" The voice rasped from the bed. "You plucked this poor child from her home, only to announce her arrival with such dramatic flare, and then you abandoned her for days at a time. Of course there'd be push back. There'd be gossip, if nothing else. You know as well as anyone how much the castle cats love new playthings..."

Malcourt winced and rose swiftly, moving to pull back the curtains from the bed's canopy. "An oversight on my part that I will rectify, I assure you. I found myself incredibly occupied, for some reason..."

There was a sound of rustling as the shape in the bed rolled into a sitting position. "Something had the audacity to distract your attention? How strange... Is that food I smell?" he asked, hopefully.

"Yes, your Majesty. Phoenix was kind enough to bring us our morning's meal."

"Did she now? Phoenix, you say? That was nice of her."

"Yes. I thought so." Malcourt gestured for Phoenix to come close. Nervously, she filled a plate from the platter and brought it to the bedside.

King Benedict - crowned ruler of Angoria, benevolent monarch to the kingdom, and Phoenix's sovereign Lord - was an unbelievably frail little man. He seemed almost sunken in on himself as he lay in the over-sized bed, relying on the support of countless pillows to keep him propped up.

He had white bushy eyebrows, and surprisingly thick hair that stuck out in several directions from sleep. He looked haggard with jutting cheekbones and sunken eyes, and Phoenix remembered that he'd been sick for some time, but his smile to her was one of welcome. She gave him an awkward curtsy, and would have spilled the food in his lap had Malcourt's hand not steadied the plate.

"Now, now," the King said, with a wave of his pale bony hand. "I don't stand on ceremony before breaking my fast - especially if it messes up my bedclothes!"

Phoenix blushed furiously, but the King's eyes crinkled at her as he accepted the plate from Malcourt. "So, you're Phoenix. You're the one Tolen's been telling me about. You've had quite the adventure getting here, haven't you?"

He took a bite of his grilled bread and raised his eyebrows for an answer while he chewed. Phoenix curtsied again before she belatedly remembered that she wasn't supposed to. "Yes, your Majesty," she said, her face hot.

"Now who's upsetting her?" Malcourt asked mildly, handing the King some juice.

The King made a face as he accepted the mug. "Shouldn't you be off doing something important?" he asked, wiggling the fingers of his free hand. "Casting or Calling or whatever is it that I keep you around for?"

Malcourt gave a short bow. "Nothing is more important than that of the health of my King," he said, elegantly.

The King gave a long-suffering sigh and rolled his eyes at Phoenix. "And you're sure you want to stay here?" he rasped.

Phoenix, shocked by the ease with which the two men mocked one another, could only open her mouth. When no sound came out, she closed it again and managed a single nod.

The King chuckled. "Well, that settles it." He swallowed his food and looked at her seriously. No trace of humor remained in his expression, and Phoenix was alarmed at the sudden change of mood.

"Phoenix, I owe you my most sincerest thanks. As you've undoubtedly heard, I have been sick for some time. Malcourt left a season ago on what we all considered to be a valiant last-effort on his part. A complete shot in the dark, if you will. Luckily for me it worked or else I wouldn't be here anymore, which I'm sure is irritating my enemies to no end."

"How unbelievably tragic," Malcourt murmured.

"My point," the King continued, casting a look at Malcourt, "is that I wouldn't be here without you. It was your quick thinking during the attack that saved not only Master Malcourt's hide, but mine as well - and for that I can never repay you. Angoria is in your debt - as am I. Anything you want is yours. Anything at all. Please, don't hesitate to ask."

They both looked at her expectantly. Flustered at being put on the spot, she could only swallow.

The King owed her a debt? What did that mean? Was she supposed to ask for something, or was that just a formality? What could she possibly ask for? Her mind was blank, but they were waiting for her to say something so she cleared her throat.

"I'd like t' stay here in th' castle, your Majesty."

The King glanced at Malcourt, then raised a bushy eyebrow. "Is that it?"

"Well," she swallowed nervously, wondering how far she could push it. "I, that is, Muler, I mean, needs a place t' stay, too.

If he could have a place in th' stables... And Kit..." She trailed off, feeling uncertain.

The King looked at her a moment. His other eyebrow rose to join its counterpart on his forehead. "You're asking me to let your donkey stay in my well-established stables? And your - what is it? - dog to stay on my grounds?" He looked at her for another moment, then made her jump when he burst into laughter.

Phoenix tensed, and Malcourt once again removed the King's dishes from harm's way. The two waited for him to re-cover.

"You're right about her, Tolen," the King said once he'd re-gained his breath.

Malcourt gave a little smile. "I know," he said, simply.

Phoenix didn't dare ask what was said.

"My child," the King said, waving at Malcourt to return his food. "It would be my honour for your companions to stay here as well. I only laugh because it is absolutely no trouble for them to do so." He picked up his glass and took a sip. "No. I will think of something nice for you. In the meantime, if you think of anything, you come to me straight away. I mean it. Promise?" He wasn't satisfied until she'd whispered a promise.

He gave a dismissing wave. "Now, do as you will and enjoy the rest of your day. You'll get settled in soon enough. Especially once Malcourt stops dallying and sees to your schedule."

"I think it's time for more medicine, Your Majesty," Malcourt said tonelessly. "After all, I did spend all that time procuring it for you."

The King made a face and plucked a piece of fruit from the tray, popping it into his mouth instead.

Master Malcourt rolled his eyes and gave her a nod. Phoenix clapped a hand over her mouth and hurried from the bedchambers.

***

Mid-day went by quickly. Buoyed by Malcourt's assur-
ances, and by the King's great kindness, Phoenix spent her free
time tending to errands. She dared to bother Minna again to
borrow a needle and thread (the woman was incredulous: "Borrow? Borrow! My dear, I insist that you help yourself! You're
doing me a favour, after all."), and she spent a relaxing hour
mending and washing her clothes.

"It's strange," she remarked to the ever-present Kit, while
hanging her washed articles in the drying room. "People here
pay a lot o' heed t' their clothes. Dirt's more frowned on than
idleness." Kit didn't open her eyes, but gave a thump of her tail
to show that she was listening.

Phoenix walked to the window and threw the shutters
open. A fresh breeze fluttered around the small room, clearing
out the musty smell that had accumulated after days of being
closed off.

A loud shout made her pause and stick her head out the
window. Multiple voices chorused an answer, and Phoenix
craned her neck to see Captain Rolf running drills with the boys
in the exercise yard.

Kit jumped up with a throaty growl and turned around
in a circle. "Smell th' fresh air, do ya?" Phoenix asked her. Kit
pranced to the door and looked back at her.

"Oh, all right, then." Phoenix opened the door, and Kit pre-
ceded her down to the yard.

The sun shed little warmth this time of day. Wrapping her
arms around herself as she crossed the field, Phoenix leaned
against a fence post as she watched the boys run through their
training.

They stood paired off in the drill field, the grass worn away from countless footfalls against the earth during practice runs. Each was armed with a wooden weapon in an attempt to best the other.

"Sloppy!" Captain Rolf roared. "Richard! Guard your side - it's wide open! If this were a battle you'd be dead."

"Yeah, Rich," Alan mocked from his spot in the drill. "Learn how to guard!" The next moment, the boy who Alan was sparring with feigned with his staff, then twirled it and used the other end to trip him up. Alan fell with a grunt.

"It's a good thing you're already a Runner, Alan," the Guardscaptain called over his shoulder, "because if you don't learn how to shut your mouth and learn something that's all you'll be good for on the battlefield."

Alan flushed angrily. Ignoring his partner's helping hand, he jumped up on his own and snapped a comment to the boy. Phoenix couldn't hear the exchange, but by the look on Alan's face she could tell that he said something nasty.

The other boy's expression was cool and unchanging. With a shrug, he turned his back on Alan and made his way off the field. The other partners remained where they were and continued with their drills.

Alan glared and watched him go. A moment later, with an angry snarl, he picked up a rock and threw it at the boy's back with all of his might.

Phoenix stepped forward. "Watch out!" she yelled.

Surprised, the boy stopped mid-step, his attention snagged by her warning. At her shout, heads turned to see the commotion. The rock continued to speed through the air until, to Phoenix's surprise, it stopped a hand's length from the boy's head.

There was a sharp pop, as if the rock had struck an invisible wall, and then it split in two and fell to the ground.

With an angry roar, Captain Rolf lurched forward and

grabbed Alan by his shirt collar, nearly lifting him off the ground.

"My apologies, Apprentice Camden," the Captain said to the other boy through clenched teeth. "Apparently some of my recruits are still lacking in manners. If you'll just leave the matter with me..."

"Of course, Captain," the boy, Camden, replied. "I welcome you to deal with it however you see fit.

Captain Rolf nodded abruptly to Apprentice Camden, then turned and yelled at the others to start their solo drills. Red in the face, he dragged Alan off to the other side of the yard.

To Phoenix's surprise, Camden changed direction and walked over to where she was standing. "Thank you," he said to her formally, giving a slight bow. "Most here would not have bothered to try and warn me." He glanced back at the rest of the boys. "I'm Camden." He held his hand up, palm out. An ornate ring on his hand captured her attention momentarily as the large orange jewel caught the light.

"Phoenix," she replied, holding her palm up in greeting, "and Kit." She gestured to the pup sitting at her side. Kit gave a low woof at the attention.

Camden nodded to Kit. His expression was curious at her appearance, but he showed no apprehension towards her.

The boy seemed familiar now that he was closer, but Phoenix couldn't place him. He wore a form-fitting grey jacket that shifted easily with his movements, allowing him the swift maneuvers that were necessary for the drills. She couldn't recall seeing him in the hall for meals, but he also didn't seem like someone who would sit near her table. He was roughly her age and height in front of her, but he stood with a level of self-confidence she had never seen in someone so young. His skin was pale, like most people who lived at Angor, and he smoothed his brown shaggy hair behind his ears unconsciously as he looked at her. His eyes, she noted, were his most discerning feature. A dark edge circled the lighter grey, like the line of the horizon containing a storming sea. His gaze was the quiet before that storm.

"Phoenix?" He looked surprised. "I thought you looked familiar. You arrived with Master Malcourt. I took your mount from you the night you arrived." He still wore the same unruffled expression as before, but his look had increased in intensity as he assessed her.

His look was calculating but not unkind, she decided. Remembering what Malcourt had said about her belonging here, she met his gaze easily. "I remember. You took Muler t' th' stables for me. Thank you for doin' tha' an' allowin' me t' get settled." She gave him a smile, secretly pleased with the way that she handled herself.

Inclining his head, he remained motionless as Kit sniffed the tips of his boots. "Will you be staying long?" He asked, watching Phoenix curiously.

Phoenix leaned back against the post. "At least for th' snows. I told Master Malcourt I'd stay tha' long, and then we'll decide after tha'."

The Apprentice's eyes narrowed slightly. He was silent a moment while he stared at her - stared through her, Phoenix realized - and then he focused on her again. "You're here to study with him. Master Malcourt asked you to come to the castle." Phoenix couldn't decide if he was asking a question or making a statement, so she only nodded. His expression of calm faltered, and she could see several emotions cross his face – hints of surprise, resentment, and even hope – before they stilled once more and disappeared under the blank mask he wore.

He bowed to her formally. "It was a pleasure to finally meet you, Phoenix. Thank you for warning me about Alan earlier. However, if you'll excuse me," he held his hand up in parting before turning and striding towards the castle.

Phoenix watched him leave. "Wha' a strange boy," she murmured to Kit. Kit wagged her tail and headbutted her legs as if agreeing with her.

A bell rang from inside Angor. The boys shuffled off to replace their weapons and to leave the yard. There was no sign of Captain Rolf or Alan among those who were leaving the field. She noticed that none of the boys made eye contact with her as they passed.

With a shrug, Phoenix patted Kit on the head. "Go see Muler," she told her, pointing to the stables. "I'll come an' visit later." She watched as Kit trotted off before walking to the hall.

Rae was already waiting at their usual spot. She waved to grab her attention, and Phoenix slid next to her with a smile. Elise and Sophie joined them only a moment later. "Nice clothes," Sophie greeted Phoenix, sliding into position on the bench across from her.

"Minna was kind enough t' help me out," Phoenix replied, noting how the girl smiled at the mention of her Master.

"So, Phoenix," Rae began, her eyes glinting mischievously, "how was breaking fast with Prince Hallan this morning?"

Elise squeaked in shock and everyone sitting around them paused their conversations to stare.

Phoenix blushed furiously. "He jus' had me carry th' trays is all," she muttered, shooting Rae a glare. "I wasn't there long."

"Why would he get you to do it?" a nearby boy asked scornfully. "You don't even got a rank!"

"Oh, stuff it, Rodney!" Rae said, throwing her napkin at him. He ducked and opened his mouth to retort, but - upon seeing Brianna and the other girls swooping towards them - he shut his mouth and turned away, doing his best to look invisible.

"Uh oh," Elise said, watching as Brianna drew closer. "Someone's on a warpath."

Brianna marched unerringly towards Phoenix. "You!" She hissed, coming to a halt. Her green eyes were ablaze with spite. "I don't know who you think you are, but you need to mind your own business!" Jenny looked around quickly and hushed her, but Brianna paid the girl no attention. "I heard about your little stunt in the yard. I bet you think you're so clever for getting Alan in trouble. If you think for one instant that-"

"Ah! Phoenix - There you are." Phoenix looked up from Brianna's tirade to see Prince Hallan striding purposefully towards her, cutting easily through the assembled girls who parted for him in shock. "We didn't get a chance to finish our talk from this morning."

"Your Highness?" Phoenix asked, confused. Belatedly she wondered if she should stand and bow to him.

"Your Highness," Brianna greeted the Prince with a graceful curtsy. Her voice was syrupy-sweet, showing no trace of the venom it had held a moment before.

"My Lady...?" He gave her a bow in return.

"Brianna," she said, smiling coyly. "Eldest child to Lord Byron."

"Lord Byron, you say? Duke of Sommervale?" He smiled in return. The Prince took Brianna's hand and brushed it against his lips formally. "I've heard great things about your father, my Lady. Such a pleasure to meet you."

"The pleasure is all mine, Your Highness," Brianna cooed.

Rae turned her head and made a silent gagging motion. Jenny fixed her with a glare and Rae gave her a smirk in response.

The gong to signal the meal rang. Everyone dispersed and

made their way to their seats: Brianna with a hostile glare to Phoenix before joining the excited whispers of the other girls; Prince Hallan with a smile and a promise to find her later.

Phoenix was aware that everyone was staring at her. Pretending not to care, she inspected her new tunic for dirt while she waited. As soon as a plate of meal rolls reached her, she snatched the nearest one and bit off a large chunk of it to distract herself. The others, seeing that she wasn't going to talk, fell to whispering among themselves.

"She seems excitable," Rae remarked mildly over the whispering, serving herself a large helping of root vegetables.

"She's mad tha' Alan got in trouble." Phoenix accepted the dish from Rae and scooped some onto her plate before passing it along down the table.

"Oh?" the three girls asked, leaning in close.

"Yeah. Earlier at drills, Captain Rolf caught him throwin' a rock at Camden's head. He was none too impressed - said he had no manners."

"You saw it?" they breathed. All three were looking at her wide-eyed.

Phoenix shrugged with surprise. "Th' whole courtyard saw it."

"Was there blood?" asked Rae.

"Or thunder?" breathed Elise.

"Or lightning?" squealed Sophie.

Phoenix rolled her eyes. "It was just a rock..."

"No, silly! From Camden. When he gets mad..." Sophie shuddered.

"What happened to the rock?" Elise asked in a whisper.

Phoenix blinked. "Well, I dunno... it just - stopped."

"Stopped?" the girls asked.

"Yeah." Phoenix thought back. "It was gonna hit his head,

but it broke instead. Right in th' air."

Sophie shuddered again and made the sign against evil. Rae hissed at her to stop it, and when Sophie retorted sharply Elise shushed them both. "Stop making a scene."

Phoenix continued to eat her meal. She helped herself to sliced fowl as the platter made its way back down her side of the table, using her fingers to catch the drippings that ran down her chin. She was even one of the first to grab a rindfruit as they made their rounds. Excitedly, she peeled it with her fingernails and pulled a juicy segment from its core.

"I don' see why he'd go an' do somethin' so nasty," Phoenix said, popping the fruit into her mouth. She paused a moment to enjoy the explosion of juice as she bit through the taut orange flesh. "Camden's nice. Alan was bein' sooky that he beat him in drills is all."

"Nice?" Elise asked. "You mean, you talked to him?"

"'Course." Phoenix bit into another piece of the fruit. "He talked t' me first," she recalled. "Why?"

"He's strange," Sophie said, with a dismissive sniff.

"People like us aren't supposed to talk to people like him," Rae said seriously.

People like them? Phoenix stared at her. "Says who?"

"It's not like she could have ignored him if he spoke first," Elise said in a consoling fashion.

"But still-" Sophie began, before Rae cut her off.

"Everyone says so, that's who," Rae told her. "You don't see any of us wandering up to the Head Table and striking a conversation, do you? It just isn't done. They have rank, and we," she gestured to those around them, "do not."

Elise and Sophie nodded seriously in agreement.

Phoenix frowned. Was it possible that Camden hadn't known that she was bloodless? Would he have bothered speaking to her in the first place if he did?

"It's still stupid," she said sullenly. No matter what she did here, it always seemed to result in a scolding.

Rae shrugged and turned her attention back to her meal.

Irritated, Phoenix propped her head against her hand and took her time to watch those around her.

Those at the Head and Masters' Tables were relaxed and laughing among themselves. They seemed full of energy, appearing overly animated as they talked, trying to out-do each other with amusing anecdotes. Those sitting at the lower tables, much like herself, were slower-moving, and seemed more weary from the day. Many of the younger ones were reading or writing furiously on their ledgers, trying to free up some dorm-time before bed.

Phoenix thought longingly of the quiet of her bed. She wanted nothing more than to pull the covers over her head and escape into the softness of sleep. Her eyes drooped, and she could feel a numbness creeping through her body. She would have been content to doze at the table, but Rae's sharp elbow jabbed itself in her ribs and chased the fuzziness of sleep from her head. Belatedly, she realized that the evening's announcements had started, and that her name had been called.

"You're to meet with the Bookmaster in the library," the unknown Master droned on from the front of the Hall, unaware that his subject had not been paying attention.

The girls looked at Phoenix quizzically, but she could only raise her hands helplessly, feeling just as confused about the summons as they were.

"And Miss Elise, also of the girls' dorm," the Master continued, "you are to meet the Mastercaller at his tower after meal's end. Be prompt, please. It doesn't do to keep our Mastercaller waiting..." His voice was stern, but he was looking in the direction of the younger boys. By the way that they fidgeted under his gaze, Phoenix guessed that his comment was directed more to them than to Elise.

A few of the noblewomen chuckled softly, as if the Master had said something humorous. Phoenix looked curiously at Elise, but Elise didn't seem to find the situation funny. Instead, Phoenix watched as the color drained from her face. Sophie looked worried and gave her friend a comforting pat.

The bell chimed to signal the end of the meal. There was bustling and the scraping of benches as dismissed workers left the tables. Scullers came after them in a wave from the kitchens and began to remove the table settings.

Phoenix turned to ask Elise what had given her such a fright, but, without saying a word to anyone, the girl had leapt up and was hurriedly making her way from the hall.

No one said anything. Even the boys sitting around them watched silently.

The first to move was Sophie, who, solemnly, used her hand to make the sign to ward against evil.

CHAPTER 10

The library smelled of stale dust. It reminded Phoenix of the storage cellar back in Avondale - except that it was high above ground, and it was filled with parchments instead of turnips, but the musty odor was much the same.

Large, ornate windows stretched along the walls, casting a wide array of hues across the floors and shelves. Unlike the windows in the hall, the colored glass did not depict scenes or pictures, but was filled instead with abstract splashes of color.

"Lanterns, please," an older gentleman called from the large desk at the front of the room. His voice carried easily in the hushed silence. He wore a deep green sweater and peered over a pair of spectacles that were perched on his nose. Phoenix had heard of them, the strange glass device that improved peoples' vision, but she had never seen them before. She found them fascinating. His white hair was combed neatly, his beard trimmed short, and he exuded the quiet authority of a Master when he spoke. "No open flames. Candles in the lanterns, please!"

The man nodded to several juniors, and handed lanterns to the few who came forward to get them. Others gathered their work and exited quietly through the double doors to return to their rooms.

"Would you like a lantern?" the man asked pleasantly, smiling at Phoenix. "It's getting rather hard to see in the dark."

"Um, n-no, thank you - well, yes, actually - but I think I'm t' see you? If you're th' Bookmaster, that is." Phoenix looked around carefully, half-expecting Master Weston to charge out from among the shelves and protest her very presence.

His moss-green eyes appraised her, their few flecks of hazel popping in the light. "Ah, yes. You must be the infamous Phoenix." When she nodded hesitantly, he handed her a lantern. "Third row on your left."

"Thank you," she said gratefully, accepting the lantern.

She walked through the aisles slowly. The shelves were filled with countless books of different shapes and sizes, most of which had the same strange symbols on their spines as the ones on Master Weston's walls.

When she reached the third row, Phoenix could see a woman restocking the shelves from a wheeled cart that groaned when she pushed it. Phoenix appraised the mountain of stacked books, impressed that not one toppled as they moved.

The woman wore a knit purple cardigan and was humming quietly to herself while she worked. She paused with a smile when she noticed Phoenix coming towards her.

"S'cuse me. I'm lookin' for th' Bookmaster..."

"Well, you've found her!" The Bookmaster laughed pleasantly, her blue eyes crinkling. "You must be Phoenix, then?"

"Yes, Master." Phoenix managed to dip into a graceless curtsy. The jerky movement caused the lantern to throw light unevenly on the shelves around them.

The Bookmaster waved off the formality. "You're newly arrived; I haven't seen you before." She paused and studied Phoenix's face for a moment, as if committing it to memory. "I was asked to set aside some books for you - they're down in the back. So, come along; I'll give you the grand tour." Pushing the cart so that it was out of the way, she led Phoenix through the shelves of parchment and bound ledgers.

The Master pointed out different reading subjects and seating areas as they went. Phoenix smiled and nodded, attempting to memorize everything that she was told. There were only a few people present in the library at this hour, and the Master spoke quietly so as not to disturb them, but Phoenix found that even though she was the one who remained silent she was still the recipient of several annoyed looks.

Eventually, they came to the center of the room. Over-sized chairs were grouped around multiple tables in front of a large, grated-in hearth. "At first I was surprised by how old you were," the Bookmaster admitted; her voice soft from years of working in a quiet place. "I was expecting someone at least half your age." She smiled kindly. "But, I guess everyone has to start somewhere."

She gestured to a small stack of books resting on the table next to them. "You have to get a beginners' ledger from Master Weston, but these will do for now." She took the lantern from Phoenix and set it on the table. "Any questions?" she asked.

Phoenix stared at the books, feeling overwhelmed. "So, I'm t' take these t' Master Weston...?"

"Tomorrow morning, when you go with the rest of the girls for your lesson."

Phoenix felt her heart sink. She was hoping to be able to avoid more humiliation in front of Brianna and her friends.

The Bookmaster smiled warmly. "If you need any help at all - at any time - you come look for me, okay?"

Phoenix nodded, then smiled shyly. Remembering her manners, she attempted another curtsy. "Thank you, Master."

"You're very welcome. It was a pleasure meeting you, Phoenix. Don't be a stranger!" The Bookmaster smiled and, turning, disappeared among the bookstacks to return to her work.

Phoenix waited for her to disappear from view before leaning against the table and lifting the cover of the first book. The characters scripted on the page made no more sense to her than they did the previous morning. With a soft sigh, she let the cover drop down and close the book.

"You obviously haven't had much practice with that curtsy," a voice said dryly from one of the study chairs. Phoenix jumped and turned to see Camden rising easily despite all of the materials he carried. He'd startled her, but she didn't admit it as he joined her next to the table. His eyes were a dark grey in the lantern light, and he was looking at her so strangely that she was beginning to wonder if what the girls had said about him earlier held any truth.

"I didn't get much practice onna farm," she informed him, feeling defensive.

He set his things down and lifted her books to look at them. "Beginner's level?" He asked, surprised.

Phoenix shrugged self-consciously. She felt strange meeting his gaze, so instead she looked at the text on his large books as if she could figure out what they were.

"I don't understand," he said, after a beat of silence. "You can't read, and yet such a strong fire burns inside of you."

Phoenix raised her eyebrows. He was focused on her, but it seemed as though he was looking through her again instead of at her.

"Wha' d' you mean?"

His grey eyes became intense as he took a step closer. "Your fire... your Power... is very strong. I can *feel* it when I look at you." He reached out as if to touch her, then drew his hand back hesitantly. Phoenix wasn't sure, but she thought she saw the gem in his ring glow briefly in the light. "Are you one of the old folk?" he asked suddenly.

"Old folk?" she asked.

"Yes. You know: sirens; dragons; body-shifters. Those who roamed the land long before man came along."

Phoenix was astonished. "You think I'm a dragon?" she asked, incredulous.

"Well, it would explain your curtsy," he said mildly. She gaped at him, and Camden had the grace to look shocked at what he said. A surprised smile spread slowly along his lips.

Phoenix couldn't help but laugh, and Camden joined her a moment later, though he seemed more relieved by her reaction than anything.

He peered at her a moment longer, then picked up his reed quill and scratched something onto a strip of parchment. With a small smile he handed it to her.

She took it carefully, mindful of the wet ink, and looked at it helplessly. "I dunno wha' tha' says," she admitted.

Camden leaned close and, with the tip of his finger, pointed to each symbol and read it out for her. When she still didn't get it, he circled the word with his finger. "It's your name, Phoenix."

In awe, she repeated the letters back to him and he nodded. "Memorize it, if nothing else. It's the most important word you need to know."

She looked up at him. His face was close to hers, and she could feel his soft breath on her cheek. Camden didn't move, but he seemed caught off guard that she still stood there.

It wasn't surprising, she thought to herself, if others reacted to him the same way that Sophie did at the mention of his name.

"Thank you," she said simply, and she carefully folded the now-dry scrap and tucked it in her tunic.

To her surprise, Camden blushed. "You're welcome," he said, straightening.

A bell chimed somewhere in the castle. Camden rearranged his things and handed Phoenix her lantern. "Late call," he said.

Phoenix accepted the light and scooped up her books with her free hand. She looked at him awkwardly for a moment. "Will you be in th' hall for next-meal?" she blurted.

Camden gave a reflective smirk. "Perhaps." He managed a small bow. "Goodnight, Miss Phoenix."

"Apprentice Camden," she replied. Phoenix was proud of the fact that she barely wobbled with the curtsy she gave him, but he shook his head in amusement as he made his way from the library. His soft laughter echoed back at her, and she couldn't help but smile.

***

Phoenix exited the library, returning her lantern to the front desk on her way out. To her surprise, Kit was sitting in the hallway waiting for her. The pup's bushy tail started wagging as soon as Phoenix closed the door behind her.

"You shouldn't be here," she scolded quietly, patting the dog affectionately on the head. Kit's sense of smell must be amazing to find her so easily in Angor's walls.

She looked around but the hallway was empty and quiet. Phoenix clicked her tongue and started down the corridor. Kit jumped up and trotted easily at her side.

Phoenix had found the castle confusing in the light of the day, but now she was completely lost. Endless grey stone walls stretched before her on either side; every passage looked the same as the next. Phoenix found it impossible to discern any point of reference as they went.

The candles on the walls flickered as they passed - causing the light to shift on the stone. Her own shadow continued to grow and shrink depending on her proximity to the quivering flames. The quiet was making Phoenix uneasy.

"Everyone's p'rolly in their rooms already," she said softly, as if talking too loudly might disturb them, "jus' like we should be." She hesitated before going down a short flight of stairs that she didn't remember from before. Surely if the library was up high, she must have to go down to get back to her destination.

"I'm not sure where we're goin'," she told the pup. "I wish someone was around t'ask…"

As they continued down the hallway, Phoenix's need to turn around grew with each step.

The books in her arms were getting heavy. She tried shifting their weight every few steps, but it did nothing to help. When felt like her arms could no longer lift them, Phoenix decided it was time to turn around. The corridor up ahead was dark and dusty with unlit candles hanging from the walls. She was loathe to get lost and be in the dark at the same time.

"Kit," Phoenix called the pup to her.

She waited a moment but Kit didn't turn around, continuing down the dark corridor.

"Kit!" Phoenix said, more insistently. Kit continued to ignore her, sniffing at the base of the wall. With a huff, Phoenix shifted her books again and took a step backwards. "C'mon. It's time t' go. We're gonna get in trouble."

Kit whined softly but didn't move. Phoenix gave a sigh and walked over to her, grumbling. "Wha' izzit now?"

Kit was sat on the floor, half in the shadows, facing the wall where a large painting was hanging.

"It's jus' a paintin'," Phoenix told her. "C'mon."

Kit whined again and barked at it.

"Shh!" Phoenix hissed. She stepped forward to grab the pup, but paused as the picture captured her attention.

The painting was large - much larger than the height that Phoenix stood - and intricately done. The frame was gilded and ornate, though tarnished, and the colors within the image were well-preserved despite its age and forgotten state.

The scene depicted was one of a young woman, smiling, and rocking an infant in front of a window. The woman was beautiful, Phoenix thought, with long dark hair and wide green eyes. She looked familiar, but Phoenix was unable to place her.

The child in her lap was reaching up and laughing. She had tight ringlets of berry-blond hair, and her eyes were the same green as the woman holding her.

"S'just a paintin'," she repeated. Patting the pup on the head, Phoenix snapped her fingers and turned back the way that they'd come. "C'mon. We gotta go."

"What are you doing here?" a harsh voice demanded, making Phoenix jump.

Captain Rolf stood in the centre of the hallway, blocking the way which they had come. He glared at Phoenix, both hands resting easily on his heavy belt as he stood as unmoving as the walls around them.

Phoenix stood nervously under his glare. She moved slightly, hoping to obscure the Captain's view of Kit, but his eyes were already focused on the pup.

"Were you not informed," he asked, scathingly, "that beasts are not allowed to roam Angor's halls?" His eyes narrowed accusingly at the books in Phoenix's arms, as if holding them was somehow a personal affront to him.

"We got lost," she began in a weak voice. "I was called to the library after meal's end..." She trailed off at the look on his face and shifted her weight uncomfortably. The Guardscaptain's expression changed drastically at her choice of words. His face darkened and he moved to the side so that she could pass him, which he indicated for her to do with an angry jerk of his chin.

"I will escort you back to the dorms," he said formally, in a controlled tone. "You shouldn't be running around the castle this late without supervision."

The way he said it seemed to imply that only she was not allowed to walk around by herself, but the look on his face encouraged her to swallow her retort. "Thank you," she said instead.

Moving quickly, she walked with Kit at her heels. Instead of leading the way, Captain Rolf followed behind her like a churlish shadow. Phoenix realized that he was doing it in order to keep the two of them in his sights.

"Go left," he ordered abruptly. She turned without comment and walked down a small hallway that led to a well-lit area. She could feel his eyes boring into the back of her skull and she did her best to move quickly so as not to aggravate him further.

The way back seemed much shorter than Phoenix remembered, though being escorted in such a fashion somehow also made the walk seem endless. The Captain directed her down a set of stairs that led out to the back courtyard. With a glare, he unlocked the metal door and held it open silently. Phoenix led Kit to the door and crouched down.

"Go see Muler," she told the pup softly, stroking her soft ears. Kit wagged her tail and gave Phoenix's hand a lick before bounding off into the outside.

Standing to watch her go, Phoenix felt a *pop* and watched as a large shadow cross the courtyard in the direction of Malcourt's tower. It was hard to make out the shape in the dark, but she could see large wings flapping backwards to slow its descent as it landed on one of the windowsills.

Phoenix frowned. Pip seemed massive in the dim lighting.

"Hurry up," Captain Rolf barked at her, looking sour as he continued to hold the door open for her.

Shifting her books, Phoenix slipped back inside to the stony warmth of the porch. The Captain pulled the massive door shut with a loud clang. Phoenix felt her ears vibrate painfully from the impact, but wisely she didn't say anything.

With heavy steps, the Guardscaptain led the way towards the dorms. Even in the late hour, the Captain showed no signs of leaving duty for the night. He was not wearing the armour that he wore when Phoenix had first met him. His garb was a thick heavy leather, and his sword scabbard was freshly polished where it hung from his belt.

They reached the dorms' staircase. The Captain went up as far as the landing that separated the two dorms, the boys from the girls, but he did not continue onward.

"Take care not to wake the others," he ordered her as she passed. "They don't deserve to have their rest interrupted just because you can't follow the rules."

His words followed her up the stairs. Phoenix said nothing and closed the door behind her, shutting out the sound of the Captain's voice, enjoying the small sliver of satisfaction that she was able to dismiss him in such a fashion.

The common room was dark and silent. Dying embers glowed in the hearth and cast a soft light in the immediate area. Gratefully, Phoenix set the books down and rubbed the feeling back into her arms.

The girls had been in bed for a while now, and the thought of waking anyone - especially Mistress Ruby - gave her pause. She couldn't deal with anyone else's disapproval.

Sighing a second time, Phoenix sat on one of the couches. She was not looking forward to tomorrow. The idea of seeing Master Weston again, or the idea of dealing with the mocking that Brianna would subject her to, filled her with a sense of dread. She thought back to what Sophie said and felt slightly relieved. Perhaps the girl was right. Perhaps in a week she would be settled.

Phoenix lay on the couch and positioned her feet towards the warmth of the embers. She was too tired to search for a spare blanket, so she tucked herself into the cushions as much as possible. She wouldn't wake Mistress Ruby, she decided. Once the waking bell rang she would slip upstairs to her room in the commotion and no one would be the wiser.

Pulling out the strip of parchment that Camden had given her, she peered at it closely. "Phoenix," she murmured to herself. Tomorrow she would memorize it, she promised herself. It seemed like the best place to start.

Carefully, she tucked it back into the pocket of her tunic. Feeling more resolve than she had in awhile, Phoenix willed herself to relax. Finally, after a while, she closed her eyes and fell asleep.

CHAPTER 11

The warmth was suffocating.

A thin wail cut through the room. Phoenix could hear a familiar voice call out in desperation. A small child wandered into view, searching frantically around her.

"Mommy!" she wailed into the emptiness.

Phoenix felt her heart lurch in her chest.

It was the girl from the painting. She was older now, about five years, though her face remained almost identical to the laughing infant in the portrait. Her long hair hung in thick curls that reminded Phoenix of her own.

"Mommy!" she sobbed, looking scared.

"Hey," Phoenix called to her softly.

The girl jumped at the sound of Phoenix's voice. Gulping back her sobs, she walked over to Phoenix. Her wide eyes were a brilliant green against her pale face.

She stopped before Phoenix and held out her hand. Phoenix reached out to take it, but the child dropped something into it instead. Phoenix opened her hand to see her necklace resting in her palm.

She fumbled at her chest where her pendant hung. "How did you..."

Suddenly the girl began to shrink, as if dropping away from Phoenix down an unseen hole. She screamed in pain.

"No!" Phoenix lunged for the girl's hand. Phoenix felt as though she were being lifted by an unseen force. She soared upwards and the girl quickly disappeared into the darkness.

"No!" she cried again.

Suddenly her feet were on solid ground. The air around her was hot and rising in temperature. Waves of heat pressed against her, settling against her skin and weighing down her hair. They snaked down her throat and into her chest, making it hard for her to breathe. Smoke hung around the room like a thick fog, acting as a wall that forced the scorching warmth back towards her. Muted firelight illuminated the heavy air around her randomly.

Phoenix started to choke as she stumbled around blindly, trying to escape. She could hear the sounds of frightened animals somewhere nearby.

Coughing, Phoenix held her sleeve over her mouth. Something caught her foot and she stumbled, barely catching herself in time as she fell, her hands saving her face from hitting the wooden floor.

Crawling, Phoenix turned around to see what made her fall. Through the smoke she could see an arm resting on the ground. It was outstretched, fingers extended stiffly as if grasping for something. Phoenix grabbed the hand and shook it repeatedly. "We've gotta get outta here," she managed to choke out between coughs.

A screeching metal sound pierced her ears when she tugged the arm again. When the person didn't move, Phoenix crawled closer to see if she could help. She waved her arms to clear the smoke and saw that it was a man wearing an Angor guard's suit. The guard remained unmoving, and it was only then that Phoenix noticed the ashen color of his skin. She peered closely at his face. His eyes were stretched wide open, uncomprehending as they stared ahead sightlessly in the burning room.

Phoenix screamed. Aghast, she threw herself backwards so that she was no longer touching the corpse. Frantically, she rubbed her hands against her arms, as if she could somehow erase the feeling of his flesh against her skin. Burning pain blossomed between her fingers and her shoulder blades.

The surrounding inferno had reached her. Phoenix started to scream as the fire licked at her bare feet, climbing slowly up her legs. She thrashed, hitting frantically at the flames.

Something shook her violently and she screamed again. In the distance, she could hear someone calling her name over the roar of the blaze around her.

Something struck her feet and she fell flat on her back.

"Harder, Rae. Use it again!" a woman's voice shouted above her. "Use that blanket! It's almost out!"

Phoenix opened her eyes.

She was lying on the couch in the common room. Mistress Ruby's hands were on her shoulders, shaking her awake, while Rae used a blanket to smother the flames at the foot of the couch. Phoenix could see the rest of the girls she had woken, glaring at her as a rumpled huddle in the doorway.

Elise rushed forward and splashed a glass of water over the couch pillows. Rae peered at it carefully and, after making sure that the fabric was no longer smoking, dropped the ruined blanket on the floor.

Rae sat next to Phoenix on the couch. "Are you all right?" she asked, pulling her into a hug. Phoenix nodded silently, and Rae began to rub her back while the hot tears poured down her face.

"Mistress Ruby..." Rae began, softly.

"Quite right, Miss Rae." Mistress Ruby straightened and fixed a look on the hostile group of girls. "Everyone back to bed," she ordered briskly, watching them without pause until they shuffled off, climbing up the stairs with sullen backward glances.

Mistress Ruby took another blanket and wrapped it around Phoenix's shaking shoulders. "Rae, go to my storage and get some tea, please. I think the thistle root one would be best. My kettle should still be warm."

Rae nodded and, with a squeeze to Phoenix's arm, walked down the hall to Mistress Ruby's room.

The Mistress Ruby took her place, rubbing Phoenix's arms to help distract her from her sleep-terror. "It's just a bad dream," she told her, with a comfort that surprised Phoenix. "You're safe. Just breathe."

Phoenix gasped, sucking air into her lungs. Desperately she tried to suppress the tremors that wracked her body, the searing pain in her scars distracting her.

Rae returned with a warm mug and Mistress Ruby held it to Phoenix's lips. The smell was awful and she gagged slightly in protest.

"It will calm your nerves," she insisted, not removing the cup. "It will help you to sleep."

Too tired to protest, Phoenix gulped the drink without pause until it was finished, coughing at the awful taste it left in her mouth. A moment later, a fuzzy warmth spread up her spine to pool in her head.

"I made it strong on purpose," Rae said, from somewhere far away. Phoenix was conscious of standing, with each arm around a different set of shoulders as she was escorted from the room.

"Here we are," a voice said, penetrating the cloud that had wrapped itself around Phoenix's senses.

She felt her body fall a short distance before it was caught by a firm surface, and gentle hands maneuvered her expertly into her bed. Phoenix was barely conscious as Mistress Ruby pulled the sheets over her and tucked her in for sleep.

CHAPTER 12

Phoenix opened her eyes. Sunlight streamed through the window, illuminating the room and the backs of her eyelids with a soft glow. Groaning, she rubbed her face and turned over.

She was in her bed. The books that she had been carrying the night before had been stacked neatly on the floor next to her clothes, which had been replaced by her new sleepwear after she had been brought upstairs.

A questioning chirp and the sound of rustling wings drew her attention to the hearth's grate. Pip was perched there, her large yellow eyes blinking slowly as she watched Phoenix sit up. She opened her great wings, and, with a flap, glided easily to the foot of her bed. Slowly, flipping her wings to her back, she minced her way along the sheets and up Phoenix's leg.

Her large talons were gentle as she rested on Phoenix's knee. Peering into Phoenix's face, Pip tilted her head so far to the side that Phoenix feared her neck would snap. The owl's head continued to turn until it was almost completely upside down, then she blinked and chirped again, as if asking the girl a question.

Phoenix smiled. Slowly, she outstretched her hand and ran a fingertip down the bird's chest. "Good morning t' you, too," she greeted Pip softly.

"Mid-day," Rae corrected from where she was sitting at her desk, startling Phoenix, who had not noticed her there before.

Pip ignored the other girl. She righted her head, and, quickly - as if afraid of being seen - rubbed her cheek against Phoenix's hand. The next moment, the owl launched herself from Phoenix's knee and disappeared through the open window, her massive wingspan barely making it through the stone opening.

With Pip gone, Phoenix had no choice but to turn her attention to Rae's curious gaze.

"How are you feeling?" Rae asked, leaving her desk to bring Phoenix a glass of water.

"Fuzzy," Phoenix admitted, drinking the water gratefully. Her mouth was parched, and her body felt like it was made of stone. "How long have I been sleepin'?"

Rae shrugged. "Mid-meal just started." She grinned when Phoenix groaned. "Don't worry about it. The weather shifted this morning so today is an orchard day: all the lessons were cancelled. And, thankfully, since Tessa said I was to stay with you, I was able to catch up on my dormwork. Oh! Guess what!" She waited for Phoenix to answer, but continued on when the girl only blinked at her. "Elise's going to be your new teacher! That's why she was summoned after last evening's meal! She's never taught anyone before - but they thought you'd be good practice. And at least you won't have to deal with Master Weston anymore."

Rae made such a face of disgust that Phoenix couldn't help but laugh, the sound that rasped out sounding foreign to her ears.

She sat on the edge of Phoenix's bed and picked at her blanket with her fingers. "So... what happened last night?" Rae finally asked.

"I dunno," Phoenix admitted. "I was late returnin' an' I didn't want t' wake anyone, so I lay on th' couch for th' night. I thought the fire was out..." Feeling confused, Phoenix frowned at the prominent singe marks on her boots.

Rae looked unconvinced, but she shrugged. "Well, it's a good thing you were yelling - otherwise no one would've woken up. You might have caught on fire!" Her eyes were wide, and Phoenix wondered whether she was being serious or not, but then she cracked a smile and the two of them began to giggle.

"C'mon," Rae told her. "We should get something to eat before we head out."

"Head out?" Phoenix asked, rising from the bed to redress in her discarded clothes.

"Yeah. We have to join the others in the orchards. We can't take the whole day to - that's a pretty necklace!" Rae exclaimed, interrupting herself to point to the pendant where it hung uncovered by Phoenix's underclothing.

"Thanks," she said, quickly slipping the pendant under her tunic before she belted the shirt around her waist. "My family left it fer me," she explained hurriedly. Marla had told her to always keep it hidden, as many would not agree with a farmgirl having something so precious. Phoenix had always kept it safe.

"I wish my family had given me something so lovely," Rae said wistfully. She opened the door to their room and led the way from the dorm to the kitchens. "Tessa said she'd put some food aside for us, since she didn't know when you'd wake." Phoenix was touched and surprised by the woman's thoughtfulness, since she knew how busy the Kitchenmaster was.

"Was Mistress Ruby mad 'bout last night?" Phoenix asked, worried that she had to deal with someone else who was set against her.

"Doubt it," Rae said, shrugging. "She's had to deal with worse. You should have seen Brianna when she first came here. She was such a wimp!"

"Really?" Phoenix asked, finding it hard to picture the dark-haired girl being anything but a bully.

"Totally." Rae's doe eyes sparkled. "She was always taken care of at her father's manor. She never had to do anything for herself until she came here."

"Oh. Why'd she come here, then?"

Rae shrugged. "Same as all the other nobles: learning how to be a proper Lady to grab a rich Lord." She rolled her eyes.

"What about you?" Phoenix asked, only belatedly realizing that she had no idea about the girl's family, and hoping that she didn't take offense to the question.

Rae grinned. "Just the opposite," she told her.

Phoenix didn't have to time to tease apart her answer as Rae pushed open the doors to the kitchens, a the sudden smell of cooking food assaulted Phoenix's nose. Her stomach growled loudly in response.

Tessa was ahead of them, orchestrating several of the young boys into separate groups. "Now, Shane. You and Jeff take these baskets to the North quadrant. Yes, on the cart. Bring the full ones back to Anna at the second set of sinks. Billy, same goes for you and Ty - except you go to the Northeastern quad. Yes, on the cart. Yes, right now. Bring the full ones back to Anna. Yes, she's at the sinks. Thank you." The woman dismissed the four with a wave in the right direction, then paused a moment to watch them go. She wiped her hands in her apron and turned to see Rae and Phoenix waiting for her.

"Ah. So you're awake, are you?" She smiled. "Fetch the food from the holding oven, please, Rae. I'll get Phoenix set up here."

Rae nodded, and Phoenix followed Tessa to a table that was out of the way. Tessa indicated for Phoenix to sit, and she brought a pot of tea and several mugs to her table.

"I heard you gave everyone quite the scare last night," Tessa said, pouring three cups of the drink. Phoenix blushed and dropped her eyes to the table with embarrassment. Strong fingers grasped her chin and lifted her head, and Phoenix was surprised by the warmth of the woman's skin.

Tessa dropped her hand and looked at her a long moment afterwards. "We all have troubles in our lives, Phoenix. Sometimes they come out funny in times of stress. It's nothing to be ashamed of."

Phoenix looked away and shrugged. "It don't feel tha' way," she told the woman.

Tessa pursed her lips, then gave Phoenix's hand a quick pat. "I know. But you'll get used to it eventually. Soon enough you'll be settled enough that you won't care about what anyone thinks… except for me, of course." The woman winked humorously and Phoenix gave her a smile in return.

Rae returned with a tray of food for the table. She and Phoenix filled their plates and ate hungrily. Tessa sat with them for a while, and even cut herself a slice of bread from the loaf.

Phoenix barely tasted the food as she shoved it in her mouth to fill her starving belly. She had eaten well last night, but she was strangely ravenous for someone who'd only missed morning's meal.

When the girls began to slow down, Tessa waved Alan over to the table. He came and stood by the three - his attention fixed solely on Tessa, as if by ignoring Phoenix and Rae he could somehow will them out of existence.

"Alan, you are excused from your next set of duties. I need

you to take these two to the orchards to join the rest of the girls."
Alan's expression became sullen, and Tessa fixed him with a
stern eye. "Is that a problem, Runner Alan?"

At his title, he straightened under her gaze and shook his
head. Phoenix thought that he mumbled something, but she
was unable to make it out.

Tessa gave him a reproachful look, but she set down her
cup and returned to the stoves without saying anything more.
It wasn't long before she could be heard shouting orders over
the commotion.

Alan huffed and relaxed his posture. "You two done yet, or
what?"

Rae took a judicious sip of her drink. "Maybe. Maybe not.
What's it matter to you?"

He glared at her. "I just don't want to be stuck in here with
you, is all."

"You mean, you can't wait to get back to Brianna. Right?"

Phoenix watched as Alan's face darkened several shades.
He turned smartly on his heels and marched towards the kitchens' double doors. Rae smirked and watched him go with a roll
of her eyes. Phoenix looked around quickly to see if anyone else
had noticed the exchange, but everyone was too busy with their
tasks to pay them any attention.

Rae shrugged and rose. Grabbing empty baskets from a cart,
the two left the kitchens and followed Alan across the courtyard
to the orchards.

Alan marched ahead of the pair by several lengths. He refused to look back at them, trying to make it seem as though
they weren't walking together while following Tessa's orders.
The pace was brisk, and it wasn't long before the three exited
the courtyard through the massive doors that led into the outer
yard.

The grounds were beautiful. The sun was shining with uncharacteristic warmth, though the wind had a chill bite to it. Phoenix didn't care. She let her empty baskets swing in her hands, happily enjoying the walk.

They reached a fenced perimeter. Phoenix could see hundreds of trees were planted in rows, and even though many of the branches were entwined, the trunks were spaced far apart that they could be walked around with ease. The bright splashes of colors in the leaves were beautiful in the sunlight. Small birds flitted excitedly between the branches in the commotion, and Phoenix paused to watch a small lizard skirt along the path next to her. It paused to look up at her when her shadow passed over it. Intrigued, Phoenix stared at the lizard in awe. It darted off the path as quick as a blink, and climbed easily up a tree until it was at eye level with her. It stopped, hanging easily onto the branch, watching her.

"Phoenix!" Rae called from up ahead. "C'mon!"

With one last curious look at the lizard, Phoenix hurried to catch up. She rushed past groups of juniors who were stacking baskets full of fruit, while the younger children tended to the laden carts. Several chaperones issued orders to direct the chaos.

Alan walked past them without a word, ignoring the adults who were calling for his attention. He ducked under a short tree and cut across the planted rows. With a shrug, Rae followed him and motioned for Phoenix to do the same.

The dorm girls were gathered loosely in a group. There was no fruit on the ground that Phoenix could see, and the others had begun to pluck the remaining under ripe ones that still clung to the branches. Elise caught sight of them and turned to wave them over. Alan pushed past her, causing her to glare after his retreating back, but she smiled at the girls as they approached.

Sophie was with her, but when she caught sight of Phoenix she grabbed her basket and hurried away.

A mocking tone rose shrilly from the adjoining row of trees. Brianna's voice came from the direction where Alan had disappeared, filtering into the area where the group was working.

"She was positively hysterical!" Brianna gushed. Phoenix could see that she was sitting on a large boulder, her baskets lying empty at her feet. Jenny and the girls were gathered around her, snickering as she continued with her tale.

"Mommy! Mommy!" her voice called mockingly, as she clasped her hands in an exaggerated expression of distress. She ended on a high pitch that sent the others into a fit of laughter. Brianna's triumphant eyes fixed on Phoenix, and the girl's pretty face turned into a vicious smirk. "Did you find your mommy after, Phoenix?" she asked, her voice honeyed.

Phoenix felt her cheeks turn hot as she realized that the group was laughing at her. She turned quickly so that they wouldn't see the sudden tears that came to her eyes.

Elise and Rae stepped close to Phoenix and the three headed towards a different area of the orchard.

"Ignore them," Rae said, handing Elise an empty basket. "It's not like she's actually good for anything, anyway." She said the last part over her shoulder, directing her words to Brianna.

A sudden hush fell upon the group. "At least the bloodless urchin has parents, sculler!" Phoenix winced as Brianna shrieked, her words lashing after them with fury. Everyone around her erupted into another fit of laughter as Rae's cheeks flushed a hot pink.

"Warty toad!" Elise swore with surprising heat, linking her arm with Rae's as they walked towards an unclaimed picking area. Phoenix was shocked by her language, but she followed her example and linked her arm with Rae's other arm and swung her basket with false cheerfulness.

"Ignore her," she said, echoing the girl's earlier words. "She dunno wha' she's talkin' about."

"Warty toad," Elise swore again, huffing.

"She's jus' jealous," Phoenix added. "Her parents turned her into a toad an' she's mad tha' yours didn't. That's th' whole reason they sent her away."

Phoenix received incredulous stares from both girls. There was a shocked moment of silence, then Elise surprised them both by bursting out laughing.

"Can you just imagine...?" her voice shook as she tried to regain control of herself.

The three had stopped walking. Phoenix became aware of Rae's arm shaking in her own. A moment later, Rae began giggling uncontrollably, and Phoenix could feel her lips twitching in response.

"Pass the pudding, Tadpole," Rae said innocently.

Phoenix couldn't help herself. Forgetting Brianna's nastiness, as well as Sophie's apparent desertion, the humor of the situation took over. She burst out laughing with Elise while Rae wiped her eyes, and the three had to wait to catch their breath before they could start collecting fruit.

CHAPTER 13

The amount of tree fruit in the kitchens was staggering. Rows upon rows of baskets were stacked along the walls, many of them perched precariously on top of one another as they struggled to hold their contents. Some of the columns stood taller than her, Phoenix realized, feeling daunted by the task. She held her basket and stared around in disbelief. Scullers and castle-folk alike were scurrying around like workerbugs to get their assignments done. Tessa stood in the thick of it - like the eye of a storm - directing everyone around as if she were controlling an elaborate dance.

Tessa caught sight of her and Rae, and gestured for them to go to an adjoining room.

"C'mon," Rae said, setting down her basket. Phoenix did the same and followed her to another fruit-filled room. "Tessa wants us to start with the sorting." She stopped so abruptly that Phoenix nearly bumped into her. Rae put her hands over her face with a groan.

Phoenix looked wide-eyed around the room, mouth hanging open. She understood Rae's distress. Mountains of fruit surrounded them. "We gotta sort all tha'? We'll be here fer days!"

"Only until the others finish washing," Rae said, trying to be hopeful. "Then they'll help out." She led Phoenix to a stack of fruit next to three large bins. "Waste, cooking, and whole," Rae instructed, touching each bin in turn.

Phoenix nodded. She was used to the routine from Avondale, just not the quantity she had to sort. She grabbed an apron and got to work.

It wasn't long before Elise and Sophie joined them. Elise handed Rae and Phoenix a kitchen knife each. "Tessa says we're to cut the bad spots out of the cooking ones," she told them.

"She would," Rae rolled her eyes.

"At least it's not as bad as last year," Elise commented, slicing a bruised piece from a fruit.

"As if! We have twice as much to do this time!"

"Ha!"

Phoenix smiled as they fell into an animated discussion comparing the two harvests. Elise argued that the weather had been better last year, while Rae maintained that more fruit had survived to harvest this year. Neither of the girls seemed intent on proving their point, and were more so debating for the fun of it.

The task wasn't hard. Phoenix found that she could let her mind wander while her hands sorted the treefruit automatically. Others joined them, and the noise of many idle conversations filled the room. Many were laughing and singing as they did their work, adding to the relaxed atmosphere of the labour around them. It was a completely different environment than Phoenix was used to.

The work continued on until the prep for evening's meal began. Phoenix could feel her stomach growling as she finished off the last of her current fruit pile. Rae looked around and sighed, wiping her brow with the back of her hand in an exaggerated fashion. "Phew," she said. "I'm glad that pile's done. I think my fingers were about to fall off." She winced and stretched them several times as if making sure they were still there.

Phoenix? Malcourt's voice rang clear. *Will you meet me in my study, please?*

"Where is it?" she asked, without looking up from her work.

"Where's what?" Sophie asked sharply, speaking to her for the first time that day. She eyed Phoenix suspiciously.

In the top level of the North Tower.

"The one across from the dorms?"

Yes.

"Is what across from the dorms?" Elise asked.

Phoenix looked up and wiped the dried juice from her fingers. "Malcourt's study? He wants me t' meet him there."

The three paused their work to stare at her. Sophie's face flushed as she looked around the room uncomfortably.

"I thought you were going to eat with us," Elise protested mildly.

"How do you know you have to meet him?" Rae asked. "You've been with me all day… Are you trying to get out of fruit duty?"

Phoenix snorted at the expression on her face. "Wha'? And miss all this fun?" She swept an arm around the room, gesturing to the treefruit that still had to be sorted. "He pro'lly don't wan' me fer long."

Phoenix? Malcourt's voice seemed much softer now.

"Yes?"

Bring me a treefruit, please.

Phoenix slid her gaze around the room to discover that Malcourt had already left. With a shrug, she took a moment to look through the whole bin for the best fruit. "I dunno why he didn't choose his own fruit," she muttered.

Rae's eyes widened, and Sophie turned and walked away

without a word. Phoenix chose a fruit and, shrugging to Elise and Rae, left the kitchens.

The tower was not far. It was floors above the kitchens, and Phoenix had to go down a hall that she had never walked before - though she admitted to herself that those outnumbered the ones she had traveled - but she knew enough by now to tell where the dorms were in relation to the hall. Hugging the inside wall, eyeing the unmoving statues of the gargoyles that stood on guard, she hurried across the courtyard to the large tower where Malcourt waited, slipping back into the castle through a side door. She smiled when she reached the entrance, feeling proud that she had found it on her own.

The hallway leading to the tower was deserted. Not even scullers milled around the halls, and the rooms leading up to it were barred and locked. Phoenix wondered if anyone ever entered the wing.

She entered the base of the tower. Her footsteps echoed in the silence, calling back to her as she walked curiously around the perimeter of the foyer, inspecting every carving and symbol in the stone walls.

A large winding staircase in the center of the floor was the source of illumination for the room. The stairs themselves were cut into an intricately carved pillar of stone that spiralled up into the next floor. The layers of the grey stacked stones looked as though they had been sanded down to a seamless structure, carved and imperfectly textured to make it seem as though a giant tree trunk had sprung from the very rock itself and wound its way to the top of the tower.

Massive carvings of branches stretched along the ceilings and the walls. They folded over one another by the base, twisting thickly before veering off in different directions and connecting to the various symbols that had been carved into the walls.

Phoenix ran her gaze over it in awe. She placed a hand against the trunk, unable to tell if the structure was alive.

The soft glow of candlelight danced around the top of the stairs, and Phoenix ascended to the next floor.

Immediately to her right was the entrance to a large room. Phoenix was unsure that this was the study, as it was easily as large as the castle library, but the other rooms on the floor were barred shut.

She peered into the open room.

The amount of books rivaled that of the library. Large candles lined the walls. Pools of old drippings had gathered beneath them, causing wax stalagmites to grow from the stone floors. New candles had been pressed atop the old ones instead of removing them. Phoenix guessed that the scullers did not venture this far into the tower. It made her wonder if she was even supposed to be here.

The tall candles glowed softly in the darkened room. Phoenix took a hesitant step forward, and, immediately, more candles lit themselves ahead of her to light her way. Taking that to be a good sign, she clutched the treefruit nervously and began to search for Malcourt among the stacks of books.

A soft hoot alerted her to Pip's presence. Phoenix turned and walked in that direction.

She found them in the center of the room, surrounded by tables and large chairs. Malcourt was sitting cross-legged on a large striped cat skin before the hearth. He looked relaxed, she thought, noticing how many of the lines on his face had receded and appeared less sharp. Pip was on a perch by a chair, preening her tail with an intent vanity that amused Phoenix.

Master Malcourt smiled and gestured for her to come closer. Phoenix stepped forward hesitantly, holding out the treefruit. He accepted it, inclined his head in thanks, then balanced it on his bent knee.

Phoenix's attention settled on the uneaten fruit.

"It was a test." Malcourt had the grace to look apologetic. "I wanted to see how well you could Hear me."

Phoenix paused. "A test?" She dragged her gaze around the study. The fire had consumed most of the logs in the hearth; the layers of ashes under the grate rested in haphazard piles. And Master Malcourt... it was obvious he had been here for some time. He was too settled for someone who had to hurry ahead of her.

The weight of the revelation bloomed in her chest. "You weren't in th' kitchens, were you?"

Malcourt shook his head. "No, Phoenix. I was here during our conversation. I wanted to see if you were able to Hear me. You didn't disappoint." He picked up the treefruit by its stem and twirled it idly. "Your Calling is very strong for someone who has never used it before... though you will have to learn not to answer out loud. I assume your friends were taken aback?"

Phoenix blinked. A few days ago she'd worked the harvest, struggling to carve herself a home in a place that only wanted to use her. Now she slept in a castle and heard secret voices in her head - and it was being treated as though it were a commonplace occurrence.

"I know it's a lot to take in," he said softly, seeing she was overwhelmed. He motioned for her to sit, an offer she accepted gratefully. "It's always a jolt when it first happens - even if you're expecting it." His voice was compassionate as he spoke. "Everyone feels this way at first."

"'Expecting it'?" Phoenix asked.

Malcourt steepled his fingers, resting his chin upon them. "Do you know who you really are, Phoenix?"

The question caught her off-guard. It brought back flashes of her younger self: sneaking out after dark to search the Cobber's collapsed house; climbing through the charred rubble for the smallest memento of her former life; forcing herself to endure the teasing of Millie and Jobe for the scattered shared laugh that made her feel as though she belonged.

The flames guttered in the hearth. Malcourt didn't flinch, his gaze steady as he waited silently, giving her time to sort through what she was feeling. Finally she shook her head, the admission all the more agonizing from the unexpected vulnerability that followed it.

He looked unsurprised. "I thought not. There's something inside you, Phoenix. Something rare."

"A fire." Phoenix ducked her head self-consciously when Malcourt's eyebrows rose to meet his hairline. "Tha's wha' Camden says, anyhow."

She'd agreed with him. She'd felt the truth of the statement settle in her bones. And she'd begun to wonder if she hadn't known all along. There had always been a whisper of something unknown that had remained hidden until she came here. Something that had begun to stir when she felt that first faint *pull* towards Malcourt's cave in the clearing. Something that had awoken.

Malcourt watched her, assessing her reactions. "You would do well to listen to Camden. He usually knows what he's talking about. More than any Junior Apprentice should - and I'm not just saying that as his Master. Though," he gave a little smile, "I am exceedingly proud of him."

Phoenix returned the smile, secretly relieved that someone else in the castle showed kindness to the boy.

"However," Malcourt tapped his chin, "we are not here to talk about Camden. We are here to talk about you. At least that was the plan..." He looked to Pip, as if the owl would join the conversation, but she continued to ignore the two without pause.

"You said tha' some people... expect wha' happened to me?"

"Ah! Yes. Thank you." The Mastercaller paused for a moment, as if unsure how to continue. "Some people - children - are raised expecting to develop the Calling. I was, my Master was, and Camden was... to a point." He frowned at a memory, but seeing her confused look he continued with a wave of his hand. "It's in the blood, Phoenix. Most noble families carry the Old Blood in some form or another. The older the blood, the stronger the Calling. Not so strong as it was back when Man shared the Land with the Old Folk, but it can manifest in many different ways; the most common of course being the Hearing - like how you first Heard me when I *called* to you.

"When trained properly, those with the Calling can strengthen their abilities. Oftentimes they develop a Talent - a type of ability that is stronger or more prevalent than the others - such as healing, or fire... usually when they don't mean to. It can activate with stress or emotional turmoil. Like a bad dream, for instance."

Phoenix blushed when she realized he was talking about her. She rubbed her thumb between her fingers self-consciously and wondered if anything happened at Angor without his knowledge. "But, if it's in th' blood... does tha' mean I have it? Could I use it to find my family?" Phoenix felt a glimmer of hope at the prospect. She'd never dared to dream that she might have family still living.

Malcourt's blue eyes were thoughtful. "More than that, Phoenix. Your Calling is too strong - especially for one so young who hasn't had any guidance. I would wager both your parents came from old blood based on how your abilities act out."

Phoenix felt her hope turn to disbelief at his suggestion. "But, why..." All of her life she'd accepted that she was Bloodless. Any hope of finding out who she was had died with the Cobbers. But if it turned out she wasn't Bloodless - if she could somehow trace it back to her family...

"Why would they live on a farm?" Malcourt finished her thought, drumming his fingers against his knee. "I don't know. I can only guess that they were hiding from something." He set the treefruit on the rug, careful to leave its curled leaf intact. "Though I honestly can't imagine what two noble-bloods would be hiding from. If they were Callers I definitely would have heard of it. Every Caller would have. Unless the Calling skipped their generation..." He stared off momentarily, considering the different options. Phoenix remained silent, watching the curiosity flicker in his expression, how the intrigue that animated his face was pulled by the undercurrent of excitement. She understood why he was adamant that she come with him.

"You knew from th' start, didn't you?"

Malcourt smiled slowly, and Phoenix was surprised to see that he was embarrassed. "After you collapsed, I could *feel* that there was... something about you - I just didn't know what. I still don't know what. But I knew I couldn't leave you there alone, and I'd decided to go back to look for you if you decided not to return with me... once the King was healed. However," he clapped his hands so loudly that Pip ruffled her wings and berated him with an angry hoot. "Sorry, love," he apologized to the owl. "However," he started again, lowering his voice, "that is not why I *called* you here. I do intend to find out - and I am quite resourceful when I put my mind to it, by the by - but we currently have more pressing matters to attend to!"

The Mastercaller rose fluidly before she could respond, his

expression serious after his grand proclamation. He walked to a small desk that nestled into a stone alcove, resting his hand on the top of the table for a moment. Phoenix could hear a soft click, and an unlocked drawer slid open. He carefully removed a thickly-folded cloth and set it on a large desk in the center of the room, pushing aside the scrolls and parchments that had already staked a claim to the surface. He beckoned for Phoenix to join him as he unfolded the rich material.

A small pile of jewels rested in the middle of the cloth. They were cut into various shapes and sizes, their colored light blending together and casting small rainbows around them. Carefully, reverently, Malcourt used the tip of a finger to separate them; pushing them apart from one another so that they no longer touched.

Phoenix held her breath. She was afraid that any sudden movement on her part would somehow cause harm to the treasure before her.

"Do you know what these are?" he asked.

Phoenix looked at them thoughtfully and shook her head. "No, but I think I saw Camden wearin' one." She remembered the strange ring on his finger from earlier.

Malcourt nodded. "Exactly so, Phoenix. These are focus stones. Apprentice Callers use them while in training. They act as a conduit when they're learning to use their Power. They also act as a shield to protect the wearer; they absorb excess Power if too much of it builds up."

"Too much of it?" Phoenix looked at the stones nervously, feeling the familiar tension stretch along the scars between her shoulder blades.

"Nothing you have to worry about just yet," he smiled. "Sometimes, when in training, it's possible for a Caller to get too absorbed in what they're doing. Power will build up, and once it reaches a certain point it can't be dismissed easily. It has to go somewhere. The stones can help to focus it so that it doesn't become destructive. It also helps the wearer to avoid unintentional outbursts." He let her look at them a moment longer, watching her. "Do you have a favourite?"

It was another test. Phoenix squared her shoulders and forced herself to consider each of the stones before her. They were all mesmerizing. They twinkled like colored stars against the backdrop of the dark cloth, but eventually she felt a pull towards two of the brilliant gems. Afraid to choose them both, she pointed to the smaller of the two. "Th' green," she admitted at last, ignoring the purple that looked almost black in comparison.

"Hold out your hand," Malcourt commanded.

She did so, and Malcourt carefully placed the gem in her palm. Immediately, a strange jolt caused her arm to tense. With a yelp, she jerked her hand back, causing the stone to fall past the desk and land on the floor. "Oh!" she exclaimed, surprised by her reaction. She anxiously cast about for the fallen treasure.

Malcourt chuckled. "Don't worry, Phoenix. That can happen now and then. You should have seen me my first time holding one. I nearly threw it out a window!"

He located the gem easily and placed it firmly back on the cloth. "So, that one's eliminated, but I'm sure you'll find one that suits you. Unfortunately, that means that you're going to have to do it again."

The next hour passed with Phoenix touching the different stones, and Malcourt watching and judging her reactions. Sometimes she was able to pick them up and hold them. Other times she could only place a finger on them before the discomfort made her jerk her hand back. The longer that they continued, the more convinced Phoenix became that she could hear a faint hum coming from the stones. It got to the point that she could tell before she touched a certain stone whether it would be uncomfortable or not.

They finished when Phoenix eliminated the last one. Dejectedly, she sat with her hands in her lap, looking morosely at the cloth before her and feeling as though she had failed.

"None of them appealed to you?" The Mastercaller carefully set the final stone back with the others.

"They're all beautiful!" Phoenix said, hurriedly, so as not to give offense. "They just..."

"Don't sound right?" When she winced, he nodded understandingly. "These aren't the only focus stones in Angoria, Phoenix. Worry not. We'll find you one. We'll just have to try again."

Phoenix stifled a groan. She ignored her frustrations. Her head ached from the constant humming around her, but the need to finish this for Master Malcourt overrode any objections. If she couldn't complete one simple task, why would he ever agree to help her?

"This one was the closest," she offered helpfully, picking up the dark purple stone. "If there are others like this...?"

He shook his head. "Unfortunately, that's not how it works."

Phoenix dropped it back on the table. As it fell, it hit the original green stone and ricocheted off of it. The noise that the two made on impact caused her ear to twitch. She was grateful that the noise didn't add to her headache.

Malcourt narrowed his eyes thoughtfully. "Do that again," he told her.

Phoenix, mindful not to chip the gems, let the two strike off of each other again. The result was a clear bell-like sound that echoed inside her head.

"Open your hand." Malcourt's complete attention was on the stones. Once she did so, he picked up both gems and held them in his hand. His expression turned to one of discomfort. His jaw tightened in pain, and, hesitantly, he placed them in Phoenix's hand. She winced, expecting the end result to hurt.

Instead, the pitches shifted. Like tumbling sand, the stones shed their vibrations until the two notes purred in harmony, reveling in the strength of the chord. The hidden whisper, the one that she had only just discovered, no longer whispered. It had begun to hum.

It coiled itself around the base of her spine, its warmth a promise of things yet to come. Maybe, just maybe, she always had this strength inside of her. And maybe now, by accepting it, she would finally have the freedom to find out who she was.

Calm spread over her body, and Phoenix couldn't help but smile in relief.

Triumphant, Malcourt jumped up and rummaged through a pile of scrolls on the table and pulled a small hide bag from beneath them. Wordlessly he placed it in Phoenix's empty hand.

Carefully he picked up the remaining stones and placed them back on the thick cloth. He folded the material back over itself in order to keep them contained.

"Do you remember the night we stayed in the field?" he asked her.

Phoenix swallowed and nodded. "Th' night we were attacked?" she asked. She could still remember her feeling of fear when the men had ambushed the campsite where they had all been resting.

Malcourt nodded. "Did you happen to notice what I was doing while you and Sylvia were setting up the fire?" he asked, returning the stones to the table and locking the shelf with a soft word.

Phoenix thought back. She remembered the explosion of the light as the attacker had thrown his powder against Malcourt's protection circle.

"Drawin'," she answered, looking up to see if that was what he meant. "A circle, around th' camp. An' somethin' else, too, I think?"

He smiled at her. "Very good, Phoenix. Well done." He walked over to the hearth where Pip was preening and extended a finger to her. The owl chirped at him conversationally and waddled forward, rubbing her feathered cheek against it. Malcourt smiled and said something to the owl that Phoenix was unable to hear. He seemed relaxed as he stood there, silently, while Pip rubbed her beak against his finger.

"Power is a deeply personal thing, Phoenix," Malcourt said at last. "Everyone's manifests in a different way. However, with the proper training and study, it can be a limitless force under your control. And I will train you to control it. Do you understand?"

Phoenix looked at the focus stones that she still held in her hand. The lines of her palms tingled slightly where they touched. The vibrations had spread down her arms and caused her hair to stand on end, but she found the tingling feeling calming more than anything.

"Wha' did you mean by 'manifest'?" she asked. She closed her hand around the stones, causing them to hum softly against her skin.

Malcourt stroked Pip's pale chest before pulling a scroll from the shelf next to him. "'Develop', I guess you could say. 'Act out', even. Those of us who have Power develop what we refer to as a Talent; a certain inclination towards one of the many components that can be affected by our abilities. We can train ourselves to use other avenues, of course, but it takes more effort when compared to those which come more naturally."

He returned to where he had been sitting and, once again at eye level, studied her face carefully. "Unfortunately, there can be consequences... like the need for new footwear, for example." His eyes dropped down to her scorched boots, as if reading her thoughts.

Phoenix ducked her head. She had been thinking about the dream that she had had, and how the arm of the couch still waited for Master Minna's expert ministrations to remove the marks where the fire had taken hold.

She cleared her throat. "So tha' was my fault?" she asked, remembering the faces of Brianna and the others as they glared at her for interrupting their sleep.

Malcourt shook his head and patted her knee softly. "I think 'fault' is too strong a word in this case, Phoenix. It implies forethought and assigns blame. Did it come from you? Yes. I won't do you the disservice of pretending that the fire was not brought on by your unusual dream - but it certainly wasn't your fault. I could no more blame you for that than I could blame someone for sneezing. You reacted naturally to a circumstance beyond your control. Anyone who thinks otherwise... well... is a fool."

His voice ended on a strange note, and Phoenix realized that, while he had conveyed the meaning of his message properly, he had not expressed it quite in the way that he had wanted. Phoenix could picture Brianna's scowl easily, though she was hardly the only one to ever treat her so thoughtlessly. She thought back to Avondale, and the way that the people there had crossed themselves whenever the fire had flared up around her; the way they whispered about her when she was still within ear shot; Millie's unnecessary cruelty. Phoenix had to admit that most had been unkind to her. She felt a pang in her chest when she realized that they had been right all along. Perhaps she had been causing terrible things to happen without even realizing it!

The room was hot. Pip shrieked with indignation and launched herself to the back of a large chair. She dug her claws into the thick material and flapped her large wings repeatedly, causing Phoenix's hair and their clothing to move erratically in the resulting drafts.

The soothing pulse of the focus stones in Phoenix's hand halted. Instead of a hum, they became silent and shocked her so abruptly that she yelped and dropped them on to the thick fur beneath her.

"Are you all right, Phoenix?" Malcourt asked, reaching for her hand. He inspected her surrendered palm, but seeing nothing of note, his gaze slid bemusedly to the candles along the walls and the hearth behind him.

Phoenix's eyes followed his. "Oh!" she said softly in the darkening room.

The candles hanging from the walls had melted away to nothing. The once tall cylinders of tallow had melted into the pools of wax, extinguished in most cases where the wick had been doused in the hot liquid. Even the hearth fire, with its massive supply of logs, had expanded and burned itself out so that all that remained was a charred bed of glowing embers.

"Pip!" Phoenix said suddenly, turning to look at the angry owl who was glaring at the two balefully.

"Is fine," Malcourt said reassuringly. "She might have a singed tail feather or two, but she'll be all right. She got a bit of a fright more than anything... though she is used to such random happenings by now. She's being a bit dramatic, if you ask me."

Pip squawked what Phoenix thought sounded like an oath at Malcourt and turned her back on the pair. Without a sound, she spread her wings and flew to the opposite end of the room, putting a massive case of books between her and the humans who were sitting together on the floor.

Malcourt chuckled softly to himself. "She'll get over it... eventually." When Phoenix looked worried he added, "I've certainly had worse accidents with her. However! The best thing about accidents - I find - is that they provide an excellent learning opportunity."

Malcourt unwound a strip of hide from the scroll and looked around the room searchingly. He motioned to the wood pile, and two small sticks rolled down from the pile and across the floor towards them. Phoenix watched, amazed, as they positioned themselves to keep the scroll from curling back in on itself.

Malcourt chuckled at the expression on her face. "Learning that little trick took much longer than I care to admit, but it's absolutely fantastic at parties."

"Could I learn to do somethin' like tha'?" Phoenix felt her initial apprehension turn to excitement.

"That and so much more, my dear," Malcourt smiled.

"Could I learn t' do a bindin' spell?" she plucked the name from her memory, thinking of Oliver, the man they had brought to the castle in the back of the wagon.

Malcourt looked surprised. "Yes, I believe you could. It takes a lot of work, Phoenix, but I think that you are more than capable of it."

She straightened her spine. It had been a long time since anyone had displayed such a level of confidence in her, and Phoenix vowed that she would not disappoint him.

"I'll do m' best," she told him. "Promise."

"That's all I ask. Now then," he tapped the scroll on the floor between them, "I want you to tell me what you see."

Phoenix assessed the image. The parchment was faded and creased with age, but the picture on it was vibrantly colored as if freshly painted. It was a mismatch of lines and colors - some drawn haphazardly, some with expert precision - which formed no discernible meaning that Phoenix could find.

She studied it silently, hoping to understand what it was that Malcourt wished her to see. It reminded her vaguely of the windows in the library - lines of colored glass without any obvious pattern - but eventually she had to admit defeat.

"I dunno wha' I'm supposed t' be lookin' for," she confessed, frustrated at her inability to complete the task.

"Ah," Malcourt replied, as if she had said something clever. "Have you ever seen one of these before, Phoenix?" When she shook her head he smiled widely. "Such youthful innocence: how lovely. No, no need to blush. It's perfect, Phoenix. You have so much potential, and no ill-conceived notions or habits for me to correct. It's truly refreshing.

"This parchment is a source; something similar to the runes you saw me drawing around our campfire. A source is an instrument that channels Power into a specific purpose outlined by the image."

Phoenix widened her eyes in disbelief. "This picture can do tha'?"

Malcourt chuckled. "If you can see it. Not every source works for every Caller, and not every Caller interprets every source the same way. Sometimes it can take years of study to activate one. Especially if it's one that lies outside of the Caller's Talent.

"This one, however, is a basic one. It's used only for training. Sources like this are used in the Academy to determine whether a person has Power or not. Symbols are hidden in the image, and it's the job of the trainee to block out the extraneous information. Children with blood - and sometimes those with-out - are tested with beginner sources to see if they can activate it.

"This source is a little different. I already know you have Power, and I can certainly suspect your Talent; I chose this particular parchment because it should bring that Talent out." He tapped the sheet. "I want you to *feel* for your favourite spot and start from there," he told her.

Phoenix frowned at the image. The colors and lines were such a jumble that no one spot stood out in particular. There were bold slashes of crimson that tapered into orange to become thin strips of yellow; thick golden lines that were scripted so precisely that they looked almost like the symbols in her books; blue and purple waves that could pass for either oceans or clouds; and bright orange markings that somehow threaded through the entire piece to integrate with every color present.

"Here," she said, placing her finger across from a squiggle that might have passed for some sort of bird. "I dunno why, but this blue spot stands out."

Malcourt inspected the spot and gave a satisfied nod. "That's as good a place to start as any. Now, trace a path, using your eyes, from that spot so that you've explored the entire source."

Phoenix concentrated on the blue patch. Choosing her path, she slowly traced through the lines and colors painted on the scroll. Once finished, Phoenix looked up at Malcourt expectantly. "Was somethin' supposed t' happen?" she asked, seeing the expression on his face.

"Eventually, yes, something will happen - but rarely does it happen the first time. Sometimes it can take a week or more," Malcourt said.

"A week?" Phoenix couldn't imagine having to spend so

long looking at the same image over and over again.

"Sometimes," Malcourt acknowledged, "but not always. Shall we try again?"

When Phoenix nodded he smiled and pointed to the small patch of blue. "Start in the same spot, but instead of choosing where to look, let the source choose for you. Let it pull you in the direction it wants you to go."

Phoenix didn't understand what he meant, but she concentrated on the blue patch and started the process again.

The only sound in the study was their breathing. The weak light cast from the the hearth illuminated the details on the parchment, but she knew that that wouldn't last long. The sky outside of the tower was already darkening.

Phoenix pushed the distraction from her mind. She ignored the chill in the air around her; ignored the sound of Malcourt's breathing, and that he was waiting solely on her. She clenched the focus stones in her fist, feeling a limited sense of peace as she glowered at the blue patch in front of her. She was tempted to trace the same path as before, let her eyes wander over the parchment to explore the picture. Instead, she waited.

Everything stood still. Phoenix concentrated carefully on the patch of color and ignored everything else. Nothing else existed but the source.

She couldn't say how long she had been sitting there - how long Malcourt had watched her silently - when a soft tingling spread up her arms and across the hair along the back of her neck. Unbidden, her eyes followed a light curve of ink and slowly slid across the scroll until they rested on a fuzzy patch of yellow.

She gasped and jerked back, causing her attention to shift away the source. Malcourt looked at her expectantly with raised eyebrows, but remained silent. Phoenix set her jaw and tried again.

Starting again at the splash of blue she willed herself to relax. Almost instantly, she felt the same tingle and her eyes slid to the same yellow patch.

She was careful to keep her breathing deep and even. Phoenix waited again for the strange tingling feeling to guide her in the right direction.

Unbidden, her gaze skimmed downwards, then jerked abruptly to the left and paused on a red that reminded Phoenix of bush berries. An instant later, her eyes drifted across the page again.

Every time her eyes moved, Phoenix could *feel* the tingling energy spread a little further along her body. Any time she felt her attention waver, or her frustration rise, she carefully pushed the feeling aside and renewed a neutral concentration on the source before her.

Finally, once she felt her eyes had traced the whole parchment, with the hair along her arms and neck standing on end, she felt the built-up tension leave her body. Phoenix slumped where she sat, exhausted.

The source on the table glowed brightly, each color activating and disappearing before her eyes. The calm surface of the parchment rippled like a pond, and a bright orange droplet rose from the waves to hang in the air like a small sun. Slowly it grew until it became fist-sized, then the outer layers cracked and peeled away, disappearing like petals on a breeze.

Phoenix held her breath. Fire erupted from the center and crawled in different directions along the edge of the sphere. Like a torch being lit, the flames danced along the globe until they crashed together and merged into a single flickering light.

The flaming ball hung in the air between them, illuminating the room. Malcourt seemed impressed, Phoenix thought, his blue eyes assessing both her and the little fireball thoughtfully.

Beneath it, the source had returned to a normal piece of parchment. The ripples had disappeared, and the original colors had returned more vibrant than before.

Malcourt extended a finger and tapped the globe. He jerked his hand back and inspected his finger for burns.

"Can you touch it?"

Curiously, Phoenix lifted her hand. Mindful of the scars on her fingers, she reached towards the globe and was surprised when she felt no heat. The sphere moved slightly, just staying out of reach. She used both hands to move the fireball around without touching it. "It keeps movin', but it's not hot!"

He nodded. "Not to you, at least. Its energy is yours, so it can't hurt you. If the flames were to spread however..." Malcourt glanced down and hurriedly removed the source. "Can you extinguish it?"

Phoenix frowned. She looked around for a glass of water but saw nothing that could help. She tried to catch the flaming ball, but every time she grabbed for it it moved beyond her touch. Phoenix reached behind it and herded the sphere back towards her. When it was close enough, she blew on it as if extinguishing a candle. Instead of disappearing, the fire expanded and the newly-enlarged globe flew backwards into the hearth, rolling along the underside of the mantle until it fell into the extra pile of wood.

Phoenix jumped up with a yelp as a thin trail of smoke uncoiled from the stack of firewood.

Malcourt waved his hand. Phoenix felt a tingling sensation, and the smoke stopped abruptly. Malcourt motioned for her to sit and snapped his fingers. The fireball immediately rose into the air and floated back to where they sat.

"*Call* it to you," he instructed.

"How?" She eyed it warily as it floated before her.

"Hold out your hand. Envision it resting in your palm."

Phoenix did as Malcourt said. She pictured the ball of flame floating closer to sit in her offered hand. The globe moved closer, then stopped with a twitch. Phoenix glared at it and pointedly looked at her hand, willing it to move. She waited, but it did nothing.

"I can't make it move anymore," Phoenix said, feeling exasperated.

"Tell it to," Malcourt replied. "You will have to use words until you can learn to control it with just your thoughts."

Phoenix repeated the process, her glare fixed on the globe. "Come."

"Command it."

"Come!" Phoenix ordered. She felt a surge; another tingling sensation. The fireball whizzed towards her without hesitation. Her triumph faded once she realized that it wasn't slowing down in speed. Phoenix ducked and held her hands in front of her face. "Stop!" she cried in panic.

There was a pause. Phoenix lowered her hands to see that the fireball had stopped a finger's length from the tip of her nose. She stared in wonder at the tiny sun burning before her, the flames mesmerizing her the longer she watched. It reminded her of her sleep-terror, and the burning inferno that had surrounded her. Phoenix rubbed her scars with her thumb and drew back with a shudder.

"Very good, Phoenix. That's enough for one day," Malcourt said soothingly. Phoenix looked up to see his bright blue eyes watching her closely. He extended his hand. "You're not in any danger while in my tower, Phoenix. I will protect you. There is no need to worry." Unbidden, her eyes moved to the woodpile. Following her gaze he chuckled. "I have many protection wards in place should you lose control of your Power."

Phoenix pushed her apprehension aside and nodded. Seeing that Malcourt had kept his palm extended, she placed her hand in his.

His touch was gentle. He cupped her hand and turned it so that her palm was facing upward.

"*Call* to it again," he murmured, lifting his other hand to outline the air above her palm. "Stop it here."

Phoenix picked a spot in the air and calmed her breathing. She found it easier with Malcourt holding her hand steady, as if she could draw from his control. She pressed her fingers together self-consciously so that he would not touch her scars.

She gazed unblinkingly at the fireball. "Come."

Without hesitation, at a much more reasonable speed, it floated forwards and stopped in the spot she had chosen. It flickered above her hand, lighting up the creases in her palm without heating her skin.

"Very good," Malcourt praised her. "Do you have your focus stones?"

Phoenix picked them up with her free hand and nodded.

"Drop them into your other hand."

She lifted her hand so that it lined up with her palm above the fireball. At Malcourt's nod, she opened her fingers and let go of the focus stones. The multifaceted gems caught in the light, looking like colored stars as they plummeted through the fireball to land in Phoenix's waiting palm.

Sparks shot from the flames and arched like lightning bolts into the focus stones. Phoenix's instinct was to snatch her hand back, but Malcourt held it steady against the onslaught. Phoenix was shocked to discover that aside from a light tingling sensation, nothing touched her skin. She watched as the fireball shrank into thin air and disappeared without so much as a puff of smoke. The focus stones hummed softly, then became quiet in her hand.

Phoenix let out her breath, unaware that she had been holding it. "Did I do good?" she asked shyly.

Malcourt laughed softly and closed her hand around the focus stones, his blue eyes bright as he looked down at her. "Amazing, my dear. You did amazing! You truly have no idea. I can't even explain it. You wouldn't believe me if I tried!"

He jumped up with a sudden energy that surprised her. "We have much to do! You are much stronger than I'd even hoped. I have to devise tests! And lesson plans! Your stones need to be modified. The wards need to be updated. And I must create a... completely... fireproof room for you to practice in." He listed off the tasks with a boyish exuberance. "But first," he announced, whirling back towards her grandly, "I will escort you to the dining hall. Calling is hungry work, after all."

As if on cue, Phoenix's stomach growled so ferociously that she laid a hand on it to try and silence it. She blushed, and the log in the hearth was consumed so suddenly that the flames barely lasted long enough to give off any light.

Malcourt tipped his head back and laughed. "You, Apprentice Phoenix, are the most curious thing."

And because of his delight in her abilities, the way his face lit up with excitement, Phoenix felt her apprehension dissipate. She had wanted to leave her old life behind, wanted to figure out who she really was, and if the best way to do it was to embrace what frightened her about herself, then she was going to give it her all. She would face the consequences head on. For the first time that she could remember she made a promise to herself, that with Malcourt's help, she would find out exactly who she was.

PART II
CHAPTER 14

Phoenix slumped against the cool stone of the window-sill. She rested her head in her hand as she stared out over the courtyard, her attention snagged by the mud-splattered caravans that sought entry at the gates. The few beginning shoots of grass that had appeared after the snows melted had long since been churned back into the earth by the giant wooden wheels of the laden wagons that had arrived a week ago. The commotion of all of the extra bodies in the castle - the bleating animals and squabbling vendors - had hung heavy in the practice room despite the locked panes of glass. She rubbed her temple in an attempt to dissipate her building headache.

"You're not concentrating, Phoenix," Camden's voice chided her, breaking through her waking-dream.

"It's a foolish thing to concentrate on." She remained facing the window, watching Kit playing with the new dogs that had arrived.

Kit had grown a lot over the cold season. The dog was all leg, knotted with muscles that bulged thickly from the long bones, stretching her as tall as the older hunting dogs, rounding out her frame as a working dog - but her strange fur pattern and rounded ears had remained unchanged during the last few months of growth. She still drew strange looks and hissed whispers when she walked the halls, marking the dog as something to steer clear of. Phoenix was careful to avoid peak times when they walked through the halls, opting instead for the quiet sanctuary of the tower.

Camden took a few steps forward. "That's not for you to decide," he said primly, attempting once again to draw her attention back to the task at hand.

Phoenix straightened and turned towards him. His grey eyes were darkly serious as he frowned at her from across the room. He still held the practice rings that they had been using before taking their break. He looked more moody than usual, she thought, noting the boy's pale complexion. Hints of shadows had spread under his eyes, a dark match to the new lines of sleeplessness that had already engraved themselves in his young face.

"The banquet is only a few days away. We have to practice. We have to get it perfect."

Phoenix sighed and pushed herself back into a standing position. She had learned the hard way that everything always had to be perfect with Camden.

King Benedict had personally requested for the pair to take part in the festivities of his birthing celebrations, and even though she felt a fierce desire to do anything that His Majesty asked of her, Phoenix had begun to resent that Camden continually forgot how his command over his Power differed from hers.

She rolled her shoulders, wordlessly returning to her position. It was a silly juggling routine that Master Malcourt had devised, designed to mimic the acts of the court tricksters in order to entertain their audience. It started off light-hearted and comical, but slowly increased in intensity so that flaming objects were flying around the hall - courtesy of the powers of the

Apprentice Callers.

Phoenix knew it was a polite reminder to the Manor Lords of the power that the King commanded. She also knew to keep that observation to herself, and had only nodded when Master Malcourt had informed them of their involvement.

A ball whizzed past her head. Camden had started without warning, hoping to catch her off-guard. He often did things like that: purposefully goaded her to see how far she could be pushed. He knew that her Power was linked to her anger and he liked to see the results of that. It was an annoyance, but she always did her best to ignore his attempts just to annoy him in return. His fascination with her had changed to that of competition since she had been named as Malcourt's second Apprentice. She often wondered if he resented her because of it.

Camden lobbed another ball at her. Deftly, she caught the weighted projectile and threw it high in the air. It bounced off the ceiling and ricocheted at an awkward angle across the room. She could *feel* the swell of his Power as he *called* the sphere back towards him, simultaneously throwing another one at her. She caught this one as well, but held it with both hands before throwing it, her insides snarling in anger and exhaustion. "Stop it," she snapped.

The ball burst into flame as it sped towards Camden. Her breath caught as, like always, she felt the fear creep in that this would be the first one to burn him.

He caught it easily, showing far less apprehension than she anticipated while faced with trying to catch a flaming object, and she could *feel* the layer of air that protected his skin from the heat of the sphere. He released it, watching it float a moment in the air, letting the fire burn brightly before him, then he clapped his hands over the object with another surge of Power - extinguishing the flame before it touched his skin.

"Don't use two hands to cast the flame. Just one. Otherwise it'll look sloppy," he scowled at her as he held the cooling ball.

Phoenix felt a stab of annoyance. "I don't know how," she reminded him, exasperated.

"Do it anyway," he retorted. Without warning, he threw the second ball at her with a flick of his hand.

Instinctually she caught it, her anger flared up as her temper got the better of her. She cursed at him. The ball burst into flames in her hand, the flickering light that snaked around her fingers growing steadily.

A twitch from her focus ring cautioned her to calm herself. Phoenix felt a shield reach out from the stones, snagging her Power and dispersing the fire into nothing. But not before the ball was charred beyond use. She glared at Camden.

A slow smile spread along one side of his mouth. "Interesting," was all he said.

Phoenix bit her tongue and somehow managed to hold back her noise of disgust.

Camden held his hand out and directed all of the equipment across the room. Cases opened on their own, and the juggling balls and hoops hopped back into place, effectively putting themselves away for the Apprentices.

Phoenix looked down at the blackened ball she held, feeling a pang of remorse. With a sigh, she threw it in the garbage and walked to her desk.

She gathered her reading books and placed her ledgers on top of them, helping to clean up the study before they left. As Apprentices, they were only allowed to practice their Power in designated areas in the tower. Malcourt said it was because he had placed extra safeguards in case their workings got out of control, but Phoenix had a sneaking suspicion that it was also as a courtesy to the close-minded castle folk that lived within

Angor's walls.

The window is open to my rooms. You're welcome to wait for me there. Malcourt's voice was strong in her head though he was nowhere to be seen.

"Why would it matter if the window is open?" Phoenix asked Camden, hoisting her books into the crook of her arm with a grunt. Sometimes she surprised herself at how much she had read. A season ago she never would have thought it possible.

Camden locked the cases and gathered his own study material. "What do you mean?" He tilted his head. "What window?"

"In Master Malcourt's rooms." When he looked confused, she shrugged a shoulder. "He just told us to wait for him there." His expression darkened and she realized that their Master had only *called* to her. "You were busy. Sometimes I can't Hear when I'm busy casting." She added the last part to mollify him. In truth, she never had trouble Hearing either of them, but he seemed to accept this as reasonable and nodded.

"We'll go there to wait for him," Camden said.

Phoenix bit back a smart remark as he strode from the room. He always felt the need to take charge, which was especially irritating in situations where it wasn't warranted. However, bringing it up now would be more energy than it was worth. She decided to ignore it and followed him from the room.

Master Malcourt's rooms were located in the top level of the tower. Phoenix locked the practice room behind her and began the climb up the winding staircase, patting the trunk of the stone tree as she went.

The three Callers mainly kept to themselves. There was rarely a need to venture into Castle Angor other than to sleep - or the odd time that Tessa needed and extra set of hands in the kitchens. Phoenix tried to join her friends for meals whenever she was able to, and sometimes she could convince Camden to join now and then, but mostly her days were lessons and practice within the tower. It was lonely sometimes, she admitted privately to herself, but she also felt encouraged to see how much she had been able to learn during the cold season.

Phoenix slowed to a stop and motioned for Camden to do the same. She could hear a melody, beautiful and high-pitched, coming from Master Malcourt's room down the hall. It reminded her vaguely of singing birds as they flitted in between the branches of the trees in Avondale.

Camden stared at her in surprise as neither of them had ever heard music come from their Master's chambers.

Abruptly there was a loud crash, and the music halted. Phoenix gave Camden a confused look. Master Malcourt would have had to pass the practice room to get to his rooms before them. Phoenix narrowed her eyes distrustfully at the closed door. She knew he kept his rooms sealed. Only he - and those wearing focus rings - were able to open the door. How did someone get inside?

Camden put his finger to his lips and set his books down quietly. Phoenix did the same and moved a step closer to Camden. She waited, watching, while Camden cocked his head, as if he could somehow hear more from the occupant of the room. Finally, he shook his head and inclined his head towards the door.

"Master?" Phoenix knocked on the door. Silence was the only thing that greeted her. Camden motioned for her to stand back, moving in front of her to open the door. His body posture had slipped into a defensive position, and Phoenix felt relief at the sight, knowing that he was a trained fighter.

The room remained silent. Camden entered slowly with

Phoenix close on his heels. No lights in the room were lit. The balcony doors were wide open, the gusting wind continually blowing the curtains around their frame. A side table next to the window was tipped over on to the floor, and rolling around from the force of the wind. Phoenix inspected the room but found nothing else that seemed to be out of place.

Cautiously, Camden approached the balcony and drew the doors closed. He bent down and picked up the fallen iron table, inspecting it for any damage from when it tipped over. A movement in the shadows caught Phoenix's attention out of the corner of her eye.

"Camden!" she screamed.

The figure darted towards the door. Camden pivoted and threw open his hand. A gust of wind whipped past Phoenix and threw the intruder towards the corner of the room. He connected against the stone wall with an audible grunt.

Phoenix paused. She couldn't make out his form, but his shape seemed wrong, as if his cloak had somehow tangled on the smooth wall behind him. She and Camden stood their ground, positioning themselves between him and the door, neither one wanting to move towards the intruder without knowing what kind of weapons he possessed.

Phoenix waved her hand, *feeling* for the embers in the hearth across the room. Immediately they came back to life, flames flaring against the stone and illuminating the room. The candles around the room followed suit and lit themselves one by one until everything was bathed in light.

Phoenix gasped, her eyes going wide. Camden's jaw clenched as he glared at the intruder, his hand diving for his belt knife.

The face that glared back bared his fangs and let loose a terrible growl: his expression matching so many of the stone creatures that Phoenix constantly saw hanging from the parapets of Castle Angor.

The creature stood effortlessly before them, his body locked in unnatural stillness as he took in their positions. His expression was as serene as any of the statues that adorned the walls of Castle Angor. He watched them through narrowed eyes as though they were the ones intruding. His slate-grey skin was a few shades lighter than the stone wall behind him, his hide-bound hair only a few shades lighter again, and Phoenix could see how easily he could blend into the background should the shadows favour his position.

His clothing was drab, made from thick layers of sewn animal hides, but the metal cuffs that he wore around his forearms were well-crafted and etched with an intricate design. Two curved blades were sheathed across his chest, their short edges curled inwards towards the handles that intersected across his abdomen. Phoenix felt a thrill of fear when she saw them, thankful that they had given the gargoyle space in the small room.

Gargoyle.

What Phoenix had mistaken for a cloak was his half-extended wings that brushed the wall behind him. They were half-retracted as if to shield him from an attack. Double hooked claws were nestled at the apex of each wing.

The gargoyle snarled at the two and pressed his wings to his back, easily flipping into a crouch. His dark eyes settled on Phoenix. The irises were a stark contrast against the rest of his coloring, the diamond slits of his pupils growing larger as he assessed her, and she was shocked by the depth of them. His gaze was not wild like she had expected, but was intelligent and calculating as he measured her up like a cat watching a mouse. He tilted his head, the angle predatory, and he waited.

Something primal inside Phoenix roared at her to run. To

back out of the room. To scream. She probed the instinct and was surprised to discover that it wasn't fear, but necessity that stiffened her muscles in anticipation. Master Malcourt would be arriving soon. She had to warn him.

Instead of running, she took a step forward.

His nostrils flared in surprise, a quick movement that had neutralized so quickly that Phoenix wondered if she'd imagined it. She would have missed it if she'd blinked.

The gargoyle smirked. He sniffed delicately, his lips parting to reveal elongated canines. "You smell delightful," he purred.

Phoenix blinked in surprise. His voice was like quicksand for her senses. It clung to them, dragging her down so that she almost drowned from the shock of it, her attention fracturing as she struggled to make sense of the sound. The voice that came from such a foreign-looking creature was unbelievably... *human*.

She could see it for what it was - a ploy to unsettle her.

Without breaking eye contact, he tried to slink around them on all fours, his focus again on the door behind them. Camden darted forward, shooting another blast of air at the gargoyle to force him back. He took up position between Phoenix and the gargoyle, drawing his knife from his belt.

The gargoyle remained motionless. He remained crouched, locked in preternatural stillness in the silent room. Phoenix was almost positive that the wind had not touched him this instance. His hair ruffled as if caught in the breeze, but his body was unaffected by the force.

He grinned, an expression that looked surprisingly human on his face even with visible fangs, and rose fluidly to stand before them.

He was taller than the two of them, even without the wings, and his build was equal to that of Camden's. Physically he had the advantage.

With a flap, he folded his wings against his back, hooked the top joints around his arms, and hung them between the armoured spikes on his shoulders. The arrangement made it look like he was wearing a cloak, and Phoenix found the visual humorous for some reason.

The gargoyle placed claw-like hands on his hips and regarded the two. "Well, now," he purred. His voice was deep and surprisingly young-sounding. Amusement danced across his features.

The three stared each other down, unmoving, each assessing the other. The gargoyle crossed his arms, waiting. Camden stiffened an instant later. Phoenix whipped her head towards him in surprise, then it hit her.

A subtle cold crept across the room. It spread from her extremities, kissing her fingertips before caressing up along her arms to her torso. It was not intense - more so annoying - but she could see that Camden was rooted in place, an intense expression of fear upon his face. It took her a moment to realize that the cold was coming from the creature.

The gargoyle strode forward, his eyes focused on the door once more.

Bile rose in her throat. Phoenix had no concept of how to fight him, but she knew that she couldn't let him escape to attack Master Malcourt, or anyone else in Angor, for that matter. She stayed still until he walked past, then, forcefully, she launched herself at him and knocked him to the ground.

He gave a muffled grunt of surprise. Phoenix did her best to keep him pinned to the floor, but he was much stronger than her and she found herself struggling. He snarled at her like an animal, snapping his teeth a hand-span away from her face.

Gathering her strength, she thrust her fist at his face with her full force. He caught it easily, engulfing her hand in his large talons as he held her attack at bay. She attempted to free it with her other hand but he caught that one as well. His tail snaked around her leg and pulled her to one side, easily rolling her over as their hands remained locked around each other's wrists. Phoenix grunted and brought her knees up, attempting to use their strength against him as she tried to twist her arms out of his grip.

He opened his wings to steady himself. A wingtip clipped the side of her face as he maneuvered himself back into a position of power.

The sudden pain of the blow made Phoenix angry. Her Power leapt into her hands, dancing against her fingers that she had locked around his forearms. He yelped with surprise. Wrenching his arms he broke himself free from her grip, throwing her away from him. Phoenix could see two red handprints burned into his arms.

He jumped back into a crouch, tail lashing while he perched on all fours. Phoenix rolled over and jumped into a standing position, balancing on the balls of her feet while she glared at him. Adrenaline pounded through her body. She balled her hands into fists, feeling the muted warmth of the growing flames tickling her palms. She hesitated only a moment, waiting for the heat to grow between her fingers, then when she was ready, she launched herself at him with a furious cry.

One foot left the ground, the other propelling her body forward, but she never reached her mark. Two arms wrapped around her waist and held her fast, pulling her back in the opposite direction. Fiercely, she twisted against the person holding her and attempted to break free.

"That's enough of that," Malcourt's voice told her firmly.

Phoenix stilled and turned to see her Master holding her in

place. Releasing her, he placed a hand on her shoulder, both to calm her and to ensure that she didn't try to attack the gargoyle again. The gargoyle, for his part, rose fluidly and snapped his wings against his back. His face was infuriatingly calm. His expression was unruffled and showed no sign that a fight had just taken place. He looked at Malcourt expectantly, but Phoenix could see that his posture was still on the defensive.

Camden, freed from the creature's Fear, shook himself and rubbed his arms as he stood next to Phoenix. She could feel the cold rolling off of him as he glared openly at the gargoyle.

"Now, then," Master Malcourt said, attempting to take control of the situation. "Would someone be so kind as to tell me what's going on?"

Phoenix remained motionless, arrested by the tone of her Master's voice. She let the flames extinguish in her hands and lowered her arms to her side, but she continued to watch the gargoyle carefully.

Camden pointed forcefully at the intruder, losing his composure. "This *creature*," he spat into the tense silence, "broke into your rooms, Master! Phoenix Heard you tell us to meet you, but it was here when we arrived so we tried to get rid of it." His tone made it seem as though they were trying to remove a bug before their Master arrived. Phoenix glanced at him quickly, and the open hatred on Camden's face was enough to give her pause. "It attacked Phoenix and it may have done the same to you - or worse - if we hadn't arrived first!"

Malcourt frowned disapprovingly at the two Apprentices. "You know that you are forbidden to enter them without my permission."

Camden flushed slightly. "We would not have, Master, but we heard the lizard inside and worried for your safety."

The gargoyle shifted, standing to his full height. "Who are

you calling a lizard, boy?" he snarled softly.

Phoenix was surprised by how melodic his deep voice was. She would have thought him human if she hadn't known the difference.

Camden, as if answering a challenge, clenched his fists and took a step towards the gargoyle, raising his palm towards him. The hair along Phoenix's arms began to prickle. The air in the room, and even the powerful winds outside Angor's walls, became still and quiet.

Phoenix could *feel* the intensity of the Power that Camden was building under his control.

Master Malcourt stepped forward and gripped Camden's shoulder, and Camden's Power immediately dissipated. The tension in the air relaxed, and Phoenix found that she was able to breathe much more easily.

Outside the wind once again began its angry howl.

"Enough, Camden," Malcourt said soothingly. "There will be no more fighting here. I was asking Rorin to wait for me here. And he," Master Malcourt stressed the word in mild rebuke, "is here by request as my guest."

Camden wrenched his arm so forcefully from the Master's grip that Malcourt stumbled slightly.

"Guest?" he demanded angrily. "Friend!" Camden's gaze narrowed on the gargoyle for a long moment, then he pressed his lips together, his jaw clenched. Shooting Malcourt a look of betrayal, he turned on his heel and marched from the room, slamming the door behind him without so much as a backward glance.

The silence in the room was uneasy in the wake of his departure.

Rorin raised an eyeridge at Camden's exit, then crossed his arms and looked at Phoenix expectedly. Phoenix glared distrustfully and shifted her weight, standing her ground as she prepared to stare the gargoyle down.

"Are your hatchlings always so emotional?" he asked Master Malcourt.

Master Malcourt sighed softly and ran his fingers through his hair. "Forgive him," Malcourt said to the room. "He is still young, and his pain runs deep."

The gargoyle inclined his head slightly, and Master Malcourt turned to Phoenix with a rueful look. "We really need to find a way to keep you from eavesdropping, Phoenix."

He said it mildly, but his annoyance was clear. "Yes, Master," she agreed, hanging her head. None of this would have happened had she not Heard him earlier.

Malcourt patted her arm with a smile. "Not your fault," he told her, his voice soft, "I should have figured it out by now."

"Maybe you humans should try whispering," the gargoyle suggested blandly.

Phoenix stared at the gargoyle, while Master Malcourt pinched the bridge of his nose with a sigh. "Rorin, may I introduce Apprentice Phoenix. Phoenix; Rorin. Rorin is a Searcher, and an added safety precaution for the upcoming celebrations." He fixed Phoenix with a serious look. "He and his flight will be in attendance at the festivities, so you two have to play nice."

Phoenix looked at Rorin with suspicion. She could tell that he was still put out by their tussle. He was inspecting the wounds on his arms critically, and he frowned at the Master-caller. "That depends," he said.

Master Malcourt frowned at Rorin. "On?"

"On however long Apprentice Callers have been training to break the Fear. Is this something that you've been teaching her, Malcourt?" His tone was even, but Phoenix thought that she could detect a subtle hint of tension in the question.

Master Malcourt blinked in surprise, looking first at Phoenix before back at Rorin in confusion. It took Phoenix a moment to identify the expression. She had never seen Master Malcourt confused before.

"No," the Mastercaller admitted with ease. "I wasn't aware they could do that."

"Not them," Rorin corrected. "Just her." His eyes almost glowed as he shifted to concentrate solely on Phoenix.

His expression was unreadable, but if he was trying to intimidate her she was unimpressed.

"Ah," Master Malcourt said, looking curiously at Phoenix. "There are no secrets here, Rorin. Phoenix is... well, she's special. Her Power reacts differently from anyone I have ever encountered. It's been a delightful learning curve for the two of us, to be sure, but sometimes surprises crop up every now and then. She is a Firecaller. Perhaps that has something to do with it?" Master Malcourt's eyes lingered a moment on Rorin's burns before they slid to her.

Phoenix did her best not to blush under her Master's scrutiny.

"Besides," the Mastercaller continued. "When would we have ever tested any '"training'?"

"Perhaps," Rorin conceded. He seemed to find Malcourt's explanation satisfactory and shrugged off his concern. "How exactly will this girl-child help?"

Phoenix bristled at his words and she glared at Rorin. As far as she could tell they were the same age. Who was he calling a child?

Master Malcourt laid a calming hand on Phoenix's shoulder. "Phoenix has an incredible Talent for Hearing - as is evident by the unfortunate confrontation you experienced earlier. We need eyes and ears everywhere, and she is one of the few who carries my absolute trust."

Phoenix blushed at the praise and smiled at her Master. Malcourt smiled down at her in return and squeezed her shoulder.

Rorin regarded her with interest before his eyes flicked to the closed door. "And your other hatchling?"

Phoenix, tired of his condescension, opened her mouth to say something sharp.

Malcourt spoke before she had the chance. "I had intended to tell him at a better time - both of them, actually - so I am not sure if Apprentice Camden will help. His history with gargoyles is volatile at best. He might come around... eventually."

Malcourt frowned, lost in thought as his eyes roamed the room vacantly. Noticing the toppled furniture, he righted a chair and sat, gesturing for the other two to seat themselves. Phoenix accepted his offer, but Rorin continued to stand, leaning against the wall in a relaxed manner.

Malcourt rested his ankle on his knee. "Phoenix, what do you know about the Gargoyle War?"

Phoenix's glance flicked to Rorin, who stood only a few foot-lengths from her Master. "Just that it happened when I was a babe," she answered. She had grown up hearing about it, of course. Everyone had. But nothing in particular stuck out in her mind. "Only a few soldiers settled on the farm after the fighting stopped. Avondale wasn't affected much."

"No, I don't suppose it was," Master Malcourt said thoughtfully. "Do you know how it started?" When she shook her head, Malcourt inclined his head to Rorin, offering for him to tell the story. When Rorin shook his head, Malcourt continued.

"Not too long ago - in the beginning of your lifetime, I believe - humans and gargoyles used to co-exist. Gargoyles were nomadic, and traveled in tribes. They used to move around

Angoria, trading with humans from different parts of the land. It wasn't always peaceful, but we were allies; as best as any two different species could be.

"King Benedict and the Gargoyle Queen Moralla were good friends. She even stood for him when he married Queen Helena. They all grew close, and worked tirelessly to quell the disputes between gargoyles and humans. They hoped that eventually the two races could live together in harmony.

"Queen Helena gave birth to a daughter, Princess Penelope. King Benedict adored her as much as he adored her mother. Queen Moranta was smitten with the Princess, and King Benedict named Queen Moranta her Royal Protector... her guardian, if you will."

Phoenix looked at Rorin, who nodded his affirmation.

"And..." Phoenix prompted, when Master Malcourt became lost in thought.

He sighed. "It was Princess Penelope's succession ceremony. The one where she would sit on the throne for the first time to be formally acknowledged as Angoria's heir. Queen Moranta had been invited as an honoured guest, and she brought her hatchling daughter with her. It was the intent of the monarchs that the Princesses would be raised alongside one another. That way they would grow as equals and the realms would finally know true peace between them."

A snort from Rorin interrupted him. The gargoyle's expression had darkened. Anger narrowed his eyes, but Phoenix was able to detect an underlying sadness in his features. "It was the perfect opportunity, in hindsight," Rorin said, his voice surprisingly soft.

"In hindsight it was," agreed Master Malcourt.

"Opportunity?" Phoenix asked.

"To break the alliance," Rorin growled.

Something tickled the back of Phoenix's memory. Pausing, she thought back to when she'd first arrived at Castle Angor. She could remember what Sophie said when they were sitting down to meal. She had said that the King had lost his Queen...

Phoenix gasped. "They were murdered." It was a question more than a statement. When the two nodded in confirmation, she became horrified. "And the babes?"

Master Malcourt's expression was bleak. He shook his head.

"Queen Moranta never returned," Rorin said into the silence, his tone somewhat defensive. "Neither her nor the Princess."

"The blame shifted back and forth for months. Humans and gargoyles kept fighting until King Benedict enacted an uneasy truce, commanding the humans to stand down to allow the gargoyles to leave. We were forbidden to follow them.

"The King lost his family and his best friend. He was heartbroken," Master Malcourt said sadly. "As we all were."

Phoenix hesitated a moment, then rested a hand on his arm. "I'm sorry," she said, simply.

Master Malcourt smiled and gave her hand a squeeze.

Rorin cleared his throat impatiently, and adjusted his wings against his back.

Malcourt nodded and ran his fingers through his hair. "This was important for you to know the details, Phoenix, despite how long ago it happened. Do you recall when we first met, how I said that I was on a mission?" When she nodded, he continued. "The King was very ill. It took all of the best-trained Healers in Angoria to keep him alive, but he still continued to worsen. I consulted with Sylvia, and, deciding that something wasn't right, we set out on a journey.

"It was a hunch, really. A long shot at best, but we knew we had to try.

"There's a rare fruit that grows in the Crystal Forest, beyond the Northern Passage. When treated correctly, it can counteract even the deadliest of environmental reactions. It's what saved him."

"Environmental reactions?" Phoenix asked.

"Poisons," Rorin supplied.

Phoenix gaped at the gargoyle. "Poison?"

Rorin narrowed his eyes at her skeptically, as if he was wondering about her mental abilities. She shot him a dark glare in response.

"That's where you come in, Phoenix," Master Malcourt said, smoothing over the tension in the room. "King Benedict has recovered well, but only with Sylvia's expert ministrations - and because of your quick thinking which saved my life."

Phoenix felt a flare of satisfaction when Rorin shot her a look of surprised respect.

"Unfortunately, that is not the end of it," Master Malcourt continued. "The original assassin was never recovered. The one behind it all. We believe that he will strike again - publically - now that the King is healthy. Prince Hallan has remained here, still to the benefit of the King. He will not rest until he catches his sister's killer."

"And neither will we," Rorin said, the steel in his voice edged with anger. "We will avenge our Queen."

Master Malcourt nodded in acknowledgement. "All of our efforts have been renewed. The King's birthing celebrations creates a unique problem, however. People will be coming from all of Angoria to pay their respects. That means that unknown numbers of people will be coming and going as they please. It will be a large task to keep track of them all, as well as protect the King at the same time."

Rorin was watching her. The casual way in which he was leaning against the wall suggested an attitude of indifference, but his gaze was too intense to fool her. She was being tested.

"If the King dies," Phoenix said, thinking out loud, "then the war would start up again, wouldn't it? He's the reason the fighting stopped. The only reason the gargoyles were banished instead of killed?" When Master Malcourt nodded, she continued. "But who would take over Angoria? King Benedict has no heir..."

She blinked as realization clicked everything into place. It wasn't about the Gargoyle War at all. Maybe it never was. King Benedict was the last of his line. The secrecy, the misleading poison, and the quiet discovery of the cure all made sense. They were trying to flush out the assassin's entire operation. "Someone is trying to take over the kingdom."

Rorin shared a look with Malcourt, and his mouth twitched into the smallest of smiles. Phoenix wasn't sure, but she thought that she could make out a set of pointed fangs peeking from between his lips.

Master Malcourt gave a tight smile. "It's been hard to keep this quiet - harder still without knowing who I can trust. That's why I reached out to the gargoyles. They have nothing to gain from the King's death. In fact, it's in their best interest to help us keep him alive.

"You're one of the few I can trust, Phoenix. I trust you with my life. I trust you with the King's life. And I trust that you will put aside your differences and work with the gargoyles. We need you. Your King needs you. I need you. Help us to save his life before the kingdom is destroyed and Angoria is plunged into civil war."

CHAPTER 15

"What's the matter with you?" Sophie snapped. "You've been acting weird all day!"

It wasn't often that the four girls were able to sit together for meals anymore, so Sophie's irritability was visibly dampening their mood. The Masterclothier had her run ragged altering clothing for the guests of the King's birthing celebrations, and it was not hard to see that the girl was tired.

Tensions in the castle had been running high over the past few weeks. With all of the new arrivals it was hard to find space to move around - let alone somewhere to enjoy some peace and quiet. Many had begun dining in their rooms instead of coming to the hall for meals.

"Yeah, Phoenix," Rae said, biting into a crusty loaf. "What gives?"

Phoenix had been craning her neck to look around the room, trying to see if she could find someone who looked suspicious. Most of the new arrivals were chatting excitedly amongst themselves, but she took particular notice of Duke Ellington, a distant cousin to the King from his mother's side, who was sullenly seated by himself. However, she reasoned with herself, he was probably just travel-worn from his long journey.

"Just seeing who's around, is all," she said innocently.

"Anyone in particular who you were looking for?" Elise asked, her brow raising sardonically.

Phoenix shook her head hurriedly. She had been looking for King Benedict, in truth, but she knew that the King still rarely frequented the hall for meals anymore. He was still recovering from his illness, and he usually spent his time going between his chambers and his meeting room. She often met with him there, usually at his request - he always wanted to know how her studies were progressing - but she found that the mood of the hall was always more jovial when the King was in attendance.

"Did you finish your dorm work?" Elise asked her, interrupting Phoenix's train of thought. Phoenix groaned inwardly, but she must have made a face because Elise scowled. "I assigned that almost a week ago!"

"You're almost caught up!" Rae said encouragingly. "You're pretty much on Sophie's level!" She then ducked with a grin as the tan-skinned girl launched a seed pastry at her head.

"Hey!" a voice protested from somewhere behind her, and the four girls had to cover their mouths with their hands to keep their giggling from giving them away.

"I'll be glad once these celebrations are over," Sophie said, once they had all caught their breath.

"Are you kidding?" Rae asked incredulously. "I can't wait to celebrate! Music, games, fancy clothes, dancing... Not to mention all the food."

"Speaking of fancy clothes," Elise said excitedly, "what are you guys wearing?"

"I've been saving up, so you know it's going to be perfect," Rae said, nudging Sophie with her elbow. "I just know my seamster is gonna make my dress extra special!"

Sophie rolled her eyes in exasperation. "And I got my material forever ago. So that just leaves you, Elise, since we all know that Phoenix doesn't need to worry about her clothes," she said somewhat snidely.

They all knew what she meant. The King had been supplying her wardrobe all throughout the cold season, stating that whatever she may want or need he was only too happy to give.

Phoenix shrugged self-consciously. "I just figured I'd wear my new Apprentice tunic and trous set," she told them.

The girls stared at her. "You can't wear trous to a royal ball!" Rae exclaimed. "You're a girl!"

"Thanks for the update," Phoenix retorted. "I was wondering when you'd notice." Elise burst out laughing and poked Rae in the ribs, who made a face and swatted the girl's hand away. "Besides," Phoenix continued with a shrug, "I'm also an Apprentice." The Apprentice title meant enough to her to forgo the need to dress up in impractical clothing.

"So you're just gonna wear your Apprentice bands around?" Sophie demanded, pointing to the silver stripes on her tunic sleeves that identified her rank.

Alan arrived before Phoenix could answer. He puffed, slightly out of breath as he slowed his speed. His own sleeves now displayed the blue double-bands of a senior Runner.

"Prince Hallan requests your presence in his chambers," he said formally to Phoenix, his voice clipped from trying to keep the proper tone while talking to her. Everyone within hearing distance went quiet.

"What?" Phoenix asked in surprise. "Why?"

"How should I know?" Alan shrugged. "I'm just the Runner." He rolled his eyes and, as if to prove a point, turned around and ran back out of the room.

"Gettin' some new Blood, are ya, Phoenix?" A boy down the table jeered at her.

Phoenix felt her face turn red.

"You shut your mouth, Roger!" Rae shot back at him in outrage. She turned her attention back to Phoenix, who was sitting there dumbfounded, and promptly kicked her under the table. Phoenix jumped and rubbed her shin. "Well? Get going! Keeping him waiting isn't going to help you find out what he wants!"

Phoenix shot to her feet and stepped back over the seating bench, nearly tripping over it in her haste to untangle herself from the table.

"Sure there wasn't anyone in particular you were looking for?" Elise asked again with a clever smirk. Phoenix gave her a withering look before winding her way through the people and out of the hall.

The Prince had never summoned her before. He often sat in on the King's council meetings, she knew, as he was so dedicated to taking care of His Majesty that he made sure that he was available on a moment's notice - much to the chagrin of the court ladies who had been trying to distract him. He always seemed too preoccupied with his duties to notice them batting their lashes at him whenever he passed.

It made sense now that she knew he was still dedicated to catching the Queen's killer. Though she could not blame the ladies for trying. The Prince was strikingly handsome. It was a wonder that he was still unattached. He could have any woman that he wanted, and yet his devotion to King Benedict - and his mission, as Master Malcourt called it - had yet to waver.

Then again, she thought with a smile, the King had a way of looking out for the oddballs in his court. It was not hard to guess where his unwavering loyalty had come from.

Something brushed her thigh. Phoenix looked down to see Kit trotting along at her heels. She smiled and patted the pup's large head affectionately. Phoenix had long-since become accustomed to the pup's uncanny ability to find her within the castle; mostly arriving at times conveniently when Phoenix was alone and needed company. She would make a good hunting dog, Phoenix thought, had she ended up on a farm instead of with her.

"You're smarter than you're given credit for, you know," she told the pup. Kit flicked her rounded ears forward and gave her tail a wag.

The corridors were full of people milling about talking to one another. It was awkward walking the halls lately. The newcomers rarely noticed Phoenix, so she often had to maneuver herself around the unmoving bodies without giving offense. Those who had been there awhile had learned to recognize her by sight, and they often gave her a wide berth after learning of her Caller designation.

Aloof expressions were withdrawn as people caught sight of Kit, most conversations stopping mid-sentence. Noblewomen turned pale. They immediately stepped back and put as much room between themselves and the pair as was possible in the cramped space.

She was a sight, Phoenix had to admit. Her large rounded ears gave her the appearance of a wild animal - as did the large colored spots along her back - but Phoenix knew it was her giant size which was the most off-putting. She had gotten large rather quickly, but it was easy to see that she had more to grow before she was done.

Phoenix felt everyone's eyes on her as she walked past. She ignored them as best she could and led Kit through the hallway towards the royal quarters. She could hear muttered disbelief about her chosen path, but the speakers were quickly hushed so as not to let her hear them.

Phoenix sighed and tucked her curls behind her ears. Let them stare, she thought, straightening her back. Castle Angor was her home. They couldn't hurt her here.

Phoenix ran up the side staircase quickly, using her long legs to advance two steps at a time. Reaching the proper level, she turned and entered the giant wing that was set aside for royalty.

King Benedict's chambers were down a corridor to her right, while living quarters and entertaining rooms connected to the large foyer were set aside for visiting guests. They took up several floors in total, and standing in the open room made her feel exceptionally small.

Phoenix hurried through the foyer and jogged up a small set of stairs that led to the connectors for the adjoining areas. Abruptly she was stopped by two men in strange uniforms who were guarding the double doors.

"State your business with the Prince," commanded the first guard with a snarl.

Phoenix was caught up short by his rudeness and blinked at him in surprise. "Apprentice Phoenix to see His Highness?" She all but asked, giving a courteous bow as she spoke. She was still incapable of the graceful curtsy that came so easily to other girls.

The door opened a crack, and Prince Hallan stuck his head out to peer into the hallway.

"Ah, Phoenix. There you are." The Prince fixed the guard with a serious look. "Apprentice Phoenix is always welcome to visit me, no matter what time of day. Understood?"

The guard drew himself up and clapped a fist over his heart. "Yes, Your Highness," her replied while the other guard saluted.

Nodding in satisfaction, the Prince opened the door wide

and waved at Phoenix to enter. She slipped past the guards with Kit at her heels, and the Prince shut the door firmly behind her.

"I must apologize," he said, making a face. "Kenneth and Jamie came with me from Kaltor. They can be quite... protective." He gave her a winning smile, and Phoenix was reminded why it was that all of the ladies of the court continually sighed over the Prince.

A flicker of annoyance marred his expression - so quickly that Phoenix thought that she had imagined it - and she looked back towards the door to where the guards stood. Instead, she saw that Prince Hallan was looking down at her side.

"Kit," Prince Hallan greeted the dog, bowing to her with a small show of respect.

"Oh!" Phoenix exclaimed, looking down at the dog who had followed her into the grand rooms. "I didn't realize..."

The Prince brushed aside her embarrassment with the wave of his hand. "Nonsense! I'm sure she'll behave..." He smiled again when she nodded. "Have you eaten? Shall I send for something?"

"N-no. Thank you." Phoenix was unsure what to do with herself so she could only smile. The reason that the Prince had summoned her was still not apparent, but she was sure that it wasn't to share a meal.

Prince Hallan nodded and offered her a chair, which she sat in gratefully. He then pulled another chair close and sat across from her. He ran his fingers through his dark hair, brushing it back from his face almost nervously. "Thank you for indulging me just now, Phoenix. I must admit that I'm in your debt."

"Your Highness?" she asked, confused.

He smiled at her. "I'm still curious, you see. About you, that is. You're a very rare mystery, Phoenix. I can see why it is that Malcourt - Master Malcourt, I mean - brought you here. He must find you fascinating. I know that I do." He stopped to look at her and Phoenix felt as though he were studying her. It made her uncomfortable at first, but she could feel her cheeks become warm from his attention.

"Master Malcourt has been very kind to me," she told him, feeling defensive. She felt momentary resentment for the suggestion that she was nothing more than the puzzle of her past.

The Prince inclined his head in acknowledgement to her loyalty. "He's an incredibly compassionate man," he agreed easily. "And he has a good eye. In fact, everything he touches seems to turn to gold." His voice was unreadable when he said the last part, and Phoenix was unable to tell if he was being humorous or not.

"I just wanted to make sure," he continued, "that he was doing right by you. That you were not lacking or wanting for anything."

"Right by me?" Phoenix shifted in her chair.

Prince Hallan's eyes moved across her face as if searching for something, and Phoenix couldn't help but notice what a deep green they were. She held her breath while he looked at her.

"I want to find out where it is that you came from," he told her, his voice firm enough to bring her to her senses. Quietly she let out her breath. "You have the Blood," he continued. "Anyone sensitive enough to it can see that. I'm just wondering why he has yet to locate your family. Not that he'd want you to go, of course. But usually he is much more resourceful. You've already been here an entire season..."

He trailed off with a frown, letting that hang between them as he watched her.

Phoenix attempted to hide how hurt she felt by his suggestion. The idea that her Master had been purposely stalling his investigation had never occurred to her. But the Prince had a point. Why was it taking so long? For such an unorthodox event - for two Callers to disappear - it was hard to believe that their absences would not have been noticed. And the Mastercaller had so many connections throughout the kingdom... Perhaps he'd already exhausted them. Perhaps he was not searching abroad for the answers.

But she hadn't asked. She'd been so content here, studying her Power and spending time with her friends, carving out a home for herself, that she'd hadn't thought to ask for an update. He deserved for her to do that before jumping to conclusions. He had been so kind to her. Surely he would have told her if he'd found something.

Phoenix drew herself up in her seat. "It doesn't matter where I'm from," she said with quiet dignity. "Master Malcourt was one of the only people in my life to ever show me such kindness. Even if I were to find out where I'm from I wouldn't want to leave. My friends are here, and my studies are far from finished. Just because you're from somewhere it doesn't mean that you belong there. This is where I belong."

Prince Hallan watched her quietly as she gave her impromptu speech, her words ringing with the truth that she felt. He was relaxed, and his expression was disarmingly friendly, but his eyes watched her with an intensity that she had never experienced before. She didn't know what it meant, but she was conscious of a warm feeling that was growing along her spine.

Prince Hallan smiled. "You're very smart, Phoenix. You've blossomed so much during your short stay with us here. I'm excited to see how much more you progress with your studies." Phoenix felt her cheeks heat into a blush. "Malcourt must place an incredible amount of trust in you," he continued. "You must find it overwhelming at times."

His compassion seemed so genuine that Phoenix felt her eyes fill with tears. "Sometimes," she admitted quietly, surprising herself by doing so.

He nodded, unsurprised by her admission. "It can be hard: coming to a new place; taking on too much to feel like you belong. That's why I asked you here, Phoenix. I felt as though you could use a sympathetic ear - someone to talk to if you need any help. After all, I went through the same thing when I came here not too long ago."

His smile was tender. She couldn't tell if it was meant for her, or because of a memory that had surfaced while he spoke, but his attention was fixed so thoroughly on her that Phoenix felt her head spin.

Prince Hallan moved to the edge of his chair, the movement fluid and unhurried. He leaned in close and placed his hand on her knee. Phoenix felt a soft warmth spreading through her body from the simple touch. She was acutely aware of the light pressure of his fingertips against her leg, and a strange feeling hitched in her stomach.

"What about now?" he asked, his face only a hand-span from her own. "With the King's birthing celebrations so soon, you must be feeling apprehensive about something."

Phoenix was conscious of how close he was. The warmth of his breath on her face. The pounding of blood in her ears. The smell of the Prince was intoxicating, and she found herself so caught up in his closeness that she was having trouble concentrating on anything else. She stared at him blankly for a moment before his question registered. Belatedly she opened her mouth to answer, but she found it difficult to form the words that he wanted.

He watched her mouth, his too-green eyes flicking their attention to her face when she didn't speak. Her breath caught, and she could only watch as he lifted his hand to touch her cheek, his palm curved to cup the side of her face.

A sharp pain cut through her confusion and her body went cold. With a yelp that startled them both, she jerked back and looked down to see that Kit had firmly entrenched her teeth into her thigh. Phoenix jumped up quickly, knocking her chair over backwards, and dislodged the dog's mouth from her skin.

"Ow!" she said loudly, using her hands to bat where the dog's head had been. Kit had already let go, and she had since positioned herself between Phoenix and Prince Hallan.

Kit's fur was stiff with fury, bristling in a way that Phoenix had never seen before. She growled a threat at the Prince, and Phoenix was shocked at her ferocity.

"Stop that," Phoenix told her angrily.

"Are you all right, my dear"? Prince Hallan asked, concerned. He had risen abruptly at her outcry, but had since composed himself enough to offer her a helping hand with picking up her chair. Kit pressed her ears back against her head and, with a savage snarl, lunged at the offending hand. The Prince jerked his hand back in time for the pup's teeth to clip together audibly in the air.

"Toads!" Phoenix swore. She grabbed Kit's scruff and jerked her back next to her heels. After she had the dog secured, Phoenix turned to Prince Hallan and tried to stammer out an apology. "Your Highness," she began, mortified. She didn't even know where to begin.

The chamber doors crashed open, and Kenneth and Jamie burst into the room. They brandished their swords and advanced towards Phoenix. She stood still and held on to the snarling Kit, who tried to lunge at the men.

The Prince held up his hand and the two men stopped in

their tracks.

"I'm fine," Prince Hallan said with a dismissive flick of his hand. His voice was almost angry as he spoke to the guards. "Phoenix's... friend... is more protective of her than I'd realized." He rolled his eyes at his own oversight, then winked at Phoenix with a smile.

The two guards did not move and continued to glare at the two.

"Anything else?" The Prince asked the pair, somewhat sharply.

The guards sheathed their swords and stiffened into a salute. "Yes, Your Highness," the other guard said. "Captain Rolf is here to see you. We can tell him to return later, if you are busy..."

"No!" Phoenix protested, feeling flustered and dragging Kit to the door. "We should go," she said, glaring down at the dog with embarrassment. She tugged forcefully on the dog to pull her out the door. "We've taken up enough of your time."

Prince Hallan sighed with regret. "Very well, Apprentice," his voice took on a formal tone. "But next time, perhaps, you could leave your champion behind?" His words were teasing, not mocking, and his expression held such longing as he watched her go that Phoenix could feel her flush deepen. She ducked into a sloppy bow and yanked the growling dog out into the corridor.

"What a surprise," a sardonic voice said behind her. "Apprentice Phoenix. Why is it always that wherever you go trouble seems to follow?"

Captain Rolf stood tall in the foyer glaring at her suspiciously, an expression of distrust settled on his face.

"Animals roaming the castle?" he asked scathingly, reminding her of the time he'd found her lost in the back corridors of the castle. His eyes ran over the silver bands on her sleeves and he smirked. "You don't get to ignore the rules because you're a Caller, girl. You might think that you're above the rest of us, but I know your Master knows better. I'm sure that he wouldn't like to hear that his reputation was marred by your constant disobedience. Neither would the King, I imagine."

Phoenix glared at him. Kit, who was finally behaving, stood obediently at her heel, so Phoenix let go of her and rested her hand on the dog's head protectively.

"Always bringing trouble," he continued, as if musing out loud. "And you came across your current Master at such an opportune time. It's all very convenient when you think about it. Tell me - why shouldn't I suspect that you were sent here to kill the King?"

Phoenix was so enraged by the suggestion that a jolt of heat ripped through her entire body. The palms of her hands burned with anger. She clenched her fists to try to extinguish the Power, but the heat spread along her knuckles to the tips of her fingers instead. It connected with the ring, causing the focus stones to flare to life and absorb the heat of the flame - cooling both her skin and her temper.

Calmly she opened her hands. Wisps of smoke curled from her palms and rose into the air. She counted herself lucky when the Captain didn't notice her lack of control. She continued to glare at him, but she kept her voice even as she spoke. "I could ask the same of you," she told him.

Those were not the words that she had meant to say, but they leapt out of her mouth before she had had a chance to stop them. She was surprised by her own insolence, and she dreaded knowing that Master Malcourt would hear of her being so disrespectful, but she kept her gaze steady as if she had meant to say it all along.

The Captain's expression changed drastically. His head snapped up and he glared at her scathingly. His face darkened and he leaned in slowly to whisper at her. "Watch yourself, girl, and know that I will be doing the same. Rest assured that as soon as I find a way to get rid of you you will be gone."

Before she had a chance to ask what he meant, he whipped the corner of his cloak over a shoulder and strode purposefully into the Prince's chambers. The guards shut the double doors behind him.

Kit snorted her displeasure and Phoenix turned her glare on to the dog. She snapped her fingers and marched down the hallway angrily, exiting the wing and returning to the main section of the castle. The bite on her leg stung, she was jittery from all of the embarrassment that she'd just experienced, and it was all she could do to keep her temper in check while she walked - stomped - back to the main section of the castle. She kept her breath steady in an attempt to calm herself. It certainly wouldn't do any good to burn Angor down before all of the celebrations.

Reaching a side door, Phoenix flung it open so forcefully that it crashed into the adjoining wall. She pointed out into the courtyard. "Go," she told Kit firmly.

Kit looked up at her with a soft whine and gave her tail a friendly wag.

"Go!" Phoenix yelled. Kit tucked her tail between her legs and took off across the castle grounds.

Phoenix pulled the door shut with a satisfying clang.

Tired and shaking from the day's excitement, Phoenix rubbed her arms and headed to the dorms.

Everyone was in the common room. Despite all of the extra activities at Angor, it was lessons as usual for the other girls.

"I'm so sick of all this ledger work!" Maggie wailed, rubbing her face with exasperation. "How am I ever supposed to meet the visiting noble boys when I have to do all of this work? Did you see Duke Ellington's son? He's so handsome!"

Jenny snorted. "If you ignore his nose."

Maggie's face flushed when some of the other girls laughed.

"Now, Jenny," Brianna said, surprisingly reproachful. "Maggie would do good to land him. After all, we can't all get a Prince, can we?" She smiled with self-satisfaction. "Besides, Maggie," she continued, "lessons are important. They're what separate us ladies from the lower classes." Brianna's eyes followed Phoenix meaningfully when she spoke.

Phoenix ignored her and crossed the room to sit with Elise and Sophie, both of which greeted her in a friendly fashion.

"What happened to your leg?" Sophie asked. Phoenix looked down to see that a small spot of blood had seeped through her clothing to show up on her trous.

Elise looked concerned. "Did that happen when you were with the Prince?"

Phoenix grimaced and perched on the arm of the couch. "Kit got a little too excited," she grumbled with embarrassment.

Both girls' mouths opened with surprise. Sophie looked aghast. "She didn't..."

"No!" Phoenix held out her hands to ward off Sophie's look. "She only bit me, thankfully. I didn't realize she was so protective." She said the last part mournfully, feeling embarrassed about the whole situation. Her stomach hitched when she recalled how close the Prince had been sitting before Kit had interrupted them. Phoenix felt her face getting hot.

"She's probably just excited about all the new people," Elise said kindly. "Our dogs used to go crazy whenever new smells came into the house. She probably felt that she was doing her duty."

"Duty or not," Sophie sniffed, "what were you thinking - bringing her to Prince Hallan's quarters like that?"

A shriek of fury stopped Phoenix before she could answer her. Brianna had jumped up and was glaring at them from across the room. Angry red blotches spread across her face, and Phoenix felt a small twinge of satisfaction at the unflattering complexion of the other girl.

Brianna took two swift steps towards them. "And what were you doing in the Prince's quarters?" she hissed at Phoenix. Her voice was low, but the fury in it carried easily throughout the room. Everyone became quiet, and only Jenny dared to watch the confrontation.

Phoenix pressed her lips together. She realized that the longer that she refrained from answering, the more antagonized the dark-haired girl became.

Brianna, who was used to others listening to her without question, was becoming more incensed by the moment. Phoenix found it difficult to feel sorry for the girl.

Sophie fidgeted with her needlework next to her, and Brianna's storming eyes snapped to her quickly. "And you," she spat at the nervous Sophie, "how dare you not come to me with this knowledge sooner."

Sophie's body went rigid, and she paled as Brianna continued to glare at her. An interesting accomplishment, Phoenix thought, seeing at how the girl's skin was tan to begin with.

"Leave her alone, Brianna," Phoenix told her. She was tired. Her body ached, and she was on edge from being attacked by both friend and foe. It had already been a long day, and she just wanted to get some sleep. Already she could feel the familiar dull ache forming between her shoulder blades. She didn't have the patience to deal with Brianna acting like a spoiled child.

"What?" Brianna hissed at her, outraged.

Now everyone in the room was watching. Phoenix didn't know if any of them had ever stood up to her before, but by the look of Jenny's smirking face, Phoenix could only guess that she was the first in a very long time.

"Leave her alone," Phoenix repeated, tired of the girl's sulky behaviour. "Maybe if you stopped yelling like a hysterical child you might be able to hear better. I know we all would."

Elise gasped. Brianna took another step forward, and Phoenix wondered if she was going to try to hit her. All eyes were on her, however, and she watched as Brianna struggled to bring herself under control.

Brianna drew herself up. Her eyes turned vicious as a mocking smile slid across her face. "What do you know, anyway?" Her voice was rough with repressed fury. "You walk around here like you're so special. Enjoy your little dream while it lasts. You have the standing of a slop bucket - you're nothing but glorified trash. You, and your pathetic friends, and every freak Caller in this place!"

"You take that back!" Phoenix cried, rising to a standing position. She was used to Brianna ragging on her, but her friends?

"Make me!" Brianna told her triumphantly, reveling in the fact that she had finally succeeded in angering her. "Everyone knows it's true! You three," and she gestured to them with contempt, "are only here to learn your manners. You're lower than those sad animals you dragged here. You have no future. The best you can do is to hope to serve someone like me." Brianna's beautiful eyes narrowed with hatred as she took another step forward. "And trust me - I will gladly make sure that you are on my service, personally."

Phoenix glared at the girl's wicked expression. Her temperature rose as a steady knot of anger grew inside her stomach.

She knew by now how it worked at Angor. Those girls not lucky enough to marry, or to keep their Apprenticeship, were kept on as wait staff for the noble ladies. The only alternative was for them to return to where they came from, which was something that Phoenix would not do. Unfortunately, with only their Lady to vouch for them, waiting girls became reliant upon their mistresses in order to survive.

Phoenix also knew that she wouldn't allow the latter to happen to either her or her friends. That was a vow she made silently to herself.

Phoenix took the half-step to close the distance between them. She was taller than Brianna, which forced the shorter girl to look up in order to keep their eyes locked. Brianna's face was flushed, and Phoenix realized that she had been unintentionally heating the air around her. Instead of making herself calm down enough to cool off, Phoenix continued to warm it.

Slowly, she brought her arm up. The Caller's stripes on her tunic were easily visible against the darker material of her sleeve. Brianna winced slightly but she did not move, and Phoenix had to admit that she was subtly impressed by the girl's ability to stand her ground.

"I will never serve the likes of you," Phoenix said to her evenly, "and that is a promise."

Brianna opened her mouth to respond in kind, but Phoenix, with a noise of disgust, spun on her heel and walked away from her without another word, The heels of her boots clicking on the stone floor.

"Don't you turn your back on me, Apprentice!" Brianna shrieked after her in outrage. "You come back here this instant!"

Phoenix continued walking down the hall away from the common room. Mistress Ruby exited her room as Phoenix walked past it.

"Miss Phoenix," she greeted her.

"Mistress," Phoenix responded respectfully.

"I feel as though I always miss the excitement whenever you are around, Miss Phoenix." Mistress Ruby raised both eyebrows slightly as she regarded her.

Phoenix gave her a slight bow. "I cannot help the excitability of those around me, Mistress."

Mistress Ruby looked at her silently for a moment, then, with the smallest of smiles, gestured for her to continue on her way. She turned then and made her way to the common room to calm her charges.

Phoenix continued uninterrupted up the stairs and to her room. Sighing softly, she walked to her bed and gratefully lay on top of the covers, using her pillow to cover her head and shut out the extraneous light around her.

The door opened as two sets of footsteps entered the room. She heard noises coming from both Elise and Sophie's desks, and the three girls occupied themselves quietly without a word to one another.

CHAPTER 16

Phoenix was still in her bed, lying face-down, when the sun rose the following day. She did her best to ignore it, tossing under the covers in an attempt to claim as much extra sleep as possible.

Her stomach's eventual protesting was what finally woke her. Her rest had restored her energy, but it had done nothing to make her feel refreshed. She had had her regular sleep-terror again - her scars once more were screaming in protest - only this time gargoyles had appeared in it to add to the confusion.

Phoenix sighed and rolled over, staring vacantly at the ceiling while consciousness chased the sleep from her eyes. She used her thumbs to try and rub the itch from the scars between her fingers.

It was delightfully quiet. Phoenix was grateful for the fact that the room's windows opened onto a private courtyard. It was one of the few places on Angor's grounds where large crowds of people or caravans would not gather.

Phoenix's stomach growled again, and she rose in order to satiate it. She winced slightly when the fabric of her trous pulled the dried blood from the cut on her thigh. With a sigh, Phoenix threw the clothing into her washing bag with the other dirty articles. She made a mental note to wash everything tomorrow so that her finest would be ready in time for the King's birthing celebrations.

Changing quickly, Phoenix hurried from the dorms and down to the kitchens.

The hearths were hot, and all the cooks were busily getting ready for mid-meal. Phoenix knew that Apprentices were not supposed to be in here picking at the food - especially before a meal started - but Tessa had told her that she was welcome to do so at any time. Her appetite had increased dramatically over the past season, but she had been told that it was normal for Callers to eat more since they used so much energy with their Power.

Phoenix ate quickly so that she could escape before she was noticed. All the kitchens were working overtime in order to feed all of the hungry mouths, and it wasn't uncommon that a station cook would berate her for being lazy in order to try and to get her to help out. Tessa always found a way to intercept before it became an issue, but Phoenix hated distracting her from her immediate tasks.

She was just finishing her bowl of broth when Camden strode into the room. He was dressed in his regular Apprentice stripes, but his eyes seemed particularly stormy this morning. He must've had a rough eve, Phoenix thought, judging by the expression on his face. Ignoring everyone around him, he took a plate and filled it quickly without so much as a word to anyone. Phoenix saw a few black looks pass among the cooks, but he received no reprimand for his actions.

Phoenix raised her arm to get his attention. Catching her eye, Camden stiffly made his way towards her and seated himself at her table.

"Where have you been all morning?" he asked her, putting a large piece of cheese in his mouth. He seemed overly disapproving, but Phoenix couldn't tell if it was because of the cheese or not.

"I slept in," she told him shortly. He opened his mouth to berate her, but Phoenix picked up one of his bread rolls and held it in front of his mouth in an attempt to block his speech. Sullenly, he pushed her hand away, so, with a shrug, she took a bite of the roll herself.

"You look exhausted," she told him, noting the darkening circles under his eyes. "Do you even sleep anymore?"

He glared at her but didn't answer. Instead, he took her mug and drank her tea as payback for eating his bread roll.

Phoenix hid her smile by finishing the roll. "When did you want to practice today?"

"After evening's meal," he told her, around a mouthful of hot broth. "We're supposed to be running drills all day, so I don't think we'll get any other time for it."

"Drills?" she frowned.

He blinked at her. "You didn't Hear Master Malcourt?" He raised an eyebrow and Phoenix frowned. She never missed a *calling* from their Master. "He's suspended all of our normal lessons for the next two days. He wants us to concentrate on learning combat drills because of the incident from yesterday morning." He trailed off with a hard look, then shot her a sly smile. "You probably would have Heard him had you not slept so late..."

Phoenix chose to ignore the last remark. She waited for Camden to finish his meal then brought their dishes to the sinks. She would have cleaned them, but one of the washers whisked them from her hands and shooed her out of the way.

She smiled her thanks and returned to Camden, and the two walked easily together towards the courtyard.

Camden led the way outside and into the pale sunlight.

The smell of horses was strong, and Phoenix found herself

wistfully thinking of visiting Muler and hiding away in the stables.

Several of the new youths had assembled in the courtyard to try their hand at the beginner drills. Phoenix knew that boys flocked to Angor every year to try out as squires and pages in the hopes of eventually becoming a soldier or ranking as a Knight. From the eager grins of those assembled, many of them planned on getting a head start before tryouts.

Captain Rolf made a point of glaring at her as she approached, but she made a point of ignoring him in return, taking up the position he begrudgingly indicated. Camden stayed up front, but she was placed in the back with the smaller inexperienced youths.

The boy standing next to her gave her a surprised stare. "Hey! You ain't supposed to be here!" he whispered at her. He had wide-eyes and a disarmingly youthful face.

She blinked at him. This was where the Captain had told her to go. "What do you mean?"

"'Cuz yer a girl," a voice drawled next to her. An older youth was standing next to them. His sandy-blond hair was dishevelled and his skin was the color of someone who spent a lot of time under the sun, but his clothing was better than most of those assembled. He had no obvious indicators of ranking and Phoenix found herself annoyed by his haughty expression.

"Then you won't have no trouble keepin' up!" she challenged, drawing herself up to match his height.

He smiled confidently and took his position next to her.

A hush fell over those assembled as Rolf stood in front of them. His raised voice projected easily as he began to call out the different movements. He first demonstrated each defensive position while naming it, then he crossed his thick arms as he led the group in runs between them.

At first the Guardscaptain called the positions slowly, pausing to allow everyone to take the stances, then he bellowed them with increasing speed. The more experienced boys in front kept up easily, their muscle memory taking over to keep their bodies flowing, but those in the back ranks were finding it difficult to keep coordinated with the movements.

Phoenix and the blond boy were easily matched. He'd obviously had practice before. He knew all of the positions, but the faster they came the more he faltered. She could tell that he was watching her and trying his hardest to beat her.

The younger boy on her other side tapped out and went to sit on the sidelines. A larger crowd of people had gathered, and many were leaning against the surrounding railing to watch. A few were calling out encouragement to the ones they knew who were still remaining.

Phoenix gave up listening to Rolf and concentrated on Camden's lean form. He moved easily from position to position, and she found that by watching him and ignoring what Rolf was saying, it was easier for her to keep up and make the appropriate movements.

She was still having trouble with the more difficult poses, her muscles were not strong enough to support them - which surprised her, as she had no idea that Camden's were - but she found that she could mimic them with relative ease. It got to the point that she could anticipate what Camden was doing just by his subtle beginning movements.

More and more youths tapped out. The youngest were the first to go, followed quickly by those who were already bored. Soon enough it was only her and a handful of others.

She was getting overheated, and her legs ached from all the crouching, but the blond boy still stood next to her so she refused to give up. Finally, when it was apparent that no more of them were going to retreat, Rolf called a halt to the exercise.

"And that," he boomed, loudly enough for everyone around them to hear, "is how Angor learns to protect its people!" He sounded proud, but seemed to Phoenix that he was scowling at both her and the boy left next to her. Looking around the yard, she realized that he was the last outsider remaining.

A loud cheering followed his words. The spectators around them burst into furious applause, many of them moving forward to congratulate those who had taken part.

The boy next to her grinned. Impetuously, he brushed back his sweaty hair and held out a palm in greeting. The movement left his face unobstructed, and Phoenix was caught short by the sight of two glinting amber eyes that glowed against his tan skin. "Alexandri," he told her.

"Phoenix," she replied, holding out her own palm in return.

"My Lady," he said, somewhat formally. She realized the humor in his tone, as she had just completed what noble-girls would have never attempted, and she couldn't help but grin in return. Nonetheless, he bowed to her courteously.

"Apprentice," she corrected, pointing to the stripes on her sleeves.

"My Lady Apprentice," he amended, still in a bowing position. His words danced with humor and Phoenix couldn't help but smile.

His amber eyes flashed and he turned her hand over. She thought he would press a kiss to her palm, but instead he sniffed delicately at her wrist. "And such an interesting scent." He grinned at her when her eyebrows shot upwards. "I assume that you live here at Angor?"

Phoenix wondered where he was from that the smell of the castle clung to her so strongly. She nodded. "I came here five moons ago."

He looked delighted. "And already an Apprentice? As well as a warrior?" The last part was said jokingly, and his grin for her was friendly. "You must tell me all about it," he murmured. His look was a mix of curiosity as well as admiration.

Phoenix was reminded of Prince Hallan and how terribly their meeting had gone. It was all she could do not to wince.

Camden jogged over to them, panting lightly from his exertions. "We have to go," he said to Phoenix, pointedly ignoring the fact that she was talking to Alexandri.

She was surprised at his rudeness. "Apprentice Camden," she said, by way of introduction to Alexandri, as if that could somehow make up for his bad manners.

Alexandri bowed stiffly. "Apprentice," he acknowledged, in a less than friendly tone.

"Trader," Camden responded in the same tone. He did not move to bow to the boy, but instead turned back to Phoenix. "We have to go. Now."

Phoenix frowned. As senior Apprentice, she knew that Camden outranked her - barely - so she had to defer to him in castle matters.

She looked to Alexandri, desperate to explain the situation so as not to cause insult, but he was just looking at her with amusement. He seemed to know how the ranking occurred in the castle.

Alexandri gave a stiff salute to Camden, emphasising it as if to mock him. He then spread his fingers in farewell to Phoenix. "Lady Apprentice," he said, with an impetuous wink. "Until next time." Giving her a crooked smile, he left the two and walked over to join his friends who waited on the railing. They whistled and clapped as he reached them.

Camden's expression was dark, his grey eyes stormy as he

watched Alexandri leave. "C'mon," he said, striding forward.

Phoenix lurched after him, her long legs catching up quickly. "What in the toads is wrong with you?" she hissed quietly, so as not to attract the attention of anyone.

"Me?" he shot back, just as quietly. "What's wrong with you?"

"What do you mean what's wrong with me? You were unbelievably rude to him!" She didn't bother keeping the anger from her voice. Camden's pushy attitude was getting to her, and she had had enough of everyone telling her how awful she was.

"So? You're not supposed to be talking to his type, anyway."

"His *type*?" Phoenix asked loudly, outraged. Heads turned towards them and Camden shot her a furious glare, but Phoenix realized that she no longer cared how moody he became. She pressed her lips together, refusing to apologize for her outburst.

They continued walking in silence. "He's a trader. They're not to be trusted," he said, finally, once they had gone back to being unnoticed. "They're nomads. They make their way around Angoria overselling their wares that they either stole, or got for next to nothing."

Phoenix snorted. "If they're thieves then why aren't they locked up?" she asked stubbornly.

Camden made a frustrated sound. "They aren't all thieves. Just most of them. They're not trustworthy people. They don't have morals like you or I."

"That's foolish. Who says?"

"Everyone says."

"Well everyone is stupid!" she snapped, her tone aiming the insult directly at Camden and letting him know who she thought everyone was.

He sighed with exasperation. "Phoenix, they don't look to any Manor or serve any Lord. They are a law unto themselves. They have no Blood, but they do not work for anyone who does. They pay no dues. It's not proper."

She stubbornly refused to back down. "Why do you even care? What does it matter?"

"Because they're commoners! Commoners can't just go wandering around doing whatever they please. They have to serve someone."

Phoenix went cold at hearing Brianna's nasty sentiments echoed in his words. She felt as if she had been kicked in the stomach. Camden was not supposed to be her enemy. He was supposed to be her friend. How could she be friends with someone who held her in such low regard?

Camden stopped and turned to see what was keeping her. It took an instant for his expression to turn from one of annoyance to one of regret. Too late he realized what he had said, and, arrested by the look on her face, his expression turned to distress.

"Phoenix... I didn't mean..." His voice was apologetic. "You know I didn't mean you," he said, softly. He took a step towards her and extended a hand.

She brushed it aside. "No need to worry about my feelings. I'm just a commoner," she said flatly.

"Yes, but-"

"And I have no Blood."

"But you're here now, and-"

"And we can't all have the good fortune of growing up in a house of splendour," she interrupted. She was angry now, and she felt the need to lash out and to hurt him as he did her.

"Phoenix, please," he pleaded with her. "You know I wasn't

talking about you."

"It's fine."

"It's not-"

"What you said was all true, *my Lord*. Every word. Don't you fret none about th' feelin's of us common folk," she drawled. "We ain't gonna bother you none."

Phoenix mimicked Alexandri's example. She bowed in a grandiose display of mock respect. "I'll take my leave of you, *my Lord*," she told him. "I wouldn't want to take up any more of your precious time. All of your noble friends are surely waiting."

Camden looked miserable but Phoenix refused to care. She turned smartly on her heel and marched away without a backward glance.

CHAPTER 17

Phoenix stood in Muler's stall, tracing the multi-directional whorls in the hair along his neck. She still felt the sting of her exchange with Camden hours later. Phoenix knew her temper had gotten the better of her, but she refused to feel badly about her outburst.

Still, she wished that it had never happened in the first place.

Phoenix had purposely lost him in the crowd, ducking into the stables without a second thought.

Muler had been excited to see her - Kit not so much, as she was still sulking from the scolding Phoenix had given her from the incident with Prince Hallan - and he showed this by continually reaching his head around to lip at her sleeves, snorting comically from the effort. She tried her best to calm the donkey, but eventually Phoenix admitted defeat with a laugh and let him tire himself out.

"We'll go for a run as soon as all this madness is cleared away," she promised Muler quietly, once he had settled down. Phoenix leaned against him and used her fingers to comb out his short mane. She relished the quiet reprieve, feeling as though she were finally able to catch her breath.

Everything was non-stop lately. She'd been shuffled from

one lesson to the other all season, only pausing to practice or to sleep. It had been a lot to take in.

"Life's gotten so confusing," she confided in a murmur. "Everything here is different. Even the people are different. They're so concerned with rank and standing... I feel as though I'll never get used to them. Not completely." Muler listened quietly. He watched her attentively as she spoke, flicking an ear back now and then to show he was listening.

"And I'm so angry all the time," she continued in a whisper, almost afraid to speak the words out loud. As if saying them would give them the power of truth. As if she could ignore the feeling otherwise.

She ran her fingers across his back, pushing against his hair and scratching gently at the skin underneath. "Ever since I started training with Master Malcourt, everything seems to be rubbing me the wrong way. Maybe that's part of the learning, I dunno... It makes me nervous sometimes. It's good - don't get me wrong - but it's also good that we left Avondale when we did."

Phoenix was quiet for a time. She shuddered to think what could have happened if she had stayed at the farm without a focus ring. If she had gone to live with Samuel without being able to control her Power...

She watched the light glint off of the silver band as she scratched Muler. The dark green stone had been separated expertly into slivers, the tiny shards arranged like leaves around the main stone, the deep purple gem cut to display mesmerizing multi-hued facets that had been hidden within the stone. Phoenix had been touched by how beautifully her ring had been made, and she took great care to keep it clean as a show of gratitude.

Phoenix was acutely aware of the warmth coming from

Muler. She only realized how tense her body was when the muscles in her back finally began to relax, the scars between her shoulder blades protesting when she rolled her shoulders. She rubbed the back of her neck and was surprised when tears sprang to her eyes.

She stood there for a time, half-standing and half-leaning against the donkey. She was tired, as always, and hungry again, but the idea of leaving her little sanctuary seemed too much to bear. Like the eye of a storm, it was a sharp contrast against the activity churning around her.

A quick movement caught the corner of her eye. Phoenix turned her head to see a small lizard scurry out of sight up a nearby wall, chased into the shadows by the sound of approaching footsteps.

Stablemaster Sean's ruddy complex came into view as he poked his head into the pen. He gave a huff as he took stock of the enclosure, the sound of displeasure not a reflection of Phoenix's presence, though he gave her a scowl before checking on the rest of the pens. He was accustomed to seeing her come and go, and while he looked as though he would prefer not having to deal with her, he never bothered saying anything to her one way or the other. She took it as an unspoken truce between them - likely brought about by Master Malcourt or the King intervening on her behalf. After all, it had been her one request of King Benedict when she had first met it.

"Did'ja find it?" the soft voice of the stablehand easily cut through the sleepy silence of the stables.

"No," Sean grumbled at the girl, sounding peevish. "Go check the slop pile. Someone must've left the bucket there."

"But I already checked- " The protest died away as they moved back down the hall, away from Phoenix and the pens.

"Then check again," Sean's roar was enough to set the horses nickering in protest. "Slop buckets don't jus' disappear!"

The sound of hurried footsteps were quickly swallowed up in a blanket of silence.

Sighing softly, Phoenix gave Muler a final pat and a nose rub before pushing herself into an upright position. Kit had finally crept closer, so she ruffled the dog's fur with a kind word and left the stables.

Conscientious of how dirty she was in the waning sunlight, Phoenix took up a light jog to get back to the dorms quickly, taking the stairs two at a time until she reached her room. She pushed the door open with a bang, grateful that the room was empty.

She frowned at the Apprentice outfit she had set aside. It was finer than what she currently wore. Around the castle it was customary to have the bands stitched into regular tunics to show rank, but the Apprentices were able to wear their regular clothing with it. The outfit was different in that the bands were worked into the fabric of the top as well as the bottoms, creating a uniformed look that was reserved for more formal functions.

Phoenix rubbed at a speck of dirt with her thumbnail. She wouldn't be able to visit the washing room and the bathing room before she had to report to the kitchens. With a sigh of deliberation, Phoenix grabbed the outfit and ran down the hall.

She wasn't supposed to wash clothes in the bathing room, but... she wouldn't get caught with everyone out. And it was for a special event...

Phoenix shed her clothing without hesitation.

She clutched her Apprentice outfit against her body and pinched her nose, sliding into the recessed bathing pool that was somehow always warmed. She swiftly washed the sweat and dirt from her body, scrubbing away any remnants of her drills in the courtyard, as if she could scrub away her spat with

Camden by doing so. When she surfaced, she scrubbed at the dirt under her nails, undoubtedly accumulated from rolling around on the floor with Rorin yesterday morning. "Whatever would the nobles think?" she murmured to herself with amusement.

She used special care when using the tallow bar to scrub her Apprentice clothes. The bar flaked easily, the pieces soft as they fizzed against the wet material. She refused to embarrass the King or Master Malcourt by having a sloppy appearance, so she kept scrubbing until the bar had disappeared into a small nub and she was satisfied that every small stain or smudge had been removed from the material. When the clothing passed her inspection, she threw on her kitchen clothes and hurried to the drying room.

The windows were shuttered tightly in an attempt to keep the chill of outdoors from creeping into the barren stone room. The breeze would not make her clothes dry faster - it might slow it down, if anything - but it would make sure that her clothes smelled fresh, and Phoenix was tired of the stuffy smell that the cold season had brought to Angor.

She flung the shutters open and pinned her shirt and trous to a rack by the windows. Happy with their position - close enough to catch the air and sunshine, but not close enough to fall out the window - she reported to the kitchens.

Tessa stood silently in the centre of the main room. The Kitchenmaster's usually composed face was frowning in concentration as she crimped several dozen pie crusts. She twirled the dishes to expertly indent the edges with a press of her thumb, sliding each completed crust to the left for cooking before taking another from the right.

Silently, Phoenix tied back her wet curls and donned an apron.

A large fire broke out in one of the roasting pits. Grabbing a bucket of water from the washing station, Phoenix ran towards the flames and doused them quickly, mouthing a quiet word of Power to bring the rest of their heat under control. She felt a small thrill of surprise when the silent command worked, and the flames that were untouched by the water sizzled back into glowing embers. Maybe she was finally learning to control her Power.

"Don't let the drip tray overflow," Tessa called matter-of-factly to the workers at the roasting station. "We don't need to build the King a new castle for his birthing day." Her words made light of the situation, but her tone was cradled in annoyance.

Tessa's eyes met Phoenix's and she shot the girl a grateful look. Her gratitude was short-lived as she jerked her head the next moment, motioning for Phoenix to attend the vegetable station behind her. Phoenix had no sooner taken position then she was set to work peeling a mountain of root vegetables and dumping them into pots of boiling water.

Phoenix continued on like this for over an hour, peeling and carrying the veg to the stoves to cook. She paused now and then to shake her hands and stretch some feeling back into her cramped fingers.

Tessa's voice rang out. "Fifteen minutes until service!" As if echoing her, the bell to signal the servers rang a moment later.

"Places, people!" Tessa called.

Everyone scrambled in a race against time. Workers rushed to finish their foods while scullers tripped over one another to load their platters with the fresh items.

Too quickly the gong reverberated through the kitchens and service began. Scullers with heavily laden platters minced their way through the doors and into the dining hall, bringing out the pre-meal dishes of breads and soup. It had barely begun before Phoenix heard a shout behind her, followed by a large crash.

Everything stopped. The silence hung heavy. "What is it?" Tessa demanded. "What happened?" She wiped her hands on her apron and hurried to the source of the crash.

A sculler sat on the floor gingerly clutching his foot. Next to him, a shattered pitcher leaked red wine everywhere.

Tessa signaled the nearest worker. "Help him get to the infirm. Have one of the Healers see to his ankle." Everyone paused what they were doing to watch as the sculler was pulled to his good foot and limped from the kitchens.

"Someone get a rag and clean this up. We don't need another accident." Tessa scanned the crowd. "Now, then. Who can I..." Her eyes landed on Phoenix. "Perfect. Phoenix, I need you to take over and serve wine to the noble tables."

Phoenix blinked. She was no server. "But I can't -"

"You most certainly can. And you have to! You're the cleanest of the lot."

Phoenix frowned down at her clean tunic. She darted her gaze around in a desperate attempt to find someone in cleaner attire, but she had to admit that what Tessa said was true. Everyone but her had been cooking all day.

"Thank you," Tessa said when Phoenix gave a resigned sigh and flipped her waist apron around to the cleaner side. Tessa poured another decanter of wine and wiped it carefully before handing it to Phoenix. "Wipe after you pour, dear. It'll do no good to stain anyone's clothing."

Tessa turned her attention to the other workers. "Don't the rest of you have something to do?"

Immediately the kitchens resumed their normal level of activity.

Tessa turned back to Phoenix with a smile. "There's two refilling tables on either side of the hall for when you run out. Walk carefully, but quickly. It's important you don't keep anyone waiting."

Phoenix squared her shoulders and exited the kitchens to the short hallway that took her into the dining hall.

The doorboy nodded to her and helped her through the entranceway to the hall. Phoenix was immediately assaulted by the cloud of noise that had been blocked by the heavy wooden doors. The diners were talking loudly and laughing throughout the room. Most had taken their seats, but Phoenix could see a few of the late arrivals - mostly the younger ones - trying to slip towards their tables as inconspicuous as possible.

Phoenix had only taken a few steps when a noble gave her an impetuous wave. With a resigned sigh, she walked to him as quickly as possible.

"Now, my dear," the nobleman was saying to the young lady seated next to him, only a few years older than herself. "You said that you are unattached? However can that be for one so beautiful as you? ...What is it that you said your father does?" He smiled at her admiringly, his eyes shrewd. He tapped his glass in a command to Phoenix, then proceeded to take no notice of her as she filled it for him.

"Oh, no," the girl protested with a smile, tossing her head as he slid the wine glass towards her. "I positively couldn't!"

"Nonsense," he said dismissively, snapping his fingers for his own glass to be filled. "I insist! We will toast to the health and title of your father."

The girl blushed and clinked her glass against his.

Phoenix wiped the decanter and moved on.

The striking of the gong signaled the start of the main meal, and Phoenix struggled to fill the empty glasses presented to her before the scullers beat her to filling their plates.

When she came to the Head Table she was delighted to find that King Benedict presided at the center of the table. Prince Hallan sat to his left, and a beautiful blonde noblewoman, presumably of high stature, sat next to his left. She was doing her best to trap his attention, but he barely seemed to notice her as the brilliant green of his eyes followed Phoenix's every move.

The woman frowned and, feeling scorned, followed his gaze to see what she was competing with. With a sneer of annoyance, she gave a curt signal for Phoenix to fill their glasses.

Phoenix blushed and hurried to do so.

The noblewoman turned back to Prince Hallan. "So hard to find good help these days, is it not, Your Highness?" She leaned closer to him, all but purring as she spoke.

The Prince didn't appear to notice. "Apprentice Phoenix," he greeted her, his voice a deep murmur. "How delightful to see you again. Whatever are you doing serving tonight?" His eyes twinkled at her and she could feel her blush deepen.

"Helping out, Your Highness," she said, holding the edge of her apron out to bob in a graceless curtsy. She caught her balance in time before she spilled any wine. "I was helping Tessa in the kitchens. I was only supposed to cook. I'm not a server. But there was an accident. Everyone's fine, but..." she trailed off awkwardly, wondering why she was telling him about it.

"But you decided to go beyond your duty." A smile played across his lips. "Admirable."

The woman turned a venomous glare in Phoenix's direction. "Your Highness is the one who is admirable - taking the time to converse with such lesser folk."

Phoenix stiffened at her words.

"Not at all, Lady Marianne," the Prince rebuked her mildly. "Phoenix here is in a class of her own. She is lesser to no one."

He gave Phoenix a smile filled with such warmth that her breath caught in her throat. Her knees felt weak, and Phoenix had to tighten her grip on the wine pitcher in order to ensure that she did not drop it.

Lady Marianne appraised her, looking unimpressed. "Really?" she asked with obvious disbelief.

King Benedict noticed her before anyone could respond. "Phoenix! There you are, dear child," he greeted her.

"Your Majesty," she responded gratefully.

He beckoned for her to come closer, so she smiled at the Prince and his companion and walked to the King's other side, firmly putting him and the Prince between her and Lady Marianne.

She was happy to see him in such good health. He leaned heavily on the arms of his chair, and he was able to sit upright with the help of a large cushion, but his face was lively and full of energy. He had even put on weight.

"Joyous early birthing day, Your Majesty," she said, offering to pour him a glass of wine.

He laughed and waved the drink away with a grand flourish. "Thank you, my dear. But why are you serving?" He took her hand and squeezed it warmly. "You should be celebrating! All of this is possible because of you, you know."

"Apprentice Phoenix knows the value of a hard day's work, Your Majesty," a deep voice interjected. Master Malcourt had appeared from behind them and, with a deep bow to the King, seated himself in the chair at his right.

Phoenix was amused by his choice of clothing. The Master wore majestic robes - the wealth of which rivalled the clothing of the King - that were dyed a deep purple, as well as thick gold rings on both hands, each one polished to absolute perfection. His usually unruly hair had been slicked back so that nothing was out of place, and even his ever-present facial hair had been shaved away to smooth skin. Phoenix had never seen him so grand. If it weren't for the twinkling of his blue eyes, she might not have recognized him.

Master Malcourt inclined his head towards her. *The guests come in part for the show*, he told her soundlessly, his silent voice dry.

Phoenix bowed to him to hide her smile. "Master," she greeted him formally. She made sure that her expression was schooled properly before she came back up.

"Actually, Your Majesty," Malcourt continued. "I think it would be in all of our best interests if Phoenix were to serve us tonight. With your permission, of course. It seems to me that there would be a lot less fuss if she were to take care of our food personally."

His words were simple enough, but he gave her a meaning-ful look that confused her.

"Ah," the King said, with shrewd understanding. "Of course. Whatever you think is best, Tolen." He gave Phoenix's hand another squeeze and dismissed the sculler that was on his way to serve them.

The sculler, confused, shot Phoenix an angry glare that made her wince.

Malcourt took the wine pitcher from her and slipped her a small disc. "For your troubles," he said, loudly enough for any-one who was listening to overhear. *Use this to check the food. Find what I can't detect. If you see something, make sure no one touches it*, Malcourt told her, his attention still fixed on pouring himself a glass of wine.

Phoenix bowed deeply in silent acknowledgement before she hurried to the kitchens.

Tessa frowned when Phoenix returned to the kitchens.

"What's wrong? Marcus said you took his serving duties. Why aren't you serving wine?"

Phoenix shrugged a shoulder "I'm to serve the Head Table. By request of King Benedict, I mean." She looked at the Kitchenmaster sheepishly before admitting: "I didn't get a chance to serve wine to the Masters' Table..."

Tessa sighed. "Chloe," she singled out a sculler cleaning one of the prep tables. "If you please..."

The girl nodded quickly and rushed out into the hall.

Phoenix grabbed a platter and walked quickly to the ovens to select fresh bread rolls.

"The Head Table's food is over there," Tessa called after her, pointing to a table with platters of the best cuts of meat.

Phoenix eyed them carefully, taking a few steps forward. How did Master Malcourt want her to check them? She opened her hand and looked at the strange disc he'd passed her. She held it up to the light to inspect, but could find nothing of interest on the surface of the smooth glass. Phoenix let her hand get hot, probing it with her Power to see if anything happened. Nothing did.

"What are you doing with that looking glass?" a voice next to her elbow asked. Phoenix nearly jumped at the sound of Rae's voice.

"You know what this is?"

Rae gave her a long look. "Obviously. It's a looking lens. Elise uses them all the time to read small parchment print."

Phoenix frowned. "Parchment print?" That didn't help her. Unless... She held the lens up to her eye. Malcourt had to remain inconspicuous. He had to look like he was in the dark, at least in front of all the guests, so that he could draw out the assassin. He had already cast detection spells on the King, but if there was something that he didn't ward against...

Phoenix turned her attention to the food that was set aside for the Head Table. There, scattered across the platters, hidden drops of liquid shimmered a sickly red against the plated food.

She dropped the lens, and the glowing layer disappeared from sight, invisible to the naked eye.

Rae watched her lift the lens to her eye again, scanning the entire area before putting it away. "What is it?"

"It's getting cold is what it is," Tessa replied. She took a step forward, reaching for the platter closest to her.

Phoenix grabbed Tessa's outstretched arm without thinking, stopping her in her tracks. She could feel the tension of the grip, how Tessa snapped her attention to where Phoenix's fingers dug into her flesh, to the focus ring that was prominently displayed on her finger.

The woman stilled. Her breath came fast in the terrible silence that followed, but Tessa made no move to break away from Phoenix's grip.

"Phoenix," Rae began, remaining motionless. Phoenix hated the sound of her name on her friend's lips, as though Rae were taming a wild animal, or calming a temperamental child.

Phoenix slid her gaze calmly to Tessa's wide-eyed stare. "Don't. Touch. Anything," she breathed.

Tessa made no move other than to nod her head once.

Phoenix snatched her hand back with an apology. She hid her wince when Tessa lifted her free arm up to the light, as if inspecting it for damage, then seemed to think better of it and looked at Phoenix expectantly.

Did you find something? Master Malcourt's voice felt like a lifeline in the tension of the room.

"Yes," Phoenix answered out loud, unable to speak silently so that only her Master could hear her. Despite her affinity for Hearing, she was still unable to get past the roadblock of Calling without speaking.

Tessa shot her a look for her cryptic response. Rae shrieked and ducked as a large set of wings sailed past her head. Pip flapped several times to position herself on a chair back, chirping with annoyance at the errand Malcourt had sent her on.

Both women jerked when the owl settled her gaze on the platters that Phoenix pointed to. If the owl's sharp beak wasn't reason enough not to cross her, the way in which she continuously lifted her taloned feet to adjust her position would certainly deter anyone from getting too close.

Phoenix walked to the spit and grabbed a knife. She began to cut thick slices from an untouched haunch that had just finished cooking. "The Head Table doesn't want those ones," she told Tessa apologetically, hacking somewhat stylishly into the meat.

Tessa watched Phoenix thoughtfully. "Oh?"

When Phoenix nodded without any further explanation, Tessa wordlessly took the knife from Phoenix to slice the meat properly. Rae gave Pip a wide berth and hurried to dish up fresh vegetables to go with it.

"Rae," Tessa said to the girl, once they had assembled new dishes for the Head Table, "who was using that table?"

Rae's doe eyes looked thoughtfully at the table that Pip now guarded. "I can find out," she offered.

When Tessa nodded, Phoenix hoisted the new trays onto her forearms and tucked a finger beneath them. "They need to wash their hands," she cautioned the pair. "They can't touch anyone. Or anything." She didn't know what was used on the food, but she didn't want to risk anyone else getting sick.

Tessa paled and nodded as Phoenix and Rae pushed their way back into the Hall. They shared a look before disappearing in different directions, Rae to round up the workers and Phoenix to serve the Head Table.

She bypassed the Lords who were calling for food and more wine. She ignored the scullers who offered their assistance with what she was carrying - even if she sorely needed their help to carry such a heavy weight.

The hairs on the back of her neck prickled, distracting her. Turning, she could see Captain Rolf glaring at her from across the room. His thick arms were crossed in front of his chest, and he was watching her so closely that Phoenix resisted the urge to offer him one of the serving platters to carry.

Lady Marianne was grudgingly listening to an elderly Lord sitting at her right ramble on about fishing twine while Prince Hallan spoke with the King. By her sullen expression, Phoenix could only surmise that the Prince had continued to spurn her overt advances, and that she was less than pleased at being forced to hear about the large fish which escaped the Lord's net.

Master Malcourt nodded for her to serve everyone, but otherwise he was tied up speaking with an animated Lady that was talking with him eagerly. He listened courteously, but his eyes constantly scanned the room.

When she had finished, she and Malcourt shared a brief look that had her taking her position behind him. If he was unable to monitor everything then she would stay and help him.

She was sent back to the kitchens now and then to get more food and drink, refilling the untouched wine pitcher was her first task, but otherwise she found it relaxing to be able to watch the room without getting caught up in it.

Seated almost directly in front of her in the centre of the hall was Camden. Phoenix's eyes rested on him momentarily, assuming that he had been placed there strategically in order to watch the room, but his eyes were downcast and he was picking at the food on his plate. The man next to him, who Phoenix could identify as a Lord from his finery, snapped at Camden, and Camden straightened immediately in his chair. A boy, the Lord's son, by the look of it, glared at Camden from the other side of his father.

Camden was sitting with his uncle.

Phoenix's frown towards the two went unnoticed.

Camden looked across the room and their gazes locked. Even at this distance she could see the stormy grey of his eyes. Forgetting her earlier anger, Phoenix offered him a smile and splayed her fingers in greeting. His eyes lightened and his whole demeanor changed. He raised his hand quickly in response.

The juniors were the first to leave. They were herded back to their dorms by their Masters before the rest of the guests started to leave. Phoenix noticed Mistress Ruby in a doorway. She marched primly into the room and led a thin-lipped Brianna back to the tables to sit next to Jenny. A moment later, a scowling Alan came back into the hall from the same exit.

Phoenix hid a grin behind her hand knowing how upset they would be by such an injustice.

Jenny whispered something to Brianna and both girls turned to look directly at Phoenix. The expression on Brianna's face was nasty, but it brightened into a wicked smile as Jenny said something in her ear. Both girls burst out laughing, and Phoenix felt an uneasy feeling grow in her stomach.

The uneasiness was interrupted when Mistress Ruby clapped her hands and herded the girls back to the dorms.

It was at least a half-hour before others started to leave. The lower tables and the Masters' Table were the first to clear out, leaving many of the nobles and royals remaining to talk to one another. Phoenix shifted her stance every few moments to try to give her feet a rest. She tried her best not to do it too often, but she was tired and her legs were starting to hurt.

Master Malcourt noticed and came to her rescue. "Thank you for serving, Phoenix," he murmured. "Please take the platters back to the kitchens and tell Tessa that I will visit her later; then the rest of the evening is your own."

Phoenix bowed gratefully and gathered the dishes. As she was leaving, Prince Hallan reached out to rest a hand lightly on her arm. "Marvellous job tonight, Apprentice Phoenix. It's not often I come across a girl with such a wide array of talents such as yourself."

Lady Marianne sniffed audibly next to him.

"Thank you, Your Highness," Phoenix stammered. She could feel warmth through her sleeve where the Prince touched her.

"Let me know when you're free so you can come by again," he invited with a murmur. "I don't get to see you nearly as much as I'd like."

Malcourt frowned and looked between her and the Prince. Blushing, Phoenix bowed as the Prince released her arm, and she hurried back to the kitchens and away from the eyes that she felt burrowing into her back.

The quiet inside the kitchens was surprising and delightful. The remaining scullers were seated and talking quietly amongst themselves, the leftovers from the feast spread out across several tables, piled high next to clean plates and dishes: all of the leftovers except the ones by Pip, who was making sure the table remained untouched under her watchful eye.

Phoenix scraped the untouched portions onto the sharing platters and brought the dirty dishes to the washing station.

"Phew!" the washer said, using a soapy arm to wipe her brow. It was Rae, dressed in wet washers' clothes, scrubbing the dirty dishes with clean water.

Phoenix just blinked at her. "You're still here?" she asked, incredulously.

Rae made a face. "My old uniform got so dirty that Tessa suggested that I do something that would keep me clean." She grinned when Phoenix burst out laughing, grateful for the girl's ability to brighten her mood. "Anyway! That's enough of being clean for one night, if you ask me. I'm famished!"

Phoenix grinned and the two went to the sharing tables to grab their meal, allowing Phoenix the opportunity to flag down Tessa and relay her message from Malcourt.

"I should take some scraps for Kit," Phoenix said to Rae, when she was finally able to sit down. Groaning happily, she stretched out her legs and kicked off her boots. "That's better," she said with contentment.

"No kidding. Why didn't you come back?" Rae asked, following suit and kicking off her own footwear. She slipped off her wet apron and flapped her arms comically in an attempt to shake loose the excess water in her sleeves.

"Had to stay with the Head Table," Phoenix said, smearing a thick layer of spread on to a piece of bread.

"Ah. That's why Brianna was looking so murderous earlier," Rae said, her eyes dancing. "I heard about the other night..."

Phoenix groaned. "Do people do anything around here besides gossip?" she asked, somewhat testily.

Rae smirked. "You tell me," she retorted. Phoenix grimaced and took a large bite of her bread. "Besides," Rae continued while she was chewing, "it's not like she hasn't done anything to deserve a bit of discontentment now and then. She's certainly caused enough of it."

Phoenix had to admit that that was true.

The girls sat in silence for a moment, just eating and enjoying the rest after such a long day. She couldn't help but frown when she remembered Brianna and Jenny laughing at her earlier.

"Brianna being awful means that everything is normal. I'll start to worry if she becomes pleasant," Rae told her. "Don't mind her," she added, when Phoenix nodded. "She can't do anything too horrible. Being sent home would be the ultimate insult to her - and to her father. She would never do anything to jeopardize her position here. Y'just need to avoid her for awhile, is all."

"I've been trying," Phoenix said bitterly.

"She's just sore because Prince Hallan prefers you, is all," Rae said blandly, laughing when Phoenix blushed.

"He does not!" Phoenix protested. The Prince would never prefer her over all of the beautiful Ladies chasing him.

"He is rather handsome," Rae said, admiringly. "I know I sure wouldn't mind him as a suitor."

"You can have him," Phoenix retorted with mild outrage. "Then I wouldn't have to deal with Brianna. Or Captain Rolf," she added in a huff, remembering their conversation outside the Prince's quarters.

Rae frowned. "Rolf? What do you mean?"

Phoenix folded up a few slices of meat and shoved them into her mouth. "He's always watching me," she complained. "He shows up wherever I go. And he's always glaring at me." The relief of finally telling someone about it turned her tone sharp. "He's mean. He gives me the creeps. And he's been doing it ever since I met him. Even more since I saw him lurking around the back hallways-"

"You what?" Rae asked, wide-eyed. "When? Where?"

"A few months, when I first got here. I got lost when I left the library. You know, the night when I..." Phoenix trailed off, remembering the sleep-terror she had experienced in the common room.

"The back hallways!" Rae squeaked, looking aghast. "They're forbidden!"

Phoenix rubbed her face. "Well, I know that now. I obviously didn't then. It was an accident."

Rae looked serious for once. "No. I mean that they're forbidden to everyone," she clarified.

"Everyone?" Phoenix asked. "Then what was Rolf doing there?"

Rae stuffed a roll in her cheek and pursed her lips "That is the question, isn't it?"

CHAPTER 18

The back corridor was dark and deserted. The layer of dust on the unused stones seemed to swallow up all sound as the two crept carefully down the hallway.

"Are you sure this is a good idea?" Phoenix asked Rae in a whisper. It felt strange being surrounded by such emptiness while the rest of the castle was bursting with activity and life. "What if we run into trouble?"

"You tell me, Apprentice Caller," Rae whispered back, and Phoenix couldn't help but find her friend's faith in her abilities somewhat disconcerting. "Are you sure this is the right way?" Rae asked.

"Pretty sure," Phoenix answered without conviction. It had been a long time since her encounter with Rolf had happened, and she had since tried to put it out of her mind as best she could.

The candle that Rae held abruptly blew out.

"Toads," Rae swore as they were swallowed by the darkness. Phoenix took the candle wordlessly and pinched the flame back to life with her thumb and forefinger. "I've got to learn how to do that," Rae joked, her voice sounding weak in the dim light. Phoenix didn't have a chance to respond as the next instant Rae screamed and leapt backward.

Phoenix tensed and pivoted. A brief thought had her reaching for her Power, rousing it with ease until her fingertips grew warm. Phoenix felt a thrill at how she was able to *call* upon it and wished that it always happened that easily.

She stood still, eyes narrowed as they adjusted in the unreliable darkness. A familiar wing-shaped form stood in front of them, his dark outline a pale shadow next to the open window that had been the source of the breeze.

"Toads!" Phoenix repeated Rae's earlier oath, glaring at the creature.

"Gargoyle, actually," Rorin said coolly. Despite his condescension, Phoenix heard a note of humor in his voice.

The light that illuminated them shook violently, and Phoenix reached out to take the candle from Rae's hand. The girl's body shook with tremors as she stared openly at the gargoyle, her mouth agape with silence - for once.

Phoenix had to admit that the sight of him was unnerving in the half-light. He was at rest, to be sure - Phoenix could see the relaxed stance of his shoulders, and both his tail and wings were hanging loosely to graze the floor - but the glint off his wicked curved blades, the way that the light caught his eyes like that of an animal… it was enough to give Phoenix pause.

Rorin crossed his arms languidly and tilted his head at Rae. He raised a brow ridge with amusement. "Is she all right?"

Phoenix made a disgusted noise at him and laid her hand on Rae's arm. "It's okay, Rae. He's not going to hurt us. He's here to help."

"Help?" Rae squeaked, still trembling violently. "You sure do attract strange friends," she told Phoenix, weakly.

Phoenix was brought up short when she considered Rorin as a friend, but for Rae's sake she didn't dispute the claim. "Takes one to know one," she retorted instead.

Rorin opened his wings and Rae squealed in fright. Instead of moving, he crossed a wingtip over his chest and bowed to Rae. "I am called Rorin," he introduced himself. "And you have nothing to worry about. Any friend of the Lady Phoenix is a friend of mine."

"Apprentice," Phoenix muttered, correcting him sourly. If Lady Marianne was any indication of what Ladies were like, Phoenix felt insulted to be compared to one.

They both waited for Rae to say something, but the girl remained frozen so Phoenix introduced her instead.

"What are you doing here, anyway?" Phoenix asked Rorin.

"Watching you," he replied, casually adjusting his wings.

Rae squeaked again, but Phoenix frowned and narrowed her eyes. "Why?"

He gave her a crooked smile, the tip of a fang poking out the side of his mouth. "You were quite the center of attention when you were in the hall earlier. It piqued my interest." When Phoenix blinked at him in confusion, he raised his eye ridges in surprise. "You didn't notice?"

Phoenix shook her head. She shrugged, trying to dispel the unease that she felt. She had spent so much time watching out for King Benedict that she hadn't thought to watch out for herself.

"Could be just the prestige of being the new castle Caller and all, but you were certainly interesting to a large number of people." The gargoyle cloaked his wings around him, the large membranous skin folding easily, compressing into a space that seemed too small for their size. The hooked talons at their apex hitched into his shoulder guard, nestling easily between the metal spikes that adorned the armour. "I was watching from the rafters," he continued on, pushing away from the wall to stride down the corridor. The girls exchanged looks and, with a shrug, hurried to catch up with him.

"You must be incredibly long-sighted," Phoenix remarked, struggling to keep the candle flame lit with their brisk pace. Rae, unusually enough, remained silent.

"Most gargoyles are," he shrugged. "We tend to see beyond your limited human vision." His voice was somewhat smug, but Phoenix couldn't contest that statement considering his ease in navigating the blackness of the corridor ahead of them.

"No wonder you can sneak around unnoticed," she countered instead.

Rorin surprised her by smiling to himself. "Indeed."

"What's that?" Rae asked, breaking her silence and pointing ahead of them.

The painting that Phoenix found last time was coming into view. This time she noticed a metal plaque at the bottom of the frame as the light from the candle caught on the dusty surface.

"Queen Helena and Princess Penelope," Rae read next to her. "The Day Before the Name-Giving Ceremony."

"Name-giving?" Rorin asked.

"Yeah," Rae squared her shoulders and turned towards Rorin. "When royals are recognized formally as having the Blood. Don't you gargoyles have something similar?"

Rorin's face was impassive. "Something similar," he conceded, "though nothing so needlessly formal."

"Needless?" Rae scoffed.

Rorin leaned closer to inspect the painting, and Phoenix felt a small pang of jealousy at how well he was able to see it in the darkness. She thought about illuminating the area with her Power, but immediately decided against it as she didn't know if she could control the flame this far from the tower. She somehow doubted the King's good graces would extend to her burning down the forbidden areas of his castle... Or Master Malcourt's, for that matter.

Rorin cocked his head at the painting before sliding his attention back to Rae. "We are a matriarchal people. It's easier to track lineage that way."

"Matri-what?" Rae asked.

"They trace their Blood through the females," Phoenix told her, half-paying attention to their conversation, remembering the word from one of the books that Malcourt had given her to read. Phoenix was studying the painting with a renewed curiosity. Something about it seemed strangely familiar, but whatever it was continued to slip around in her mind, eluding her.

"Is what you're looking for near here?" Rorin asked, interrupting Phoenix's concentration.

Phoenix gave up on the painting and turned her attention back to the two. "Yes. There was a room - somewhere around here - that Rolf was sneaking out of."

"Captain Rolf? Guardscaptain Rolf?" Rorin asked. When the girls nodded he curled his lip. "That's unsurprising."

Rae stared at him. "What does that mean?" She narrowed her eyes suspiciously.

The gargoyle shrugged a shoulder. "He's always so sure of himself - so superior. He acts as though everything in your castle is his business to know."

"That's because everything is his business to know," Rae said, defending him staunchly. "Besides, what do you mean by 'always'? How often are you even here?"

The gargoyle gave her a slow smile, and Phoenix couldn't help but notice that the tips of his long canines were visible between his lips. "More often than you will ever know," he told her in a purr.

Rae shuddered and stepped closer to Phoenix.

"Anyway," Phoenix said awkwardly, breaking into the following silence before it could stretch any further, "we have to find the door-"

"That door?" Rorin interrupted, pointing into the shadows where Phoenix could see nothing. "Unless of course there's a second, hidden, doorway somewhere?"

Phoenix shot him a withering glare and stalked in the direction he indicated. As she stepped closer, the light from the flame of her candle caught the metal door handle and reflected off its dirty surface with a dull sheen.

Resolutely, she grabbed the handle and gave it a hard yank to open the heavy door. Nothing happened. She quickly tried again with more force. The door moved slightly, but it stopped with an abrupt clang that jarred her arm.

"It's locked," she told the two needlessly, wincing as she rubbed her arm.

Rorin stepped forward and grasped the handle. Phoenix was surprised to note that his hand only had three digits as opposed to five, but that thought was pushed aside as he pulled on the door with surprising force. He was much stronger than she remembered. The door made a grating noise, and there was a loud sound of metal scraping off of metal as he attempted to force the door open despite the lock.

After a moment of exertion he stopped.

"Shhh!" Rae hissed, looking over her shoulder. "Someone might hear you."

"So?" Rorin asked, nonchalantly.

"There's no one around, Rae," Phoenix reminded the girl comfortingly.

"Can you break the lock?" Rorin asked Phoenix, ignoring the other girl's fears.

"What do you think I am, a blacksmith's hammer?" Phoenix asked with exasperation.

"No," he said, as if she were simple, "but perhaps a forge. Can you not melt the lock?"

Phoenix was glad that it was dark so that her blush could go unnoticed. However, judging from the amused twitch of the gargoyle's expression, she was unsure as to whether he could make out skin color in the dark or not.

She stepped forward and took a deep breath. Phoenix knew that she was not supposed to use her Power outside of the tower as there were no safety precautions save her own focus ring. Still, she reasoned with herself, this was an important cause - the very life of the King could depend on what they found.

Grasping the handle, Phoenix closed her eyes and calmed her breath as Master Malcourt had taught her. Carefully, but with determination, she sought for the Power that rested inside of her.

She closed her eyes and visualized a pool of liquid fire residing in her belly. She pictured herself slowly feeding the flame, fuelling the fire until it expanded, boiling up her arms until the contents overflowed through her skin and spilled out into her hands. There was a soft hissing, and Phoenix opened her eyes in shock as steam rose into the air. She was never able to get her Power to work without being upset.

An orange glow spread from the handle and seeped through the metal mechanism of the door. The metal glowed angrily, the heat palpable in the air, though the feeling of burning didn't touch her skin.

When she was satisfied, Phoenix clamped down on her Power and dropped her hand. "Careful," she cautioned breathlessly when Rorin stepped forward to take her place. The gargoyle ignored her.

There was a sharp sizzling when Rorin gripped the handle, making Phoenix wince, but he immediately twisted the knob and a loud cracking sound could be heard. The girls jumped from the noise, but Rorin calmly set the previously-glowing doorknob in Phoenix's hand. The gargoyle's skin was ice cold, and Phoenix was shocked to find that the knob was frozen solid.

"You may want to melt that back into place afterwards, Apprentice," Rorin murmured. Before she could respond, he reached his arm through the hole and clicked the lock open from the inside.

The door swung towards them with an ominous creak.

It was a storage closet.

The room was smaller than Phoenix was expecting. The three peered inside, but when Phoenix held the candle up all that could be seen were rows upon rows of shelves containing glass jars.

An acrid smell assaulted Phoenix's nostrils, and she coughed lightly in an attempt to clear the burning sensation.

Rae stepped forward to read the labels on the jars. "Barknut... Darkroot... Banebore... Some of these are poisonous. This one is missing!" She pointed to an empty space on the shelf, the circular pattern in the dust showing where a large jar had rested until recently. A shadow of a stain pooled on the empty shelf. The remnants of the oily liquid shimmered in the dim light, and Phoenix knew at a glance that it was what had been used on the meals for the Head Table.

"This one too," Rorin pointed under the bottom shelf, where the larger containers were kept. The floor was damp. Whatever had spilled there was what was causing the smell.

Rae stopped in her tracks, as though the act of standing still would somehow ward herself against any possible danger. "I don't understand."

Phoenix and Rorin exchanged grim looks. "It makes sense

to keep people out of these corridors," Rorin said.

"And to keep the doors locked," Phoenix added.

"But why would Captain Rolf come here?" Rae asked the two. "The main storage room is full of herbs. Why would he want something so dangerous?"

"That is the question, isn't it?" Phoenix responded, echoing the girl's earlier words back at her.

Rorin nodded. "And, for the more important one: now that we know, what are we going to do about it?"

***

Phoenix attached the handle back to the door - sparing a moment to wonder if it would work again - and the three hurried away from the dangerous room in the forbidden corridor.

Rorin, upon reaching the window, opened it and bid them good night, slipping lithely through the opening and disappearing from sight. Phoenix and Rae ran to the window to watch as he disappeared. They gasped in unison as he dropped like a stone before unfurling his large wings and - with a powerful flap - soared upwards and disappeared out of sight over the rooftops.

Phoenix wordlessly closed the shutters behind him.

The lights were bright in the main corridors, and Phoenix and Rae winced slightly as they rounded the corridor into the well-lit foyer. The activity was deafening in comparison to the quiet that they had become accustomed to.

Can you meet me in your tower? Phoenix Heard Rorin ask, presumably to Master Malcourt.

Of course, her Master replied. *I will be there momentarily.*

"Well," Rae said, looking around quickly, "I should probably get back to the kitchens. I'm sure there's a lot of pre-prep to do for the morning..."

Phoenix nodded, clenching her jaw to stifle a growing

yawn.

The girls smiled at each other and went their separate ways.

It wasn't until Phoenix had begun climbing the stairs to the dorms that she Heard Malcourt *call* her.

Phoenix, can you come to my rooms please?

She groaned quietly to herself and turned around. "Of course, Master," she spoke aloud, knowing that he could Hear her.

Camden, can you come to the tower please? Malcourt *called.*

Yes, Master, Camden replied respectively.

The stone tree was sluggish when she arrived,shifting its branches to allow her to access the upper floors. Phoenix patted the gnarled trunk in thanks before dashing up the makeshift stairs.

Rorin and Master Malcourt were already waiting. Her Master was pacing the space in front of the hearth with agitation, his hands clasped behind his back. He looked up as she entered, and he gave her an acknowledging nod - as if they hadn't just seen each other recently - but he turned back quickly to his own thoughts.

"Phoenix," Malcourt said. He had changed out of his finery that he had worn to the dining hall, and now he was back in his customary loose tunic and trous. He looked weary, and a half-finished glass of wine was resting next to him on the side table. "I've heard that you've been busy."

Phoenix blushed under his gaze. "Yes, Master," she said.

Camden came in then. He was brought upright when he saw that Rorin was there. His face darkened, but he took the seat that Master Malcourt gestured to without a word. He shot Phoenix a tentative look, but she ignored him and kept her attention focused on Malcourt.

"Rorin was already telling me about your little adventure this evening," Malcourt continued, looking at Phoenix. Phoenix could see Camden narrowing his eyes at her in her side-vision, but she ignored his reaction. "I'd like to hear your side of it," he said.

"Yes, Master," Phoenix said. She paused for a moment, unsure of where to begin telling the tale. Then, taking a deep breath, she started at the very beginning when she met Rolf in the clearing all those moons ago.

She talked about his suspicions of her; his general attitude towards her - which went far beyond the general mistrust of Callers; his rudeness; the way she caught him sneaking around the forbidden hallways, and the way that he had been on guard around her ever since. Lastly she told him of his accusations outside the Prince's chambers; how he believed her to be the assassin, and how he would do everything he could to make sure that he found her guilty.

Master Malcourt said nothing while she spoke. He did raise an eyebrow, however, when she talked about being outside Prince Hallan's rooms, and she felt herself blush all the more because of it.

"I know he's just doing his job," she added, after there had been a moment of silence, "to protect the King. Well, that's what I thought, anyway. But since seeing the room..."

Camden's eyes darkened at the mention of the room but she said nothing.

"He's spending too much time concentrating on one girl," Rorin said, ignoring the fact that Camden spoke at all. Master Malcourt looked at the gargoyle curiously, so he continued. "All of his concentration is focused on her. I watched him in the hall tonight. He was studying her as she tended the Head Table - as if suspecting to find her guilty of something."

"Or trying to find a way to make her guilty of something."

Everyone turned to Camden when he spoke. The boy's eyes were stormy. "It's no secret that Captain Rolf dislikes Phoenix," he said. "He always has. He was watching her in drills this morning - glaring at her, practically. He seemed disappointed that she completed them so well."

Phoenix felt hotly uncomfortable in the large room. She hadn't known she was being scrutinized that intensely.

Master Malcourt frowned and tapped his fingers against the wooden portion of his arm rest. "This is a very serious accusation, Phoenix," he said as last, fixing the girl with a stern look. "If something like this gets out then there's no taking it back."

"Yes, Master Malcourt," she said, bowing her head in embarrassment.

"So," he continued, "while I don't condone the act of vigilante investigation, it seems as though this was the best course of action." Phoenix's head came up with relieved surprise.

"Now, you all must realize," Malcourt said, holding up a finger, "that there could be any number of reasons as to why Captain Rolf was in the forbidden corridors - as well as the storage closet. However," he inclined his head to Rorin to acknowledge the gargoyle's earlier point, "I must admit that his interest in Phoenix seems very suspicious. It does seem highly suspect that someone in his profession - someone as good as him in his profession - would spend such time concentrating on one individual, no matter how convinced he was of their guilt."

Malcourt frowned again and tapped his chin in thought. "But it just doesn't make sense. Rolf has always been loyal to the King. He would have nothing to gain by his death, and there's no reason to think that Phoenix would want for that to happen, either. So why watch her?"

Phoenix was relieved that Master Malcourt believed her,

and that she had both Camden and Rorin to back her up.

"Because he knows who the real assassin is," Rorin said.

A stunned silence settled over the room. Malcourt's expression went blank and he pressed his lips together. Phoenix could tell that he was thinking about the statement carefully, but she could only guess that by his furrowed brow that he could not find dispute with the claim.

"But then why is he always keeping track of me?" Phoenix asked with confusion.

"He would need a scapegoat," Master Malcourt said, slowly, "if this is in fact what is happening."

"Scapegoat?" she asked.

"He's waiting for you to screw up," Rorin told her, his expression bleak. "He wants to find you doing something wrong; something that he can blame you for, as an excuse to blame you for everything. He needs you as a cover up."

"We can't let that happen!" Camden burst out angrily.

"We won't," Malcourt said swiftly. He looked between the three. "This is serious," he told them, "and it's an incredibly delicate situation. If we're wrong, it can potentially allow the real assassin to escape. But, if we're right..." He sighed at the gravity of the situation.

"Phoenix's safety must not be compromised," Rorin said decidedly, giving everyone in the room pause. When Phoenix blinked at him, the gargoyle gave her a crooked smile. "You're okay - for a human. It would be beneficial to the diplomatic relations between our races if you stayed alive.

"Thanks," Phoenix said dryly. She could see Camden make a dirty face.

"'Diplomatic relations' or not," Master Malcourt said, "Phoenix's safety must not be put at risk; yet if she were to suddenly disappear than we would tip our hand."

"Then I shouldn't disappear," she said simply "I can take care of myself," she added when Master Malcourt frowned at her proclamation. "I'll be careful."

"And I will watch over her," Rorin told Master Malcourt, looking at Phoenix with amusement. "I'll even try my best to keep her out of trouble."

Malcourt thought about it for a few moments and, finally, sighed. "Very well, then. There's really no help for it. There are others who are aware of the situation as we are, but in this case it may be hard to know where their loyalties lie." The look he gave Phoenix was tinged with worry. "Still, I would feel better if it were not you."

His voice was very soft when he said it, and a quiet note of protectiveness was in it.

"I will stay with her, Master," Camden volunteered, puffing himself up a bit to appear taller in his chair. His voice was deadly serious as he spoke. "I will keep her safe."

Rorin's eyes shifted to Camden, his expression still amused, but he did not say anything to the boy. Opening his wings slightly, he walked to one of Malcourt's windows and lifted his leg to rest on the window sill.

"That settles it, then," he said. "I will watch Phoenix, she will watch Captain Rolf, and the boy will stay near her in case I cannot get to her in time." Rorin smirked slightly as Camden gave him a black look. "And you, Malcourt, are free to watch over everyone else. We are all capable of Speaking to you if necessary."

Master Malcourt eventually had to concede with the gargoyle's impassive logic. When he agreed, Rorin bid them a good night and dropped out of sight through the window. The Master sighed and pinched the bridge of his nose with discontentment and bid them a good night.

The two Apprentices rose and quickly made their way from his room.

"Phoenix," he called after her before the door had closed.

"Yes, Master," she asked, sticking her head back into the room. He looked weary, and worried, but he gave her a soft smile.

"Be careful, my child. I would be inconsolable if something were to happen to you. Would you do that for me? Be careful?"

Warmed by his concern, Phoenix blushed. "Of course, Master. Anything for you."

He closed his eyes and nodded his head slowly. She went to close the door behind her, but not before his voice followed her into the hall. "Keep Kit with you as well."

Phoenix shut the door. She discovered Camden waiting at the top of the stairs, his scowl directed at the stone tree that continued to guard the staircase. He looked up at the sound of her approaching footsteps, then shot a look of annoyance at the trunk in front of him as the large branches twined around themselves to create a railing down into the now-unobstructed stairwell.

He turned and they walked down the stairs together. Camden didn't say anything, and Phoenix was too tired to start a conversation with him, so they continued on for a time in silence. Finally, after he had finished his brooding, Camden broke the quiet.

"Why were you hanging out with a gargoyle?" he asked. His expression was blank, but his voice quivered as he spoke. She was unable to tell if he was angry or hurt.

She shrugged one shoulder, too tired to rehash it. "Why not?" she asked instead.

"Because he's a Searcher. You know what that is, right? A

spy. They can't be trusted," he told her seriously.

"They?" she prompted, feeling that he wasn't referencing the gargoyle's occupation.

"Gargoyles," he said flatly, impatient at her need for clarification.

"Well, we can't be trusted, either," she said crossly. "Humans, that is," she added before he could pull the same stunt that she just did.

"And you're going to trust your life to one of them?" Camden asked as they walked down the stairs. "They're murderers!"

Phoenix bit back a sigh. "Says who?" All she had wanted to do after meal's end was to climb into her bed, and several hours later she was still up and running about. She didn't feel like having Camden on her case, too.

"I do," he spat, showing uncharacteristic ire. Phoenix said nothing and continued down the stairs next to him, waiting for him to calm down. She could tell that he was waiting for her response, so when she didn't give one he spoke again. "Gargoyles murdered my parents."

Phoenix's foot missed a step and she was forced to grab the stone railing to keep herself from falling. "What?"

He didn't meet her stare. "Back when the war first started. You were probably too young to remember, but the fighting was savage when the gargoyles were first banished from Angor. There were battles everywhere.

"My father was trained in combat. He always led the men to slay the beasts when they came nearby or to roost on his lands.

"One night there was an attack. Lizards had banded together to ambush the manor in the middle of the night - when they knew that everyone would be asleep. They had planned to take everyone by surprise. I remember my mother, coming into my room and waking me up in the middle of the night. She bundled me up tight and took me downstairs to hide me in the cellar. She told me not to leave until she came to get me."

"Camden..." Phoenix began.

He turned his angry eyes to look at her. "She never came back," he said, with a hard finality. "It wasn't until my uncle," he said the word with a sneer, "Lord Nelson, found me three days later that I even saw sunlight again. Those monsters killed everyone, and I was left behind - to live - with him."

Phoenix rested a comforting hand on his shoulder. She understood, now, why he was so opposed to Rorin; why he showed an open hostility to the gargoyle whenever he saw him.

"Camden," she began again, gently, "The Gargoyle War was exactly that - a war. There was a lot of fighting. People lost their lives on both sides."

Camden jerked himself away from her touch. "They're not people!" he spat, nearly falling down the stairs himself in an effort to confront her.

"Camden..."

"You think what you want," he said, turning to continue down the stairs. "But I know what I know. You tell your new friend to watch himself. If I have any reason to believe that he is any sort of threat..."

"Oh, what are you going to do, Camden?" she snapped, tired of his posturing. "Blow him over?"

Phoenix knew that his particular Talent was a sore spot for Camden. While she and the Master had more innately powerful Talents - her with fire and he with the power of energy - Camden's was more understated than most. He could manipulate air currents flawlessly, but unfortunately, to his own desires, they were not powerful enough to affect much else.

His eyes darkened, and Phoenix wondered if she had

pushed him too far. He reached the base of the staircase and strode across the base of the tower, his boots echoing on the stone with each footfall.

"Just tell your lizard friend to watch himself," he told her over his shoulder, barely pausing before he pushed open the door and exited the tower.

Phoenix watched him as he walked away. She felt defeated. Camden was one of the few people in Angor that she had considered to be her friend and now he might never speak to her again.

With a sigh, and a yawn, Phoenix left the tower in the opposite direction as Camden. She headed to the dorms and, finally, to her bed.

CHAPTER 19

A soft movement buried into Phoenix's consciousness and jerked her awake. Silence smothered the room as she lay motionless in her bed, ears straining for anything out of place in the bedchamber. The even breathing of her sleeping friends was the only sound in the quiet room. Her eyes were useless in the darkness, and she briefly debated trying to light a candle with her Power before deciding against it. No need to recreate the excitement of setting the common room on fire.

There was a nudge against the blankets. Phoenix tensed, her foot resting against the bed to launch herself out from under the covers, when a cold, wet nose pressed itself against her arm.

Phoenix relaxed with a smile and made herself more comfortable, burying herself into her blankets with a sigh. Her mind became quiet, and her consciousness slipped back into a sweet and dreamless sleep.

Morning arrived with more celebration than was customary - or appreciated. Multiple trumpets led the charge in a penetrating fanfare that sounded as though it were coming from inside the room, announcing the arrival of the sun as it rose into the sky. Messenger drums pounded the breaking dawn to announce to all that the King's birthing day, the day of celebrations, had arrived.

The girls stirred and groaned around her. "Must they be so loud?" Sophie complained, burying her head under her pillow with a groan.

"How else will everyone get ready in time?" Elise chirped, launching her pillow at the shorter girl's bed. "Hey," Elise pointed at Phoenix's bed, "how'd she get in here?"

Phoenix shifted, her hand brushing against coarse, warm fur, and realized that Kit was still in her bed.

"Through the door, obviously," Sophie quipped, rubbing the sleep from her eyes before she threw Elise's pillow back at her.

"It was closed at last call. What did she do, open the door and trot on in?" Sarcasm sounded strange coming from Elise's lips, and Sophie told her so.

Phoenix ignored their squabbling and frowned down at the dog. Kit, seeing that she was awake, thumped her tail against the sheets. Phoenix didn't know how the dog was always showing up.

"Maybe the door wasn't fully shut?" Phoenix suggested.

The others had already forgotten the conversation and had moved on to the evening's festivities.

"I don't know how to wear my hair," Elise lamented, twitching her bed furs straight before she laid out her attire.

Phoenix sat up and stretched languidly. She watched as the other two went around the room, setting out their formal garments and getting ready. She was amused to see the effort that they were putting into their appearance. Their dresses alone must have cost a sum that was larger than their statuses could usually afford.

"You sure you don't want to join us, Phoenix?" Elise asked, pausing the braiding of her hair and looking over at the girl.

Phoenix nodded and hauled herself out of bed. "I'm sure,

thanks."

"What are you wearing, Phoenix?" Sophie asked, shrugging out of her sleep wear and beginning to brush her hair.

She shrugged. "My formal Apprentice uniform." The girls raised their eyebrows, and Phoenix shrugged as she pulled her boots out from under her bed. "My boots are new."

Elise giggled - not unkindly - and removed the silk scarf that covered her hair. "Well, when you get yourself ready, I'll be happy to do your hair for you if you want."

"Me too," Sophie chimed in with uncharacteristic kindness.

Feeling warmed by the offer, Phoenix nodded her head with excitement as she hauled on her boots. "How about I get us all food and then we can get ready together?" She hopped up and smoothed the wrinkles from her clothing, grateful that no one noticed that she hadn't changed into her sleep clothes the night before.

Elise and Sophie clapped excitedly as Phoenix dashed from their room, Kit bounding next to her at her heels.

The kitchens were a flutter of activity. Orders were flung back and forth with ease, raising in volume in an attempt to drown out the general noise of chopping and banging from the various stations. Phoenix was unable to see Tessa, so she quickly ducked out of sight from searching eyes and scrambled to grab a platter of food before it all went out.

While she was loading up a plate with eggs, a heavy pitcher of tea was placed on her tray. Phoenix looked up to see Rae, her hair tied back and her face sweating with the heat.

"You're gonna need this," she said with a wink.

Phoenix frowned. "Aren't you joining us?"

Rae shrugged. "I'll be out of here soon. I stayed late yesterday..." she trailed off, and the girls exchanged a grim look at the reminder of their adventure last night. "Which is good, because I need to wash and get ready." Rae mirrored Elise and Sophie's excitement, and Phoenix smiled to see her friend so happy.

"Why don't you do that now?" Phoenix offered. "I don't have much to do - I'm just wearing my formal uni - so I can take over here and you can go ahead and get ready."

Rae clapped her hands excitedly. "Really? Thank you! You'll need to help Anna baste the fowl, and probably shape more dough rolls, but that should be it!"

Excitedly, Rae gave Phoenix a quick hug and dashed out of the kitchens and up to their room with the serving tray in her hands.

Phoenix chuckled to herself and pulled an apron from the storage bin and reported to Anna.

The work was fast-paced, but not taxing. She found that her mind could wander while her hands automatically completed their tasks.

Phoenix decided that she would try and smooth things over with Camden. She was tired of their constant bickering. They had to practice together before the celebrations, and they would continue to work with each other far into the foreseeable future. The idea of always being at odds with him, or them having to tiptoe around each other felt like a stone sinking in her stomach. She liked Camden. She wanted things between them to be easy, even if she had to force the two of them to figure it out.

An order was shouted out for Master Malcourt and King Benedict, and Phoenix hid a smile at the thought of her Master watching the King so early in the day. She wondered if he'd remained in his tower. Knowing him, he probably used the cot in the King's chambers, keeping watch during the long night.

Time passed, and before she knew it she had finished her work. Washing her hands, Phoenix tossed her apron in the dirty pile up and snagged herself some food before exiting the kitchens. She also grabbed some extra to give to Kit, who had been sitting patiently at the main kitchen doors and waiting for her. Once the dog had dared to follow her into the kitchens and Tessa had thrown a fit - as well as a pot - at the pup. Kit had not ventured into the kitchens since.

Phoenix hurried back to the dorms to get ready for her practice with Camden. Smoothing things over with the other Apprentice would go more easily if she were on time, so she wasn't paying attention to where she was going, and in her haste she bumped into a youth who was wandering through the corridors. Stammering out an apology, she held out her hands to steady him so that he wouldn't fall over.

He was about her age. His clothes were dusty from travel. She could tell they were new, as though he had gotten them specifically to wear while visiting Castle Angor, but they were not extravagant like many of the other visitors. He looked familiar, and she tried to place him against all the new faces that had arrived recently.

He blushed. "My apologies, Miss," he said, giving Phoenix a practiced bow. "I didn' see you there."

"No, it's my fault," she assured him. "I was in a hurry. I didn't look where I was going."

He looked uncomfortable, his cheeks tinged with embarrassment while he refused to meet her eye, and Phoenix felt sympathy for him, remembering how long it had taken her to learn how to act in the castle.

"Are you lost?" she asked kindly. When he nodded she offered a smile. "Don't worry about it. It took me moons to learn my way around this place. It's tricky."

"It is," he agreed with relief.

"I'm guessing you're looking for the dining hall?" When he

nodded again, she stepped to the side to gesture down the corridor. "The kitchens are just past those doors - they go down a level - but you don't want to go there. Just walk a ways further and there'll be a passageway to your right. Follow that to the end of the hallway and you're there!"

"Thank you very much," he said, bowing to her again with the same stiff little bow.

"You're welcome! Enjoy the festivities!" Phoenix splayed her fingers in farewell and headed towards the dorms again - this time at a much slower pace. She noticed, when turning the corner, that he was standing there and staring after her in disbelief.

He had probably caught sight of Kit.

She wracked her brain to think of when she saw him last, but the familiarity kept teasing itself away from her. He was probably one of Alexandri's friends from sparring practice yesterday, she decided at last, already pushing the exchange from her mind as she eyed the sun's location in the sky.

Taking the stairs two at a time, Phoenix hurried back towards the dorms.

***

Phoenix padded from the bathing room. She clutched the thick towel around her, tightening the soft cocoon around the tingling she felt from her rushed attempt at scrubbing the smell of the kitchens from her skin.

Kit trotted next to her happily, her wet paws pressing prints on the stone as they walked down the empty corridor.

A strange smell caused Phoenix to wrinkle her nose. She waved her hand in front of her face to displace it, but the action did little to help. The further she walked, the stronger it became. Kit snorted from the smell.

Phoenix opened the door to the drying room and found

that it was strongest inside. The windows had been shut since her last visit, shuttered tightly against the wall so that the foul scent was amplified in the stuffy room.

Trying not to gag, Phoenix took a hesitant step forward and looked around. She could find nothing that was the cause of the smell. She could find nothing in the empty room. Her outfit was missing.

Frantically, she peered around the room, even going so far as to open the windows - as if her uniform had decided to drop out of the three-floored opening. She frowned and looked around.

"Maybe someone brought it back in the room," she said reasonably to Kit, fighting the panic that was rising in her throat. "They probably came in to close the windows and dropped it off."

Deciding that that was what had happened, she shut the door behind her and returned to her room.

The smell grew even stronger as they continued. Eventually she was forced to cover her mouth and nose with her hand as she walked to keep herself from gagging. She had no idea what could be causing such an odour - especially in the girls' dorms, where everything was kept completely clean and tidy. It smelled almost like rotten fish, she thought, remembering the smell of the leftovers from a few days ago. Rotten fish that had somehow been combined with a dirty stable. The smell of decay clung to the back of Phoenix's throat.

The stench came from the bedroom. Pinching her nose, Phoenix pushed the door open all the way and stopped midstep.

Rae, Elise, and Sophie were all kneeling on the floor, scrubbing the object that was undoubtedly the cause of the horrible smell. There was a bucket of steaming soapy water and a bucket of what Phoenix assumed was slop, all of which were surround-ed by dirty used brushes. Puddles and chunks of filth were all over the floor where the dirty bucket had spilled over.

Next to her, Kit sneezed.

"Hurry up," Rae said, facing away from the doorway as she worked. "She'll be back before we know it." The three girls were in their under clothes as they scrubbed, their dresses hanging up across the room at a safe distance.

"What the sweet jumping toad is causing that horrible smell?" Phoenix asked, stepping into the room. Her voice sounded strange, she knew, having her nose pinched as she spoke, but she couldn't help it. She didn't understand how the other girls could handle the smell.

Rae jumped at the sound of her voice while Elise squeaked with fright and dropped the brush she had been holding. So-phie just sat back on her heels and sighed, frowning at Phoenix with a strange expression. It took her a moment to realize that it was a mixture of sorrow and pity.

There, crumpled on the floor between the three girls, barely recognizable, was Phoenix's uniform.

The outfit had obviously been soaking in the bucket for some time. The bucket that Phoenix now recognized as the one missing from the stables. The uniform was beyond redemption, whatever was collected had undoubtedly absorbed permanently into the fabric. Even if the girls managed to wash it clean, there was no way that the horrible smell would ever disappear.

"What?" Phoenix was so dumbfounded that she dropped her hand to her side. She winced as the smell hit her full force. "How... ?"

Rae jumped up and gave her a hug. "Oh, Phoenix. I'm so sorry. I found it when I went to bathe. All the windows were closed and your clothes were just lying in this... bucket," she wrinkled her nose at the filth, face twisting in disgust.

"We tried as best we could," Elise chimed in. "We wanted to clean it for you, before you noticed, but we couldn't. It's been soaking too long..."

There was an uneasy silence in the room as everyone stared at the filthy outfit.

Sophie made a loud noise of frustration and threw her brush at the dirty heap. "It's all Brianna! I know it is! Her and her rotten little lackeys. She's been put out of sorts ever since you came here. She can't stand anyone else getting any attention!"

Sophie's fit of anger was completely uncharacteristic for her, which momentarily endeared her to Phoenix before the melancholy set in.

Phoenix just stared at the ruined clothes. "But why would she..."

"Because she's awful," Sophie spat.

"Sophie's right," Rae said quietly. "Brianna and Jenny have seemed particularly suspicious the last few days."

Phoenix nodded numbly, remembering the way the two had been laughing at her during evening's meal.

"Not that we can ever prove it," Elise said, bitterly.

"Not that we can do anything about it, either," Phoenix muttered.

Sophie narrowed her eyes and clapped her hands together with a strange show of authority. "Never mind that, now. We've got to get Phoenix a new outfit," she declared.

The three stared at her.

"What?" Elise blinked.

"You heard me," Sophie told her.

Rae frowned. "Sophie, none of us are the same size as Phoenix. She's so..."

"Gangly?" Phoenix asked darkly.

"Tall," Rae supplied quickly.

"So we'll ransack the discard room!" Sophie said with a mischievous smile. Her voice took an innocent tone. "After all, who else would have a key to it at this time of day?"

Rae cheered and Elise clapped, and Phoenix felt herself smiling despite her rotten mood.

"Go to your lessons, Phoenix," Rae turned her about and pushed her out the door while Elise tossed a mostly-clean outfit after her. "We'll take care of everything here."

"But what about the mess?" Phoenix asked, clutching her towel, looking helplessly behind her at the slop on the floor.

"You leave that to us," Rae said, her eyes dancing. "I think I heard Sophie talking about what we should do with it earlier."

Elise and Sophie grinned. The door closed in Phoenix's face before she could ask any more questions, the definitive sound of a lock clicking had her swallowing her objections as she stared at her barred chambers in disbelief. Kit huffed and, with a shrug, Phoenix ducked into an empty room to change.

***

The stone tree shifted behind Phoenix as she stepped onto the floor. The branches rolled back onto themselves, twining together to obscure the fabricated stairs that were paramount in accessing the higher floors. Stone tendrils clung to the wall like hanging decorations, interwoven as thoroughly as a spiderweb, while the buds of leaves peeked out from their vantage points.

Phoenix gave one of the vines a pat of thanks, convinced as always that the tree settled more quickly because of it.

She was the first to arrive at the practice chamber. The area was empty except for the kindling targets that stood around the perimeter of the room, and except for the large box of floating rings that Camden used for practice.

Feeling jittery, Phoenix launched into a pace to calm herself, concentrating on the motions of her legs carrying her across the room, the impact of her boots against the stone floor. Despite her best efforts she was unable to make it work. Her body still shook with anger, the heat of it flickering between her fingers.

Settling in Angor had been a challenge. Learning how to integrate herself into the castle's routine while having to work constantly on her lessons to catch up with her peers - she had pushed a lot aside in order to get to where she was. That would be her last mistake. Now she was done. Brianna's nasty prank was the final straw.

Phoenix was fed up with the snotty girl attacking her at every turn. She had tried to downplay the situation for the past few moons - tried to avoid a direct confrontation that would shame her Master - but she could see now that that was no longer an option. Phoenix would have to figure out a way to deal with the girl on her own terms.

Her anger overwhelmed her and she punched a target, reveling in the satisfaction she felt when it burst into flame, breaking apart from the force of the heat that sprung into life. She snatched a fallen piece and hurled it at a second target. She glared at the piece as it sailed through the air, pinpointing her Power against the stick as it spun across the room.

Wicked delight snaked down her spine as the second target also caught fire from the impact. She couldn't help but feel a small kernel of pride glow in her stomach at her newfound trick.

The sound of clapping startled her and she whirled around. Master Malcourt and Camden had arrived without her noticing, and as Phoenix fought to control her emotions, the flames behind her guttered into nothingness. They stood in the doorway. Camden was looking at her with a muted show of respect, but Master Malcourt beamed openly while he clapped.

"Very good, my dear," he congratulated her. "You learned that much more quickly than is customary."

"Master?" Phoenix hastily wiped the sweat from her brow, feeling embarrassed that she had broken the targets without permission.

"It takes a while to learn to direct Power," Camden explained, removing his fancy overcoat to hang it on a wall hook. The threaded design that was stitched into the dark fabric flashed in the light "It took me almost twice as long."

Phoenix shrugged, feeling self-conscious. "All I did was keep my focus on the piece I threw," she disagreed.

Master Malcourt nodded in acknowledgement. "You'd be surprised how long that can take some Apprentices... despite how simple it seems in hindsight."

He shrugged off his overcloak as well, hanging it next to Camden's. His outfit was formidable. He wore a long, dark cloak which hung past his waist, matching the tempered steel of the sword scabbard that hung from his belt. She had never seen him wear one before, noting how odd the weapon looked on her Master. His tunic underneath was a deep red, the dark embroidered patterns caught the light of Phoenix's dying flames - much the same as Camden's did - and flashed ominously with the movement.

Master Malcourt watched her assess his clothing and made a face. "Acting is sometimes part of the Calling duty, Phoenix," he told her dryly. "It's always more prudent to impress others without the need for demonstrations. It's usually a lot less messy, as well."

Camden removed his under vest and sat cross-legged on the floor. He was dressed as most nobles were, in one of the outfits that Phoenix always found to be silly and overly ornate. It was a dusky blue, a color borrowed from the sky that trailed the setting sun. A color which strangely accented his alert grey eyes. What impressed her was that Camden had his Apprentice stripes added to the sleeve of his coat. Phoenix wished that she had thought to do that.

He caught her watching him and tilted his head, his eyes shifting greys as he appraised her. "I'm surprised that you're not changed as well." He raised an eyebrow. "Aren't girls supposed to spend half a day preening themselves?"

"We're not birds," Phoenix retorted before ducking her head and muttering something about getting ready after. She crossed her legs as well and sat down a few hand-lengths away from him.

Camden blinked in surprise. "You're not wearing that, are you?" When Phoenix shrugged a shoulder despondently, he looked aghast. "You can't wear something like that!"

Malcourt joined them on the floor, sitting with a grace that spoke of the countless times he had spent taking part in the exercise. The three of them sat in silence for a moment, forming the shape of a triangle with Master Malcourt seated at the top.

"Where is your dress, Phoenix?" Master Malcourt asked gently. "I've been so preoccupied that I didn't think to check in on you. I keep forgetting that this is your first royal ball."

Phoenix rested her chin in her hands and picked at the scorched debris on the floor to avoid looking up at him. "I did have something," she admitted. She felt a wave of emotion as she tried to explain what had happened, so she stopped talking to try to swallow the lump out of her throat.

"Did?" Master Malcourt prompted.

Phoenix glanced up, but she was unprepared for his concern and froze before she could avert her eyes again. His sapphire gaze was shadowed as he assessed her, darkening the distress that was evident on her face.

Phoenix realized that she had let him down. Not only would she disgrace him at the ball, an important event despite how impermanent the nature of it was, but she was not fitting in like he had assumed.

The revelation was like a punch to the gut. Silence hung heavy in the room as moments passed before she opened her mouth in an attempt to answer.

She surprised everyone, most of all herself, when she burst into tears.

Once Phoenix started she was unable to stop. Her mind seemed to separate herself from her body, coolly assessing her reaction as her body heaved out the frustration and sorrow that she had buried for so long. It got to a point that she couldn't tell where it ended and she began - when the hardships of her time at Angor bled into her previous life at Avondale, when the feeling of lacking, or being less than had become ingrained in her sense of self.

Phoenix tried to get a hold of herself at first. Embarrassment crept through her at the thought of being so vulnerable in front of Master Malcourt and Camden, at losing control of her emotions. She was tired - so tired - and the idea of having to fight against herself was too much. Giving up, Phoenix rested her head in her hand as tears escaped down her face, not caring about how foolish she looked.

Warm fingers wrapped around her empty hand. The one that she used to steady herself against the floor like an anchor for her heaving body. A pair of arms encircled her shoulders and pulled her close with a gentle tug.

The heat of Malcourt's body soothed her as her shoulder rested against his. He made comforting sounds in his throat, murmuring lowly as if trying to calm a wild animal. "Spoke too soon, did I?" Master Malcourt asked softly as he rocked her.

Phoenix's shuddering sobs were her only answer. The only sound in the room. They rattled out of her swollen throat, her streaming tears dampening her tunic. Eventually she cried herself out, yet still Malcourt did not let her go until he was satisfied that her hiccups had disappeared and her breathing returned to normal.

Camden still cradled her hand, a strange show of concern for him, and she offered him a shaky smile of thanks.

Master Malcourt patted her back softly as a comfort. He let her go when she shifted with embarrassment, withdrawing easily to give her back her space. No one had held her like that since she was a child.

"Now, my dear," Master Malcourt said firmly, steepling his fingers, "I want to hear all about it."

Phoenix dashed the tears from her eyes with a deep sigh. Squaring her shoulders, she told him all of the problems she had encountered. She started with how her outfit for the royal ball had been ruined, threading the story backwards to explain all of the animosity that she had been subjected to since her arrival at Angor.

The words tumbled out of her unchecked until she found herself fighting for air, as though by purging the air from her lungs she would also somehow rid herself of the sorrow inside of her. When she finished, Phoenix felt as though a weight had been lifted off of her. It left her feeling lighter even if she didn't feel any better. She rubbed her face with her hands and watched Master Malcourt with shame. She had been careful to keep names out of her story, careful to keep everything vague without having to use specifics, but she made certain to elevate the statuses of Elise, Rae, and Sophie - who had been her staunch friends since the moment of her arrival.

Malcourt sighed and ran his fingers through his hair. "I

wish you had told me sooner, Phoenix," he sighed, admonishing her kindly. "I would have done something about it much earlier."

Phoenix shook her head. "I didn't want to involve you, Master," she told him quietly. "I still don't. You have bigger things to worry about - we all do. It's just foolishness. I didn't want it to distract you when it's my responsibility to take care of it myself."

Camden snorted, and Master Malcourt gave her a small smile. "Ah, but it is my concern, my dear. I brought you here after all. Your well-being is paramount - and that includes your happiness."

"It's hard out in the castle sometimes, Master," Camden shifted, speaking up for the first time. "So many don't understand us - we are either met with fear or hostility - and it's hard to go through it every single day. It wears us down. And I know," he said, holding up a hand as if to ward himself off of the Master's displeasure, "that that is part of being different. It will always be that way, but certain courtesies are not afforded to Apprentices like they are to Masters."

Malcourt pursed his lips. "I had hoped," he began, after a moment's thought, "to use it as a learning experience for the two of you, but I see now that it was unnecessary. I forget that you have both already faced such trials from where you came from: you, Phoenix, at Avondale; you, Camden, from your uncle."

Phoenix peered at Camden with interest, but the boy's face was closed off and his expression was unreadable.

"If you will allow me to make it up to you, I will certainly try," Malcourt continued. He paused for a moment, and Phoenix wondered how he could possibly say that could fix the situation. He looked at the two Apprentices with concern for a moment, then gestured around the room, indicating the expanse beyond it as well. "Move into the tower," he said simply.

They both stared at him.

"Move into the tower?" Camden repeated at last, his voice full of disbelief. Phoenix, for her part, only blinked.

"Why not? It's certainly big enough for the three of us, if not more. You have your choice of empty rooms. You could each have your own space. It's a good idea... if you like it, I mean."

Master Malcourt continued to look between the two for a response, but he was met only with stunned silence. He cleared his throat. "Or not."

"Of course we will!" Phoenix and Camden chorused out of sync with one another. They laughed and Phoenix clapped her hands with excitement.

"Kit, too," Master Malcourt added, before Phoenix could open her mouth to ask. "It makes perfect sense to keep her close. Besides, that way we may be able to avoid her biting anyone else..."

Phoenix flushed with embarrassment from Master Malcourt's teasing.

"Never mind, my dear. These things happen. She is still young." He smiled and gestured for the two to return to their spots on the floor, shifting his own position so that their seated triangle became unbroken.

Obediently, despite their excitement, Phoenix and Camden rested their hands palms-up on their knees and attempted to relax their bodies.

Phoenix's mind raced. She was momentarily distressed when she realized that she would no longer share a room with her three friends, but the idea that she would no longer have to put up with the torment of the other girls in the dorm. And maybe - just maybe - she would be able to use her new position to help out her friends as well. Maybe she could get them all out of the dorms, and into a much more relaxed environment.

A kind voice interrupted her meditation. It was soft despite its intrusion into her consciousness, a probing thought as she unwound the tension in her body to focus on her lessons.

Don't worry, Phoenix, Master Malcourt told her. *Everything will work out. I promise.*

Phoenix didn't know if it was the sense of belonging that washed over her, or the contentment that she felt sitting quietly with the other Callers, but the rest of her sorrow disappeared so thoroughly with his assurance that even the nagging tension between her shoulder blades vanished.

With her body finally relaxed, Phoenix smiled as, for the first time, she slipped effortlessly into the proper mindset for her training.

CHAPTER 20

Rae, Sophie, and Elise were waiting in their room. The three girls were dressed so beautifully that Phoenix felt a lump come to her throat seeing the care that they put into themselves.

Rae wore a rich purple gown that hung off her shoulders. The waist was drawn in with a pale belt that rested above her hips, hugging them loosely so that the skirts of the gown tumbled to her ankles, unencumbered by her movement. Her hair was pinned to the side so that her curls cascaded down one shoulder.

Sophie wore a deep brown dress accented with gold. The two colors cascaded together like swirling waves. The dark brown ebbed into the shimmering gold, rippling across the dress to accent her neckline and her skirts in a rich border. She wore a matching gold headpiece, the fabric woven around an open-ended band that wrapped around her hair, starting from the top of her head and disappearing out of sight under her loose hair. It wasn't hard to tell how hard she had worked on incorporating the different fabrics into her outfit.

Elise was stunning. The girl wore a vibrant form-fitting red dress with an asymmetrical neckline. Matching ribbons were woven into the capped sleeves, crisscrossing around her arms to weave into a single strand by her wrists, the edge of them looping around a finger to keep everything in place. She wore her hair unbound. The dark coils, free to move naturally, tumbled from the crown of her head to frame her face with a volume that astounded Phoenix. A single golden comb swept the shorter ones in the front to the side, securing them so that they stayed out of her eyes.

Phoenix blinked rapidly. "You look amazing," she breathed. She couldn't begin to guess how long the girls had been saving up for their outfits.

The three smiled at her and blushed.

"We found these for you," Rae said, stepping aside to show Phoenix the articles of clothing laid out on her bed. "We didn't know what ones you'd like, so we brought them all so you could choose."

The pickings were slim, but she could tell that her friends had tried hard so she took her time sorting through the mismatched outfit pieces, careful to pick the ones in the best shape. Eventually she settled on a long skirt and plain tunic that went well enough together, but once she tried them on it was obvious that they were both too big for her.

"I can do a little bit of quick altering," Sophie offered, pinching the material together in the back of each item. "It won't be a great job by any means - I won't have time to style it correctly - but it will work well enough for tonight."

"Wouldn't everyone be able to see that?" Elise asked the shorter girl. "She can't very well go around with pins sticking out of her!"

Sophie stuck her tongue out at her friend before rummaging through the storage trunk at the foot of her bed. "I can throw in a few quick stitches," she retorted, giving off the air of one who had been mortally offended. She lifted an item from the trunk and handed it to Phoenix. "You can also borrow this, if you want."

Sophie held out a shawl. Phoenix took it carefully, her fingertips barely pinching the edges of it as she stared in amazement.

The shawl was a pale cream color, its material stitched together in such a way that Phoenix couldn't help but think of it as a silky spider web that had been draped over her hands. The edges of the lace caught where she'd split her knuckles from punching the practice target.

"It's beautiful," she whispered.

The other girls stared. "Wherever did you get that, Sophie?" Rae asked, reaching out to run a finger along the silky strands.

Sophie shrugged self-consciously. "I made it a while ago."

Elise's jaw dropped. "You made this? Did you show it to Master Minna?"

Sophie flushed. "I didn't think it was good enough."

"Sophie!" Elise cried, shocked at the girl's self-depreciation.

A knock at the door interrupted them. No one visited them other than Mistress Ruby, who always rapped a warning before entering immediately afterwards. The girls looked at each other curiously before Rae stepped forward to open the door.

She was met by Alan's sour expression. He stood at the threshold looking uncomfortable. He held an intricately wrapped package, both hands cradling it securely while his arms were extended so that he wasn't holding it too closely. He was obviously being careful not to drop it, but the look on his face showed that he wished that he could. His lip was curled in a sneer.

"You're not supposed to be here," Rae told him with authority. The exchange reminded Phoenix of the first day she arrived at Angor, and she found herself grinning at the boy despite herself.

Alan ignored Rae and looked straight ahead, as if he could also ignore the fact that the room was occupied by the four girls.

"Package for the Apprentice Caller," he said, his voice hoarse. He held it out in front of himself as if trying to distance himself from it as much as possible, but when Rae attempted to take it from him, he jerked it back so that she wouldn't touch it.

Stunned silence settled in the room. Rae assessed the Runner with a shrewd eye. He wouldn't meet her gaze - or anyone's, for that matter - and he refused to take another step into the room.

"Did someone get in trouble for not delivering this before now?" Her voice was soft as she reached out again; this time she tapped the corner of the box where the ribbon was crumpled. "Or perhaps for opening what doesn't belong to them?"

Her voice was sweet but her pale brown eyes were flat as she crossed her arms.

Alan's expression didn't change, but he paled noticeably under their scrutiny. "It got lost," he muttered, defensive.

It was false bravado. Phoenix had seen Apprentices with the same expression on their faces, usually after being brought to task by a Master. If Rae's assumption was correct, if the Runner had been hiding something that should have been delivered before now, Phoenix didn't have to guess which Master had intervened on her behalf. Especially not after the scene she had caused at the tower.

Sophie snorted and Elise shushed her. Rae stepped back as Phoenix walked forward to accept the parcel. As soon as her fingers touched it, Alan snatched back his hands as if he couldn't bear to touch it an instant longer.

He peered back at them over his shoulder, sniffing with a smirk. "What's that smell?" he asked, his expression innocent.

Rae spat something nasty at Alan under her breath and slammed the door in his face. She clenched her fists. "If I had Blood..." she began, narrowing her eyes.

"Never mind that," Elise clapped her hands with excitement. "Open your present, Phoenix!"

"Yeah!" Sophie and Rae chorused excitedly, all but pushing her to one of the beds.

"Who is it from?" Elise asked.

"I have no idea," Phoenix told her, insanely curious as to who could be sending her a gift.

"I bet it's a secret admirer!"

"I bet it's the Prince!"

The girls giggled excitedly and Phoenix felt her face warm. "I bet it isn't," she shot back, not altogether convinced that it wasn't.

Phoenix tugged on the ribbon that was coiled around the wrapping. The thin sheets of the patterned parchment fluttered away to reveal a thin wooden crate, the interior cushioned in a thick fabric to protect its prize.

The girls gasped in awe.

It was a ball gown. She unfolded the dress with care and held it up for everyone to see.

It was pale green in color. Embroidered vines accented the neckline and sides, adding a muted look of elegance to the background. In the forefront, white-filled flowers surrounded by purple petals were stitched in a wind-blown pattern around the leaves. The center of each flower cradled a small gem that caught in the light. They twinkled in unison as she moved, the soft fabric shifting easily at her touch. Phoenix caught her breath when she realized that the pattern matched her focus ring perfectly.

Rae and Elise looked at Sophie questioningly, but the girl raised her hands in surprise. "I have no idea," she told them, staring at the stitching with appreciation. "Master Minna said nothing about it..."

The room went quiet, then Elise broke the silence with an excited whisper. "Try it on!"

Phoenix, nervous that she might somehow damage the fabric, changed out of her clothing to pull the dress on. Rae helped her to pull it down over her head, and Sophie stepped behind her to lace up the back with expert precision while Elise smoothed it against her underclothes.

Phoenix blinked at herself in the long mirror.

The bodice fit her so snugly that Phoenix realized that the Masterclothier must have gotten a hold of her measurements somehow. The material bunched around her waist and flowed down to hang at her ankles, resting high enough so that she would be unable to trip up in the skirts.

"Toads," Rae said with soft appreciation. "You look amazing!"

Phoenix just stared at her reflection speechlessly.

"What's this?" Elise asked, bending down to pick up a folded piece of parchment on the floor.

"It fell off of the dress when Phoenix tried it on," Sophie said.

Elise handed it to Phoenix, and she took it silently. She opened it and read it out loud for everyone to hear.

"To Phoenix. Usually it is customary to receive gifts upon one's birthing day, but the fact is that without you I would not have lived this long to celebrate it. You have truly given me the greatest gift of all. Please accept this small token as my unwavering thanks. With fondest feelings of adoration. King Benedict."

They all stared at each other. Rae picked up the box and handed it to Phoenix again. Inside, unseen earlier from all of the wrapping, was a collar for Kit with the same pattern as the gown.

"You have a gift from the King!" Rae exclaimed, grabbing Phoenix's hands and twirling her around excitedly. She stopped dancing suddenly and started laughing. "I would pay good coins to see Brianna's face when she finds out!"

Phoenix felt a slow grin spread across her face.

"That'll put her in her place!" Elise said with satisfaction.

"Oh, I have a feeling she's going to be put in her place soon enough," Sophie told them slyly.

Phoenix didn't know what the girl meant, but she didn't bother to ask as Rae made her twirl around in her gown. Phoenix winced as she looked in the mirror and realized that the back of her dress was low enough to show the raised scars on her back from being burned so long ago.

"You look perfect, Phoenix," Sophie said softly. The other two girls nodded in agreement.

Phoenix shook her head. "No," she disagreed, picking up the delicate shawl that Sophie had offered her earlier. She wrapped it around her bare shoulders and tied it loosely in the front. The end of it came down to the small of her back as she smiled at Sophie. "Now it's perfect," she insisted.

Sophie returned her smile gladly.

The four of them looked between themselves and Elise clapped with excitement. "Let's do your hair!"

The other two cheered and grabbed Phoenix's arms. With Elise and Sophie on either side, and Rae at her back maneuvering her, Phoenix was seated on the plush chair before the shared vanity.

Smiling, she sat still as her friends began to style her hair.

***

The ballroom had been transformed. The decorations were so grand that Phoenix paused on the threshold and stared. Large colored streamers draped from the rafters, swooping from one end of the room to the other like deconstructed rainbows. They swayed with the movements of the guests milling about on the floor nearly a hundred feet below, shimmering gently in the light. The candles that dotted the walls were ornamental in relation to the large hearths that blazed around the room, their soft points of light breaking up the growing shadows that separated the massive works of art that hung between the colored glass windows that filtered in the sun's waning light. It played across the hanging, multi-colored vials that were suspended from the rafters over the dance floor. Phoenix cast them an appreciative eye, calculating how they were to factor into her performance later.

Rae gasped quietly next to her. Even Sophie - standing next to a wide-eyed Elise - looked impressed. A group of minstrels took up their instruments and began to play a lively melody to welcome everyone as they entered the room.

"Isn't this wonderful!" Rae beamed with excitement. "It's so grand this year. Usually the King is quiet about his birthing day."

"He has more to be thankful for this year, I think," Elise said, pushing Phoenix's shoulder in a teasing manner, careful of Sophie's shawl that was draped over her shoulders. Phoenix insisted on wearing it over the dress the King had gifted her.

"Which I am certainly grateful for," Sophie smiled coyly, linking arms with the two. She inclined her head to the side, and the girls looked over to see several boys who had stopped mid-conversation to stare at the four of them.

They giggled and continued into the room.

The atmosphere was joyous. Jesters juggled and performed backflips to the sound of impressed applause punctuated by the clinking of coins being thrown in their basket.

Kit had appeared in their dorm room before the girls had left. Now, she stuck close to Phoenix, her tail wagging intermittently from excitement. She sniffed constantly, her round ears pricking forward or swivelling towards any sound that caught her attention. She punctuated each investigation with an excited bark.

"Hush!" Phoenix laid a hand on the top of Kit's head before she drew too much attention. Phoenix had forgotten herself in all of the excitement, but a sudden movement caught her eye as she felt a flutter against her temple. Far above the grand entranceway, high in the rafters, a figure slipped through the shadows easily as the inky darkness shifted around his body like liquid. She watched for a moment, her body tense, until the figure turned and a pair of eyes reflected the waning afternoon light as they scanned the room.

"Rorin?" Phoenix whispered, her lips barely moving.

"Hmm?" A distracted Rae asked her, turning her head to look at Phoenix. "Did you say something?"

Phoenix shook her head in the negative, and Rae shrugged and turned her attention back to the crowd.

Miss me? Rorin's voice was an amused purr as he settled into a crouch on the rafter beam, looking the part of the mysterious spy peering out of the half-shadows. *You really ought to learn to call without using your mouth. It can be… distracting.*

Phoenix gave the ceiling a glare and stuck out her tongue. She didn't know if he could see it, but his far-seeing eyes must have noticed it as a moment later she Heard what she assumed was laughter. It started as a tickle in the base of her skull, then radiated outwards until the area behind her eyes felt fuzzy. She rubbed her nose with surprised delight, and couldn't help but grin in response.

The music changed into a lively tune and space was made on the floor for those who wanted to dance. Scullers drifted around the room with serving trays filled with finger foods and drinks. Rae, her eyes dancing with mischief, took a glass of wine from one and grinned at the other girls.

Acrobats danced onto the large dais at the front of the room. They all wore painted masks and matching costumes, the garish color pairings popping against each other as they contorted in front of the audience. They gestured dramatically, communicating in short bursts of shouting, but spoke no words as they carried out their routine. Phoenix gasped with the audience as the show reached its finale: a tower of bodies that toppled one by one to twist in mid-air and tumble to their feet with a flourish and a bow. She clapped loudly when they finished.

A trumpeting fanfare drew the crowd's attention as the acrobats tumbled off the stage. A pompous looking page appeared at the top of the grand staircase - which was directly across from the main stage - causing everyone to turn around in order to see properly. Obviously delighted, he looked down through his pointed nose at the room below.

"May I present," he boomed to the crowd condescendingly, apparently enjoying the importance of his role for the evening, "our host and Royal Highness - His Majesty King Benedict of Angoria!"

The brass played a loud introduction and the King appeared at the top of the staircase. Malcourt stood immediately to his right and Prince Hallan, a step back, hovered at his left.

"Isn't this exciting!" Elise gushed as the King descended the stairs.

Phoenix nodded absently as her eyes flicked through the

crowd to gauge their reactions. Nothing seemed out of place, until...

Until a guard caught her eye. He stood in one of the entranceways, impassive as a boulder as his girth blocked the side corridor next to the staircase. He was unremarkable in the half-shadow, and Phoenix studied him for a moment trying to figure out what piqued her interest about him. There was something about the set in his shoulders that caused her to stare. All of the other guards were standing at attention, taking turns going between watching the crowd and watching the King. He, however, was not. The easy way he shifted from one foot to the other made Phoenix's spine lock. A whisper of Power stirred in response.

She took a few steps towards him and stood on the toes of her boots to get a better look. He watched the King with a bored expression, the lines etched into his face as though they were a permanent fixture. Perfectly practiced. As Phoenix watched, his expression of boredom transformed into cool detachment, but his eyes darted around him quickly in a vivid contradiction as he grabbed the knife in his belt.

"The entrance way!" Phoenix cried, her voice lost against the cheering of the crowd. Frozen, with a sea of people between her and the King, she waited to see if she had been Heard.

Next to her, Kit gave a hair-raising howl. Malcourt stiffened, his gaze snapping to where Phoenix pointed.

Got it! Rorin said, peering downwards and pointing a talon at the shadows clinging to the wall above the guard's head.

It was as if the very wall shifted in response, and Phoenix gaped as a decorative stone statue came to life above the unsuspecting guard. The unknown gargoyle plummeted onto the man. The element of surprise worked, causing the man to stumble badly as the gargoyle's talons gripped the front of the guard's uniform, holding him like a ragdoll as powerful legs launched them down the side-corridor and out of sight around the edge of the doorway. Phoenix felt a *pop* and the two disappeared completely from sight.

It all happened so quickly that Phoenix wondered if she had imagined the whole thing.

He was in a guard's uniform, Camden's voice was tinged with outrage. Phoenix looked around before she located him standing stiffly with a noble who was going out of his way to ignore him. Phoenix easily recognized Camden's uncle from the look of disdain on his face.

All the more reason to be vigilant, Master Malcourt replied grimly. He paused for a moment before adding, *Good job, Phoenix.*

Slowly, still raised on her toes, she turned in a circle. Several stone statues were perched on ledges around the room, their colors blending in with the grey stone behind them. They remained motionless where they crouched, even the fabric of their clothing refused to move in the open air, but if Phoenix looked at any one of them for long enough she could catch them blinking from time to time.

Did you think I was the only one here? Rorin asked mildly. Amusement colored his tone as he shifted back into the shadows.

"I guess I never thought about it," Phoenix admitted. The woman standing next to her - dressed in an outfit composed entirely of ruffles - stared at her openly as she talked to herself. Shifting her glance away uncomfortably, Phoenix walked ahead to lose herself in the crowd.

Phoenix *felt* Rorin's silent laughter following her.

Malcourt leaned in to whisper something to the King, and King Benedict raised his hand to signal silence from the room.

"My friends," he said, his rich voice carrying easily. "I wish to thank you for joining me on my special day! It means so much - more than I could ever express. Now, please! Enjoy your evening! I know I certainly will!" He winked at the crowd comically, and delighted laughter erupted in the room.

The party descended the stairs with the forgotten page at the top calling after them. "All who wish to seek an audience with the King privately are invited to line up outside his meeting room! He will begin seeing guests shortly!"

Those who did not leave the ballroom immediately surged forward to greet the King in person. Phoenix could see that both Rorin and Master Malcourt had their focus on the immediate crowd, so she afforded herself the luxury of relaxing for a moment.

"Well," Rae said with a curious display of pride and satisfaction when her friends had caught up to her. "He certainly knows how to make an entrance!"

"Yes, Rae," Elise said, dryly. "You're so lucky to be one of the treasured few who are permitted," she stressed the word, "to cut the King's vegetables." Sophie snickered next to her and Rae shoved them both playfully.

"Where shall we go next?" Sophie asked brightly. "Before Rae fills her cups, that is."

Rae made a face at the girl, and Phoenix was surprised to see that she was holding a mostly-empty cup.

"I think outdoors would be best," Phoenix said, eyeing the girl speculatively. "It would be embarrassing for us all should she start to smell of ale as well."

Rae gave Phoenix a look of outrage, and the other girls burst into laughter.

"You're right," Elise said with a deadpan expression.

"A complete embarrassment," Sophie added seriously.

Rae made an outraged noise and, laying her glass down with more force than was necessary, marched through the crowd towards the exit. The three girls laughed and followed behind her.

The courtyard was filled with merchant stalls. Every space around the perimeter of the yard boasted different types of makeshift booths that had been erected within the past week. People walked between them promoting their wares, shouting out to grab the attention of the nearest guests as they walked past.

Those with the coins to spend were milling about from shop to shop, while others were just chatting idly and enjoying the evening air. A faint breeze brought the smell of horses to them. Phoenix gave a small smile, but the other girls wrinkled their noses.

"You'd think they'd keep the horses somewhere else," Rae remarked, waving her hand in front of her face to push fresh air in front of her nose.

"Ah!" a voice said. The girls turned to see a sandy-haired boy leaning against the castle wall. His eyes sparkled as he watched them, his pale gaze assessing them thoughtfully. He pushed himself off the wall and dipped into a gracious bow. "Lady Apprentice," he greeted Phoenix gravely, his mouth quirking into an amused smile. Then he straightened and smiled slyly. "I barely noticed you. You clean up nice, you know."

"Thank you, Alexandri," Phoenix said, with a note of pretended offense. He winked at her and she smiled. "Elise, Sophie, and Rae - Trader Alexandri," Phoenix said, introducing them all to each other. "We met at the training drills the other morning."

Alexandri took Rae's offered hand and brushed his lips against it. "My Lady," he greeted her warmly.

Rae blushed and opened her mouth to say something, but no sound came out.

"There's a first," Elise muttered under her breath, and Sophie used an elbow to jab her friend in the ribs.

"Ow!" Elise hissed, somewhat loudly, and pressed a dramatic hand to her side.

"May I show you around?" Alexandri asked them all, gesturing to the field. "I can show you all of the best stalls."

"And how many of them belong to your family, Alexandri?" Phoenix asked teasingly. Alexandri only winked in response.

The girls agreed easily, so he straightened and marched them through the crowd. Judging by the looks he exchanged with many of the merchants, he did indeed bring them to the stalls of people that he knew, but her friends seemed enamoured by the items on display, so Phoenix smiled and said nothing. Even Kit showed interest at one of the stalls selling spiced meat tarts.

Above the doorway, along the sides of the darkening castle walls, gargoyle statues seemed to arrive with the setting sun, their motionless forms pointedly keeping watch over the courtyard.

The hair on the back of her neck prickled. Phoenix felt eyes upon her, and she pivoted slowly in an attempt to find the source of the gaze. She ended up turning in a complete circle, the curious looks of her friends waiting for her when she returned to her starting position, the four of them having stopped what they were doing to watch her when they noticed her strange behaviour.

"I didn't know you could dance," Alexandri said comically.

Phoenix scowled at him but said nothing.

A familiar face over his shoulder caught her attention. It

was the boy that she had met that morning in the halls, the one who had seemed so familiar, who was the source of the scrutiny. He stood only a few foot lengths away. He stared at her openly, his eyes wide in surprise and disbelief.

Phoenix frowned. "Your friend is staring at me," she told Alexandri, her voice colored with more annoyance than she intended.

"He probably wants you to buy something," he shrugged.

She shook her head. "Not the trader. That one over there. He's been following me." She nodded towards the male and they turned their heads to look at him. The boy, realizing that he was the subject of their scrutiny, ducked his head and turned to talk to the man next to him. The man had his back turned so Phoenix couldn't see his face, but she tried to make out any distinguishing features in case he had come here to be a threat to the King.

"My friend?" Alexandri asked, confused. "I've never seen him before in my life."

Sophie furrowed her brow. "Then who is he?"

"He was staring right at you, Phoenix," Rae said.

"Maybe he's interested in meeting you," Elise supplied.

Alexandri looked suspicious. "I'm usually pretty good at reading people," he said, "and I don't think that that's why he was looking at you, Phoenix. He was watching you."

"Well then" she said shrugging, trying to make light of the situation. "I guess we'll just have to watch him back and see how he likes it."

"Someone should have taught him better manners," Elise muttered.

"It's not like you did anything wrong," Rae told her reassuringly.

"I somehow doubt that," a deep voice said. Captain Rolf

was standing only a few foot lengths away with a hand resting on the hilt of his sword. He watched Phoenix through narrowed eyes.

"I've been watching you, Apprentice," he continued in his harsh voice. "You seem a bit nervous tonight - looking around a bit too much, if you ask me."

Alexandri raised a brow. "And why is it the Captain of the Guard is spending all his time watching a young girl instead of looking for any real threats?"

"Watch your tone, Trader," the Captain snarled, his nostrils flaring. "I don't need some Bloodless boy telling me how to do my duty."

Alexandri's face stiffened and he glared at the Captain. Several people around them had slowed down to watch the interaction between them.

Rae glared at Captain Rolf's smirk. "Why don't you go and bully someone else!" she demanded hotly.

"You forget your place, cook," he retorted, emphasizing her title.

"No. You forget your place," Phoenix told him, her voice angry. They had the attention of the crowd, and she watched as Rolf's face darkened by several shades of red.

"How dare you!"

"After all," she continued, ignoring his outrage, "was it not one of your guards that was just taken into custody?"

His expression turned to surprise and he looked at her suspiciously. Everyone else was staring at her in wonderment for her accusation. "How could you possibly-"

"Thief!" someone cried out loudly in the crowd. "Thief!"

Alexandri winced. "Uh-oh," he said quietly under his breath.

A murmur of surprise and shock rippled throughout the

crowd. Phoenix looked quickly around but saw no one moving or running away. She saw all of the merchants lay their hands on their sword hilts and stand in front of their stalls defensively. The gargoyles hanging on to the stone scanned the yard, but none of them moved so Phoenix could only assume that they also could find no one.

"Guard! Arrest th' thief!" A man elbowed his way through the crowd to where Captain Rolf stood. Impetuously he looked up at the tall man. "This child stole from me an' I demand justice!"

Alexandri's look of confusion shifted to panic as Captain Rolf shot his hand forward and grabbed the boy by his front collar. "With pleasure," Captain Rolf said with a serpentine smile.

Phoenix frowned. The familiar boy who had been staring at her early was there, watching her again with that same look of disbelief. Recognition dawned on her slowly as she realized who the boy was. She opened her mouth in surprise.

"Not him," the man scoffed. "Her!"

A stunned silence fell on the group.

Phoenix turned her attention back to the group to find the man pointing a meaty finger at her.

Captain Rolf smirked. He relaxed his grip on Alexandri and took a step towards her.

A ferocious snarl erupted from Kit and she crouched in front of Phoenix. She looked terrifying, her ears flattened against her skull in a way that all familiarity of the animal had evaporated, and Phoenix felt a twinge of fear on a primal level that surprised her.

Alexandri also stepped forward, his expression shifting to the human equivalent of Kit's predatory stare. His hand rested on the hilt of his belt knife.

The man was familiar. Slowly, as if willing her apprehension to change the man's identity, Phoenix raised a steady gaze to her accuser. Speaker Thomas's angry glare bore into her, his face arrested in an expression of triumph. Next to him stood Jobe, the boy who had been watching her so diligently.

Speaker Thomas pointed at her, signalling her out to everyone who was watching. "Arrest her! She's a runaway, an' a thief! She lied t' remain here without consequence, an' I demand t' see th' King about it!"

CHAPTER 21

Pompous ass, Phoenix heard as the progression left the main foyer. A mental snort was the only response, and Phoenix could only assume that she was privy to a conversation between two gargoyles.

Need any help with your new friends? A lazy voice asked above her. Phoenix glanced up, her eyes barely making out Rorin's outline in the shadows, his tail a darkened grey where it intersected with the dim lighting in the rafters, peering down at the progression with interest.

A knot of dread formed in Phoenix's stomach as the King's meeting chambers came into view. "Don't you dare," she muttered at him.

"Hush your mouth, girl," the Guardscaptain growled. "Keep moving. No need to insult us further with your disobedience."

Phoenix pressed her lips together. She balled her fists, focusing on the burning in her palms as her nails left half-moon marks in her skin.

There was a rumble of outrage as they skipped ahead of those already waiting. "See here!" a nobleman protested, stepping forward to stop them as they passed. A single look from Captain Rolf had two guards moving to block the man's path.

Phoenix could feel the dark looks thrown at her back as they bypassed the line entirely.

The Captain nodded to his guards and they moved the line back from the entrance of the foyer, ushering Phoenix and her group into the room. One of the men guarding the chambers entrance saluted the Guardscaptain, then slipped in through the double doors to alert the King's page of his new visitors.

The room went quiet as a well-dressed noble was escorted from the chamber and back out into the foyer. "But I wasn't done!" he protested.

Captain Rolf smirked and grabbed Phoenix's elbow, wrenching it as he dragged her into the meeting room. Kit snarled and launched herself at the large man, diving for the offending hand. Rolf kicked the dog aside as easily as he would swat a fly.

"Kit!" Phoenix cried. She attempted to twist out of the man's grip, but the hand gripping her arm was too strong. "Let me go! I didn't do anything!"

Captain Rolf dragged her behind him, but not before she saw Jobe separate himself from the group with a frown. Phoenix watched him kneel next to Kit before the door slammed shut between them.

She tried not to stumble as the Guardscaptain pushed her forward.

The meeting room was not as grand as she was expecting. A large dais was the focal point. On it, a single high-backed chair commanded the attention of the room. Intricate, carved designs wove their way around a crescent orb that sat recessed in the top of the chair back, as if paying homage to a rising moon. Before it was open space for people to bring their grievances to the King, as often happened, when there was dispute between Manors and Propers.

The King was seated in the chair - a throne really - with Malcourt standing at attention by his side. They were both watching the doorway to see what was so important that their previous meeting should be interrupted. But when Captain Rolf and Phoenix came into view, King Benedict frowned and sat up in his chair.

"Rolf," he scowled. "What is the meaning of this?"

The Captain's grip tightened, and Phoenix attempted once again to wrench herself free. Fueled by desperation, her Power rose to the challenge, causing her skin to turn hot to the touch against the perceived threat. Captain Rolf snarled and released her, throwing her towards the dais.

Phoenix struggled to catch her balance, stumbling a few steps before falling. Her knees barked in protest as they connected against the hard stone.

Master Malcourt was next to her instantly. He extended his hands to her and carefully helped her to her feet. "Are you all right, my dear?" he asked softly.

"Master," she whispered, tears springing to her eyes. "I'm so sorry..."

He gave her a reassuring smile, then leveled a glare at the Guardscaptain. "Explain yourself." Malcourt's voice was almost unrecognizable with fury. "Now."

"Quite right," King Benedict's expression was a mask of royal disapproval. "Get on with it."

Captain Rolf bowed respectfully to the King. "Of course, Your Majesty. The presence of a thief was reported moments ago. Since the accused is someone known to you, I thought it best to bring them to you, Your Majesty, as is proper with those who actually have the Blood."

"Rolf," Master Malcourt said warningly.

Captain Rolf ignored him. "This... child... came to us under false pretences. She's a thief and a run away - a common criminal. And you," he snarled accusingly at Master Malcourt, "welcomed her with open arms."

Master Malcourt pivoted slowly. All courteousness had disappeared from his face, his expression thunderous.

The King raised his bushy eyebrows. "Surely you don't mean Phoenix?" His tone was of mild disbelief. "What is the proof?"

Captain Rolf bowed again. "Of course, Your Majesty. May I present Speaker Thomas of Avondale; the man who alerted me to the girl's true identity."

At the mention of his name, Speaker Thomas stepped forward and gave the King a well-practiced bow. "Yer Majesty," he greeted the King. "I'm Speaker Thomas of Avondale Farm."

"Not the Head Speaker of the Proper?" Master Malcourt's expression was unreadable, but Phoenix knew the question was meant to rattle him.

The Speaker stiffened. "An' who might you be?"

"Tolen Malcourt," he said, almost amicably, inclining his head towards the man. "Mastercaller of Castle Angor; Advisor to the King."

Speaker Thomas's gaze flicked from the man's face down to where he was still holding Phoenix's hands and he swallowed audibly, visibly uncomfortable.

"The charges?" King Benedict prompted, seemingly bored with the posturing of the two men.

Speaker Thomas drew himself up. "This girl, Phoenix, used t' live on th' farm. Her caretaker, m' dear friend Marla, passed on 'bout a year ago, an' ever since then we - th' people o' Avondale - took care o' her, not askin' fer no thing in return."

"Tha's a lie!" Phoenix protested, easily slipping back into the Speaker's dialect. "I worked hard for m' keep. T' say other wise is dishonest!"

"Accordin' t' you, you did," Speaker Thomas snorted. "What do a girl know 'bout workin' hard?"

"And according to you, what actually happened?" Master Malcourt slid his hands into his sleeves, his stance casual. He seemed completely unfazed by Speaker Thomas's accusations.

Speaker Thomas took a breath, fixing Phoenix with such a look of contempt that she realized that his speech was just as well-practiced as his bow. "She ran wild," he stated. "She went wherever she wanted whenever she wanted, withou' thinkin' 'bout anyone else. She claims she helped wit' th' harvest, but it was not near enough to cover her own food supply - let alone that of her beast, or their room and board. I had t' turn down a foaling mare 'cause her useless crossbreed was takin' up space!"

Phoenix felt like a blow had landed. She opened her mouth in protest, but Master Malcourt shook his head and she said nothing.

Let him talk, my dear. It's easier for us if he gets himself into trouble. Phoenix blinked at her Master and he winked. *You doubt me?*

"Never," Phoenix whispered emphatically.

"Hush," Captain Rolf growled.

"She put on airs," Speaker Thomas continued, not noticing the exchange, "as if she had Blood. Which she don't. She has no one t' vouch for her."

He smiled self-importantly. "I knew she didn' have nothin' goin' for her, Your Majesty. I knew she had no way t' pay us back for our generosity - so I set up a deal.

"An nearby goat herder was in need of a woman to tend his home and children. I made an arrangement with him in order to secure her future, but th' ungrateful brat ran off, leavin' us with a pile of debt and a broken word on my part." Speaker Thomas fixed Phoenix with a glare. "She's nothin' but a thief an' troublemaker, an' I couldn' ignore m' duty t' inform you of such a person livin' in your court, Your Majesty!"

"You mean you couldn't ignore your duty to get what you've decided you're owed," Master Malcourt snorted.

Captain Rolf made a disagreeable noise in his throat and stepped forward. "Your Majesty," he implored. "Could we not continue this discussion in private? If the Mastercaller is permitted to disrupt this hearing because of his misguided emotional attachment to this girl-"

Master Malcourt snapped his arm up before Captain Rolf had taken another step. His palm was flattened and facing towards the Guardscaptain so quickly that Rolf's righteous indignation faltered.

Phoenix knew that such a gesture from a Caller was considered a very serious sign of aggression. At best it was a promise of violence. At worst...

Captain Rolf, understanding the message as Phoenix did, did not move. The entire room held its breath.

Master Malcourt turned his head, slowly, to face Speaker Thomas. "What did the Head Speaker have to say about this arrangement?"

Speaker Thomas looked deflated. "Th' Head Speaker?"

"Yes," Malcourt said. "What did he have to say about it?"

"'Bout wha', exactly?" Speaker Thomas hedged.

"The arrangement." Malcourt's expression became exasperated. "The *entire* arrangement. What. Did. He. Have. To. Say." When Speaker Thomas hesitated, Master Malcourt continued. "I presume you contacted the Proper about the arrangement, as is the law? And the fact that there was a Bloodless thief leeching off the tribute you had to send? Or the fact that she had run away before paying back what was owed? Or the fact that she was even there in the first place, so that you could properly calculate an agreed-upon debt?... Or was the debt the arrangement fee you decided to charge Phoenix for your unwanted service?"

An owl screamed a challenge from the rafters. Phoenix jerked her head upwards as Pip stretched out her massive wings, her long nails biting into the wood to keep her stationary as she flapped repeatedly. Angry. Master Malcourt had to be beyond angry for Pip to have such a display of temper.

"We launched a search party," the Speaker began, answering Master Malcourt evasively. "The Head Speaker said that she had not come that way..."

King Benedict frowned. "If you launched no formal complaint, I fail to see what it is that you hope to accomplish here."

"To warn you!... Your Majesty," the Speaker added, correcting his tone.

"Your Majesty," Captain Rolf spoke up, his eyes still on Master Malcourt's outstretched hand.

King Benedict inclined his head. "Tolen," he said, reminding the Mastercaller mildly of his bad manners.

Master Malcourt lowered his arm.

"Your Majesty," Captain Rolf repeated, "the burden that the child placed upon the Speaker and his farm was his alone - not that of the Head Speaker. I'm sure that he sent his full dues to the Proper," Rolf looked to Thomas for confirmation and the Speaker nodded, "so Speaker Thomas felt no need to trouble the Proper with a problem that he had thought he had contained. He was doing the girl a favour and she used it to ruin his reputation and word as a Speaker."

King Benedict regarded Captain Rolf for a long moment. Long enough that the Guardscaptain shifted under the weight of his stare. "Is that so?" he asked in a mild tone.

"And did this favour involve any compensation in any form?" Malcourt asked Speaker Thomas.

Thomas's face turned red. "Only what it was that the girl owed!"

"And you still realize that, as a mere Speaker, you are unable to enter such an arrangement without the consent of the Head Speaker if it falls within his jurisdiction?"

"She is Bloodless," Speaker Thomas protested, his face darkening a shade. "She has no one to vouch for her."

Master Malcourt sliced his hand through the air, the force of the gesture making the Speaker jump back. He shot Malcourt a wary look.

"I brought Phoenix to live at Castle Angor. And not only did she do me the favour of saving my life - but in doing so she also saved the life of the King." Master Malcourt spoke quietly and calmly, effortlessly taking control of the conversation. "Since then she has built a home for herself here - not because of her title, but because of who she is as a person. She is also… the closest thing to a daughter that I have ever had. So, yes, there is someone to vouch for her - and that someone is me. As long as I am alive, she will always have a place to call home if she so chooses."

Phoenix couldn't stop the sudden tears that streamed down her face. It was as if a floodgate had opened up inside of her. For so long she had felt as though she were on the outside looking in, perched on the cusp of something that everyone took for granted. Now, for the first time, she was welcomed and wanted exactly for who she was.

It was as if a weight had been lifted. Phoenix pressed her chest, feeling fragile, trying to contain the growing sob that was threatening to break her open with its release.

Phoenix was barely aware of Malcourt's arms around her, holding her tightly while she fought to get control of herself.

"Sorry to spring that on you in such a public setting," he apologized against her mass of curls. "Am I in trouble?"

Phoenix laughed, the sound hitching in her throat. She wrapped her arms around Malcourt and squeezed him hard enough to make him grunt. "Absolutely," she hiccupped.

Captain Rolf scowled and Speaker Thomas's face turned a bright red. "Well," he stammered, trying to find a way around that development, "tha's now. Back then, however..." Malcourt looked at the Speaker with a stony expression and he faltered. "I mean... tha' is t' say... Surely Your Majesty can see m' predicament?"

King Benedict frowned. He looked strangely foreboding, Phoenix thought, for someone who was always so pleasant. "All I can see," he told the man, "is that you needlessly persecuted a helpless girl for your own gain. You purposely let herself get into debt - not that I'm conceding that she owes you anything, mind you, having seen her disposition for hard work, but for the sake of argument - when you knew that she had no possible manner in which to pay you back; you purposely exploited her in order to further yourself. That is what I see."

His words had a final ring to them. Speaker Thomas's face drained of all color. He opened his mouth but no sound came out. He looked wildly around the room and then at Phoenix.

Phoenix, remembering how nasty he had been to her back at Avondale, gave him her sweetest smile.

"Furthermore," the King continued, "your moral shortcomings aside - you broke the law. *My* law."

Speaker Thomas paled visibly.

"However, having said that," the King said musingly. A strange smile spread across his face and he all but grinned as he looked at Master Malcourt. "Hilarious, isn't it?" the King asked the man.

"Absolutely," Master Malcourt confirmed in a dry tone. Phoenix, who was completely lost, looked between the two men with a sense of confusion.

"Having said that," King Benedict began again, "your deplorable behaviour is what brought Phoenix to us in the first place - and because of that I am able to sit before you now at this very moment." The King frowned and tapped his lips as he watched the man. "So whatever will we do with you?"

Speaker Thomas was shifting uncomfortably as he stood in the middle of the floor.

Phoenix could see Captain Rolf standing at attention out of the corner of her eye, but her attention was completely wrapped up in the Speaker.

"Flogging?" Master Malcourt asked mildly. "He did break the law after all."

"Hm," King Benedict said, as if giving the notion some serious thought. "It gets so messy after the first fifty lashes." He made a face of disgust, and Phoenix thought the Speaker was going to faint on the spot. "Banishment? Obviously no one who breaks the law truly wishes to live in my kingdom..."

Malcourt inclined his head to show that the King's logic made sense. "Hefty fines, perhaps?" he asked. "To pay back what is owed to the stead - what he claims Phoenix owes - in order to show gratitude that Your Majesty was able to keep his life."

Speaker Thomas swallowed nervously. "I have no way in which to pay..."

Master Malcourt tilted his head at the man. "Where have I heard that before?"

"Perhaps a joust!" the King said excitedly. "We haven't had

a good jousting in a while! Especially not with a commoner. They usually have to be carried out of the field, you know."

Speaker Thomas looked sick, and Phoenix felt a strange sense of pity for him. It would have been cruel if it was happening to anyone else.

"Cast him out," Phoenix murmured, echoing the suggestion that had once been thrown at her.

King Benedict tilted his head so that he could hear her better. "What was that my dear?"

"Send him home, your Majesty... Please."

King Benedict looked at her kindly. His voice was serious and soft when he spoke. "Nothing more, Phoenix?" he asked. His eyes were soft as they regarded her. "You are well within your rights to demand more. It is almost improper to do otherwise, you know, and now that you have a name to uphold..." The King tilted his head towards Master Malcourt.

Master Malcourt just chuckled. "I've never really been a stickler for what's considered to be 'proper'..."

Phoenix felt a slow smile creep across her face. "May I be improper, Master?" she asked, almost pertly.

King Benedict burst out laughing, but Malcourt only smiled with delight. "You certainly may, Apprentice Phoenix. His fate is in your hands."

Phoenix turned her full attention to Speaker Thomas. "You will leave," she told him softly, with a small note of authority. "You will leave this room, and you will leave this castle, and you will never return. Seeing you, here, is an affront to me. You are no longer welcome in my home. Stay in your quarters tonight, away from the celebrations, and leave at tomorrow's first light.

"Not only that, but once you do return home, you are to file the necessary documents with the Head Speaker at Avondale

Proper so that he may decide on your consequences. You may be a Speaker, but you are not above the King's law!"

King Benedict smiled at her. "You were indeed right about her, Tolen."

Malcourt gave a little smile. "I know," he said, simply. And Phoenix felt for a moment that a conversation between them had already taken place.

Speaker Thomas's expression was bleak, but he acknowledged his task with a stiff bow to Phoenix. "Anything else... m' Lady?"

Phoenix was unprepared for the title, but for once she didn't correct it. "Yes," she said simply, before he turned away. They all looked at her expectantly, but their curiosity didn't weaken her resolve any. "Should another situation ever arise like that of mine; that someone is 'stealing' from you as I was - that they are a burden - I want it reported directly to Castle Angor and to me." Malcourt looked at her with interest, but Phoenix continued to stare down the Speaker where he stood. "I never want to hear of you using anyone else in the way that you did me. Is that understood?"

Phoenix felt a certain bravado as she commanded the future conduct of her former Speaker. All of the resentment that she held of his previous treatment towards her was bubbling to the surface, and she knew it was time to get rid of it once and for all.

Speaker Thomas lowered his eyes and bowed again. "Yes," he muttered.

Seeing that Phoenix was done, King Benedict waved his hand. "That will be all, then. Captain Rolf, escort our guest back to his chambers. I'm tired of looking at him. Afterwards... report back to me. You and I need to have a conversation."

The Guardscaptain, his expression unreadable, bowed to

King Benedict before grabbing the Speaker by the elbow - much as he had done to Phoenix earlier - and steering him from the room. Angrily, instead of knocking for one of the guards to assist him, he kicked open the set of double doors and marched through the waiting room and back out into the corridor.

Jobe, Phoenix saw, was still sitting on the floor next to Kit. A woman knelt next to him. Kit, for her part, seemed unharmed and was wagging her tail from the woman's attention.

Jobe jumped up at the sight of the Speaker being led away by the Guardscaptain. He shot a confused look at Phoenix before hurrying to catch up with them.

Kit, upon seeing that the doors were opened again, stood up with a whine and trotted over to Phoenix. The dog wagged her tail in greeting and knocked her head against Phoenix's knee. Phoenix dropped to one knee and wrapped her arms around the pup. "You all right, girl?"

"She'll be fine," the woman said, rising. She dusted her hands off and flicked her skirts before entering the room and bowing to the King. "Your Majesty," she said respectfully.

"Healer," King Benedict acknowledged with a nod of his head.

"Sylvia!" Phoenix exclaimed in delight and surprise. It had been months since she had seen the woman. She didn't realize how much she had missed her kind face until then.

Sylvia laughed and embraced Phoenix warmly. "My goodness, child, how you've grown! And Kit, too! I hardly recognized her." The Healer stepped back to examine Phoenix at arm's length. "You look wonderful, dear. Truly wonderful. I think that castle life agrees with you."

Master Malcourt and the King shared a look that made Phoenix blush.

"Well," Sylvia amended, also catching their exchange,

"hopefully most of the time, anyway."

Master Malcourt chuckled and patted Phoenix on the arm. "Most of the time," he said, relenting.

"Well, now," King Benedict said. He stood and stretched his arms wide."I think that that's enough sitting in the stuffy room for one evening! I mean, it is my birthing day after all."

"Of course, my King," Master Malcourt agreed.

"Very good." He took the few steps down from the dais and patted Kit soundly on the head. "I think it's high time we move to another room and sit down!"

He was being comical, and Phoenix couldn't help but laugh at his demeanour. He grinned at her from beneath his bushy eyebrows and extended his arm to her. "My Lady Phoenix. How stunning you look in your new gown. You do it justice. What excellent taste the person who commissioned it must have... whoever they might be." He gave her a boyish grin. "Would you do this old man a favour and keep him company while he shuffles the halls? I would be in your debt - again."

Phoenix smiled shyly and took the King's offered arm. "It would be my pleasure, Your Majesty."

The King patted her hand affectionately and led the way from the chambers. Master Malcourt offered Sylvia his arm as well, and, when the Healer accepted with a smile, the two followed behind the Phoenix and the King.

CHAPTER 22

The celebrations threatened to split open the brightly lit room. King Benedict watched with a mild smile playing on his lips as he puttered around the room, greeting various guests and making a point to thank the performers. A silent Master Malcourt trailed behind him; an imposing presence in the room of gaily colored outfits. He scowled when someone came too close to the King, his expression often severe enough to halt the offender mid-step, but Phoenix could tell that it was for show. His expression was unmoving except for his eyes which constantly scanned the area for threats, his gaze turning distant intermittently while he conversed with the gargoyles.

"There you are," Rae declared, weaving her way through the crowd in order to get to Phoenix. "What happened? Are you all right?" Her light brown eyes assessed Phoenix, her lips pressing together into a scowl that seemed foreign on her face.

Phoenix gave her friend a smile and nodded. "Everything is fine."

Rae weighed Phoenix's response for several heartbeats before smiling in return. "Good! Your Trader friend was asking after you. He waited with me."

"Are you sure that he was waiting for me?" Phoenix asked, feeling some small satisfaction when the girl gaped.

A lively tune picked up. Rae straightened as people began to sway with the music, but the dance floor remained empty. "Why doesn't anyone want to dance?" She sounded disappointed.

"You could always see if Trader Alexandri is interested," Elise said slyly, coming to stand next to them.

Rae blushed furiously and swatted Elise's arm. "Shh!" she hissed as Elise grinned.

Rae huffed and Elise slid her attention towards Phoenix. "All right, Phoenix?" Phoenix nodded and she tossed her head. "Good! Imagine the nerve of that man - accusing an Apprentice Caller of being a thief! What an ignorant-."

"Uh-oh," Rae said, looking off into the distance. Phoenix stood on her tiptoes to see Brianna, with Jenny and Alan in tow, barrelling her way towards them. "Someone must have found the present we left in her bed…"

Phoenix gaped at her friends. "You didn't!"

They nodded. The slop bucket had found its new home, and from the look on Brianna's face the girl was not impressed with its new location.

Sophie appeared before Brianna reached them. "We need to move," she informed them. "Now."

Phoenix groaned and closed her eyes. Dealing with Brianna was the last thing that she wanted to do today.

Trouble? Rorin asked her. The gargoyle leaned down to watch the dark-haired girl with interest, the tip of his chin barely visible in the light. *She doesn't seem too dangerous.*

"She's not dangerous," Phoenix replied, her voice carrying easily, "just problematic. She's been a thorn in my side ever since I arrived." Her friends gaped at her, and Phoenix straightened her shoulders against their incredulous looks. "And, honestly, I'm tired of her bullying me. It won't work anymore. I'm not going anywhere."

Phoenix felt the truth of her final statement resonate within her.

Elise blinked as a slow smile slid across her face, and Rae looked equal parts delighted and impressed. Neither had the chance to say anything, however, as Brianna descended upon them a scant instant later.

"Well now," Jenny said haughtily, appraising Phoenix's clothing with a critical eye. "Whose chambers did you have to visit in order to get those?"

Brianna smirked. "We all know she stole them." Her eyes raked Phoenix up and down. "There's no way she would be able to fetch such a price."

Alan and Jenny laughed at Brianna's cleverness. The boy gave Brianna an adoring look, and Phoenix was reminded of Millie and Jobe from Avondale. It made angry, but not enough to explode in the way that they wanted.

"Unlike you," Phoenix said distinctly, with what she hoped was quiet dignity, "I do not have to throw myself at every passing noble to get whatever it is that I want." Her current run-in with Speaker Thomas was unfortunate, but it had afforded her the opportunity to secure herself a place in Angor of her own accord.

Brianna's face darkened but Phoenix continued. "Since I arrived I've had to endure your constant spite towards me. You feel threatened by me because I am different, and that is unfortunate, but I no longer care. You are a child and a bully, and you have no place here in Castle Angor. You are a guest. Perhaps you are even an honoured one - you certainly have rank - but you are only a guest all the same. I, on the other hand, live here. This is my home, and you have no say in what I do while I am here - Blood or no Blood.

"Furthermore, I will never serve you. I am out of your reach, and I will do everything in my Power," she emphasized the word, holding Brianna's gaze, "to ensure that my friends are as well."

A long silence stretched between them. Jenny, and Alan gaped at her, their mouths hanging open and their eyes wide. Rae, Elise, and Sophie looked surprised, but there was no mistaking the deep satisfaction in their expressions. Brianna, as angry red splotches grew on her pale cheeks, opened and closed her mouth a few times to say something in response, but no sound came out.

They locked eyes, staring at each other silently until Phoenix could see the shift in Brianna's gaze. The exact moment that the girl realized that Phoenix wasn't going to back down.

"There you are," a deep voice interrupted, breaking into their standoff. Phoenix felt a delightful tingle in her spine at the sound of it, causing her body to go hot and cold all at once. Prince Hallan strode towards them, cutting through the crowd easily as people parted to bow or curtsy to him.

"My Prince," Brianna said sweetly. Her voice was honeyed even as she cut a glare at Phoenix. "I did not see you earlier."

Prince Hallan's brow furrowed as he inclined his head. "Lady... Brianna," he greeted her, momentarily forgetting her name. He nodded to the others before turning his full attention to Phoenix. "My dear Lady Phoenix," he greeted her, bowing to her respectfully. "I've been looking for you endlessly, but the anticipation did not disappoint. May I say how lovely you look this evening?"

Phoenix gave an awkward curtsy. "T-thank you, Your Highness. You look lovely as well." The last part tumbled out of her mouth before she realized what she was saying, and Phoenix's cheeks flamed with embarrassment. She could hear Rae cough beside her.

Prince Hallan laughed and smiled at her. "I'm delighted that you think so, Phoenix." He reached a hand towards her, but a warning snarl from Kit caused him to jerk it back quickly. "Ah, yes," he said, somewhat disapprovingly, "it seems that your little friend still hasn't taken to me."

"Kit!" Phoenix hissed, tapping her lightly on her head. "Stop that! I'm so sorry, Your Highness. She's not usually like this."

Prince Hallan shrugged off his irritation. "She has good reason to look out for one such as you, my dear."

He smiled, and Brianna glared at her with such an open hatred that Phoenix wondered if it could be seen from across the room.

"Do you think it would be possible, maybe, to get her to just watch you from a distance? I was hoping to have a talk with you privately. I promise I won't keep you long - or steal you away, for that matter. Unless you let me, of course."

The Prince's eyes were a piercing emerald as he winked at her. A small warmth crept along her spine, and Phoenix wondered what it was about the man that drew her to him so.

Brianna's expression became murderous. She moved her eyes to see Rae smirking at her, and, surprisingly, her large eyes filled with tears. She turned around hurriedly and plunged into the crowd to get away from them as quickly as she could. Jenny followed looking confused, and Alan looked sullen as he stomped along behind them.

"I've got to, um, go check on that thing," Rae said, vaguely. "Elise, can you help me to check on it? Sophie, you too?"

Elise blinked and Sophie jabbed her quickly in the ribs. "Yeah," she said. "No problem."

The two linked arms with Elise and dragged her off across

the room. Elise glanced back at Phoenix with confusion, but she allowed the girls to drag her away.

"Now then," the Prince said, offering her his arm. "Are you thirsty? I'm positively parched myself." Prince Hallan led her grandly to a refreshment station across the room. Everyone stopped to bow as he walked past, many of the Ladies paused to look at Phoenix appraisingly and Phoenix wondered silently if he was purposely taking the most indirect route possible.

"So tell me," Prince Hallan said, pouring her a cup of wine and handing it to her despite her objections. "How are you enjoying your first royal ball? You certainly look the part. All of the women here are seething inside with jealousy over you, I can tell." He smiled at her handsomely and poured himself some wine.

Phoenix felt giddy as she sipped from her glass. "People always stare at me, Your Highness. I don't think that it has much to do with the clothes I'm wearing - I think it's just a distrust for Callers in general. No one seems to ever want them around." She surprised herself with her candor, and she hid her embarrassment by taking a large mouthful of her drink.

Prince Hallan was studying her over the rim of his glass. "You know, Phoenix," he said somewhat sadly, "I do believe that you're right."

They walked slowly as they talked. A pungent, bitter aroma wafted towards them, clearing Phoenix's head momentarily, but it faded quickly as she followed the Prince.

They stopped before one of the small side hearths that helped to heat the large room, and Prince Hallan leaned against the stonework with a soft sigh.

He set his glass on the high mantle and silently offered to do the same for hers. She accepted with a nod.

"Sometimes I miss my homeland," he admitted in a murmur, and Phoenix found herself leaning in in order to hear him properly "I don't talk about it much... I don't talk to anyone much, if I'm being honest. I feel as though there's no one here that I can really confide in; no one here that I can trust." A private thought tugged at his expression, making it unreadable. "I will always be seen as an outsider here. My friends are only interested in what I am - not how I am." He looked at her for a time, silently, his expression soft.

Phoenix couldn't help but notice how easily the light of the fire played off of his body, the shadows accenting the broad shape of his shoulders. The Prince caught her eye, and she knew that he had seen her watching him. She quickly averted her gaze.

"You must know what I mean, Phoenix," he probed. "I feel like we're the same, you and I. I feel like we understand what the other is going through."

The Prince moved closer, and Phoenix felt a whisper of his fingers against the hem of her sleeve. "It's a shame that people here are so closed-minded. They get so caught up in their preconceived ideas... but maybe it's finally worked to my advantage. Maybe it's a blessing in disguise, that they are unable to see a truly beautiful thing when it's right in front of them."

Prince Hallan reached out to tuck a thick curl behind her ear, his fingers trembling slightly with the movement, and Phoenix stared up in surprise, finding it hard to catch her breath. His face was much closer than she'd realized. She was acutely aware of the brush of his fingertips against her hair, and the current that shot through her scalp with a jolt of excitement.

"You know," he continued softly, "Callers are highly revered where I come from, Phoenix. I would love to take you there so that you may experience it sometime..."

Phoenix opened her mouth to respond, but the sound died

before it reached her lips. Prince Hallan chuckled and extended a hand to her. "We can discuss it at another time. But for now… Dance with me, Phoenix."

Phoenix looked at his expectant hand and cleared her throat. "I'm not much of a dancer…"

The Prince's hand remained outstretched, insistent, as a half-smile played across his lips as he refused to back down. "I won't let you fall."

Blushing, Phoenix accepted his invitation and gasped as he twirled her onto the dance floor. She was conscious of the feeling of his body against hers, the heat of his touch and the strength of his arms around her. "You're a much better dancer than you give yourself credit for," he murmured.

Phoenix felt the room whirl around her. "T-thank you." She tried to remain composed, but she was sure her face gave away her relief when he opted for the simpler steps of the dance routine.

The Prince gave a low laugh and led her into another spin, catching her when she became dizzy. "I could do this all night," he confided. "But, unfortunately, duty calls."

Phoenix found it hard to focus. A mental chuckle invaded her mind and her attention snapped up to the rafters. "You be quiet," she muttered at Rorin.

"Pardon?" Prince Hallan asked mildly.

"Nothing, Your Highness."

The music swelled into a crescendo, and Phoenix mindlessly kept time with the Prince's movements, matching his steps as he led her around the room.

Everyone ready your positions.

Phoenix faltered, nearly tripping as the dance continued around her. Prince Hallan caught her easily. "Is something wrong?"

Phoenix shook her head, looking around the room slowly. "I think we have to move."

Price Hallan blinked. "What do you mean?"

"People are taking their positions."

Prince Hallan pulled her closer. Grasping her wrists, he peered down at her. "What do you mean, *positions*?" His emerald eyes were bright as he scanned her face.

The music dropped into silence and a hush fell over the room. Phoenix craned her head to see King Benedict standing on the dais. His head held high, he closed the distance to his throne easily. The ornate chair was almost a twin of the one in his meeting chambers. The only difference was that the crescent moon was replaced by a large pale stone that was recessed into the top of the high chair back. The stone swirled with different shades of blue that looked as though they were moving with each other. It hung like a full moon over the Angorian landscape which was carved into the polished wood.

The room held its breath, waiting, as the King sat on the cushioned seat. Phoenix stood frozen as a ripple of power emanated from the throne. In response, the orb glowed a brilliant blue. It grew brighter until the light could no longer be contained, and it shot up from the stone and through the glass dome that stretched over the high ceiling of the dais.

The beacon of light illuminated the dark sky, and Phoenix *felt* the Land sigh in relief as King Benedict's strength reiterated his hold on Angoria.

The castle cheered.

"My friends!" his voice boomed, augmented easily with help from Master Malcourt's Power. "It is time for the entertainment!"

We are almost in place.

Prince Hallan dropped Phoenix's hands. "Are you a Future-caller as well?" he joked, eyes dancing merrily.

What's going on? Rorin's voice flowed easily through the din, pooling in Phoenix's head.

"I don't know," Phoenix confessed.

Prince Hallan, misunderstanding her meaning, gave her a wink. "We'll figure it out eventually." He turned her slightly so that she was facing the King. "Find me after your performance," he commanded softly, his breath caressing the shell of her ear. One of his hands pressed to the small of her back while the other rested on her waist. She nodded, blushing, and Prince Hallan propelled her forward with a parting chuckle.

Phoenix walked woodenly to where Camden waited, ignoring the incredulous look he shot her.

Master Malcourt took charge of the room, his voice projecting easily as he introduced their act.

You humans always did love your pageantry. Rorin's tone was amused as it landed gently in her head. *Must everything be so dramatic?*

Phoenix shot a look above her, uncertain where he was perched, but counted on her roaming gaze to rake across him eventually. A huff of laughter was his only response, and she couldn't help the grin that spread across her face.

"Stop fidgeting," Camden hissed at her out of the corner of his mouth. He was doing his best to look relaxed in his new embroidered Caller's outfit, but the stormy grey of his eyes gave away the tension that lined his body.

Front and centre stood Camden's uncle, Lord Nelson. She recognized him as the man who had been sitting with Camden during last night's meal. His arms were crossed over his chest as he glared at the three Callers. His thick fingers drummed on his upper arm as he waited, undoubtedly wanting to get back to the drink and revelry. Her attention narrowed on his brazen show of irritation. Other than his son, who else had he spoken with tonight?

Lord Nelson met Phoenix's gaze, his eyes hard. Phoenix held his stare past the point of comfort, and his lip twisted into a sneer in response.

Fine. If he was waiting for her to back down, then she was happy to disappoint. She looked through him, her face a mask of boredom as she flicked her eyes away dismissively. She saw him redden out of the corner of her eye, but ignored it as Camden nudged her forward.

Malcourt had finished his speech and stepped back, allowing the two to come forward to take their places.

Camden stopped where their Master had stood, but Phoenix continued forward, slipping momentarily in a puddle of something slick before catching herself. Her face turned red as she strode across the length of the dance floor to stand at the opposite end of the room.

A feeling of unease settled over her. She glanced around, looking for what had prompted it, but could see nothing out of place.

Above her, suspended single-file on crisscrossed threads, colored glass vials hung from silver strands. They swayed softly, resting at different lengths as if a path of stars had spilled over the dance floor.

The only sound in the room was Phoenix's even footsteps on the wooden floorboards. When she stopped, the silence hung around her, expectantly, like a held breath as she turned back around to face Camden.

Her position was marked by the absence of the hanging glass. Even the light from the roaring hearths shied away, letting the shadows deepen as they twined around her skirts. Phoenix stood motionless, her muscles clenched to keep her body still as she felt everyone's eyes on her. Their curiosity bored into her bowed head from every angle as the room - the very kingdom - waited.

She sent a thought to the sleeping pool within her. A gentle nudge had the Power whispering through her veins, waking her senses as it heated her core. Phoenix reached out to it, beckoning it, and it stirred in response to her invitation.

Someone tittered behind her. Another to her left echoed the noise, and Phoenix lifted her head in their direction, reveling in the calm that flowed through her instead of the embarrassment she was used to feeling. If they thought that Callers were amusing, then she would certainly give them something to laugh about. Even the assassin would think twice before they were done.

"Showtime," she murmured to herself.

The word was an unleashing. She *felt* her Power reach out, assessing the flames within the room and tallying their strength. Starting at the dais, where they were concentrated, the candles began to wink out one-by-one. Slowly the room began to darken. Imperceptibly at first, then as a wave of midnight that crashed across the room, cresting over Phoenix and the massive harth that remained lit behind her. It roared a protest, rallying brightly in an attempt to fight, then extinguished with such a loud huff that those next to it startled with loud oaths.

The room was plunged into darkness. Not even the faintest whisper of a moving gown could be heard.

Phoenix *felt* Malcourt's approval tap against her skull. *Wonderfully done*, he praised her.

A slow smile slid across her face at her captive audience. Extending her hand, unseen in the darkness, Phoenix gestured to the glowing coal in the hearth. "Dance," she murmured invitingly.

There was a soft pop in response. A flake of the ember detached and, with a whispered surge from Camden that pulled at her senses, rose hauntingly into the air. It floated unerringly towards Phoenix and landed on one of the small mirrors on her dress, an ember living in the reflection of its spark. Phoenix controlled its slow burn on instinct as her attention settled on the embers in its wake.

Like a procession of tiny firebugs, each glowing flake settled on her skirts like a faceted jewel, pulsing with life.

The embers continued to tumble from the hearth, drifting past Phoenix, rotating in a swirling vortex, higher and higher, until they reached the hanging vials.

The first sparks touched the woven silver thread, their pinpoints of light transferring to the spun metal, then sliding down it to the wick-topped colored glass.

The room was full of falling stars. They spiralled out from where Phoenix stood, a sparkling sun in a darkened sky, slowing building a moving path of light that led to the King himself.

A murmur of appreciation swelled in the crowd. Heads turned as the dais came to life. King Benedict, Master Malcourt, Prince Hallan, and several other officials were basked in the rainbow glow as the colors blended and merged to create new hues that swayed gently with the breeze.

Phoenix let her embers die out, concentrating solely on the hanging lights and making sure that they stayed lit. She used the dim light to her advantage and wiped her palms in her skirts. Now was not the time to be nervous.

Ready? Malcourt's voice was calm and cool. If he had any doubts, he hid them easily.

Camden's response was just as cool, leaving no room for Phoenix's doubts. *Of course.*

There was a pause. Phoenix felt as though it stretched for an eternity, even if it only lasted over three heartbeats. *Phoenix?*

In response, the flames dimmed, and each light shrank to the point of a pinprick.

A breeze manifested from the still air. It snaked around the room, gathering strength as it bounced against the walls and nipped at the onlookers, raising cries of dismay as those affected hurriedly straightened their outfits.

Phoenix bit back a grin when she saw Lord Nelson cut a glare in Camden's direction as he adjusted his tunic.

That's enough, Camden, Master Malcourt's voice was not without humor while chiding him, and Phoenix was certain she could hear a poorly-disguised mental laugh from Rorin.

Camden's only response was to use his Power to pull at Phoenix's long skirts with enough force that she slid easily to the centre of the room. Stunned silence surrounded them. Camden inclined his head and, with a whispered thought, floated the wooden performance rings to their starting positions.

As one whizzed past her head, Phoenix detected the same bitter scent that had grabbed her attention when she first started dancing with the Prince.

The Prince.

Phoenix scanned the crowd, her breath stalling when she caught sight of him. He stood at the forefront of the dais, scanning the crowd as Master Malcourt helped King Benedict back to his throne. Prince Hallan's eyes were not on her as she was hoping, but focused instead on the twinkling lights above her.

You're drooling, Rorin's dry voice slid into her thoughts.

Phoenix snapped her attention up to the rafters. She made a show of fixing her hair in order to disguise a vulgar gesture that she directed at the gargoyle. She grinned when his mental laughter floated down to her.

Camden stood stiffly as he watched her, and Phoenix realized that he had been quietly waiting for her to continue. Conscious of everyone's eyes on her, Phoenix shook off her distractions and gave Camden a smile to signal that she was ready. She was relieved when he smiled back in response, and she was struck for a moment on how much his face softened when he smiled.

The reflection was short-lived as a moment later a wooden ring hurtled towards her head without warning.

Easily, the two slipped into their routine, passing their Power back and forth as if they had been training together for years. Camden's wind easily fanned Phoenix's flames, teasing them so that they burned brighter before he eventually smothered them. In response, Phoenix pitched her fire so that it travelled between the moving rings, flaring as it jumped from ball to ring, sometimes barely clearing Camden's head or her arm in the process.

The crowd gasped or murmured appreciatively. It was all for show. Between Camden's air buffer and Phoenix's immunity, there was no danger of either of them getting burned. They didn't feel the need to share that with the audience.

The routine escalated. Camden floated additional projectiles from where he had nestled them in their carrying cases. Hidden cases spread around the room opened seemingly of their own accord. Gasps in the crowd punctuated the arrival of the new rings as they flew past their unsuspecting heads.

Phoenix raised a brow at Camden and he smirked. He planted his feet apart and raised his arms, bringing the projectiles towards him.

"Dramatic, much?" she muttered under her breath, attempting to *call* to him across the floor.

Camden flashed her a grin. *You love it.*

Phoenix couldn't help but grin in response. His pale eyes flashed silver, his expression lighter than she had seen it in many moons. Could it be? Camden was actually having fun.

Her reflection was cut short as three wooden rings flew towards her, signaling the shift into the next phase of the routine.

This time Phoenix was going to keep the targets burning. She flicked her wrists and scattered them mid-air like a flock of birds. Each one skimmed past her, brushing against her outstretched hands, striking against her fingertips or an errant swish of her skirts, igniting them before they landed on the cold stone floor.

A murmur of apprehension went through the crowd as the wood continued to burn. Phoenix felt a thrill go through her at their response as the mood shifted around her. She could feel their undivided attention.

Wooden projectiles shot at her from different angles and Phoenix set them all ablaze with a single word. She didn't wait for them to get close enough to touch her. This time she used the trick that she had learned that morning, and sent the flame jumping from one projectile to the next.

Once they had caught, she withdrew her attention from the rings, removing her connection to the pulse of the flames. There was a brief sputter of protest before the fires resumed burning on their own.

Additional rings rolled across the floor. Camden's eyes followed the moving pieces as they touched off the individual fires, pausing just long enough to share the heat before continuing to their final positions. When he finished, a ring of fire stretched around the pair and surrounded them in an unbreakable blaze.

Phoenix turned her concentration inwards. She fed the small pool of heat inside of her, stoking it gently until it thrummed in her ears.

A sharp *pop* behind her caught her attention. Her concentration faltered. Phoenix glanced behind her to see that the fire had somehow spread outside of the closed ring and in a line across the smooth stone floor. She tried to extinguish it but found that she had no control over it. The fire burned differently than the rest.

Careful, Master Malcourt warned her. *Reign it back if you can't control it all at once.*

Phoenix frowned. She didn't realize that she had even created it.

Unable to snuff it out, she openly glared at the offshoot until the flames withered and died.

Remind me not to do anything to earn that look, Rorin's amused voice slid into her head.

Phoenix snorted and cast a look around the room. He was still hidden, something that continued to surprise her because of how close he sounded.

Feeling self-conscious, Phoenix brought her attention back to the floor. Almost every eye in the room was trained on her. Instead of shrinking away, Phoenix straightened her spine instead. Callers were celebrated in Prince Hallan's homeland. Maybe Angoria would start to follow suit.

Prince Hallan.

Phoenix located him and felt deflated that she didn't have his attention. His head was tilted upwards, his eyes fixated on the colored globes that hung from the ceiling.

She followed his gaze and noted that the globes had started swaying in the breeze. Camden would have to decrease the strength of his Power if he didn't want to break the decorations.

The thrum of her Power heated her veins. Her focus ring began to vibrate on a different frequency, gearing up to dissipate her Power's build-up, and Phoenix soothed it with a thought so that it didn't interrupt her.

"Rise," she said, releasing her Power.

Balls of flame immediately rose from the burning ring. The flaming globes rose like heated lanterns into the air. They were small, but plentiful enough that Phoenix could feel the temperature rising around her as they floated towards the rafters.

Try not to singe my wings, Rorin told her. *I'd like them to stay intact.*

"Baby," Phoenix muttered, while simultaneously creating more of the small globes to join the first ones and create a wall of heat. She withdrew her control so that Camden could propel them around the room.

The glass hanging above them clinked. The sound went through her and Phoenix jerked her head towards it.

The colored glass was swinging back and forth on the end of the silver threads. Another breeze snaked through the air, weaving between the globes and the rising fire wisps and tossing them into each other haphazardly.

Camden, slow down, Master Malcourt's voice was a forced calm over the clinking glass.

It's not me, Master. Phoenix felt the muted desperation in his response. *I'm not controlling it.*

Then what-

Master Malcourt's question was cut short by the sound of breaking glass.

Phoenix watched as the hanging globes shattered against each other. A thin liquid spilled out of the containers, pouring down from the ceiling like a bitter-smelling rain as it was thrown from the broken containers. The scent clung to the inside of Phoenix's nose and she opened her mouth to keep from gagging. The smell was familiar. It was a stronger version of what she had noticed while she was dancing with the Prince.

Everything happened too quickly for her to follow. She was conscious of the cries from the audience around her, the movement as the people closest to her ducked or covered their heads from the pieces of shattered glass that tumbled from the ceiling, causing a surge of movement that resembled a wave of bodies that threw themselves backwards.

Phoenix was only dimly aware of the chaos around her. Instead, she could feel where the first flecks of the strange liquid combined with the rising fire globes and the resulting temperature of the meeting. Throughout the room, she could sense the surge of strength in the flames that surrounded them.

The bitter scent clicked in her brain. It was the smell she had first found in the strange locked closest in the depths of Angor.

Accelerant. Someone had filled the vials above them with the rapidly-burning oil, knowing that they would be performing a fire show during the celebrations. They were attempting to kill them all.

She opened her mouth to scream a warning but it was too late. The strength of the liquid hit the flames and the room exploded.

CHAPTER 23

Phoenix fought for control over the blaze. Wildly, she *called* to the flames in an attempt to subdue them, trying to bring their strength to heel.

A bead of sweat perched precariously on the tip of her nose before sliding to the floor. Heat swirled around her, snaking down her throat and into her lungs, causing them to spasm as they rejected the caustic vapours that overpowered the air around her.

Gagging, she became momentarily distracted by the memory of a burning barn. The same smell that clung to her nightmares was now bringing tears to her eyes.

Muffled screaming pulled her attention back to the present. Just in time, she raised a hand to block a fire-surge before it reached her face. The flames were her own, and a bright flash of her focus ring caused them to dissipate before she could blink.

She quickly dashed her fists across her eyes to assess the situation.

The fire was contained. Camden had erected a barrier to keep it from spreading, but a quick mental probe made her realize that in his haste to keep everything enclosed he had somehow blocked their ability to *call* to anyone else. They were unable to warn Master Malcourt and the others about the danger that pooled unseen in the cracks of the floor around the room.

One stray spark and the room would ignite like a tinder box.

Thick smoke swirled in the air between them, the heat becoming unbearable without anywhere for it to escape. It was only a matter of time before the entire dome would fill and they would choke to death.

Are you hurt? Camden's voice was strained, and Phoenix couldn't tell if it was because of the effort in asking or because of the question itself.

"I'm fine." Phoenix minced towards him, skirting around the flames that lashed out at her as she passed. She came close enough to assess him visually. "You?"

I've been better. His voice was light despite the way he gritted his teeth. *Feel free to help out,* he offered, flinching back as the encroaching fire found a sprinkle of the accelerant and flared wildly next to where he'd been standing. *Sooner would be better than later.*

Phoenix rushed forward and managed to stomp out the trail that was spreading to his other side. "I can't control it. The fire isn't mine."

Camden eyes widened, shifting to a dark grey as he assessed their options.

Phoenix was finding the act of speaking difficult. "Can you drop a section of the barrier to let some of it out?"

Camden exhaled slowly before answering. *No. If I try to drop any of it the entire thing will come down.*

They stared at each other grimly. If the barrier came down… If any of it escaped…

Phoenix's mind raced. There had to be a solution.

Camden sank to his knees and Phoenix dove forward to help him to the floor. Exhaustion lined his face as he accepted her help. They kneeled on the floor together, their breathing ragged as they sucked in the air that was the least-tainted from smoke.

The sound of muffled yelling caught Phoenix's attention. Beyond the barrier she could see nobles struggling to run. The mass confusion did little to empty the room and everything to spread the bitter liquid over everyone. Puddles of it splashed with agitation as people ran between doors in an attempt to open them.

The doors were barricaded shut. Everyone was trapped inside.

Phoenix felt panic take control of her body. She was unable to move. The horror of her sleep-terror crashed into her full force, except this time she was living it. The sights and smells assaulted her senses and it was all she could do not to crumple to the floor in defeat.

Phoenix, Camden's voice was calm as he *called* to her. Helplessly she latched onto it, letting it pull her from the chaos. *We need a plan.*

Phoenix shook her head as if to clear it. Flames flared between them and he flinched back, a weak gust of wind attempting to extinguish the heat before it reached his skin.

I can't hold out much longer. Camden's voice sounded strained. *We need a plan before the barrier comes crashing down.*

Phoenix shook her head helplessly. Camden's quick thinking had bought them time, but it was all for naught unless they figured out how to save them all. Without the barrier the fire would spread and kill them all. Unless… unless it didn't…

Phoenix snapped her head up, dragging her gaze along the invisible boundary. Some puddles had been intersected, but maybe it wouldn't matter. Maybe…

It was a long shot. But it was all they had.

Phoenix took a step towards Camden, a plan already forming. "Let it."

Camden's eyes widened in surprise. *What?*

Phoenix *called* to her fire. A small flame came to life in her hand, sputtering as it fought to burn, gasping at the remaining air around them.

Carefully, cautiously, Phoenix set it on the floor. Keeping her connection to it, she urged it towards the barrier, feeding it slowly so that it could fight for space against the established fire. She watched in triumph as it took root and pooled along the perimeter in a thin line.

Camden watched her in disbelief, his breathing rapid. His expression was unreadable as Phoenix knelt on the floor, shuffling closer to him again.

"Let it fall," she croaked around the billowing smoke. She was feeling light-headed. The necessary concentration coupled with the lack of ventilation was taking its toll. "Remove the air."

Camden looked like he was going to object. His eyes flicked to the barrier, then watched as Phoenix's fire met itself next to them. Understanding dawned on his face.

If her barrier held, and if he could extinguish the rogue flames, nothing would spread. Everyone would be safe.

Everyone except for them.

He wouldn't be able to hold a shield in place if he was manipulating the air.

Camden took a shaky step forward and knelt next to her. *Stay still,* he warned her.

Phoenix gave a nod and clenched her trembling muscles. She could *feel* Camden shrinking the barrier around them, feel the heat and smoke press closer against them. She concentrated on her breathing. On keeping it steady. On Master Malcourt, and the King, and Kit, and Rae and her friends. On keeping her Power under control, and strong enough to keep them alive.

Brace yourself, Camden warned her.

They locked eyes and took a deep breath in unison.

Now.

CHAPTER 24

The sound of the barrier shattering filled Phoenix's ears. There was a whoosh as the contained air rushed into the room, the heat and smoke barreling its way into the crowd.

Screaming filled the air around her as panic took hold. The pounding against the doors renewed as the guests attempted to break them down.

Previously-muffled sounds struck Phoenix's senses with full force. Cries and curses rang in her ears. Rorin and Malcourt's questions ricocheted inside her head, each one echoing against the other now that she could finally Hear them.

It was overwhelming, but she refused to be distracted. She refused to let her control slip.

She dedicated her focus to the little ring of fire that she had held in place around them.

The sounds of destruction were swept away by the enraged huff of the inferno as Camden attempted to extinguish it.

Phoenix shut everything out. Steeling her spine, she held fast to her Power. The strength of her flames increased as they absorbed the heat from the rogue blaze, winning the fight against the expanding foreign fire as she and Camden battled it. She waited, counting her heartbeats, until it spread to a finger length from the waiting accelerant, until the heat had mingled so thoroughly that Phoenix couldn't tell where one ended and the next one began. Until the fire was close enough to reach out in an attempt to caress the explosive pool that waited for the heat as silently as death.

With a thought, and a word of release, Phoenix snuffed it all out.

The room was rocked by the resulting explosion as Camden attempted to control the backlash from the disappearing flames. At the last possible second, she *felt* Camden's air shield cling to her like a second skin. Then there was silence.

Her knees crumpled. She slouched where she had fallen, dazed, and made no attempt to pull herself off the hard stone floor. Her eyes closed and she let the sounds of the room wash over her.

Malcourt's voice swelled in her head. The demands of Rorin and the gargoyles, quieter yet more plentiful, filled in the spaces around it and made her temples throb. Phoenix remained motionless and silent, concentrating only on dragging the fresh air into her burning lungs. She started when Camden placed a hand on her shoulder. Phoenix gave it a gentle squeeze before staggering to her feet – just in time to stumble as a whining Kit barreled into her.

Phoenix... Master Malcourt's concern nearly overwhelmed her, and tears sprung to her eyes.

"I'm fine," she gasped, her breath pushing the words from her mind towards the waiting Malcourt and Rorin. She locked eyes with Camden and he gave a quick nod. "We're both fine."

The doors to the ballroom were finally pried open and the guests stampeded into the corridors. New guards fought their way against the tide of bodies to gain access to the room, causing a blockage in front of some of the double doors. Cursing and swearing filled the air again, and Phoenix and Camden exchanged a tired smile in response.

Master Malcourt had barricaded the room for security purposes and now the reinforcements were struggling to secure it.

The dais remained in lockdown. Malcourt stood poised at the front, King Benedict firmly behind him as he blocked the throne with his body. His blue eyes were dark as he scanned for threats.

The room was pandemonium. Guards attempted to push their way into the room against the guests who were trying to escape. Shouted orders fell on deaf ears and only served to add confusion to the room.

Where do you want us? Rorin's voice was tense, and Phoenix could feel the added strain from the gargoyles as they remained hidden amongst the chaos. She could tell he was loathe to reveal himself and his flight, but he would gladly do it if they would be of help.

Remain where you are for now, Master Malcourt's response was just as tense. *Your vantage point is invaluable. We just need your eyes… for now.*

The gargoyle gave a mental snort, but didn't disagree. *Let me know if that changes.*

Phoenix straightened. The chaos in the room wasn't subsiding. Guards were pushing guests back into the room in an attempt to contain everything. Tempers flared closest to the door as heated words were exchanged. Camden's uncle was red-faced as he bellowed up at a guard who towered above him. The guard slammed the butt of his spear against the stone floor and bent down, hissing a response that Phoenix couldn't hear, but she could see Lord Nelson's face drain of color.

Camden tensed and took a step forward before he paused. His eyes turned stormy as he second-guessed his impulse to intervene. Giving his head a shake, he turned his attention to the room instead. "What are they doing?"

Phoenix slid her gaze in the direction he faced. Guards refused to let anyone leave. Their hulking frames crowded the entranceways, forcing everyone to stay in the room.

She frowned. Something wasn't right.

An unseen wave went through the room. Phoenix felt Master Malcourt's Power prod against her as it began pushing the accelerant out of the way and into the corner of the room.

There was a brief break in the wave. A tiny dip to her right caused Phoenix to turn, but she couldn't see what caused it.

Kit swiveled her ears and whined, looking in the same direction.

Something definitely wasn't right.

Another dip tugged at her senses. Phoenix blinked at the sensation. A cloaked man stood across the room in a spot that she would have sworn was empty just an instant before. The hood of his heavy cloak was pulled up - a strange sight in a room of finery - obscuring his features from prying eyes.

There is a man in a cloak to the left of the dais. He is staring at the King. Camden's quiet update rang throughout Phoenix's head as he took a step forward.

He just stepped out of a circle. Rorin responded with midnight softness.

Master Malcourt's voice snapped through her skull. *A protection circle?*

Phoenix barely registered his question before she surged forward, Camden at her side. He attempted to shoulder people out of the way so that they could get through. Phoenix didn't need to Speak to know that they shared the same thought. A protection circle would only be used if someone was trying to hide themselves. And they would only be hiding if they wanted to do something terrible. Panic rose in Phoenix's throat.

The cloaked man seemed unaware that he was visible. He stood unmoving, assessing. Too preoccupied to realize that the edge of his boot had nudged past the confines of the circle drawn with soot and ash.

The people around them weren't moving out of the way quickly enough.

"Go, Kit!" she commanded. The dog was tight at her side, snaking through the crowd next to her as she went. "Go to King Benedict! Go to the King!"

Kit's answering snarl was pure savagery.

The people around them jerked away so quickly that they fell into one another in their haste.

Camden was the first to reach Master Malcourt. Captain Rolf stood on the dais next to him, a flank of guards surrounding him. They stood in line, acting as a barrier in between the crowd and His Majesty.

The hooded man crouched. A moment later he launched himself into the air, and stretched his arm back as far as it could go. He snapped it forward in a terrible show of strength, arm muscles bulging, and Phoenix saw the shine of a blade leave his hand.

"Watch out!" Phoenix cried desperately, knowing she was too far away to be of any help.

An owl screamed in outrage, and Phoenix could see Pip tuck her wings and plummet towards the head of the assassin.

A storm of things happened all at once.

Captain Rolf lurched forward in the same instant that a giant dome of yellow energy curled around the dais in a protective shield. The dagger, with a flash of red light - the same red light that had obliterated Malcourt's protection circle in the clearing all those moons ago - smashed through the shield. It broke it so forcefully that shards of energy shot off in all directions, causing guests to scream and drop to the floor in order to avoid being struck by the deflected Power.

With a sharp snap of his hand, Phoenix saw Camden step forward at the same moment that Captain Rolf reached the King. Camden's Power flickered tiredly before causing the attacking object to change course. The dagger curved upwards so forcefully that it became embedded in a rafter beam.

Captain Rolf, contrary to Phoenix's assumption that he was behind everything, stood in front of King Benedict, acting as a human shield to keep him from harm. He and Master Malcourt exchanged a look, and the ever-standing tension between them melted away as they took up defensive positions around the King.

With Camden to the side, and Kit in place next to King Benedict, Phoenix raced towards her new family to protect the King and to stop Angoria from being plunged into war.

CHAPTER 25

Phoenix slid in front of the guard barrier and turned her back to them in order to survey the crowd.

The walls around the room crumbled in several places where Master Malcourt's energy blast had struck them full force. Several people were sitting on the ground, hands pressed to wounds received from falling rocks, and two of them were lying unconscious with those next to them trying to rouse them.

The assassin was screaming. He clutched his face in an attempt to cover it from Pip's razor-sharp talons. Blood flowed from between his fingers from where the owl had gouged his face. Kit was latched firmly on to the end of his leg and snarling as she tried to pull him down to the ground.

"Guards!" Captain Rolf boomed, not moving from his post where he was protecting the King. "Take that man into custody!"

Several uniform-clad men moved towards him. The first man to reach him grabbed him by the cloak and hauled him roughly back in the direction towards the Captain. Phoenix watched in shock as the second guard, when he reached the two, grabbed the first guard's wrist and, with one fluid motion, brought his gauntlet down and broke the guard's arm. As he fell to the ground, clutching his arm, the attacking guard pivoted so that he was between the assassin and the approaching men.

The guards slid to a halt. Surprise registered on their faces as the painful sound of the protecting guard's sword was unsheathed.

"Now!" he called, his voice carrying easily over the soft moans and weeping of the wounded. He raised his sword high. "Every one! To me!"

There was an answering roar and the sound of sword hilts pounding against shields. The guards folded in on themselves as men wearing identical uniforms crashed into each other. Friend was unable to distinguish foe until they found themselves the victims of an attack.

The guard next to her fell heavily to the ground. He lay there, stunned from a surprise blow to the head, and he stared up at his attacker with glazed eyes.

Phoenix launched herself at the back of the attacker and wrapped her arms around his neck, hooking her leg around his knee to try and pull him backward. He made a choking noise and dropped his weapon. Large hands engulfed her arms and squeezed them so roughly that Phoenix gasped loudly in pain.

"I don't care what he said," the man rasped, twisting her arms painfully, "I'm going to delight in caving in your skull, Caller brat."

He twisted his body roughly and Phoenix flew onto the floor. Her elbow hit the stone with a sharp crack, and she gasped as pain lanced through her arm like white-hot lightning.

A vicious blow made her grunt. The guard's large boot had connected with her ribs, and Phoenix rolled in time to avoid another kick to her side.

Phoenix became stuck against the guard that still lay dazed on the floor. Her attacker's expression turned to satisfaction when he realized her predicament.

He took a slow step forward, deliberately bringing his foot up next to her head. Before he could bring it down, a loud scream made him freeze in terror.

The air around her grew heavy. A slate-grey shaped slammed into the man, and Phoenix winced at the sound of bones snapping. He thrashed a moment before losing consciousness.

Answering roars filled the room, punctuated by the flapping of wings and the sound of countless footsteps as those who could, fled.

The creature turned and crouched down next to her, offering her a four-clawed hand to help her up. Rorin peered down at her anxiously, all but pulling her to her feet when she clutched his talons. "Are you all right?" he asked quickly.

Phoenix surveyed herself with a quick glance, then nodded.

"Thank you," she said gratefully.

They both looked up as a man charged towards them, both weapon and shield were raised for battle and there was nothing but rage written all over his face. When he came into range, Rorin dropped down and whipped his body to the side. His tail lashed out and connected with the man's shins with a sharp crack and he dropped to the floor clutching them and howling. Another man came up behind them and swung a heavy sword towards the gargoyle's head.

"Watch out!" Phoenix cried, trying her best to alert the gargoyle as well as to grab ahold of him to pull him out of the way.

Rorin dodged easily and brought his arm bracers up to protect his face. The sword's edge slid off of the thick metal with a terrible screech that set her teeth on edge. The sword swung free and both gargoyle and human stumbled as they tried quickly to regain their balance before the other.

Phoenix took that opportunity to dart in between them and grab at the man. He regained his footing before she could reach him, and he snapped his arms back quickly in order to try his attack again. With a grunt of effort, Phoenix launched herself at him with the intent to knock him down with her body. Instead, the man pivoted at the last instant and Phoenix was forced to use her toes to push herself backwards to avoid opening her side to his sword.

He brought his arms up again to swing, but, before he could move, Rorin had grabbed his arm and wrenched it to the side. Phoenix darted forward again and grabbed the man's sword in an attempt to disarm him. When that failed she then resorted to other measures.

Phoenix used her anger to channel her Power through her fingers and into his sword. The metal became heated instantly, and it only took a moment before it became too hot to hold. the man yelped and quickly threw it down on the floor as forcefully as he could.

Rorin then twisted the man's arm to spin him around so that he was facing him. A moment later, the gargoyle landed a solid blow to the man's face and he fell unconscious to the floor.

The sounds of fighting and the clash of steel was all around them. Phoenix took a moment to assess their surroundings and so did Rorin. There were very few spectators left in the room. Everyone besides the wounded were engaged in combat, and Phoenix was surprised to note that many of the noblemen remained to fight.

A movement caught her eye and Phoenix turned to see a man attacking a young boy. He was dressed as a Trader, and Phoenix remembered him from the group of boys that had run drills in the courtyard. He was putting up a valiant fight, but he was not large enough to match the man's strength. He was continually forced backwards until, eventually, he tripped on one of the stones that had fallen from the wall. He tried to regain his balance but he could not and, despite his attempts, he fell.

Phoenix knew that she was too far away, but she lurched forwards anyway and ran towards them. the boy covered his face as the man raised his sword for a killing blow. His arms swung downwards heavily, but the sword did not reach the boy.

A terrifying scream caused the man to pause mid-swing, as if his muscles had locked involuntarily. A winged body launched itself through the air and slammed into the man, kicking him to the ground. The body, a female gargoyle, moved to stand over him.

The gargoyle was massive. She stood taller than Rorin, and her muscular form was clothed in thick boiled leather that added enough extra girth that Phoenix was surprised to see that she could still fly. Her skin was a pale lavender, marred in places with darkened smudges of blood and dirt from fighting in the hall. Her tail lashed as she regarded her fallen target.

"Tika?" Rorin asked, coming to stand beside the humans.

"I'm fine," the gargress said haltingly, as if she were unaccustomed to speaking aloud. She grinned, and Phoenix could see a flash of her fangs. "You always get invited to the best parties."

Rorin raised an eyeridge sardonically but made no reply.

Tika turned to look down at the three of them. Her eyes were dark like Rorin's, and when she fixated them on Phoenix, Phoenix was struck by the depth and age that showed in her gaze. She sniffed, evaluating Phoenix's scent, assessing Phoenix a moment before her gaze shifted to the younger gargoyle. *Take the hatchlings somewhere safe, Rorin. Leave this one to me.*

Rorin nodded and looked around to find the best path to

take. The boy, looking uncertain, stepped forward towards Tika. "T-thank you," he said to her, his voice breaking slightly as he spoke. The gargress looked surprised, then she bared her fangs in what Phoenix could only assume was a smile. "You're welcome, child," she said in a friendly fashion.

Phoenix tugged on the boy's sleeve, and the three left as Tika bent over and picked up the attacker by the front of his shirt. She held him as easily as Phoenix would hold a basket of clothes, and she could see the man's face go pale as Tika gave him a smile that was significantly less friendly than the one she had given a moment ago.

Rorin and Phoenix helped the boy get to the safety of the corridor before they began looking around. The dais was empty, and Phoenix could hear that the sounds of fighting had moved to the courtyard.

"Master Malcourt's gone," she told Rorin..

"As is the King," the gargoyle replied. They looked at each other for a long moment before they turned and ran towards the courtyard.

The field was destroyed. Carts were tipped over and various wares had been broken and strewn across the grounds. Phoenix had to hop over a pile of broken glass in order to walk the rest of the way onto the landing of the outside stairs.

"Lizard demon!" a man screamed at Rorin. The man then rushed towards them, but as he passed Phoenix she stuck out her foot to trip him. Rorin caught him as he fell and, with a fluid motion, the gargoyle flipped him over his shoulder and over the railing so that he fell into a pile of horse feed.

"I thought only gargoyles flew," a dry voice said. Rorin smirked as Trader Alexandri bounded up the stairs to join the two of them at the top.

"It's a common misconception," the gargoyle told the boy seriously.

CHAPTER 26

Gargoyles were everywhere. Phoenix had not realized the number of creatures who were in attendance for the birthing celebrations. When they were motionless they blended in so well with the stonework that it was easy to mistake them for statues if you weren't looking for a living creature. Now that they were moving, however, she couldn't help but pause to watch them in awe.

Their movement was so fluid that they appeared to be dancing. They were synchronous with their combat moves – blocking easily to let the other attack – and Phoenix could Hear the silent whispers between them that went unheard by their human opponents. The chill in the air clung to her skin, but she was surprised to see that the Fear was not affecting anyone.

Phoenix and Rorin had left Alexandri in the courtyard. The Trader was organizing his friends into different groups to find and help remove people from the fighting. Satisfied, Phoenix and Rorin turned back into the castle to look for Malcourt and the King.

Phoenix had not Heard from her Master since the fighting started.

The gargoyle was kneeling down to inspect a fallen guardsman. He was dead, Phoenix knew, but Rorin seemed more interested in his uniform as opposed to the health of the man.

"He's one of Prince Hallan's personal guards," Phoenix told him, noting the different uniform. "Well… he was one," she amended. "They came from Kaltor with the Prince."

Rorin peered ahead and growled thoughtfully. "If he was slain here, then the Prince must have come this way – and that means that the King must have been with him."

Phoenix nodded in agreement and assessed the corridor as well, as if she could somehow find something that the gargoyle's long-reaching gaze could not.

"Here," Rorin said, securing the guard's belt knife and handing it to her. "You will need this."

Phoenix nodded again and took the dagger from him. The weight of it was heavy, but it was also comfortable. It was well crafted – the blade was still sharp despite its apparent frequent use – but the thing that caught her attention was the strange emblem worked into the metal of the handle. It was strangely familiar, but she was unable to place it.

Rorin closed his wings to get them out of the way. She could *feel* a foreign tension assaulting her from the waves of Fear that the other gargoyles were sending out.

"We should go," Rorin said, his body moving to act as a shield between her and the fighting. "Their blood runs hot from battle," he said, indicating the humans around them. "The Fear will not work on them – but it may freeze you yet."

Phoenix was only too happy to leave. "Down this way." She pointed in the direction of the Royal Quarters with her dagger. It was more of a statement than a question. Trails of blood and obvious signs of fighting carved a path along the hallway. Rorin nodded grimly and the two continued on.

They moved soundlessly. It was strangely deserted where they were, despite the frenzy of activity in the adjoining areas of the castle. She was so used to the noise being dampened by distance that she yelped when a voice cut through the silence and straight through her skull. Rorin laid a hand on her shoulder and pressed a claw to his lips.

My Lord! The gargoyles are too strong! There are too many of them. What are your orders?

Rorin stopped moving and tilted his head to listen. Phoenix held her breath, hoping that when he responded she would be able to identify the man behind it all.

The silence stretched on. Phoenix and Rorin remained motionless as they strained to Hear the answer.

My Lord? The voice asked again, a hint of desperation in his tone. *My Lor-*

The voice cut off with a sickly sound. Phoenix, for a reason she couldn't identify, got the distinct impression of an invisible sword entering through her ribs and slicing through her body. She gasped involuntarily and clutched at her chest. Next to her, Rorin shuddered and she knew that he had felt the same horror.

"Come on," the gargoyle said, continuing down the hallway. "We have to find the others."

"We should check the King's Chambers," Phoenix said, clearing the revulsion from her throat. "He is the target. That would probably be the first place that the assassin would go."

"It's the best place to start," he agreed.

Blood caked the hallways. Phoenix did her best to avert her eyes when they came to a body, but she always stopped to wait when Rorin stooped to check if they were dead. Eventually, as they continued on, the gargoyle stopped pausing to check for life.

"Help me," a voice implored weakly. Phoenix could see a pair of feet sticking out from behind a stone bench. She hurried over to find Sophie hiding in the corner, her hand pressed to a bloody wound in her side.

"Sophie!" Phoenix said, leaping behind the barrier to get to her friend. "What happened?"

"King Benedict passed by," she said, coughing weakly, her usually vibrant face pale from pain. "A group of men attacked him, but I hit one of them," her voice held some satisfaction as she nodded to a dented frying pan resting next to her on the floor. "I just wasn't fast enough... Camden helped me here. Elise left to find help."

"And Rae?" Phoenix pressed.

Sophie coughed again and gave a half smile. "Where do you think I got the frying pan? We left her in the kitchens. She insisted on making sure everyone got out."

"Phoenix," Rorin urged, crouching down next to them, "we have to hurry."

Phoenix used the dagger to cut a large strip from the hem of her dress. 'Here," she said, handing the material to Sophie. "Use this as a bandage. You need to stop the bleeding."

Sophie smiled weakly and began to wrap the strip around her torso. "Thank you," she whispered.

"Here," Rorin said, taking a pinch of something from a pouch attached to his belt. He poured a small amount of powder into the palm of her hand. "Ground bloodwort. Sprinkle it on the wound. It will help to stop the bleeding."

Phoenix squeezed the girl's arm and accepted the talon that Rorin offered to help her to stand. Realizing that she still wore the shawl around her neck that the girl had given her, Phoenix removed it and draped it around Sophie's shoulders. "We'll be back as soon as we can," she told the girl. "Promise."

Sophie closed her eyes and rested her head against the wall behind her.

Phoenix felt horrible about leaving her there, but it couldn't be helped.

An image of Sophie entered her mind as Rorin projected it to the rest of his flight. "Someone will help her as soon as they're able," he murmured, nodding to a nearby window.

Phoenix had trouble swallowing the lump of gratitude that formed in her throat.

A loud crash caused Phoenix's head to snap back in the direction that they had been heading. Another crash, followed by a yell of fury, caused her and the gargoyle to take off at a run down the corridor.

There was a howl from a side room. An instant later, a man came running out of the room with a snarling Kit biting at his heels. In his panic, the mercenary ran towards Phoenix and Rorin while he tried desperately to kick the dog away at the same time. Rorin stepped forward and lifted his arm, and Phoenix watched as the man ran straight into it, striking his head on the gargoyle's wrist bracers and falling unconscious to the floor.

Kit broke off her pursuit and trotted over to Phoenix with a satisfied snort.

"Good girl!" Phoenix told her, rubbing the dog's body all over vigorously. She had to blink back the tears of relief when she saw that the dog was unharmed.

Rorin frowned and stepped over the unconscious human dismissively. "We must be close if she is here. She must have stayed close to King Benedict and the others… If only we could Speak to them," Rorin growled, his silted eyes scanning the staircase to the royal chambers slowly. "I'm assuming that the one behind all of this could Hear us, otherwise we would have Heard from the others by now."

"Rorin," Phoenix said hesitantly, "if the planner can Hear, then he probably has other Power as well." As worrisome as that though was, Phoenix was grateful that Rorin had not assumed that the others were dead.

Rorin looked grim. He nodded. "We'll have to be extra careful, then." He put a claw to his lips and nodded ahead of them. He took the lead and, gripping her dagger so tightly that her knuckles turned white, Phoenix followed him up the stairs and through the double doors.

The main room was a mess. Tables and chairs were overturned and lay in scattered pieces around the room. Scorch marks were fresh on the walls, and by their erratic patterns Phoenix knew that they weren't from any kind of natural fire.

"Malcourt…" she whispered softly.

There was a stirring near to them. The next instant, a woman jumped out of the shadows and brandished a sword at them. Phoenix's body shifted into one of the defensive positions that she had learned. She held the dagger between her and the woman instinctually. Next to her, Rorin had done the same.

The three of them stood like that for a moment, then the woman took a hesitant step forward.

"Phoenix?" she whispered hopefully.

Phoenix paused. "Sylvia?"

With a soft sob, Sylvia ran forward and pulled Phoenix into a tight hug. "Oh, child," the woman whispered into her hair, "I thought the worst when I didn't see you with the others. I just assumed…"

"Healer," Rorin said urgently, "we must find the King…"

Sylvia sniffed. "Of course, gargoyle," she said, letting her sword dip so that the tip of it was resting on the ground. It looked heavy, Phoenix thought, and she was surprised that the woman could lift it up at all. The King's emblem was etched prominently on its blade, and, having seen it often enough, Phoenix knew that it belonged to Captain Rolf.

"They fought their way into the sleeping rooms," Sylvia told them, dragging the sword back to where she had been previously standing. Phoenix could see Captain Rolf's body lying on the floor. A large pool of blood was underneath him.

"I stayed here," she continued, kneeling next to the Guardscaptain. "I've been trying to keep him alive." Her voice cracked and she said softly, "The blow was meant for Tolen. He saved his life."

Phoenix and Rorin looked at the Guardscaptain with respect. Phoenix looked at the gargoyle and he nodded. He removed the pouch of bloodwort from his belt and handed it to Sylvia. She opened it and looked inside, then closed her eyes in relief. "Thank you," she said in a whisper.

"My flight is on their way, but it will take them some time to reach you. Save him if you can," the gargoyle frowned. "One so courageous is one who deserves to live."

Sylvia nodded and knelt next to Captain Rolf's wound, sprinkling the dried bloodwort into the deep gash across his chest.

Phoenix could *feel* Sylvia's Power rally to try and mend the flesh together.

Rorin turned to Phoenix and squared his shoulders.

She nodded and, as one, the two crept towards the doors, Kit following behind them.

Phoenix peered through the crack between the doors. She could make out several shapes in the room, but she was unable to get a final count.

Her skin prickled, and she could *feel* Power being used from the other end of the room. Camden was there, a barrier of air between him and two assailants. A third, who must have made it through before the barrier had been made, was dancing around him in combat.

The two lunged at one another and locked swords with a crash of sparks. The man was larger than Camden and out-matched him when it came to strength, but Camden was much more agile and was able to maneuver quickly out of the way.

Every time their swords struck one another, the barrier flickered and lost strength. The men on the other side readied their weapons for an attack.

Phoenix no longer felt the need for stealth. Leaning back, she kicked the double doors open with a crash and charged ahead. Recklessly she ran straight towards the men waiting to ambush Camden.

The air around her became heavy. An instant later, Rorin leapt over her and, with a flap of his great wings, dove towards the closest target with a battle cry. The men, who had startled at their entrance, paused for a moment. Recovering from their surprise, they both raised their weapons and charged at Phoenix in return.

The noise was explosive. Rorin crashed into the first man. He knocked his shield away and it slid across the floor towards Phoenix. The man was up again in a flash and was swinging his sword towards the gargoyle's head. Rorin jumped back and crouched on the ground, lashing his body around quickly to whip his tail at the man's legs to trip him up.

"Watch out!" he shouted to Phoenix.

The other man was close; almost within sword's length of where she stood. Taking Rorin's idea, Phoenix waited until the man was close enough and she dropped to the ground to kick at his shin.

The effect was not the same. Instead of knocking him down, the man only stumbled for a moment before regaining his balance. His sword came and Phoenix rolled out of the way just before the steel struck the carpeted floor. She managed to grab the discarded shield and cover her face with it before the sword fell again and crashed into it, the force of the impact jarring her hands painfully. Another blow came and the shield's frame buckled under it. Phoenix made a noise of desperation. She knew that the next time the shield would splinter and break, and it would not be able to protect her.

She kicked out in an attempt to catch the man's legs, but she only managed to kick air. She pushed the shield aside and tried to scramble out of the way.

Kit launched herself at Phoenix's attacker with a snarl. She distracted him long enough for Phoenix to be able to get out of harm's way. The man grabbed the dog by her collar while she was still in mid-air, and he wrenched her sharply in another direction, slamming her down on the floor heavily.

"No!" Phoenix cried. She leapt forward and grabbed the arm that was holding Kit's collar. Quickly, she thrust her dagger into it. He yelled and let go of Kit, whipping his arm to the side to dislodge Phoenix's hold on him.

Phoenix fell to the ground, but she noted with some satisfaction that her weapon remained entrenched in his flesh.

"I'll kill you!" he roared, using his other hand to pull the knife from his arm. Phoenix jumped up and grabbed the shield next to her. He looked up just in time to see the shield come crashing down on his head. The wood splintered and he fell unconscious to the ground, the metal frame hanging around his neck like a collar.

"Lizard demon!" The other man snarled. He was leaning over Rorin, who was lying on his back on the floor and blocking him with his legs. "I'll cut out your heart and feed it to my dogs! Umph!" The man grunted as Phoenix jumped on his back in an attempt to pull him down to the ground. When she realized that her weight was not enough, she settled, instead, for trying to choke him by locking her arms around his neck.

The man twisted in an attempt to grab her. "Caller brat!" he spat, grabbing a handful of her hair. 'You're lucky he wants you alive! Otherwise…" His sword flashed up to block Rorin's knife.

Phoenix cried out in pain as he wrenched her head to the side. He brought the edge of the sword up to her neck with a triumphant grin at Rorin.

"However," he amended, "if I have to choose between her skin and my own…" He waited calmly and watched the gargoyle. Rorin growled and bared his fangs at the man. He threw down his belt knife and watched the man angrily, his eyes flashing brightly like that of an animal in the half light.

Phoenix cried out again as the grip on her hair tightened. "Control your beast, Caller," the man spat at her. Kit had come slinking towards the two. Her nose was wrinkled with a growl, and she stopped still when Phoenix waved a hand at her.

He kept his eyes on the two and backed Phoenix towards the barrier that still stood between them and Camden, where he and the guard fought on the other side. Roughly, he pushed Phoenix into the invisible wall of air.

"Make it go away," he commanded, keeping his body in between her and the other two.

Phoenix felt the cold steel of the man's blade press against her neck. She was still hanging off of him from where she had jumped onto his back to save Rorin. The man supported her weight easily, and he gave her no room in which to get down and stand on her own feet. The hard leather of his armor pressed against her, which in turn pushed her into the churning wall of air.

"Make it go away!" he snapped, pulling forcefully on her hair. A searing pain ripped across her scalp, and Phoenix knew that he had been successful in ripping out a chunk of her curls. A warm trail of blood trickled down the side of her head.

"All right!" she cried out, desperate to get her throbbing head out of his grasp. "All right. I'll do it," she promised. "Just let me go."

He released the rest of her hair, and Phoenix winced as she pressed her hand to her head. She found the bald spot easily. The skin was raw and painful underneath her fingertips.

He grabbed her arm, instead, and shoved her forward. "Hurry up,' he snapped. He kept his blade close to her and one eye on the gargoyle, who was trying to edge closer without being seen. "Or else," the man growled.

Phoenix took a deep breath to calm herself. She was conscious of the unmovable air before her, and the painful grip that the man had on her arm. She pushed it from her mind and sought her Power.

It was often difficult, she found, to *call* on it at first. Once she had it, it was easy enough to use, but making the initial pathway was what always took time.

She closed her mind against her external senses like Malcourt taught her. It came more easily than ever before. Her blood was already pounding hot in her ears, and she used the heat from it to spark her fire.

The warmth tingled in her hands and spread outwards along her fingers and arms. From somewhere far away, she was aware of her body being shaken forcefully, but she ignored it. All she could feel was the growing pressure of her Power pulsing against her skin, waiting to be released. She could *feel* the resistance of Camden's Power against hers, but she ignored it and sent her Power in another direction.

She looked at the man and smiled at him. "Catch," she said, calmly, using her voice to release it.

It all happened in slow motion.

It started off as a single flicker, but quickly it grew into a roaring flame. The heat left her skin and passed along into the hand that was holding her.

A scream snapped her out of her reverie.

The man had let go of her, his hand raw and swollen where she had burned him. The fire, no longer needing Phoenix's contact, continued to burn and feed itself. It spread to the man's clothing, growing quickly as it spread to engulf him.

Screaming with horror, he ran around the room in an attempt to put out the fire. He stumbled from the room and crashed into the stone ground of the waiting room. He rolled around, his armour making a horrible noise as he did so. Phoenix could smell the stench of singed leather and burning flesh where the fire had become trapped between his armour and his skin.

Her focus ring flashed. It absorbed the excess energy and filled in the pathway that Phoenix had created. Cut off from the source, her Power dissipated and rose off of her as smoke.

Her attacker lay on the ground, unmoving, panting and groaning with every breath. He was alive, but his injuries were severe.

Phoenix could taste the bile rising in her throat.

Behind her, Camden fumbled. He jumped up quickly, his reflexes fast despite his fatigue, but not before his attacker slashed a wound across his chest.

A red flower immediately blossomed on his chest, and blood soaked through his tunic. Wide-eyed, Camden pressed his hand to his chest and fell to his knees. His expression was blank.

"Camden!" Phoenix screamed, throwing herself at the air barrier with all her strength. Her shoulder smashed into the barrier and the air current pushed at her roughly. She grabbed her bruised arm in pain. Camden's opponent, seeing the boy kneeling on the ground, gave a wicked smile and walked towards him.

"You put up a good fight, Caller boy," the man drawled, "but I put up a better one."

"No!" Phoenix cried, pounding against the wall as the guard raised his sword for the killing blow. She feltl her hand slip through the outside force surrounding the wall, but the currents inside of it were far too strong for her to make it through.

Behind her, Rorin and Kit had launched themselves at the wall as well. They scratched and clawed at it to try and break through. Phoenix could only watch as the man stood before Camden and brought his arms up as high as they could go.

Camden's expression turned from dazed to triumphant. His free hand flicked his sword up and, before the man could move to block, Camden's blade slid through the bottom of his mail shirt and into his belly He continued to thrust upwards, and Phoenix could hear a sickening crunch as the force broke through his bones and plunged into his chest.

The man hunched over with a grunt. He dropped his sword with a clatter, and Phoenix could see his eyes lose focus. Still staring at Camden in surprise, the man fell forward as his body lost strength. Camden used the sword hilt to direct the man's fall and moved out of the way so that he hit the floor. Still sitting on the bloody carpet, he closed his eyes and the barrier flickered into non-existence.

It was too much for Phoenix. Falling to the ground, she was only able to move her hair back before she emptied the contents of her stomach on the floor. When she had finished retching, she wiped her face with shaking hands and looked around.

The place was ruined. Broken furniture and blood was

strewn about the floors around her. Her body was bruised and sore and, conscious of how weary she was, she wished that she could just hide and rest somewhere for a time.

A grey talon appeared in front of her, and she looked up to see Rorin before her, offering to help her to stand. Gratefully she accepted the help, and she was surprised at the ease in which he pulled her to her feet.

"Camden,' she said worriedly.

The boy was sitting against the wall. He had his hand pressed to his chest, and Phoenix was relieved to see that his wound had all but stopped bleeding. His face was pale from the exertion of using his Power while fighting, but he was glaring openly at the gargoyle that held her hand.

Phoenix hurried over to him. "Are you all right?" she asked.

He nodded. "I pretended that I was hurt worse than I was so that he would let his guard down. It was my only chance to beat him,"

"You scared me."

"I'm sorry." His voice was soft, and he looked so pitiful that Phoenix couldn't help but give him a quick hug.

"Ouch!" he protested.

"I can't get through," Rorin said. The gargoyle was trying to push his talon through a wall of red light. The light was blocking the entrance to the King's sleeping chambers, and every time Rorin touched it it flashed angrily.

"Prince Hallan put it up," Camden told them.

"Why haven't you taken it down?" Rorin asked.

"Because I can't!" Camden snapped at the gargoyle. "Don't you think I've been trying? I can't knock down walls!"

"Yet you can put them up?" the gargoyle asked matter-of-factly.

"That's different. I can keep air moving. I can't use it to break something." His tone indicated that the gargoyle was stupid for not knowing the difference between the two.

Rorin made a dismissive noise in his throat.

Phoenix ignored their bickering and began to inspect the wall herself.

"Well can't you just blow it down?" She heard the gargoyle ask.

"Can't you just fly through it?" Camden snapped back.

Phoenix laid her hand against the force. There was a brief moment of resistance – a feeling as though she was dragging her hand through water – and then her arm sunk through the barrier.

Gripping her dagger tightly in her other hand, Phoenix entered the room.

She could hear Kit's howling through the space that still lingered behind her, but the sound cut off abruptly as the opening closed and sealed itself behind her. She could see both Rorin and Camden pounding their fists against the wall, causing the light to flash under their hands.

Bracing herself, Phoenix turned her attention away from her friends and focused on the darkened room before her.

CHAPTER 27

The only movement in the room was a sickly red light that flickered against the walls, casting harsh shadows across the hung tapestries. The familiarity of the off-color gave her pause, but Phoenix was unable to pull it from her memory.

Kenneth and Jamie, Prince Hallan's personal guards, stood with their backs to her. Prince Hallan towered over a fallen Master Malcourt, with King Benedict standing a few feet away, held at knife point by the assassin, his thick hand pressed over the King's mouth while the flash of a dagger was held at the King's throat.

Malcourt, to Phoenix's horror, was trapped by the strange red light that flickered across his body. He was alive, but fully immobilized where he lay. Only his eyes rolled towards her as she approached.

"What are your orders, my Lord?" Kenneth asked the Prince.

Prince Hallan, who had his back to the pair, turned around slowly with a wondering smile. "Phoenix," he greeted her warmly, "however did you get in?"

The guards whirled, but Prince Hallan raised his hand and the two stayed where they were. "Now, now," he told the two. "There's no need for that. Apprentice Phoenix is a friend after

all." Prince Hallan walked between them and gave her a dis-
arming smile. "Aren't you, my dear?" he purred.

Phoenix, tongue-tied from his attention, could only blink in
confusion.

"It's not her fault she was kept in the dark," the Prince continued. "She would never hurt anyone. Would you, sweetling?
Not unless it was absolutely necessary, of course."

There was a snort behind him. The assassin stood behind
the Prince, a sneer on his lips. His thick hood no longer covered his face, and Phoenix was shocked to see that Oliver had
escaped from his cell in Castle Angor's depth. He stood before
them now, his sword steady as he held it to King Benedict's
neck.

The Prince held up a palm. "Careful," he warned Phoenix.
"We don't want to provoke anyone into doing something dras-
tic."

Oliver shifted his attention to Phoenix, curling his lip. "You
best listen to him, brat. You might live to regret it, but your King
sure won't."

"We don't want that to happen," Prince Hallan agreed reasonably. "That's why I said I'd guarantee your safety if you let
him go. It's the best option for you now that your Master is…
indisposed."

Oliver narrowed his eyes. His gaze fell to Malcourt's trapped
body. "Yes… My Master promised me great rewards if I got rid
of the King and the Prince." He said the words haltingly, as if
he were trying them out for the first time. He raised his greedy
gaze to Prince Hallan. "But it doesn't matter to me who dies so
long as I get paid."

"You're lying!" Phoenix crouched over Malcourt. "Master
Malcourt would never-"

"Careful," Prince Hallan warned her as she reached towards the light that encased Malcourt. "You don't want to touch that."

"What are you doing to him?" she demanded. Malcourt's expression was pained as he looked up at her.

Prince Hallan frowned. "I have to drain his Power, Phoenix. I have to keep him secured – otherwise he could free himself and kill the King, and I would never forgive myself if that were to happen. I'm sure you understand…"

The Prince sighed when she continued to glare at him. "Think about it. Who has the most to gain from the King's death? Malcourt, of course! The King's very own advisor! Who better to take over Angoria then one who already knows how to run it?"

He stood behind her now. He rested a hand on her shoulder, and Phoenix was instantly soothed by the touch. She looked down at Malcourt in disbelief, sinking to her knees next to him as his eyes desperately fought to hold hers.

"But... he healed the King…" Surely the Prince's mistake was obvious. "He brought me here when I needed a home. He took care of me…"

"Only because it benefited him! Don't you see? It all makes sense! Who better to avoid suspicion than one who was working so hard to save him? Of course he healed the King – he was the one poisoning him. He had the antidote all along! And as for you… Well… you're amazing, Phoenix. How can you not understand that? How could he have let you think otherwise? How could he have left you in that disgusting dorm room? You passed his protection circle in the woods without his detection – and just now you passed through the shield I erected to keep your friend safe. That's impossible!"

Phoenix felt confused. "It is?"

"You didn't know?" The Prince's expression was pitying.

"Of course not," he murmured, as if to himself. "He didn't want you to know. He was afraid you might leave and he wanted you all for himself... No wonder he didn't look for your family."

The statement clanged through her. "He didn't?" she asked in a stunned whisper. Hurt, she looked down at her frozen Master. The concentration that it took to fight against Prince Hallan's Power showed on Malcourt's face. He was unable to Speak to her because of the shield around him.

The Prince's hand moved from her shoulder to the back of her head. "He wanted to make you stay with him," he continued, his fingers sifting gently through her hair. A soft tingling spread through her body from his touch. "I want you to stay with me, too, but I want you to choose to do so."

"Stay with you?" Phoenix's confusion increased. Her body ached. She was mentally and physically exhausted. It would be easier to stop fighting. The more Prince Hallan spoke, the more he began to make sense.

The Prince's fingers grazed the spot where the chunk of her hair had been pulled out. Frowning, he withdrew his hand and pulled her to her feet.

"You've been through so much today," he murmured, as if trying to soothe her. His concern was so touching that tears suddenly filled her eyes. "Why don't you go and wait with your friends? I'll take care of all of this unpleasantness. I'll take care of you." He brushed a curl back from her face and tucked it behind her ear.

She stared up at him. His emerald eyes sparkled down at her and she couldn't help but smile shyly back up at him.

She felt strange and warm inside. Everything seemed so far away. So unimportant. Everything except the Prince, and how he was looking at her. No one had ever looked at Phoenix like that before.

He lifted a hand to her cheek.

A ring on his finger snagged her attention. It was elegant. The gemstone in the centre, surrounded by familiar symbols, caught the light as it moved.

It was a focus ring.

Phoenix frowned. He had never worn it before. Until now, she didn't know that the Prince had Power. He had shown no sign of it during her time at Angor. She hadn't thought about how he was keeping Malcourt captive, or how he'd divided the rooms with a barrier. But if he still wore a focus ring, that meant that he was in training. Or that his Power was too unpredictable for him to handle.

The symbols on his band were different. Phoenix didn't understand what they meant, but she recognized one of them. Its twin adorned the dagger from the fallen soldier.

Her brain was sluggish. She was too distracted by the Prince to concentrate, but she forced her thoughts past the fog that trapped them. Why would the Prince wear a symbol that matched the dagger that she carried? And why was the symbol so familiar in the first place?

The red light flickered off of the dagger tantalizingly where it lay forgotten on the floor. It was the same light she had seen in the clearing on her way to Angor. When red powder had been used to break Master Malcourt's protection circle during the ambush. When the captured man held a dagger identical to the one in her hand.

Her mind cleared instantly.

Master Malcourt was not the threat. It had been Prince Hallan all along. He poisoned the King. His Power had revealed them in the clearing. It was his men who had attacked them, it was his binding spell that controlled them, and his plan, now, that was being followed through. He was the one attacking the castle.

The warmth she held for him turned to revulsion in the pit of her stomach. She understood, now, what his Talent was. She could *feel* the waves of manipulation emanate from him in an attempt to tangle her senses.

With a jerk, Phoenix slapped his hand away before it could touch her face.

"No," she said, firmly.

The Prince's expression turned incredulous. "What?"

"No!" she repeated, loudly.

"No?" he demanded, his exhale turning the word into a hiss. "What do you mean 'no'?"

A wave of anger washed over her. "It was you all along," she replied, her voice getting louder with every word. She took a few steps back, grabbing the dagger and positioning it between them. "You're the one behind everything."

I am here, a voice said. *Keep him busy.*

Rorin must be nearby if he was able to Speak to her again. Phoenix glanced over to see that the barrier, the flickering red barricade that the Prince had so carefully erected along the doorframe and across the walls, hadn't jumped across the window's opening to meet itself.

Rorin had entered unseen through that window, and was slowly crawling along the ceiling to where King Benedict was being held.

"But why?" Phoenix asked, stalling; backing up so that her heel touched the light that cocooned around Malcourt. It flared, angry at the contact. "King Benedict is your family. Why would you do this to someone you love?"

Prince Hallan threw back his head and laughed. "Love?" he mocked. "Hardly. The only person I ever loved was my sister, Helena – and he took her away from me! He had to be punished. They both did."

"Both?" Phoenix asked.

"She left me for him," the Prince spat, and Phoenix fought the urge to shrink back from the wild look in his eyes. "She abandoned me for him - a stranger in a foreign land. She wouldn't come home. She refused to leave because of their child, but she belonged with me!"

King Benedict thrashed. He elbowed the assassin in the stomach, managing to free himself momentarily as the man doubled over. "You?" he cried at the Prince. "You killed them?"

Prince Hallan's face twisted. "It was supposed to be you," he snarled. "Helena's death was an accident. I never meant to hurt her. I wanted you gone - you and your heir - so that I could come here and comfort her. I would help her rule Angoria. We would never be apart again!"

With an outraged roar, King Benedict lurched forward.

Rorin gave a savage snarl and dropped onto the assassin. Oliver screamed and lost his balance as the gargoyle crashed into him.

"Guards!" Prince Hallan's face grew red as he screamed. "Kill them! Kill them all!"

Kenneth and Jamie charged at the King. Phoenix whirled and dropped to her knees next to Malcourt. "Master," she whispered. Her fingers edged past the vulgar symbol next to the barrier and touched his arm through it. Triumphant, Phoenix realized that she was able to enter this barrier as well.

"Get away from him," Prince Hallan demanded.

Phoenix slammed her hands against the shield, pushing through the resistance that fought to block her. She grabbed at Master Malcourt's hands and *pulled*. A soft glow appeared between their fingers, and Phoenix felt his hands squeeze her own. Bracing herself, Phoenix gave one final tug and pulled them free.

Malcourt's Power flashed a brilliant yellow. With an audible crack, the wrapping around him shattered into shards of yellow light. The next instant, Phoenix was pushed to the floor as a blast of red blew past her to intersect with the shield that Malcourt had conjured. Malcourt rolled to his feet and threw himself at the Prince.

Across the room, the Prince's personal guards had caught up with the King, who was doing his best to fight both at the same time. Next to him, Rorin was fully engaged in combat with the assassin.

Phoenix jumped up and darted around the Power battle. She ran to King Benedict, surprising the nearest guard by running into him at full speed. She ducked as he recovered and swung his spear at her.

The King held the assassin's previously dropped sword and blocked the fatal blow from Kenneth's spear before it hit him. While they were locked together, Phoenix ducked underneath the weapons and slashed the guard's knee with her knife. He cried out and, grabbed his leg, dropping his weapon in the process. King Benedict used the hilt of his sword to bash the man's head, and the man dropped to the floor.

There was a scream behind her that dropped into silence. Phoenix glanced behind her to see that Rorin's struggle with the assassin had led them to the window. The gargoyle was peering down over the ledge, frowning as the man disappeared from sight.

The other guard was coming up behind her. Rorin leapt over them and whipped his tail at the guard's head. The man ducked, but the gargoyle grabbed his arm and pulled him backwards. The King swung around and Phoenix stabbed the man in his side. He grunted in pain, and Rorin took the opportunity to throw him back against the wall. He connected soundlessly and did not move.

The three turned their attention to the fight between Malcourt and Prince Hallan.

The two fighters didn't notice them. They were too busy trying to stay alive. Malcourt was more powerful, but the Prince had syphoned off so much of his energy that they had become evenly matched. He had to rely solely on his training.

Rorin crouched down and the air around them grew heavy. He launched himself upwards and, with a flap of his great wings, dove towards the two. King Benedict paused only a moment before he and Phoenix ran after him.

Prince Hallan shot a bolt at Malcourt, who held out his hand in front of him to block it. A shield flickered into existence briefly before disappearing with the impact of absorbing the attack.

The Prince had moved forward during the shot, so when the shield disappeared he was the perfect distance to strike out. The metal bracer on the back of his fist collided solidly with Master Malcourt's face. Phoenix heard the crunch of breaking bones, and Master Malcourt's legs gave way under him.

"No!" she screamed.

Rorin pressed his wings to his back and dove at Prince Hallan. The Prince rolled away just in time and watched as the gargoyle swooped upward for another dive.

"Spear!" he shouted, raising his hand at the attacking creature. Light shot from his fingers and raked along the gargoyle's open wing.

Rorin screamed – sounding like a wounded animal – and his wing drooped. He fell into a downward spiral and landed heavily on the stone floor.

Smirking, the Prince walked back to Malcourt and pointed

at him with his sword. "You have no idea how long I've waited for this moment."

King Benedict leapt forwards. "Defend yourself!" The King boomed, swinging his sword hastily at the Prince.

Prince Hallan did not need to. Lifting his weapon he stabbed at the King with his lightning reflexes.

The blade cut easily through King Benedict's finery. There was a muted crunching sound as it pierced his chest. The King stood still, and Phoenix watched in horror as the Prince slowly pulled the sword from the King's body, the wet noise from the drawn-out motion was the only sound in the room. He held the sword at his side and watched King Benedict calmly.

Everyone held their breath. All that could be heard was the blood that dripped from the Prince's blade to collect in a pool on the floor.

Blood poured from King Benedict's wound. The King, staring ahead in shock, pressed his hand to his chest in a distracted fashion. His sword clattered to the stone floor, forgotten, as he inspected his fingers. Slowly he closed his eyes.

Phoenix was sick with horror. She watched as blood seeped down the King's finery, a red blossom that bloomed across his chest, soaking easily into the thin, ornate fabric.

He made no move to staunch the wound. Instead, he watched its growth with a curious expression.

Phoenix sucked in a ragged breath as tears streamed openly down her face.

King Benedict smiled sadly. "Helena," he whispered, his voice barely audible. The blue of his eyes dimmed as his expression slackened. His legs crumpled beneath him, and Rorin stepped forward to catch his body before it hit the floor.

Malcourt dragged himself over to the two and pressed his fingers against the King's neck. There was a pause, then Malcourt gently closed King Benedict's eyes.

Prince Hallan threw his head back. "I've done it!" he crowed, his teeth flashing in the light. "I've finally done it! Angoria is mine!"

His voice crackled with a hysterical edge as it reverberated around the room. Each echo dripped with the hatred that he had hidden for so long - finally uncovered, it stretched and flexed in its newfound freedom.

Phoenix clenched her fists, using them to dash the tears from her eyes. It did nothing to halt the white-hot anger that blurred her vision. Unbidden, her Power leapt to her hands and licked along her fingers, warming her palms. Without thinking, blinded with rage, Phoenix pivoted backwards and threw the crooked dagger at Prince Hallan with all her strength.

The knife sliced through the air. The Prince jerked his head back, but not before the blade grazed his cheek. Stunned, he lifted his hand to the small trickle of blood that ran down his face.

"Ungrateful brat!" he snarled, his face contorting. "Net", he spat, lifting his hand towards her.

Rorin dove towards her. "Watch out!"

Phoenix crossed her arms over her head in defense against the attack.

Red light spun from the Prince's fingers. It coiled around itself, twisting together to complete the command before launching itself at her, but the net found no purchase. It passed through Phoenix like cobwebs on the breeze.

Instead, the net wrapped around Rorin, ensnaring the gargoyle where he stood behind her. He fell heavily, covered in the same draining energy that had trapped Master Malcourt.

"Must you ruin everything?" The Prince rounded on Phoenix, causing her to stumble back. "It would have gone so smoothly if you had only listened to me." He pinched the bridge of his nose, then shrugged. "No help for it, I guess."

The Prince raised his hand towards her. "Spear!" he commanded, releasing another bolt of light at her.

Phoenix froze. Master Malcourt had shielded himself against the same type of assault earlier. But his reflexes were much faster than hers. And his training...

Phoenix shifted into a defensive stance. Drills with Rolf were a help against a physical attack, but this was entirely different. She didn't know how to make a shield. She couldn't summon the light they had used, and her fire wasn't strong enough to burn the spear...

Phoenix *called* to her Power. She dipped into the tired flames that flickered in her core. She coaxed them, pleading with them to expand. The air around her warmed in response before the heat sputtered into nothing. She was drained. She couldn't protect herself.

Phoenix squeezed her eyes shut in anticipation of the blow.

Rorin screamed, his voice raw.

The flash of light was bright even through her closed eyes. She waited for the sensations to arrive: her energy to dissipate; the heat to erupt.

Nothing happened. There was a beat of silence, and Phoenix realized that she felt no pain. Opening her eyes, the remnants of her fire guttered into darkness, replaced by an icy terror that clawed at the inside of her chest. Phoenix's breath caught in her throat.

Master Malcourt stood before her. He was hunched forward, his shoulders locked at odd angles. They rose shakily with his laboured breathing, his face becoming more ashen with each breath, but he managed to smile down at her when she opened her eyes.

"Master?" Phoenix's voice was barely a whisper.

Master Malcourt opened his mouth to answer, but the sound died on his lips. He slumped forward and Phoenix caught him, gently helping him to the floor.

"Master…" She cradled his head in her lap, gripping his shoulders tightly, as if it would keep him with her. "Just hold on," she whispered. "We'll get Sylvia. She'll fix everything. She'll make everything better. Just hold on…"

Malcourt coughed and shook his head. Phoenix could feel the wound cavity on his back. The sickly red - a color reminiscent of blood - had spread to his chest from behind. "No." The word came out as a rasp, his voice hoarse from the effort it took to fill his torn lungs with air. "Leave me here. Save yourself."

"No! I won't go without you!"

Malcourt chuckled weakly. "My dear – I am already gone." He held a hand up against her cheek. "Dearest Phoenix…"

His eyes became unfocused. Malcourt's gaze slid down her face, unseeing, and Phoenix pressed his hand against her cheek. She called out to him, begging him to come back to her.

For a brief moment his gaze settled on her pendant, uncovered since she had abandoned Sophie's shawl during the fight to the King's chambers.

His eyes widened and he reached out, laying his thumb against the teardrop gemstone in the center of her necklace. It glowed a brilliant blue, bathing his pale face with light as he looked at her in wonder.

He exhaled slowly and his hand dropped. Panicked, Phoenix grabbed at his clammy skin. "Master?"

Fumbling, Malcourt pressed his thumb against her palm. Phoenix winced as the touch burned. She held her hand up to see a glowing imprint against her skin before it faded from view.

Follow it... Malcourt's body had stopped moving. Only his face showed any life as he looked up at her warmly. *Go... find yourself.*

He took a long laboured breath and his face went slack. Phoenix could see the light leaving his eyes, two brilliant blue gems dimming into stone as he stared up at her blankly.

"Master!" Phoenix screamed, clutching him tightly. Her chest felt as though it was going to explode. "Don't go!"

Follow the trail. Survive...

His voice tapered off. The last word was an echo. Phoenix could hear it continue in her head, bouncing against the nothingness that remained. He was gone.

Master Malcourt was dead in her arms.

Pip screamed. The owl's cry was so shrill that Phoenix felt chills along her skin.

Phoenix was numb. Everything around her seemed cold, and distant. This had to be a sleep-terror. She was going to wake up and everything would be back to normal. Once she had awoken to find the couch on fire, so all she had to do-

"Poor Phoenix," a rich voice broke through her thoughts.

Phoenix watched through watery eyes as Prince Hallan prowled towards her. He ignored Rorin where he lay on the floor, almost stepping on him had the gargoyle not twisted himself out of the way.

"Everyone you care about is gone," Prince Hallan purred. "Last chance, my dear. Come with me. Rule the kingdom by my side. That is where you truly belong." He extended his hand towards her with a smile.

Phoenix looked down at Malcourt and smiled softly. Gently, she closed his eyes and set him on the ground, smoothing the hair from his face and tidying it on the top of his head. He was the closest thing she had ever known to a father. He had vouched for her, and she wanted to leave him looking at his best.

She could hear Rorin's muted struggling as he tried to free himself, but she ignored him as she watched the Prince.

She still found him handsome, and she was surprised to find that her body wanted to move towards him - to obey when he beckoned to her.

"Where I truly belong?" Phoenix's voice was empty as she took a step forward. Did she even want to belong here anymore?

Malcourt's voice echoed in her memory. *Survive.*

Prince Hallan's Talent rolled over her in unseen waves. She could *feel* it emanating from his body; *feel* it sticking to her skin in an attempt to confuse and control her senses. She tilted her head at him.

"Mindcaller?" she asked blankly.

The Prince's smile was cruel. "Something like that," he told her. She remained motionless and he grinned. "Join me," he urged again, his voice enticing. "Imagine the Power we could create with the joining of our Blood! We could give birth to a generation of rulers who will control the Land for all time!"

"I could rule with you?" she asked.

"For always," he purred. His face was pure greed as he watched her, her expression blank as he stepped closer.

Phoenix understood, now, that he was only ever interested in her because he wanted to possess her. Malcourt's motivation had always been to help her, but Prince Hallan's had been much more sinister.

Phoenix stretched her hands towards him. His Talent pressed against her so strongly that she found it hard to catch her breath. Her heart beat so quickly - too quickly - that it made her dizzy. She felt flushed from being so close to him.

The Prince grinned and moved closer. He reached out to take her hands, but she ignored the gesture and continued to reach towards him. Smirking, he moved even closer.

Slowly, carefully, she dragged her hands up his chest. Her fingers brushed against his cheek, the rough texture of his stubble scratching against her skin. The sensation seemed heightened somehow; she could feel it through every fibre of her body, the contact made her bones shiver. His eyes were brilliant emeralds as he watched her, his breath against her face was the sweetest breeze she had ever felt. Her entire body was intoxicated with him.

His Talent purred from her touch. It spread over her, trying to absorb into her, to take advantage of the attraction that she held for him - the flaw that it had used before.

The pathway formed in her mind. It was faster this time, as if the distance to its surface were reduced somehow. She barely had to think about it. The fire burned hot inside of her. Phoenix kept it there, feeling how, in a detached way, it pulled on the currents of her anger and hatred in order to feed the flames. It grew so forceful that she wondered if her skin would split open from the strength of it.

"Just imagine the things that we will do," the Prince was saying softly as he tucked a stray curl behind her ear, trying to strengthen the intoxication that he was coiling around her.

His Talent intensified, desperately searching for the attraction she held for him, for the way she had felt when she first arrived. With silent menace her Power rose to the challenge. She gave him nothing.

Phoenix smiled. She brushed her fingers against his jaw, letting the tips caress his skin as he stood there, waiting, watching her as his Talent fully wrapped itself around her in a final attempt to invade her senses.

Her Power purred at its touch, and Phoenix spread her fingers to cup her hands around his face as much as possible. The Prince smiled as she gazed up at him.

"Burn," she commanded.

He looked at her in confusion. She could feel the heat leave her fingers, like a stream trickling into the ocean. Too late, he realized what she was doing. The floodgates had opened.

Prince Hallan jerked back and began striking at her in horror, trying to get away. Phoenix's fingers burned against his cheeks, melting skin and bone alike as she pushed them into his face without mercy. He screamed, but his cry only served to increase her anger. She *felt* her focus ring extend itself in an attempt to limit her Power and contain it once again.

The pathway began to close and she fought against it with all her might, desperate to punish the man who had killed the ones she loved. Blindly, she pushed her way through the obstacle.

Her focus ring shattered. She *felt* the gems weaken and crack as her Power flowed around its buffer to continue its deadly assault.

A scream of rage and anguish tore itself from her throat. It was bestial sounding, the strength behind it wrenching the pathway open again as her Power tore through the defenceless Prince. Flames erupted on his hair and clothing, and he shrieked in anguish one final time before going silent.

His lifeless body, still burning, fell to the floor.

Phoenix screamed again, a sweet release of the Power and emotion that threatened to overwhelm her.

The heat spread from her body to the rest of the room. The fire spread along the carpet, traveling down the hall and jumping to the tapestries that hung on the walls. The inferno wrapped around the chambers, covering the room in a blanket of flames that threatened to crack the stones with its ferocity.

She screamed until her lungs ran out of air. Wiping her hands in her skirts, she buried her face in the warmth of her palms. The thumbprint that Malcourt had marked on her skin flashed in the light. Shutting her eyes, Phoenix began to weep.

Collapsing, she curled in on herself and sobbed uncontrollably. Hot tears, as hot as the fire around her, streaked down her face in an unbroken stream.

Cool skin pressed against hers. Two arms, hard as stone, held her tightly as she wept. Icy wings wrapped around her, shutting out the noise and the heat of the inferno that ranged at the edge of her senses. Comforted by the darkness, feeling completely spent, Phoenix went limp in Rorin's arms. He rested his chin on her head and adjusted himself so that he was better wrapped around her - the coldness that he created enveloping her completely, cutting her off from the fire that raged around them.

Phoenix, thankful for his kindness, closed her eyes and surrendered to his embrace.

EPILOGUE

The passing service was held two days after the royal ball.

The weather was grey and wet, a fitting atmosphere, Phoenix thought, as the Land itself mourned the death of its monarch.

The service felt endless. Phoenix found herself numb to the words as the Hooded Brother droned on, outlining the Divine Plan of the Creator and the riches that awaited the two men who saved the kingdom from a tyrant. Phoenix held Sylvia's hand while the woman wept openly, not bothering to wipe the tears that streamed down her face as the Brother began the final blessings.

When he finally bowed his head, his lecture dwindling as the last anointments were scattered over the closed caskets, a dull silence fell over the congregation. The only constant sound was the wind that battered against the mourning flags, the sound punctuated by the staccato sniffing of those around her.

Phoenix was too numb to cry. Her attention shifted to watching those assembled, to Camden who was surely influencing the wind that buffeted them, the nobles who tried to hide their impatience at figuring out their claim to the throne, the dark clouds that rolled overhead - anywhere but at the robed cleric before her, or the ornate caskets that held the bodies of the only men who had ever shown her kindness.

She was very careful not to think about what - *who* - rested in the sealed boxes before her.

A gong reverberated through the gloom, signaling the end of the ceremony.

Phoenix helped Sylvia to her feet. Tessa came to stand next to them, her eyes red, before nodding to Phoenix and laying a comforting arm across Sylvia's shoulders. Phoenix nodded in return and took her place at the front of Malcourt's casket, Camden to her left, as the two Apprentices rested their palms against the polished wood to say farewell to their Master.

The ceremony stalled as Phoenix bowed her head. Her vision blurred as she rested a hand against Malcourt's casket. The wood was a hard finality of the barrier that separated them, and this time it was a barrier that she could not break.

Camden cleared his throat and she blinked her eyes clear, swearing her shoulders as she stepped back out of the way. Several guards joined him as Captain Rolf took charge at the head of the King's casket and led the way to the royal crypt.

A double funeral. Rolf had balked at the idea when it was first mentioned, when the heads of each discipline had met together to decide what the next move would be. The designated Small Council. It had been generations since the last one had formed.

Phoenix had attended, even though the right was technically Camden's as First Apprentice. She had walked with him to the meeting, then entered without an invitation, ignoring the looks of surprise that had been sent her way. Camden had stood next to her silently, a wordless form of support as his steely gaze dared anyone to protest.

No one did.

She had watched the different Masters bring forth their

grievances, feeling the numbness spread as she watched each one vying for compensation to set right what had been lost - the payments they would never see, the years of wasted training when the noble-blooded Apprentices were summoned home.

Resources were scarce and Castle Angor was in ruins. They could not allow any favouritism to slip. They would have to tread carefully until the new ruler was discovered; this was when fresh wounds were factored into how future alliances were formed. The joined passing service would be the first of many concessions.

Phoenix turned and made her way across the courtyard, her thoughts churning as she forced the funeral behind her. She trailed an aimless gaze along the castle's broken walls as she went, inspecting every shadowed crevice for an outline of claw-tipped wings or a lashing tail. She was unable to locate any.

Phoenix strode towards the royal chambers. She'd found herself back here more times than she cared to admit over the past two days, yet each time was just as fruitless as the last. Phoenix barely slowed when she came to the shattered double doors that led to the royal chambers. Her eyes raked the ruined door frames, her attention snagging on the new notches where weapons had bit into the wood.

Phoenix steeled her spine and passed through the splintered doors, the sound of her boots echoed back at her from the empty stones. She silently cursed the ever-present kernel of hope that she would find some sort of clue as to what Malcourt had wanted her to do next.

Survive.

The memory of Malcourt's voice was clear in her mind. Her steps faltering, she pushed it aside before it could threaten to undo her.

The clicking of nails against stone alerted Phoenix to Kit's presence. The dog's usual buoyant attitude had been very much subdued, and she rarely let Phoenix out of her sight as a result. Phoenix didn't mind. She welcomed the quiet companionship. It was a welcome relief to share company with someone who didn't ask her how she was feeling every few moments. Especially since the truth was that she didn't feel much of anything if she could help it.

It had been easy to avoid, hiding in the tower with only Kit for company. No one was able to enter the tower with all of the protection barriers that Malcourt had left in place. No one except for Phoenix.

That had been a point of contention between her and Camden. He had been unable to enter the tower without Phoenix's assistance. Whatever barriers Master Malcourt had put into place had rebuffed his attempts at entry, and even though he was First Apprentice he had needed her assistance after they realized she could walk through effortlessly.

His rage had been silent, but his eyes had been the color of storm clouds. Shortly after he'd announced that he was going to attempt the Rites in order to get his Mastercaller ranking, and decided to leave on the next ship to sail to the Academy. He ended up staying for the funerals, but he made it clear that there was nothing left for him now that their Master was dead.

The blow had wounded her more than she'd let on, so she had found convenient ways to avoid him - a task made easy by the fact he couldn't surprise her by showing up unannounced. She had said enough goodbyes over the last few days. She refused to open herself up to another one.

That refusal was the reason she was currently stalling.

Phoenix rubbed her temples. Her head was pounding. She had not slept yet, and she was finally starting to feel the ill-effects of its absence. Phoenix rolled her shoulders and gave herself a shake. The last thing she wanted to do was lie down. The idea of closing her eyes...

The last time she had she'd begun to dream of Malcourt's study.

It was the first place she had gone, after everything had settled. It was just as he had left it. Scrolls and books lay haphazardly around the room, still open to the pages he was studying - the pages he had last touched. She hadn't been able to bring herself to close them. She'd avoided the room ever since while awake. She didn't want to visit it in her sleep.

Phoenix walked to the window. She pressed her palms against the cool stone of the ledge and leaned forward, savouring the scratch of the cracked edge as it bit into her thigh. She tensed her fingers, as if doing so would somehow allow her to crumble the stone in her hands.

She lifted her head.

Dusk darkened the courtyard. Phoenix stood still, feeling the weight of her exhaustion settle into her bones.

Shadows pooled across the ground, spreading from the base of the walls to stretch and merge against each other. Phoenix eyed the sun as it dipped lower against the hills. The day's light dimmed and pulled in a line of fire across the horizon, a final affront to the darkening sky before disappearing completely from sight.

Candles winked into life from the different windows of Angor. The hour wasn't late, but the castle was already quiet. Rolf had raised the question of enforcing a curfew since the attack, as if that would keep the inhabitants safe from any new threats that might descend during their time of vulnerability. As if it would somehow make up for the violence that they had already incurred. The idea had proven unnecessary in the end. Most had taken to barricading themselves in their rooms once night arrived. It made it easier for her to get around.

With a sigh, she steeled her spine and pushed her attention back into the room.

She had put it off long enough.

Kit pressed her nose into Phoenix's leg, sensing her apprehension. The girl ran her fingers through the dog's fur and gave her head a pat.

"Time to go," Phoenix murmured.

Kit whined softly and trotted ahead of her.

Phoenix let her lead the way. She didn't know how Kit knew their destination, but she was content to let the dog dictate their path, taking comfort in the easy pace and the fact that she didn't have to pay attention to where they were going. Instead, her eyes traced the castle walls as they walked. She noted every scorch mark, every new scratch and splatter of blood that had yet to be cleaned up. Footprints remained untouched in the aftermath of the battle.

They came to a stairway that plunged into darkness. No candles dotted the lower hallways. The earlier procession must have used the external entrance.

Phoenix sent a thought to the burning pool inside of her. It responded instantly. She could feel the heat rolling off of her and did her best to quell it instantly. With her focus stone broken, she had to be careful using her Power outside of the safeguards of Malcourt's Tower. All she needed was to send the remaining parapet of Angor up in smoke…

"Illuminate," she said clearly, her voice the only sound in the darkness. A fire globe grew into life in her hand. It spread until it touched the tips of her fingers, then stopped, heatless flames licking out against her hand before returning to run across its surface.

She carried it to the top of the stairs and released it into the darkness below.

The globe dropped like a stone through the centre of the spiral staircase, falling into the depth of the earth before finally coming to a halt. It hovered above the ground, twirling idly as it pushed back the shadows, a tiny sun beckoning her into the abyss.

Phoenix crept down the iron stairs into the belly of the earth. "Don't fall," she muttered, unsure if she was speaking to herself or to the metalwork that now supported her weight.

A damp cold settled against her as she trudged farther underground. For the first time in a long time, Phoenix wished she was wearing her cloak.

Her foot hit solid ground. Packed earth crunched underfoot as she strode towards the ornate metal door that loomed ahead of her.

The fire globe hovered in the air next to her shoulder, keeping up with her movements and illuminating her path.

She paused in front of the entrance, her hands pressing against the carved door that blocked her way.

Kit whined softly at her hesitation, rubbing the flat of her snout against Phoenix's leg. The movement was enough to snap Phoenix out of the dread that pooled in her core, and she gave a mighty push and opened the door into the hollowed out cavern.

Flickering torches lined the walls that stretched before them. Phoenix extinguished her globe with a word and felt the ripple of Power dissipate around her. Grabbing a torch from the closest sconce, she steeled herself and followed the main passageway.

The rudimentary corridors - if they could be called that - spiraled around in her in a mis-matched honeycomb. Each familial monument stood in the centre, an imposing presence of forced benevolence that soared above the stone markers that littered the grounds around it. Some were dotted with fresh offerings of flowers and fruit from the recent pilgrimages of the living.

Phoenix paid them little attention as she continued to the apex of the room. The statues became more ornate the further she went. The earth was tamped down from the countless foot falls that it had endured today. But now? Now it only had to contend with her and Kit.

Phoenix held her breath and stepped into the Royal Crypt.

The freshly-disturbed earth was the first thing that caught her attention. Two new caskets dominated the space. They rested above the ground on curtained tables, spaced slightly apart, where they would remain for the next week so that mourners could pay their respects before they were interred in stone.

The fire of her torch guttered into darkness. The unlit base, forgotten, fell to the floor with a thud.

Phoenix stepped haltingly towards the double caskets. She pressed a palm against each wooden surface, slowly running her hands along the glossy edge. Feeling for… What? What was she even expecting from this encounter? They were gone. There was no hint of their presence remaining. No clue as to what she should do next.

Her vision dimmed at the edges. Her fingers tingled and her hands dropped, weighted, to her sides. Closure slammed into her. It was all she could do to stay standing, all she could do to breathe.

A whispered rasping filled the air behind her and Phoenix startled at the sound. Her vision cleared instantly. She turned in time to see Kit, her body rigid, pushing against the heavy lid of a small stone sarcophagus.

"Kit! Stop!"

Phoenix leapt forward, grabbing at the edge of the heavy

stone lid before it slid off and onto the ground. Grunting, she pulled at the slab cover, wincing at the scraping and grating until she had repositioned the weight of the stone to keep it from tipping.

She exhaled loudly, letting her head drop as she rested her weight briefly against the carved stone cover. When she was convinced the danger had passed, Phoenix rolled her shoulders with relief and cast a glance down at the stone coffin.

"You're lucky," she told the small stone box with a smile. The rest of her words died before they escaped her lips, her attention caught by the relief carving of the small child that she had just saved from smashing into oblivion.

Princess Penelope's sleeping face adorned the slab under Phoenix's hands. With her attention fixated on the carving, she felt a familiar *pull* in the centre of her stomach. Without knowing why, Phoenix finished the job that Kit started and pulled the slab off of the internment box and rested it against the packed earth on a slant.

She stared at the sarcophagus. Uncertainty prickled along her spine as she stared at her handiwork. What was she doing?

Kit took advantage of her hesitation and jumped up onto the stone edge. Instantly, to Phoenix's horror, the dog wriggled her way through the crack and into the stone opening.

"Kit!" Phoenix hissed, grasping at the empty space that her tail had just occupied. "Get out of there!"

There was no movement.

Cursing, Phoenix tipped the cover onto the ground, shoving aside the disgust at the thought of having to reach into the death-soaked darkness after the dog. A soft thumping of Kit's tail caused Phoenix to pause. Instead of grabbing for Kit's collar, she *called* a fire globe into existence over their heads.

Except for Kit, the tomb was empty. No evidence of a burial

box remained around the dog, who was curled in on herself and looking up at Phoenix with a sheepish expression on her face.

Phoenix straightened. "Illuminate." Two more globes burst to life in the darkness and whizzed past her to dance over the cover of the carving. She snapped her fingers at Kit to get out - who obliged her for once - and ran her fingers all over the edges of the sarcophagus. There was not a scrape or a mark inside or out to show that it had ever been used.

"If not graverobbers, then what? Why is it empty?"

Frowning, Phoenix grabbed the cover and yanked it back over the tomb, grunting with the effort of trying to avoid scraping the stone together... and failing miserably.

Kit gave a huff, her attention switching to something else, and trotted towards the opening of the crypt. Phoenix trailed behind her, pausing momentarily to press her hand against Malcourt's burial box, feeling the polished wood cool the imprint that he had left on her palm.

"Follow it," she murmured, echoing his last instructions back to him. Or to what remained of him, at least. "I can't find 'it' to follow. I don't know where 'it' begins!"

She blinked rapidly, struggling to swallow the lump that had swelled in her throat. Unbidden, her fire globes plunged into darkness around her.

Phoenix turned and followed Kit back to the outside world. She made sure the door was shut firmly behind her.

Across the courtyard, Phoenix could see the windows to the girls' dorm. Many of them were dark, the rooms empty since the nobles had been pulled back to their Manors. The ones that remained had moved deeper within Angor's walls where it was much less isolated.

Phoenix was beginning to welcome it.

"That's where it all started..." Phoenix said softly to Kit, eyeing the dorms.

An idea formed after she digested the words. Everything had been put into motion when she met Malcourt, but before that... If there were no clues at Angor for her, nothing here that Malcourt wanted her to find, then she would have to look somewhere else.

"I have to go back to where it all started," Phoenix announced. "I have to go back to where *I* started."

Phoenix strode towards the tower, making a mental list of the things she would need. It had been nearly half a year since she had arrived at Angor. Perhaps it was time for her to travel again. She had to follow her roots to figure out who she was, and what it was that Malcourt had been trying to tell her.

"We're going on an adventure, Kit," she told the dog, who trotted easily at her side. Kit pressed her body against Phoenix's leg as she pushed through the tower's protection barriers. She pushed the door open, letting it swing on its hinges so that it shut behind them.

"We're going to Avondale."

ACKNOWLEDGEMENTS

Out of the entirety of the book, this was by far the most difficult thing for me to write. I have received so much support from so many people over the last few years that I could never fully express how truly grateful I am.

To my husband, Chad: You are my continual source of unconditional love and support. I'm beyond lucky to have you. Thank you for always checking-in, holding down the fort, and for shouldering all of the extra "Dad Duty" during this journey. I can think of no better partner for my life, and no better father to our son. Without you this wouldn't be possible. I love you.

To my parents, Paul and Alison: You instilled in me a love of reading at such an early age that I can barely remember a time before it existed. Thank you for the weekend trips to the bookstores even when the bookshelves at home were overflowing, for the amazing book suggestions (and for never coming looking for the ones you've lent me...), and for always, always, encouraging my creative outlets. Between Mom's endless supply of children's books, and Dad's edits on the rough draft, it's no wonder the story turned out the way it did. I think we did a pretty good job.

To Write Club NL: You accepted me as one of your own even though I basically showed up unannounced. (Joke's on you, you're stuck with me now.) You added a social aspect to an otherwise solitary activity, which was reaffirming and invaluable. Thanks for all the great chats, the commiserating, and for being a late-night, interactive thesaurus. Long live Cans.

To Matthew LeDrew of Engen Books: Thank you for everything. Thank you for taking a chance on a first-time author with no formal training. Thanks for all of the hand-holding during my case of "First Book Jitters," for including me into the Engen family without reservation, and for making me feel like I belong. You made the scary parts not-so-scary. I appreciate you and all that you do.

And lastly, to Amanda Labonté, my author bestie: As soon as I expressed interest in finishing this book, you basically gave me a grin and said "C'mon, we goes." And here we are. You are a blessing - and now that it's officially in print, you're able to cite it whenever necessary. It's my gift to you. You're welcome.

MORE FANTASY FROM ENGEN BOOKS

HEED THE CALL

After a heated fight at sea between twins Ben and Alex, Ben vanishes from their boat without a sound or even a ripple in the water. Unwavering in his dedication to find his brother, Alex begins the adventure of a lifetime armed only with the help of a local girl named Meg and his own mysterious musical abilities... the key to which, and to the mysteries that surround him, may be tied to the alluring song of the dangerous girl he finds among the ocean's frothing waves.

"A mysterious figure in the ocean, a suspicious loss in the waves, a riveting treasure hunt, and surprise after surprise, how could anyone not want to read this novel?"

~Alice Kuipers
author of Life on the Refrigerator Door

"Loved this book and can't wait for the next one."

~Helen Escott
bestselling author of Operation: Wormwood

"It's been a while since I've read an entire book in one day, but...Whenever I tried to put it down, it would call out to me, luring me back like a siren's song."

~Ali House
author of The Six Elemental & The Fifth Queen

"Call of the Sea seamlessly weaves together the hardships and humour of rural Newfoundland life with a fantastical storyline that will leave you wanting more. This book will not disappoint."

~Lauralana Dunne
author of Ashes

SUPERHERO FANTASY FROM ENGEN BOOKS!

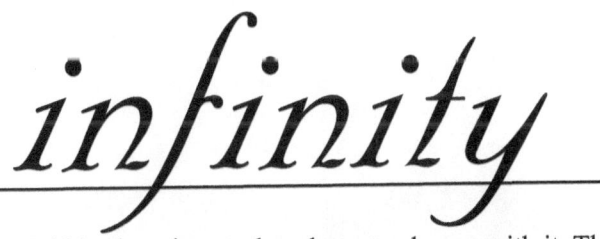

infinity

The world is changing, and we have to change with it. That was the one thing that Victor was really sure of when he started looking for special people: people who could change the possibilities of the future from something certainly grim... to something *infinitely* positive.

Now four unsuspecting people from different backgrounds and walks of life have been thrown into the mix together, and nothing will ever be the same. But there's a difference between hoping for a better world and actually having one, and there will always be resistance to change.

Book One: Infinity (October 2010)
Book Two: The Tourniquet Reprisal (October 2012)
Book Three: Exodus of Angels (April 2016)
Book Four: Garden of the 8th Circle (August 2020)

Related Books:
    light|dark (April 2012)
    Roulette (October 2009)
    The Long Road (May 2014)
    Touch Your Nose (May 2018)

Written by the superstar team of Ellen Curtis (*Compendium*) and Matthew LeDrew (the *Xander Drew* series).

Destiny doesn't wait for anyone.

ABOUT THE AUTHOR

Lauralana Dunne grew up running around the library stacks of St. John's, Newfoundland, Canada, and has been writing stories for as long as she can remember. She can often be found at different writing events around the city, typing on her phone with one hand while simultaneously fueling her caffeine addiction with the other.

She is a die-hard lover of YA Fantasy, and has been known to describe herself as a "Slayer of Imaginary Monsters."

Ashes is her first novel.